Humanity Abides – Book One

Shelter

By Carol A. Bird

This book is a work of fiction. Names, characters, places, and incidents are the product of the author's imagination or are used fictitiously. Any resemblance to actual events, locales, or persons, living or dead, is coincidental.

Special Thanks to:

Lori A. Bird – Editor
David A. Bird – Illustrator
Bob Dean - Contributor

This book is dedicated to my mother,
Julia Margaret Adams.
One of my fondest childhood memories
is of our weekly trips to the Lemon
Grove Library.

Table of contents:

PART ONE   5

PART TWO   237

PART ONE

"Every death even the cruellest death drowns in the total indifference of Nature/Nature herself would watch unmoved if we destroyed the entire human race."

Peter Weiss (1964)

<u>PROLOGUE</u>

The twisted coil of DNA - representing the code of life - splits down the middle of the tightly wound helix like rungs of a spiral ladder breaking under the weight of a heavy body. Base pairs are ripped apart. The cell writhes and contorts with the exposed and isolated DNA strands awash in the primordial soup of the cell's nucleus. RNA attaches to the DNA as lonely strands find their opposite partners and base pairs link in an ecstasy of reunion. The genetic information is copied to the RNA which then separates from the DNA and races off to carry out its function of protein synthesis. In this manner the genetic information contained in DNA is copied and utilized to form proteins, enzymes, organs and tissue.

During meiosis, or sexual reproduction, DNA forms distinct chromosomes within the cell's nucleus. As the cell divides to become an ova or sperm, one half of each chromosome pair ends up in a daughter cell. With the haploid number, or one-half the usual number of chromosomes, each cell has all the information required to create a new being when combined with a sex cell from another individual of the same species. Only then can the miracle continue.

At the moment the sperm penetrates the ovum the resulting zygote again contains the full complement of chromosomes. The DNA begins a dance of life. Chromosome pairs match up, bringing together characteristics from each parent to create a new and absolutely unique individual.

Mitosis, or non-sexual division of the nucleus that produces daughter cells identical to the parent, results in growth and regeneration of cells in a body.

During these fragile times, when cells are dividing sexually or somatically, the cell is the most vulnerable. Mutations can alter the form or function of the cell, or of the proteins coded for by the DNA. Slow, orderly mutation causes minor changes that alter the organism very slightly. If the mutation is beneficial, the organism flourishes and by natural selection passes the change onto its offspring. If not, the organism is not successful, either in living or reproducing. This evolution has proceeded for millions of years, changing and improving the life forms that inhabit the Earth.

These mutations are caused by many factors, natural and unnatural. Natural causes include cosmic radiation or genetic accidents. In modern life, more frequent or serious mutations can occur; caused by drugs, environmental pollution, chemicals in food or water, or strong radiation.

Sometimes these mutations can lead to deadly malignancies. And if the mutagen is strong enough, may sometimes lead to something worse… something much worse… something monstrous.

8

<u>ONE</u>

August 18, 10:30 a.m.
Society Islands, South Pacific Ocean

Sleek and beautiful, and gleaming white against the azure ocean, the Sea Witch sliced through an early morning glassy sea at forty knots. Spray arced from her bow, glittering with an untold number of tiny rainbow spectrums. In contrast to the beauty of the tranquil sea, turmoil reigned on the yacht's bridge as her darkly handsome skipper paced nervously, running his fingers through his black, wavy hair. Apprehensive about yesterday's unexpected encounter with a Chinese gunboat, he checked the GPS to ensure they were on course, and for the twentieth time glanced fearfully at the radar screen, searching for any evidence that the Chinese ship was still in the area.

It remained clear.

Alphonse Carelli was an excitable, hot-tempered Italian and was easily rattled by unexpected events. Yesterday's experience with the gunboat had left him frantic. He had tossed and turned all night, worried he might be prevented from delivering his valuable cargo to its final destination. The Chinese vessel, which had been detected by the yacht's radar while still several miles away, had no authority in these waters and absolutely no fathomable reason for being here.

"What the hell is he doing down here? We're thousands of miles from China, for Christ's sake!" Alphonse complained to his first mate Paul Jeter. A man of few words, Jeter had just shrugged his massive shoulders and headed below.

After picking up the load of drugs in the Philippines the Sea Witch had traveled east along the equator and then turned southeast toward French Polynesia. Carelli's plan was to spend leisure time in Bora Bora and Tahiti to divert suspicion. He loved powerboats, this one in particular. This was his second smuggling run using this craft and he was taking full advantage of these trips to live a life of luxury while sailing the South Seas. This latest assignment, smuggling the largest shipment of heroin his boss had ever imported into the United States was going to make him a rich man. Ricky Wong, after many years as a small time crook, was quickly becoming one of the most powerful Asian Mafia bosses on the west coast and Carelli was hoping to rise right along with him.

After two weeks of sailing between the islands, with Alphonse and his wife diving and snorkeling in the blue-green waters around Moorea and lounging on pristine white beaches, the Witch had left the Society Islands sailing east. They avoided normal shipping lanes and were planning on swinging north to approach the west coast of the United States from the South. Yesterday, just as lunch was being served, and while still in an uninhabited portion of the South Pacific they had encountered the Chinese ship. The yacht's captain, Cecil Jameson, notified Alphonse they had picked up the vessel on the radar. It was traveling toward them at high speed. From the ship's fly bridge Alphonse and Jeter watched with dread as the gunmetal gray military vessel approached, bouncing over the waves, until it began to slow off their port bow. "You don't think he's been tracking us, do you?" Carelli asked Jeter.

"How the fuck would I know?" He replied in his deep, gravelly voice. "You want me to break out the heat?" Jeter was six and a half feet of bulging muscle, with greasy, black hair protruding from under a filthy baseball cap. It hung down in front of his eyes and covered his ears. He wore dirty overalls with no shirt underneath, much to the chagrin of Captain Jameson and the rest of the immaculately attired crew. Jeter was always itching for a fight, and the thought of a battle - with weapons blazing, had caused his eyes to shine with excitement in the intense, early afternoon sunshine.

"No! Are you an idiot? Look at the size of the guns on that baby!" Carelli had been unable to drag his gaze away from the rapidly approaching vessel. He spoke as if to a child, "Remember, we're just a pleasure boat cruising the South Seas for recreation.

Go tell the captain and crew that everybody's to stay cool and look casual." He ordered Jeter away with a flip of his hand. "What the hell's a Chinese ship doing down here, anyway?" he repeated. In very real danger of pissing his pants, he anxiously awaited the ship's arrival.

Jeter went below. He preferred the dark recesses of the lower decks and the engine room to the bright upper levels. He was prepared, if necessary, to break open the hidden, highly illegal stash of automatic weapons. Jeter couldn't care less what Carelli thought. There was no way he was going to rot in a Chinese prison, and he didn't care if he and everyone else had to die in a hail of bullets to prevent it.

The yacht's crew came on deck ready to prepare her for boarding, but the military ship drew alongside, and to Alphonse's immense relief, didn't demand either to board or to search her. The Chinese captain, speaking perfect English with almost no accent, warned Alphonse to leave the vicinity immediately.

"Yes sir, is there some kind of a problem we should know about?" Alphonse asked deferentially.

The captain wouldn't elaborate, but indicated that Alphonse and his vessel would be at extreme risk if he didn't comply. Apparently in a hurry themselves, they swung their ship away from the Witch, gunned their engines and departed at high speed, their ship producing a wake that caused the massive yacht to roll sickeningly.

Alphonse's trembling legs had given out and he'd slumped into a deck chair, relieved that the huge shipment of heroin, concealed in the space between a false hull and the real one, had not been discovered. This smuggling run from Southeast Asia to the United States was going to bail him out of debt and make him an extremely wealthy man. His concealed cargo was worth over fifty million dollars and after cutting would be worth even more on the street. Providing this trip was successful, and the heroin delivered to the various dealers, Ricky would sell him the Witch and make him a partner, and there would be many more lucrative ocean crossings in his future.

If it wasn't successful, the Federal government would confiscate the yacht, his wife would leave him, and if the government didn't kill him, Ricky would. This job, a joint venture between him and Ricky Wong, was his last chance and he paled at the thought that he came so close to blowing it.

Arrangements had already been made to divide the goods prior to reaching domestic waters. Smaller vessels would rendezvous with the Sea Witch off the coast of Mexico, and taking separate routes, would deliver their expensive cargo to various west coast ports. The shipment was of very high quality and was promised to drug lords in three major cities. Money laundering had already been arranged and Alphonse Carelli would soon be a rich businessman living in luxury in San Francisco.

Unfortunately, soon after the gunboat disappeared over the horizon, a malfunction of one of their turbine engines brought them to a halt, and they'd drifted overnight while Jeter and the mechanical crew made repairs. This morning found them only a few miles from the location where they'd encountered the Chinese gunboat the previous day.

It probably wouldn't have mattered.

***

An Intercontinental Ballistic missile screamed through the upper atmosphere, having reached the highest point of its trajectory in a matter of minutes. Eight thousand miles down range it bloomed like a deadly flower, sending out five blossoms, each with independent propulsion and guidance systems, and each independently targeted for a predetermined atoll, or tiny uninhabited island in the Pacific Ocean.

As Carelli continued his pacing, the sea had become restless, with winds kicking up and previously gentle swells becoming whitecaps. The captain reduced speed slightly and with no indication of the gunboat on the radar, and much to the captain's relief, Alphonse left the bridge around eleven a.m. to find his wife.

Marci Carelli, tall, tanned and beautiful, turned over on her chaise lounge, exposing her shapely nude backside to the sun as the brilliant orb showered her with golden rays from almost directly overhead.

"Alphonse, honey, put some lotion on my back." Her voice was deep, sensuous.

He came over and sat beside her on the edge of her chaise, leaning down and kissing the back of her neck, breathing in the lotion's sweet coconut aroma. They looked good together. His handsome Italian features, and dark hair and eyes, contrasted with her pale blue eyes and long blonde hair that cascaded over the chaise's edge and spilled onto the deck. He squirted lotion into his hand and applied it to her back, working his way down to her buttocks where his hand lingered, caressing.

He gently pulled aside her hair and kissed behind her ear, speaking softly, feeling his own arousal, "You're going to be the wife of a very rich man, my sweet. In another month we'll have everything we've ever wanted." He continued to rub the slippery oil on her tanned back. "You know that exquisite white Mediterranean mansion on the hill? I'm going to buy it for you."

"Oh Alphonse, I love that house! Can you really afford it?" She flipped over, tossing back her hair and squinting in the bright sunlight as she grinned up at him excitedly.

Suddenly the daylight became infinitely brighter. Marci threw her arm across her face as the fierce light stabbed her eyes, temporarily blinding her.

"What the fuck?" Alphonse jumped up and ran to the rail, his arm held aloft, shielding his eyes from the brilliance. Within seconds the dazzling light faded and Alphonse stood in awe, his mouth hanging open, as he saw a gigantic explosion in the distance. An incredibly huge waterspout was climbing skyward as the ocean vaporized, was superheated, and was sucked upward into a billowing, incandescent fireball; a radiant orange, yellow and angry purple inferno surrounded by roiling gray and white clouds of steam and gases. The column of water grew, an impossible amount of water traveling upward, spreading out into a churning mushroom-shaped cloud that quickly blotted out the sunlight and plunged the day into night. He gripped the rail with all his strength.

"Oh God! Full speed ahead!" he screamed stupidly. His ears popped from the gigantic overpressure created by the blast.

He never heard the explosion.

The sound trailed far behind the light, heat, and radiation. Vacuum created by the rapidly rising and expanding gases jerked the yacht forward, drawing it downward into an enormous trough created in the sea, and then forward toward the growing maelstrom, nearly tearing his grip from the rail.

"No, no, stop!" he screamed, leaning backward, pulling on the rail as if, with his feeble strength, he could keep the yacht from the blast.

Within seconds, as though struck by a giant's backhand, the Witch slammed to a stop.

He heard Marci's terrified screams as she, her chair, and everything that wasn't tied down flew past him, sucked toward the spreading column. He was smashed against the railing, hanging on for his life . . . when something on the surface caught his eye.

"Sweet mother of God!" he whimpered. A wall was racing toward him with blinding speed, a looming tsunami of water and steam, cerulean blue capped with frothing white.

Searing thermal radiation from the rapidly expanding fireball reached Alphonse. His clothing melted and fused to his flesh. His hair disintegrated, and flash burns blistered, bubbled and blackened his exposed skin. The leading edge of the concussion wave, traveling unbelievably fast, blasted him and the entire yacht to molecules as the firestorm continued to spread outward from the blast, obliterating everything in its path.

The vacuum above continued to fill with water, gases and steam, until gravity reasserted itself and millions of tons of radioactive water came crashing back to earth, sending shock waves through the ocean, wave after wave, spreading out in pursuit of the retreating concussion front.

The target atoll was gone.

August 19, 4:00 a.m.
Newport Beach, California

"The blood of Christ…" Mark Teller murmured softly, as he tossed restlessly in his bed. He flipped over and tangled the sheets around his naked, sweaty body. *"The blood of Christ,"* he moaned louder, his spine suddenly cold with fear as he ran…ran through darkness, darker than he had ever known or had ever thought possible, as though light had been forever extinguished from his world. He sprinted, gasping for breath, through endless corridors, around blind corners and across inky intersections, searching, seeking someone - with something unspeakable in pursuit. He could hear it coming closer and could feel its hot, foul breath on the nape of his neck.

Turning over violently and flailing his arms, he tried to escape the grasp of the unclean thing in his nightmare, crying out in abject terror as fear overwhelmed him; not for himself, but for someone he thought he knew but couldn't quite recognize in the turmoil of the horrid dream.

Suddenly chilling water was all around him, in a tide that climbed up his legs, his hips, swirling by him on all sides, coming from nowhere and everywhere at once. The water trapped him, and he slogged forward in slow motion, as though his legs were embedded in concrete - the thing behind him continuing to gain ground. He heard a plaintive sob, someone in the darkness crying out his name, the panic in the young voice tearing at Mark's heart, terrifying him beyond comprehension. Who was it? He couldn't remember, no matter how hard he tried, but he yearned desperately to locate the child who seemed to believe that only Mark could save him from the hellish demons lurking in the darkness.

He bolted upright in bed, gasping unevenly, choking for breath as he jerked awake in the early dawn. The nightmare was still stuck in his mind, stubbornly refusing to fade completely. The strident ringing of the alarm clock intruded on his mental terror and he automatically reached over and hit the snooze button. His heart continued to pound as though he'd been running for his very life, and he shook his head, trying to come awake in the predawn darkness.

"*The blood of Christ.*" He shook his head and frowned in concentration. The thought frightened him but he had no idea why, or what the term represented.

The loud ringing continued and the fog finally began to lift as the fading dream finally relinquished its grip on him. Realizing that it wasn't the alarm ringing, but his cell phone, he fumbled for it in the dark, muttering "hello," in a rough voice shaken by the nightmare.

"Hi Mark. It's Will. The President wants us to attend a meeting this afternoon. Be at the plane in an hour, okay?"

"Sure, what time is it?" Still slightly disoriented, he swung his feet to the floor, flinging aside the damp, tangled covers. His bedroom window was open to a warm, summer, Southern California night, and he was soaked with perspiration.

"Four a.m. Be there at five. I'll see you then." Mark knew Will Hargraves well and he detected an uncharacteristic tension in Will's voice.

He sat on the edge of the bed trying to shake the lingering feeling of dread that had overwhelmed him and lingered even after he'd awakened. He realized it wasn't the phrase, "*The blood of Christ,*" that frightened him. In fact there was something oddly comforting about it. It was the other memory, fading quickly now that he was awake, of something loathsome in the darkness, and of a danger - an end worse than death - that caused his gut to wrench, and the hairs on the back of his neck to prickle. He reached up and massaged his neck, pressing hard, attempting to rub away the tension. Mark was unaccustomed to having nightmares and the vividness of this one had left him shaken.

He stood and headed for the bathroom, the effects of the dream rapidly diminishing. He would have to hustle to get to the airport on time. With minimal traffic due to the early hour it would take him thirty minutes to get to Hargraves Aerospace Industries in Costa Mesa.

Mark wasn't particularly surprised that the President of the United States had summoned them to Washington. Being Chief

Executive Officer at Hargraves Aerospace, a major defense contractor, he'd been involved in high-level government meetings in the past. This afternoon's meeting was undoubtedly due to the developing international tensions that began years ago when India and Pakistan rekindled the cold war by testing nuclear weapons. Other problems followed as spies were found to have stolen U.S. nuclear secrets and there was a proliferation of nuclear technology and materiel. Then came September 11, completely changing the situation forever. More recently, North Korea was testing missiles and sending satellites into orbit while Iran was moving toward developing a nuclear weapon in spite of severe international sanctions. The current inflation in the U.S. had caused China to cease buying U.S. treasuries and the Chinese were making threats about the inability of the United States to pay back the massive debt owed them. All of these problems had led up to yesterday.

Details were sketchy, but the news media reported that China, against the provisions of the nuclear test ban treaties, had conducted an atmospheric hydrogen bomb test, immeasurably escalating the international tension. Will would have more information, and Mark hoped the meeting with the President would fill in the blanks.

As he shaved, he studied his image in the mirror. He had, once again, gone to bed too late trying to complete a thorough review of three new documents the Contracts and Grants department had previously approved. Will Hargraves would expect him to be familiar with their provisions in detail. Dark circles under his eyes reminded him of the folly, at his age, of getting too little sleep. At thirty-six years old it was getting harder to skimp on sleep and still function at his peak during the day.

He grinned his lopsided grin and scolded his image, "Mark old boy, you need to get your beauty rest." He was convinced the nightmare was a result of too little sleep.

He'd noticed himself thinking more about his age lately and hoped it was a passing phase, brought on by his recent birthday and reaching the "closer-to-forty-than-thirty" age. Actually, he looked younger than thirty-six, blessed with boyish good looks, wavy dark hair, a body slimmed by regular exercise and electric blue eyes that sparkled when he smiled. His one hundred eighty pounds on a five-foot eleven-inch frame were mostly muscle, due to running almost daily and weight training three days a week.

His smile faded abruptly as his thoughts returned to the present situation. As he dressed he remembered that Will Hargraves' company had worked on Strategic Defense Initiative projects, essentially anti-missile systems, prior to the Strategic Arms Reduction Treaty signed by President George Bush. Mark wasn't completely familiar with the details but he guessed today's meeting could possibly lead to reinstatement of those, or similar contracts and he would be a very busy man in the next few months. He was right about the latter but for reasons he couldn't possibly imagine.

Opening the closet, he retrieved the overnight bag he always kept packed and grabbed his computer case with his laptop. He reset the security alarm as he entered the garage from the kitchen and glanced at his watch. 4:22 in the morning. He would make it with five or ten minutes to spare.

Mark backed his Silver Lexus SUV out of the garage and wound slowly down his quiet residential street in Newport Beach, California. His home was a small, older style Spanish hacienda, perched on a low hill, with a breathtaking, panoramic view of the ocean visible from his front porch. He'd fallen in love with the house when he spotted a "For Sale" sign in the front yard as he and a friend had jogged by just over six years ago. He had finished his run, called the broker, made an offer and moved in two months later. During the six years he'd owned it he had completely upgraded the house with every modern convenience, including a total, home automation system. It controlled the drip systems that watered the lawns and shrubs, adjusted the interior and exterior lighting and controlled the security systems that ensured his safety. Mark loved to cook and did most of his own, even when entertaining guests, but he employed a gardener, a pool man and a housekeeper. Life was good.

It was still dark, a waning moon just slipping into the ocean, as he passed the beautiful, perfectly landscaped properties of his neighbors. Their yards were filled with acacia trees, fan palms, roses and rhododendron and a profusion of other flowers, gray in the predawn darkness, which would flash into rainbows of color with the rising of the sun.

Mark had never met any of his neighbors, except to wave occasionally when they saw one another by chance. Instead, he preferred the company of a few good friends. One of these, Steve Jordan, was a fellow runner and owner of "Running Free," a Fountain Valley sporting goods store that sold running shoes, clothing and paraphernalia. When Mark wasn't flying one of the five antique planes in his collection, he and Steve were out running trails, through Trabuco Canyon in the Cleveland National Forest east of San Juan Capistrano, or in the Santa Monica or San Gabriel mountains to the north.

He left the guarded world of Newport and headed north on Pacific Coast Highway to Newport Boulevard, and then right, toward Costa Mesa and the plant.

As he pulled into his reserved parking space at the plant's main hangar, Mark noticed that Will was already there, his Black Mercedes parked in the space next to Mark's. He grabbed his computer and bag from the trunk and walked around the corner into the well-lighted, open end of the hangar, where he found Will Hargraves and five other people standing beside the sleek business jet. The others waved and went on board as Will turned to wait for Mark.

Will Hargraves was an imposing figure. Taller than Mark, at just over six feet, he had a full head of steel gray hair, a neatly trimmed white beard, and eyes that were an unusual shade of gray. His demeanor was that of a man in charge. Will flashed a brief smile as Mark approached. "Hey Mark. Let's get going. Can't keep the President waiting."

The Gulfstream V, powered by twin BMW Rolls Royce jet engines, was cleared through several intermediate altitudes before leveling off at flight level 410. Flying above a light cloud cover at forty-one thousand feet and cruising at Mach 0.8, or about 530 miles per hour, they would reach Washington, D.C. in approximately four and a half hours. With several attendees coming from the West coast the meeting had been scheduled for 2:00 p.m. to accommodate the time change.

Mark and Will were both excellent pilots and were certified to fly the G-V, but today they had a crew of three; the captain and co-captain, and a flight attendant who was busy preparing breakfast in the galley. Mark lounged in a wide leather seat across the aisle from Will, sipping a hot cup of coffee. Two other passengers, Miles Bannister, Chief Operations Officer, and Heinrich Muensch, Chief Engineer of Hargraves Aerospace, sat on a small side-facing sofa in front of Mark and Will. The men were longtime employees, having been employed at the company when Will purchased it from their previous employer. Both men were in their late fifties and both wore rumpled suits. Miles was clean shaven while Heinrich had a short beard. Miles ran his hand through thinning gray hair as Will briefed them on the middle-of-the-night conversation he'd had with Secretary of State Charles Hansen. Will and Chuck Hansen, friends in college, had known each other for over forty years and Chuck regularly kept Will informed of events transpiring in Washington.

"The situation is far worse than any of us could have suspected, with international tensions running higher than they have in several years. I assume that the escalating tensions will mean the resumption of testing and development of projects that were discontinued years ago. The technology is so different we will be basically starting from scratch."

He looked over at Miles and Heinrich. "While Mark and I are at the White House, the two of you have appointments at the Pentagon. You'll meet with General Constantine. Feel him out on the types of contracts they're interested in but don't make any commitments. Fax any paperwork they've prepared to the plant."

Prior to Mark's employment, Hargraves Aerospace Company had been involved, among other things, in "Star Wars" type anti-missile research. Will's company held over twenty patents for state-of-the-art navigational equipment, used, among other things, in guidance systems for missiles and rockets. Many of the patents were for equipment Will Hargraves had invented himself and Mark knew the highly accurate Cruise missiles utilized homing technology similar to that developed by Hargraves Aerospace over two decades ago. Will also owned several subsidiary companies whose primary businesses involved manufacturing rocket engines and laser guidance systems.

"You know Will," Mark said, "The projects you're referring to were canceled soon after I joined the company. Can you fill me in?"

"Of course. We were working on several projects for the SDI, Strategic Defense Initiative. Most of our involvement was in guidance systems. For example, the plant in Idaho was researching and designing mirror systems for directing ground-based nuclear x-ray lasers. We were also in R&D on computer guided projectiles, fired from electromagnetic rail guns that could be moved around the country on the nation's rail system, and several other less glamorous projects."

"Why were they discontinued?"

"Are you familiar with the concept of deterrence?"

"Yeah, sort of. If each country has the ability to annihilate the other, then we're balanced, and deterred from launching a first strike." Mark downed the last of his second cup of coffee.

"Mutually assured destruction," Miles added. "If each side knows his own destruction is certain, even if they strike first, theoretically they will withhold that first strike."

"Yes, that's the general idea," Will continued. "A program to develop a defense against ballistic missiles challenged these assumptions of deterrence. The SDI, supposedly providing total U.S. protection against nuclear attack would remove the disincentive to attack first. Back in 1972 and 1974, treaties allowing only limited deployment of antiballistic missile systems had been signed by the superpowers, and members of Congress believed the SDI contravened these ABM treaties. It's ironic since we kept the bargain and it's widely believed the Soviets and China went ahead and developed anti-missile systems anyway."

The flight attendant had breakfast ready on the dining-conference table, and moving to the rear of the cabin they continued the conversation over a light meal.

"The system was also too damned expensive," Heinrich said, in a slight German accent, which forty years in the United States hadn't completely obliterated. "Thirty billion dollars!"

Will continued, "In 1993 the Strategic Defense Initiative was abandoned and the Ballistic Missile Defense Organization was established. It's much less expensive and uses internal ground-based antimissile systems. Although I'm on the civilian advisory board for this organization, I've been reluctant to financially commit the company to any projects, fearing until now that Congress would pull the plug on the B.M.D.O. as well. Even now, with this undeniable breach of the nuclear weapons treaties, I'm not sure this administration is going to be willing to make any waves and fund new projects. The president is strong on defense but congress fights him every step of the way."

Mark was beginning to understand the complexities of the situation. "We're looking at years to redevelop these systems," he told them. "Are we going to have that kind of time?"

"Well, now that's the real question isn't it?" Will said.

August 19, 6:25 a.m.
Las Vegas, New Mexico

It was one of those beautiful mornings so prevalent in the American Southwest, calm and crystal clear, with Venus shining like a jewel in the indigo sky of predawn. One-half mile from Interstate 25 a coyote gained on his prey, zigging, zagging and pouncing on the jackrabbit just as it reached its burrow at the base of a twisted juniper tree. The predator snatched up the rabbit with steel-trap jaws, and with a quick shake of its head easily snapped the animal's neck, killing it instantly. With the dead rabbit dangling from its mouth, the coyote trotted off through creosote and greasewood, winding through a sandy wash to the top of a rise, where he ripped open the rabbit's jugular and gulped down fur-covered chunks of blood-soaked meat.

With a full stomach, he lifted his muzzle and yapped his satisfaction to the gleaming beacon in the heavens.

The sun vaulted into the sky, throwing lances of golden light across the desert. They speared a battered green van as it swung around the corner onto Grant Avenue and pulled to a stop in front of a dilapidated diner. The words "Desert Air" were neatly stenciled on its side. Across the street from the diner, a large digital clock perched high atop the bank read 6:27 a.m., alternating with the temperature, which read a comfortable seventy-two degrees. In a very few hours the temperature will have climbed to almost ninety, or possibly have exceeded it, considering the record breaking heat wave that currently parched the southwest.

A large bear of a man climbed down from the van and entered the diner. Walter Thompson was dressed in worn coveralls, his gray hair covered by an ancient baseball cap embroidered with the name "Dukes", Albuquerque's triple A minor league baseball team. "Morning Heather. Just a cup of coffee, please." He swung his leg over a battered stool, tossed the cap onto the counter and sat down heavily. Looking around, he nodded a greeting toward his friend Norm Ortega, a darkly tanned rancher with deep lines radiating from the corners of his eyes. Norm was another regular customer at John's Coffee Shop in Las Vegas, New Mexico. "Morning Norm." Norm's mouth was stuffed full of bacon, but he returned the nod in acknowledgement.

The counter contained plastic donut trays, equally spaced down its length, and metal holders with grease-stained, dog-eared sheets of paper that served as menus. Maroon colored booths, covered with duct tape, lined the side of the restaurant under the windows and a line of tables and chairs occupied the space between the booths and the counter. Walter looked through the wide pass-through into the kitchen and waved at John Stiles, owner of the restaurant, an ex-navy cook, and an excellent chef. Next to the pass-through, appearing totally out of place, a brand new marker board announced today's breakfast special, "Steak and eggs with hash browns, toast and coffee - $9.95."

An elderly couple sat in one of the booths and two men dressed in cammo pants and orange vests occupied the table beside the door. This area of New Mexico, though high plains, was in close proximity to the southern terminus of the Rocky Mountains and boasted excellent hunting and fishing almost year-round. The other occupant, a trucker, sat next to Norm.

Walter's weekday mornings were identical, stopping by the aging diner for coffee and conversation, and then swinging by his son's house to pick him up for work. Jerry Thompson, a partner in his parents' business, was learning to repair appliances as his father's apprentice.

"How's it going Norm? Gonna be any cooler today?"

Norm wolfed down the last of a stack of hotcakes, swimming in butter and syrup, and washed it all down with a swallow of his black coffee. "Yeah, Walter, I think it is. You won't have any work to do." The hands holding the coffee mug were calloused from many years of ranching in this predominately rural area of New Mexico.

"Shoot, that'll be the day. There are plenty of appliances in this town that need fixing." He smiled at the young woman hovering nearby with the coffee pot. "Thanks, Heather. You're an angel in disguise." Actually, though pretty and in her early twenties, she looked less like an angel and more like a hard-working lady of the evening, with smudges under her eyes as evidence of a perpetually exhausted state. Light brown hair, pulled straight back and fastened with a colored ribbon spilled halfway down her back, and she had applied thick, overdone makeup in an attempt to disguise her weariness. Heather's live-in boyfriend worked a P.M. shift at the only hospital in this town of over fourteen thousand inhabitants, and arrived home just before midnight every night to find her waiting up for him. With her shift at the diner starting at five a.m. it didn't leave a lot of time for sleep.

Walter sipped his coffee and began the usual early morning discussion. "How about those Chinese? I hear they're doing some nuclear testing. Isn't that prohibited by some treaty?" His remarks were thrown out to anyone who would listen or participate.

Norm took the bait, "There's no way China's going to pay attention to any treaties. They have too many people, and someday they're just going to snatch territory from another country and then there'll be hell to pay. I hear their maps show the entire Asian continent simply labeled 'China'."

The trucker agreed with Norm, "Yeah, they don't give a shit what anybody says. They're supposed to be friends with North Korea, but now they're fighting with them too, and everyone knows North Korea has nuclear bombs. Hell, everyone has bombs nowadays, probably even Iran although they say they don't. We'll be in big trouble if all them guys start tossin' those bombs around." He shook his head and kept eating as if it were his last meal. Walter noticed every other person in the restaurant nodding his or her head.

"No." One of the hunters chimed in. "I don't think Iran has one yet, 'cause Israel's still here." That elicited some chuckles around the room.

"That blast yesterday was something, huh?" Norm said.

The other hunter agreed, "I hear it was the biggest ever. But those guys have been testing underground bombs for years. Nobody's gonna be stupid enough to do anything really dangerous, like send 'em in our direction. We'd kick their ass."

Though Walter fancied himself a country bumpkin, he was a highly intelligent man, had in fact been Chief of Building Crafts at Los Alamos National Laboratory for many years, and although he'd retired to his own small business in Las Vegas, he had always kept up-to-date on current political and scientific events. During and after dinner every night he watched diverse news and discussion programs; local news from Albuquerque, MSNBC, Chris Matthews, The O'Reilly Factor, CNN. He was the king of the television remote. Armed with this knowledge, he believed the situation was far more serious than these people realized. He believed that they, like the rest of the U.S. population, were in serious denial of the true situation.

The conversation continued while Walter worked on his second cup of coffee. "Well, Walter, I gotta go." Norm tossed down a few crumpled bills by his check, and slapped Walter's shoulder as he passed, afraid if he stayed much longer his old friend would begin to lecture at length about the instability of the post-cold war international situation. He had more important things to do, a cattle auction to attend.

As Norm went through the door he brushed by another man dressed in a dark suit and tie. The man glanced at something in his hand, a photograph, and went over to sit by Walter. Heather approached, coffee pot in hand. "Coffee, mister?"

"No thank you, nothing for me." He turned to Walter as she shrugged and walked away. "Are you Walter Thompson?" he asked.

"Yes sir. Something I can do for you?"

"Mr. Thompson, I'm supposed to deliver this to you." He handed Walter a small package. "Your wife told me you'd probably be here, and it's very important, so I wanted to track you down. Please read the letter included with the package. I have other deliveries to make so I'll be going and I thank you for your time." He stood to leave.

Surprised, Walter accepted the package. "Hey, wait a minute. What is it?" he called after the man.

Halfway to the exit he turned and answered, "It's explained in the letter," and was out the door.

Walter briefly examined the package. It was wrapped in plain brown paper and addressed to him, although no postage had been affixed. Downing the last of his coffee, he dropped money on the counter and retrieved his cap. "See you later, Heather." She absently waved in his direction, already absorbed with wiping down the counter-top where Norm had eaten.

He pulled the van door open, climbed in, and tore the wrapping from the package. It contained both an envelope and a small metal box measuring about six inches long, three inches wide, and two inches deep, with a hinge located midway along the top, and what appeared to be a speaker on one side. Thompson couldn't find a latch, or other visible means of opening the box. He removed the letter from the envelope, and as he read it his eyebrows rose in surprise. For several minutes he sat motionless in the old van, puzzled, staring toward the mountains rising up in the northwest. Then he started the engine and slowly pulled from the curb.

August 19, 8:30 a.m.
Las Vegas, New Mexico

"Doctor, there's a gentleman here to see you, a sales rep, I think. Can you talk to him now?" The woman, dressed in a nurse's uniform, leaned around the doorjamb of the Doctor's office. She wore a starched white cap on her head, an anachronism in the 21st century and, quite possibly, the only one left in existence.

"Yes, I have a few minutes. Who's my first patient?"

"Julio Martinez at nine o'clock. His mother says he's been coughing and he's running a temp, and she's worried."

"Okay, thanks Carmen. Send in the rep, please." He placed another finished chart on the stack in front of him.

Dr. James Wiggins, Board Certified in Family Practice, had been practicing in Las Vegas, New Mexico for almost thirty years. His staff privileges were at fifty-four bed, Alta Vista Regional Hospital, along with 25 other family practitioners, internists, surgeons and other specialists. Dr. Jim, as he was affectionately called by his patients, at fifty-six, was one of the oldest physicians in town but had never considered retirement, or even diminishing his workload.

Always behind with his paperwork, his desk was piled high with patients' charts, stacks of manila folders that threatened to tumble over and bury him at any minute. He planned on getting a computer system with an Electronic Medical Record system but hadn't gotten around to it. Framed degrees adorned the wall behind his desk, and the left wall was covered with photographs of patients, many of whom he had delivered before the town grew large enough for an obstetrical specialist. Las Vegas was the County seat of San Miguel County, one hundred ten miles from Albuquerque by highway, and had grown to over fourteen thousand residents. Some days Jim was sure most of them were his patients. His caring and friendly "Marcus Welby" manner endeared him to them all.

The gentleman who entered Jim's office, neatly dressed in a dark suit and blue tie, looked forty-something, was average height and build, and appeared nervous or hurried, glancing at his watch as he crossed the room. He carried a small package in his left hand and shook hands with Jim across the desk, managing to avoid the piles of charts.

"Hello Doctor. My name is Karl Dohner."

"Hi, please have a seat," Jim offered.

The man remained standing. "No thank you Doctor. I'm here to deliver this package to you. Under normal circumstances it would have been mailed but I'm afraid we're short of time." He handed the package across to the doctor. "Please open it immediately and take it very seriously. My employer has access to current political information that most people are unaware of and I've been told to caution recipients not to consider this a joke."

"May I ask what's in the package?" Jim was a little concerned about the man's nervousness, with thoughts of Ted Kaczinski coming to mind, as he visualized a bomb blast blowing him to pieces and taking out the entire office with him.

Karl turned to go. "There's a complete explanation inside. Goodbye Doctor, and thank you for your time." He turned and strode out the door.

Jim placed the package, which was wrapped in plain brown paper, on his desk and stared at it for a full minute. With the exception of his ex-wife, he had no enemies he could recall. He couldn't imagine anyone wanting to harm him, so he shrugged, tore open the package and read the enclosed letter. "Well, if that don't beat all."

He reached over and pulled his freestanding cane, with its four rubber feet, to the side of his chair and, balancing on it, pulled himself to his feet. Once standing, he moved across the room with only a slight limp, leaving the cane beside his chair.

"Poliomyelitis," the doctor had told his parents, "Also known as 'Infantile Paralysis' or 'Polio'." The early fifties were a time of national panic over the virus that left children dead or paralyzed, and Jim vividly remembered the fear on his mother's face, as the doctor ruffled his hair and reassured him he was going to be fine. He was one of the lucky ones, a minor paralysis that had improved over the years, leaving him with only the cane and the limp as reminders that he had contracted one of the most dreaded diseases of the century and survived. It had never slowed him down and the brush with death crystallized his dream to become a doctor, as he remembered the comfort in the physician's voice and the way he ruffled a small frightened boy's hair.

He found his nurse in the small treatment room where they prepared injections and ran laboratory tests on blood and urine. "Carmen, when am I scheduled to go to Albuquerque for that continuing education seminar?"

"You're supposed to leave day after tomorrow."

"Cancel it would you? Take a look at this." He handed her the letter.

With a puzzled look on her face, she accepted the proffered letter, and after reading it, commented softly, "That's really weird."

August 19, 8:45 a.m.
Las Vegas, New Mexico

Walter coasted to a stop in front of a small well-kept tract house and honked the horn. His son Jerry waved from the front door and turned to kiss the woman behind him. "I'll be home early so you can get to school, honey," he told her. "See you later." He came down the sidewalk, veered around a BMX bicycle and climbed into the van.

"Hi Dad. How come you're late?" He tossed a tool belt onto the seat beside him as Walter made a U-turn and headed back the way he'd come.

"I had to pick up supplies at the hardware store."

"Do you think I can get away early so I can babysit while Barbara goes to school?" He glanced over at the older man. "Hey, what's the matter?" His father looked pale.

"Nothing son. I'm fine. Just a little hungry, that's all. Do you know anything about this Chinese situation?"

Jerry considered it briefly, and then admitted he knew almost nothing except what he'd caught on the television news while flipping through the channels looking for sporting events. He seldom read the paper, limiting himself to the sports page or occasionally an interesting headline. "Why, what's up?"

"Oh, no reason. Just making conversation. Is Barbara picking Pete up from the Amtrak Station today?"

"Yeah, in between her classes."

Pete, Walter and Sarah's other son, was a computer science major at The University of New Mexico in Albuquerque. Walter had never earned a degree himself, working his way to the top with elbow grease and common sense, but at Los Alamos he'd worked with some of the United States' brightest and most distinguished scientists and he was very proud that his son was going to graduate from college with a degree in a scientific field.

Jerry and Pete were as different as two brothers could be. Jerry was twenty-six years old, with light brown hair and hazel eyes, and a stocky build, while Pete was slender, more athletic looking, his hair much darker, and he had inherited his mother's blue eyes. Pete, three years younger than Jerry, often kidded his brother that if he were any shorter and wider, wandering canines seeking a place to relieve themselves would have found him irresistible. Pete stood three inches taller than Jerry at six feet. Jerry was a hard worker, and being his father's business partner was his idea of an ideal career. He'd married young, directly out of high school, and he and Barbara had a son, Jeremy, now seven years old. A good-natured man, Jerry didn't have a lot of ambition, but no one could deny he was a happy man. Pete, on the other hand, had more ambitious plans; a high tech field, living in an exciting, fast paced city, working in systems analysis, or for a major software company. He loved his family but had no intention of living his life in what he perceived as a small backwater town like Las Vegas, New Mexico.

After receiving the package this morning Walter was pleased that Pete was coming home between the summer session and the fall semester.

Fifteen minutes later, Walter pulled into the driveway adjacent to his shop and parked alongside the commercial building that housed his appliance repair business. Telling Jerry to go on ahead he retrieved the package from behind the seat where he'd stashed it, put it in his toolbox, and followed his son into the shop.

Rebuilt washers and dryers sat behind the front window, visible from the sidewalk that passed by the store front. Their prices were posted above them on the windows along with advertisements that offered low-interest rate financing and "great deals." The store was filled with hoses and PVC parts. On one wall stood a rack of heater and air conditioner filters. A counter with a cash register ran parallel to the back wall. Walter passed through the store, through the work shop, and into the attached house where his wife and son were coordinating the day's activities. Sarah's hands were full of work orders and she was briefing Jerry on the preliminary jobs for the day.

"Mrs. Talbot needs her washer fixed right away. She says she has four kids, and the laundry is multiplying and crawling out of the laundry basket, threatening to bury them all."

Jerry, smiled, "They always need everything fixed right away," he told her as he reached for the work order. "Dad, you don't look so good. I'll check it out to see if I can repair it on-site, and if not, I'll bring it in. Bye Mom." He plucked the keys from his father's outstretched hand, and headed back through the shop to the truck.

Sarah looked concerned. "Walter?" She placed her hand on his forehead. "Jerry says you're sick. Are you okay?" Walter pulled back from her hand and took out the package to show to his wife. "I told him I'm fine. You know the guy that was looking for me this morning? He gave me this." He extended the letter for her to read, poured himself a cup of coffee and leaned back against the kitchen counter to watch her reaction.

Sarah's eyes widened as she read the letter. "Do you think it's a joke?"

"I haven't the foggiest idea, but I guess it doesn't matter. If it is, we can ignore it. If it isn't, we can put it in the closet and forget about it - until it goes off that is. I guess we can worry about it then."

He thought about it for a minute. "You know Sarah, I think it might be real. Remember the job Fred Peterman offered me a few years ago? He was working on some big government project somewhere within a hundred miles of here. Wouldn't give me much information, but said it had one of the most sophisticated environmental systems he'd ever seen. I turned it down because it was a yearlong job and I didn't want to neglect the business. It could have been the facility in the letter. Makes you kind of nervous though, doesn't it?"

"It scares me to death."

"I'm glad Pete's coming home," he told her. "I think we should get the boys together and discuss it. It's kind of like discussing your burial plans; you hope you never need the information but everyone should be informed just in case."

He watched her fondly as she moved around the kitchen fixing his breakfast. She'd had health problems when they were young, but a change in climate, moving from Atlanta to New Mexico, had alleviated her asthma symptoms and they'd stayed and raised their family. The boys grew up in Los Alamos, hunting and fishing in the mountains surrounding the town, while their father worked for the Nuclear Laboratory. Retiring at fifty, when Jerry was a senior in high school and Pete was still a freshman, Walter had moved his family to Las Vegas, a small town in the high plains east of the Sangre de Cristo Mountain Range. He had friends from Los Alamos that had retired here as well and Sarah knew their wives. He didn't want to live by any big city and Las Vegas had the weather Sarah needed.

Sarah had gained some weight over the years but at fifty-four she was in good health. She colored her graying hair to a honey blonde shade making her feel and look much younger. Acting as secretary to the business, she did all the paperwork, took job orders, did payroll and even the accounting. Their lives had been good, but Walter worried about a gathering storm on the horizon. After finishing his breakfast, he went into the shop to begin the day's work, feeling powerless to stop it.

August 19, 11:05 a.m.
Washington, D.C.

Will and Mark were cleared by White House security, after having been thoroughly scanned by metal detectors, and they were furnished ID badges before being escorted to the meeting by Secret Service men. The meeting had already begun and grim countenances turned in their direction as they took the two empty seats at the twenty-foot-long conference table. Glancing around the room, Mark knew the problem was, indeed, very serious. The President of the United States, his National Security Advisor, members of his cabinet, the Chairman of the Joint Chiefs of Staff, a few Senators and several civilian defense contractors were all present. He recognized representatives from Lockheed-Martin, McDonnell-Douglas, Rockwell and Northrup-Grumman among others. He saw Will nod across the table at his old friend, Secretary of State Chuck Hansen.

Robert Stearns, the Secretary of Defense, paused in mid-sentence and nodded in their direction, "Glad you could get here so quickly, Hargraves, we've just begun." He stood in front of a 70 inch T.V. screen showing a map of the South Pacific. Stearns was sweating, although the room seemed comfortable to Mark.

Stearns continued, "You already know of the nuclear weapons test conducted by the Chinese yesterday. What you probably don't know is that, without a doubt, the blasts were the most powerful ever detonated." He took a drink of water as he waited for the murmurs to subside. "More powerful than anything the U.S. or any other nuclear power has yet developed. KH-12 satellite photos indicate multiple devices were detonated, with each warhead yielding approximately 60 megatons."

"Mr. Secretary?" One of the civilian defense contractors, waved a hand in the air. "Just how big is that?"

Stearns briefly glanced at his notes, "Back In 1952 the U.S. tested the first Hydrogen Bomb, code named 'Mike', with a first ever yield in the megaton range. Contrast that to the relatively puny yields of "Little Boy" and "Fat Man," the atomic bombs dropped on Hiroshima and Nagasaki, which measured in the low kiloton range. Then in 1954, at Bikini Atoll in the Marshall Islands, we conducted an atmospheric, hydrogen bomb test that, at the time, produced the largest yield ever at fifteen megatons. "Castle Bravo," as they called it, a lithium-deuteride fuelled H-bomb, had a fireball over 4 miles across and turned out to be even more powerful than anyone anticipated. Test crews in bunkers well outside the expected limits of its effects still received large amounts of radiation, and the explosion threatened ships they thought were way beyond the boundary of the danger zone.

'Then, in the early sixties when Khrushchev was premier, it was widely believed the Soviets had developed a 100 megaton super-bomb. It was never tested, but they did test a hydrogen bomb up by Alaska that was fifty-seven megatons. That bomb was massive and had to be carried and delivered by an airplane. By comparison, three of yesterday's five explosions were each greater than sixty megatons and were delivered by a single, long-range missile. They've managed to cram that tremendous power into a bomb no larger than our current, lower yielding ones. With our present technology, if we manufactured a nuclear device that powerful, it would require years to modify our delivery systems to accommodate the size increase."

"Do we know how many of these missiles they have?" the President, Albert Rissman, inquired.

"No sir, we don't. Previous estimates indicated they had around 450 of the old warheads, but we actually have no estimates of how many of these new ones they possess." He took another drink as though he'd been on an all-night bender and was severely dehydrated.

"Now ladies and gentlemen, here's the real kicker. Until yesterday, our intelligence community had no idea that China had developed the necessary delivery systems to be a serious direct threat to this country, especially with weapons of that size. Previously, of course, they could reach us with SLBMs, Submarine Launched Ballistic Missiles, and could also just barely reach us from Mainland China in a ballistic pathway over the North Pole, but with everything coming from the same direction we had a better chance of intercepting them. Their older missile system had a maximum range of approximately 6,800 miles, in contrast to our own capabilities of 8,100 miles." He pointed his laser pointer at a location, east of the Society Islands, in the South Pacific. "The target for this test was here."

He moved the computer mouse. The map changed, projecting photos taken from space, showing five distinct explosions, two appearing much smaller than the others. "Again, Satellite reconnaissance indicates this test was launched from the Chinese mainland and exploded, with amazing accuracy, over the South Pacific, 8500 miles away. They completely destroyed a small group of uninhabited atolls north of Easter Island."

Mark heard "Uh oh," muttered by several of those in attendance as he himself thought, less politely, "*Oh shit!*"

"The missile was an MIRV, Multiple Independently Targeted Reentry Vehicle, which delivered nuclear warheads to several different locations. In addition, we believe it utilized Soviet technology designated as FOBS, or Fractional Orbit Bombardment System, which keeps the missile aloft in earth-orbit until it's ready to descend. This has increased their ICBM range tremendously, enabling them to now reach any target in the U.S. from any direction."

"Ah . . . Mr. Secretary . . ." The Senior Senator from Texas spoke with a pronounced southern drawl. "How is it we were caught with our pants down again? After India surprised us with their nuclear tests, you would think the CIA would be more diligent. We have these billion dollar satellites with a capability of taking photos of something as small as a paperback novel, but these countries continue to catch us off guard. Can't these satellites be parked in orbit over one location?"

"Yes, Senator, that's correct. But since September 11 we have been more focused on the Mideast. There are many hot spots on Earth that require constant surveillance. Iran takes a lot of our resources. The two Lacrosse satellites are solar powered but the KH-12s require precious fuel to reposition them. We need to have suspicion of wrongdoing to justify moving these satellites over a particular spot. China is a signatory of the 1970 Nuclear

Nonproliferation Treaty. India and Pakistan aren't. We didn't expect this from China."

The senator smacked the table with his fist. "Well sir, maybe you should have!"

There was an uncomfortable silence

"Mr. Secretary, how many other countries have nuclear weapons?" one of the other civilian representatives asked.

"Until India and Pakistan, there were five with declared nuclear capability, the U.S., Russia, Great Britain, France and China. Now there are theoretically seven. But we know Israel has nuclear weapons and several middle-east countries have secret nuclear-arms programs. North Korea, of course. Other countries, including some of the former Soviet countries, South Africa, and a couple of South American countries supposedly gave up testing after signing the 1996 Comprehensive Test Ban Treaty." He emphasized "supposedly."

Stearns clicked the computer off and walked to the head of the table. "We have another problem. You'll notice that two of the five explosions were significantly smaller than the other three. Although the blasts were smaller, they were "dirtier" than the others, but with the type of radiation that destroys life without producing the massive explosion we normally see in an H-bomb. We haven't completed our analysis yet, but it looks like these two warheads delivered neutron bombs." Stearns took another drink of his water and sucked in a long breath.

The same man raised his hand again. "I thought all the nuclear powers were trying to lessen the amount of radiation in bombs, to make 'clean bombs.'

"Yes, that's true, and that's the idea behind the neutron bomb. The radiation is different from that produced by fission, as in atomic bombs, or fusion as in Hydrogen bombs. That radiation can linger for years, decades and even eons, depending on the isotope and can contaminate the earth, making it uninhabitable. Even though a neutron bomb produces a significant amount of initial radiation, consisting of extremely high-speed, penetrating neutrons, it does not increase the power of the blast, and it dissipates much more rapidly than normal radiation. The concept is, that it delivers a "sterilizing dose" of radiation, killing life, while leaving structures intact, and after a suitable amount of time, usable. This is why they are considered "clean" in comparison to hydrogen and atomic bombs. Neutron bombs use the fusion process like H-bombs do, and like H-bombs, normally need a fission device, or an atomic bomb, to detonate them. Although the explosion is much smaller, the high-energy neutrons destroy life in an area far beyond the blast radius."

"How many of you have heard of Red Mercury?"

He paused as most of those in the room raised their hands, and then explained for the others, "This is a substance, mercury antimony hydride, produced by subjecting mercury to massive irradiation. When detonated by conventional means, it creates a huge amount of heat and pressure and can actually be used, in turn, to detonate a neutron bomb.

During the Reagan administration the U.S. produced around a thousand of these bombs, but they were never deployed because of objections by European nations, and were dismantled during the Bush administration. We believe China, Russia, Israel, South Africa and others have this technology and may maintain an arsenal of these bombs. With Red Mercury the main concern is that a suitcase size neutron bomb becomes a real possibility. It would eliminate the need for an atomic fission device to detonate it. A neutron bomb could be delivered to a site in a very small package and set off outside the Capitol Building, for example, killing everyone inside. We were more concerned about it as a weapon for terrorists and were unaware it had reached a point of development where it could be used in a weapons systems and delivered by missiles, but we believe the Chinese have used Red Mercury in these explosions."

He downed the last of the water, gulping several times before continuing.

"This means, to summarize, that the Chinese have developed some kind of God-damned super-weapon, a system capable of delivering it to other continents with amazing accuracy, and they obviously don't give a damn who knows about it."

The President stirred in his chair and addressed Charles Hansen. "Mr. Secretary, get together our formal denunciation and contact the U.N. Security Council. They, and we, will be imposing the usual military and economic sanctions. I believe they should be stronger than those imposed on Pakistan and India. Even worse than those we have placed on Iran."

"Yes sir. We wanted to brief you on the situation first. Something should be released to the media right away, as they're getting impatient."

"Well, we certainly don't want them speculating." The president turned to his press secretary, "Tell Jamison to set up a press conference." He turned back to the table, "Comments, gentlemen?"

Mark saw Will's face darken and knew what was coming. "My suggestion is we dust off the plans for defense systems we all shelved years ago and get back into production. Your damned test ban treaties have left us in an extremely vulnerable position." This was slightly unfair since Rissman had come out of nowhere, and was elected on the basis of his strong stance on defense. After other administrations had traded nuclear weapons technology for campaign funds, the electorate wanted no more of that type of leadership.

"We're all familiar with your objections to the treaties, Mr. Hargraves. This is hardly the time for 'I told you so'." This statement came from the Chairman of the Senate Armed Forces Committee, Henry Simms, a jumpy looking man with thick glasses perched on an oversized nose. He was glaring at Will over the rims as though he were a naughty boy.

"Senator, I've gone on record as being in favor of non-proliferation agreements. The only objection I've had to disarmament has been our unilateral abandonment of research and development necessary to keep us even with the other side. What we must do now is resume the R&D as quickly as feasible, if it isn't already too late."

There were nods of agreement around the table. Edward Hermann, head of Western Airmotive Corporation concurred, "Will's right. I know we've been through this argument before, but it's time we faced the facts. Our companies have all had projects underway that were canceled because of disarmament treaties. It isn't just a matter of the loss to our companies, this latter incident illustrates the folly of believing the ban would ever be observed. First, France tests underground weapons in 1996, then India in 1998, with Pakistan retaliating, and now China."

Simms cleared his throat, "It seems you gentlemen could be a little more concerned about world peace and a little less concerned about your pocketbooks."

This brought an immediate protest from a number of voices around the table. "Gentlemen please! Let's keep our discussion aimed at a solution to the present dilemma." Rissman spoke up and the room quieted immediately.

"Mr. Hargraves, how long would it take you to recommence your companies R&D?"

"Of course there would be a considerable amount of work, but we could get started at once. I can have complete proposals prepared in a couple of weeks. Many employees who worked on those projects are still with me, but I would have to have assurances of a congressional appropriation."

"Mr. President, I must protest!" Simms jumped to his feet, his face red, "You have no right to resurrect any of these programs without authority from the Congress. This could seriously hamper current negotiations with governments who are not part of the disarmament treaties. Keep in mind that the countries of the old Soviet Union have thousands of nuclear warheads and they'll be threatened by any increase in arms production on our part."

"Mr. Simms, entering into these negotiations with other countries is precisely the reason we're in this predicament. We stopped our research and development while China and other countries obviously pushed forward with theirs, and now they've caught us flatfooted. Until all countries comply with the non-proliferation agreement, we're compelled to move ahead with our own research and development. I want all the companies that had major contracts canceled when the ban went into effect to resubmit paperwork."

"But Mr. President. Considering what we've just been shown I think it unwise to provoke the Chinese until all diplomatic solutions have been exhausted."

The president looked at Simms for several seconds and then pointedly looked away.

He turned to the Secretary of Defense, still standing with arms folded at the head of the conference table. "Bob, I want the programs screened to evaluate our "state-of-the-technology." Stay in contact with these gentlemen, utilizing their expertise. Mr. Hansen is going to Moscow to get a handle on their reaction to China's testing. I'm certain this will result in Russia continuing their own testing, if not more of the old Soviet states. We'll continue to work through the U.N. Security Council to salvage the test ban treaties even if there's been a setback and I'll get with congressional leaders to start seeking appropriations. I'm meeting with the Joint Chiefs in an hour."

The president stood, the others following suit, and he left the room accompanied by several of the other attendees. Will and Mark had started toward the exit when Simms approached them. "Hargraves, I've fought too long and too hard for these test ban treaties. The United States hasn't even ratified the Goddamn Comprehensive Test Ban treaty that's been signed by 149 other countries! This must be accomplished. We have a chance to get the other countries on board if we don't panic over this thing. I'm warning you, don't fight me on this or you'll end up never getting any government contracts again."

"Don't threaten me, Henry. We're only going to evaluate discontinued programs. I'm a businessman, believe me, we won't be spending money until your colleagues appropriate the funds. You just continue your negotiating and leave the important work to us."

Will and Mark left him standing in the room alone, and made their way to the limousine. As they drove toward the airport, discussing the implications of the meeting, Mark could see more dark clouds forming in Will's eyes. When Will got angry, things happened. Usually gentle and cultivated, Hargraves could be absolutely ruthless when necessary, and he generally got what he wanted.

Hargraves had made his fortune in the aircraft industry while still a young man. He earned flying money by working in his father's hardware store, then haunted the flight school, hanging out with pilots and volunteering to help the mechanics, to stretch his one hour of flying time into half a day's entertainment. He learned everything necessary to pass his ground school exam without spending a cent. An excellent pilot, he obtained his license while still a teenager, and when his father couldn't afford college tuition, Will joined the Air Force. He took classes at night, and flew every chance he got.

After his discharge, he obtained a position with a small aircraft company in Orange County, California. Continuing to attend college at night, he earned an engineering degree while in his late twenties, and soon became head of the company's testing and development division. The owner of the company, in dire financial straits, died unexpectedly three years later leaving behind a wife and a young son. Unable to support the business financially, the widow sold the company to Will. These events were of paramount importance to Mark since the dead owner and his widow were Mark's parents.

Now deeply in debt, Will turned to his father's good friend Maurice Whitfield for financing. Maurice had been in aircraft for many years and felt that Will's innovative designs, and his ambition, would give him a handsome return on his money. Will met Maurice's daughter, Katherine, at Maurice's home in Palos Verdes and they immediately fell in love. Katherine, only twenty-five when they'd met, was polished and sophisticated beyond her years and she loved flying every bit as much as Will.

He renamed the company, and modified its emphasis to defense-related projects, building it into one of the largest and most respected in the industry. A hands-on owner, his personal involvement kept the company efficient and productive, and regardless of his reputation as a ruthless businessman he took good care of his employees. He continued to employ many of the people who had worked for the former owner. Mark knew it had been

Will's wife, Katherine, who had softened Will's ambition, keeping his life in perspective.

"First thing tomorrow morning, depending on what Miles found out at the Pentagon, I want the database searched for the old contracts. We need to have preliminary specifications ready to submit to Washington in a couple of weeks; or sooner if possible. We need to get a jump on the competition. I think we'll mostly be starting over since the technology has changed so drastically"

They rode in silence for the duration of the trip to the airport. Will seemed to be distracted and Mark was thinking about the nightmare from this morning. He was having difficulty recalling the details but remembered vividly the terror.

Finally Will broke in on Mark's thoughts, "Mark, I want you to keep in constant touch with me. Carry your cell phone at all times and don't go off on one of your mountain runs or do anything that will put you out of touch for very long for the next few days."

"Yeah, no problem. My phone gets great reception. Are you coming to the plant tomorrow?" The limousine pulled into the executive terminal at Dulles Airport.

"No, I'll be at the house. Chris is coming up from San Diego and I want to see her before she leaves."

"If you want to see Chris, you'll have to move fast." Mark chuckled. "How long is she staying this time? I'd really like to see her myself." Mark had been in love with Will's daughter for as long as he could remember.

"Why don't you come by the house tomorrow? She's going to at least stay the night. I hope I can convince her to stay a few more days until this problem's resolved."

Mark frowned, "Are you that worried about this?"

Will suddenly looked older than his 62 years. "Yes I am, Mark. Damn worried. This may be bigger than anyone imagines. Why do you think China tested this weapon? They've tipped their hand, making the entire world aware of their capabilities by testing both H-bombs and neutron bombs together. I'm sure they just needed one successful test. Now they know their weapons are operational. If it hadn't worked, they could just say "Oops, we made a mistake" and the world would go ahead and forgive them. Because that's what we do. We never hold anyone accountable for anything since we pulled out of Iraq and Afghanistan. Everyone is too tired of confrontation. And this Red Mercury, enabling them to kill life and preserve the property for future use? China has a hell of a lot of people, well over one billion, and it's been rumored that they, and Russia, have built shelters to protect huge numbers of their population. They are seriously upset that previous administrations' "quantitative easing" has destroyed the value of the debt we owe them. They've already quit buying our bonds and they want to be repaid. Our current inflation is killing the dollar." He paused and gazed out the window.

"Instead of biting the bullet and cutting spending on entitlements, or trying to reduce the deficit, they kicked the can down the road and just kept spending. They bought an election with the promise to take care of the voters from cradle to grave, just like the European system. We could have had a less painful let-down by balancing the budget. Instead we kept trying to give everyone something for nothing, and now we're broke, and China isn't about to let us default on our debt. I think they want their money one way or the other.

"If they want to preserve structures why use hydrogen bombs at all? They're going to blow everything to smithereens." Mark said.

"They would need to disable our retaliatory capability by destroying major cities, military installations, missile silos, and the like. The neutron bombs aren't as powerful for destroying that type of infrastructure. The additional radiation produced by the neutron bombs would destroy life in areas not crippled by the hydrogen blasts. The MIRVs can carry up to ten independent missiles. They wouldn't need to have warheads on all of them. Some could deliver the Red Mercury detonated neutron bombs or even biological weapons. Then, after a suitable period, they just move in."

"God Will, You don't think they actually intend to use it?" Mark was shocked at Will's implication.

"I certainly hope not, but what were they thinking? I talked to Karl Dohner three days ago. He's out flying all over the Western U.S. making deliveries."

Mark suddenly realized Will thought this was very serious indeed.

August 19, 2:00 p.m.
Las Vegas, New Mexico

    Barbara Thompson drove into the bus/train depot. She parked her car in the short-term parking and entered the terminal with a few minutes to kill. She stopped and bought a Diet Coke and a newspaper and found a seat in the shared waiting area, scowling as she read the headline that proclaimed:

"U.S. Accuses China of Nuke Testing."

    The U.S. denounced today, the testing of an aboveground nuclear device over the South Pacific Ocean by the Chinese government. The test is a clear violation of the Comprehensive Test Ban Treaty.

    Neither Russia nor any of the other former Soviet states have issued statements at this time, but Secretary of State Charles Hansen is reported to be traveling to Moscow for a meeting with the Russian President.

    The President of the United States is conferring with his advisors today to decide on a course of action and to evaluate appropriate sanctions. Reliable sources indicate the test caught the U.S. completely off-guard. Apparently, according to the same sources, the blast was more powerful than the Chinese were previously thought capable of.

    Global concern over radiation has nuclear scientists scrambling to measure the effects of the test and the United Nations is sending an international team to monitor the situation.

As she read other stories about carjacking, rape, murder and an increasing number of home invasion robberies she wondered what kind of world they were creating for Jeremy to grow up and live in. Things were becoming worse every day as welfare was slashed and the food stamp program had been cut in half.

Glancing at her watch, she gulped down the remainder of the Diet Coke, left the paper behind, and followed the arrow "to trains," passing through the door onto the platform just as the train from Albuquerque was unloading. Pete disembarked, and turned to speak with the girl behind him. They seemed to be together as they headed toward the door where Barbara waited. Pete spotted her, his face lighting up with a grin, and he rushed over and hugged her so hard he nearly crushed her. Pete did everything with a lot more enthusiasm than her husband Jerry did. She noticed a small earring in his left ear that hadn't been there when he came home for Easter.

"Barbara, I'd like you to meet Sandi Baker, a friend from school. Her parents are on vacation in Europe and I convinced her to stay with us for a few days until they get home."

Sandi took Barbara's outstretched hand. "Hi Barbara. Nice to meet you, I hope it won't cause any inconvenience. Pete can be very convincing."

"No problem at all. Glad to have you. If you can get along with Pete, you're welcome."

"Oh, thanks a lot Barb. I'm an angel, everyone gets along with me." They collected their luggage and headed to the parking area.

Barbara was curious about Sandi. She really didn't seem to be Pete's type. He was very good looking and quite extroverted, while Sandi, although certainly not bad looking, seemed rather plain, and spoke with a soft, shy voice. Her light brown hair hung below her shoulders, no hint of waves or curls, and her wide set eyes accentuated her look of shyness. She didn't appear to be wearing any make-up. Barbara particularly wondered how Walter and Sarah, who could be a little old fashioned sometimes, would react to Pete's bringing this girl home.

"How long will you be here?" Barbara asked Sandi.

"I guess about a week. Pete promised to take me hiking for a couple days."

Pete threw the bags in the back of the Wagoneer and they all climbed in, Pete taking the back seat. "I was telling Sandi about me and Jerry backpacking every summer and she seemed interested. Can you believe she's never been?"

"Yeah, I sure can. You guys have never taken me, even when I begged, remember?"

"It was a guy thing, Barb. We haven't backpacked since last summer so I figured this would be a good opportunity. There's only a couple of weeks before I have to return for my final year. Hey, How's Jeremy doing?"

"He's trying to be independent at the age of 9. He's not being very successful." She laughed.

Nothing was very distant in Las Vegas and it took only a short while to reach their destination. Barbara dropped them off at Walter and Sarah's house and asked them to make her apologies, as she had another class to attend. She was in her sophomore year, working on her teaching credential at New Mexico Highland University.

Pete tried to think of a delicate way to approach his parents about the backpacking trip. He and his brother had hunted and fished in the nearby Sangre de Cristo Mountains every summer since moving from Los Alamos, but summer school had interfered with this annual pilgrimage and he was eagerly anticipating some quality time in the wilderness. His folks would be disappointed he was leaving again so soon, but Sandi would be going home to Phoenix when her parents returned and this would be their only opportunity.

He'd met Sandi in one of his classes, a beginning course in illustration. He took it as an elective, hoping it would be useful in his engineering classes, but he was terrible at it and had reluctantly admitted he would forever be compelled to do his drawing using computer CAD programs. He would have dropped the course if Sandi hadn't tutored him and they'd become good friends during the last semester. She'd recently had an emotionally difficult time breaking off a relationship with her boyfriend and Pete had lent his support. He discovered her parents were out of the country and on the spur of the moment invited her to go backpacking with him.

They came through the front door of the shop and his mother, who was working at the front desk, jumped up and threw her arms around his neck. She blubbered something about "finally home" and "my baby" and finally stepped back to wipe away a tear. She smiled at Sandi and looked a question at her son.

"Mom, this is Sandi, a friend from school. I invited her to stay a few days while her parents are in Europe."

They exchanged greetings and went into the living quarters. "Have you had lunch? I was just about to fix your father's. He's running late or he would have eaten by now."

"No, we haven't. We saved our appetite for some home cooking. I'll put my stuff in my room. Is Jerry's old room made up?" She assured him it was and he left to put their things away.

"Mrs. Thompson, I appreciate your letting me stay. I don't particularly like going to my parents' place when they're away. They moved to Phoenix while I was away at school and it just doesn't feel like home to me." She leaned against the kitchen sink while Sarah prepared sandwiches and soup for lunch.

"It's no problem at all, we have plenty of room. Have you known Peter for very long?" She sounded casual but Sandi, who was already a little embarrassed and concerned about what Pete's parents would think about her and Pete going camping, could feel the questions coming. Fortunately, Pete returned to rescue her, hugged his mom and winked at Sandi over Sarah's shoulder.

They heard the front door slam and Walter entered the kitchen, his grin splitting from ear to ear as he grabbed his son's hand, pulling him into a bear hug. Sandi could see the resemblance, but where Walter was large boned and heavy, Pete was tall and slender and, she thought, extremely good-looking.

After introductions and settling down to eat, Pete asked how the family business was doing. Walter laughed, "Are you kidding? It's 92 degrees out there. The air-conditioning part of the business has been booming. I'm glad you're here. I could use your help."

Pete gave a sideways glance at Sandi and plunged right in, "I'll be able to help quite a bit when I get back, Dad. Sandi and I are going backpacking for a couple of days before she heads for Phoenix. I hate to leave when I just got home but it's our only chance since I have to go back for the fall semester in two weeks." Feeling uncomfortable, Sandi carefully studied the remains of her tuna sandwich.

Walter hesitated, looking slightly disappointed, then said, "Well, I guess that's okay, Pete. I know how much you miss those mountains."

Pete breathed a sigh of relief. His father was the most understanding man he'd ever known. It was clear his dad was wondering about his relationship with Sandi and probably disapproved of his going camping, just the two of them, but he would never put Pete on the spot in front of company. They carried on a desultory conversation, catching up on family news as they finished lunch.

"Hey, how's my truck? Did Jerry have any problems with the new engine?" Pete had blown the engine just before he was due back at school and had to take a bus to Albuquerque much to his embarrassment. Sandi had provided transportation during the summer session, which had contributed to the time they'd spent together, and Pete promised he would return the favor and drive her back to Albuquerque when she was ready to fly to Phoenix.

"No, it only took him three days. Your truck is good as new."

"Great! Jerry's the best mechanic in town." He stood up, having trouble keeping the excitement from his voice, "Come on Sandi, we'll go start getting the gear ready. I'll ask my brother if we can borrow his pack and sleeping bag." Amused, Sandi followed him out the side door toward the garage where Pete's Ford Ranger was stored.

Walter turned to Sarah, "Sandi'll be gone in a few days and we'll tell Pete and Jerry about the box when he gets back from his trip. What do you think about that earring?"

Sarah just grinned at him.

Early that evening a mound of camping gear, including a backpack, fishing pole and tackle, sleeping bag, flashlights and old bags of dehydrated food, loomed in the center of the living room floor. Pete was on the phone, talking to his brother. "Hi Jerry. Yeah it's the kid. Hey, when you come over tonight can you bring your backpack and mummy bag? I have a friend visiting and we're going camping tomorrow morning." He listened to the reply and then said, "I knew you'd be jealous. Cool, see you later."

Sandi helped Sarah prepare dinner as Walter listened to his son's phone conversation. He disapproved of Pete going off to the mountains with this girl but knew it wasn't any of his business. After all, it was the 21st century and Pete lived in a university environment with a completely different set of rules and mores than Walter grew up with. Pete had always been headstrong, but other than a few minor problems, had never disappointed his parents. Well, there was the time the boys threw the cherry bomb in Mrs. Morales' mailbox and blasted it to several large pieces of deadly shrapnel that nearly decapitated Pete as he and Jerry frantically pedaled away on their bicycles. The local Sheriff allowed Walter to compensate her for the damage with the stipulation the boys apologize to Mrs. Morales. Leaving her home, they barely got out the door before the boys had erupted in paroxysms of laughter. Walter had cuffed them both good. Punishment consisted of cleaning the garage, an almost impossible task, and working without pay for two weeks in the appliance store doing clerical tasks, the most insufferable thing in the world for two teenage boys.

"Son, how long will you and Sandi be gone?"

"We'll drive up to Eagle Nest tomorrow morning, pack in and camp tomorrow night, and hike back out the next afternoon. We should be home by day after tomorrow in the evening and I'll be ready to help you in the shop the next day. Sandi's never backpacked before and I don't think we should push it for her first trip. She might never want to go again." He guessed what his father was thinking. "Sandi and I are just friends, Dad. She just ended a relationship and she needs a friend."

But Walter was worried about much more than just the girl. He was concerned about the package he'd received this morning, and he was worried about China testing Hydrogen bombs... and he was damned worried about what the Russians would do about it.

August 19, 3:00 p.m.
Cheyenne Mountain, Colorado

Leroy Jefferson had a problem. He stood at his console, trying to control his breathing and clasping his hands together to calm their trembling. It was worse today. He listened to a news broadcast prior to coming on shift, and because of reports of Iran getting close to having the bomb, and the on-going war against terrorism, and because of nuclear tests being conducted by China, it was much worse today. Leroy paid very close attention to the news; you might say he was a news addict.

Part of his problem was that Senior Airman Leroy Jefferson was claustrophobic, and the other part of his problem was that he was stationed at the NORAD Alternate Command Center deep within Cheyenne Mountain in Colorado.

Despite the circumstances, Leroy considered this the best assignment he'd ever had. The energy of the place was incredible and Leroy, stationed here for almost a year, considered himself personally in charge of protecting the United States of America from enemies foreign and domestic. He took his responsibility very seriously.

But, unfortunately, he had this bad case of claustrophobia and was barely able to maintain control from day to day. Last year, after receiving orders for NORAD, the North American Aerospace Defense Command, he'd made an appointment with a civilian psychiatrist, having heard that "systematic desensitization" sometimes worked with simple phobias. The process involved gradually confronting the sufferer with situations close to the feared ones until he was no longer phobic. It cost him a fortune and was completely unsuccessful, undoubtedly because he had to report to Cheyenne Mountain long before he had the opportunity to finish the therapy.

Most of the command had been moved out of the mountain to Peterson AFB in Colorado Springs and he hoped he would be stationed there. But as luck would have it he got assigned to the Alternate Command Center in the Cheyenne Mountain Nuclear

Bunker. He was okay most of the time, able to convince himself this large room he worked in was open space above ground. The claustrophobia kicked in when the space was smaller than a normal size room or when he perceived a danger.

Leroy's console was one of several positioned in a line facing several huge screens at the front of the room. There was another line of workstations behind him at a slightly higher level. A constant babble of voices filled the air as data was accumulated and reports were given on troop movements, fleet reassignments and incoming satellite transmissions.

Getting to work every day proved to be a major challenge as the jeeps carrying him and his co-workers entered the mountain through the pneumatic blast doors and traversed a network of tunnels large enough to drive massive trucks through. On most days he was able to stare straight ahead and ignore the panic building within him. On occasion though, when there were reports of international tension, he knew he'd never make it and he feigned illness, attending sick call to avoid being in the mountain just in case something should happen. Usually, though, he just went to work and shook.

This morning, he had considered calling in sick, but on other occasions when there were similarly frightening reports he'd managed to get to work, worrying that calling in sick too often would call attention to his problem. During the Iraq War he had actually been counseled for poor attendance and he'd been stationed above ground at the time!

Leroy monitored his console, feeding data to the mainframe computer and checking it against that received by his co-workers at other terminals. He continually evaluated data from a variety of sources including E-3A Airborne Warning and Control System, or AWACS aircraft, which were essentially flying radar installations. He received other data from ADCOM, the U.S. Aerospace Command that supported the mission of NORAD, a joint U.S. and Canadian organization.

Detection and tracking devices used by these various agencies represent some of the most sophisticated monitoring devices on the planet, and include magnetic, thermal, chemical and acoustical sensors, radar and sonar, laser beams and high-resolution optical devices that use both natural and artificial illumination. This equipment resides on the ground, in the air, at sea and on satellites. The monitors at the front of the room display that information, as well as the current locations of U.S. military vessels and aircraft. The entire defense system is computer-controlled and Leroy was one of the guys it reported to.

He looked up from his terminal just as the indicator light on the wall changed to Defcon 3. He hadn't been too concerned when it changed from Defcon 5 to Defcon 4 following the Chinese test the day before, but he was definitely concerned now.

"Oh my God," he muttered under his breath, as he fought down a surge of panic, and swallowed convulsively to force the acidic bile back down where it belonged. Cold sweat broke out on his ebony forehead, his stomach lurched, and he realized he seriously needed to take a leak.

"Easy Leroy," he told himself, "It's been there before. It's been there lots of times. Even worse." He had seen it at Defcon 3 and even Defcon 2 in drills. He knew it had reached Defcon 2 once before, for real, during the Cuban Missile Crisis. DefCon 1 would indicate imminent or actual attack. The indicator, of course, had never reached Defcon 1.

"Maybe it's another drill. Yeah, that's it. It's probably a drill. Please God, let it be a drill. It's almost time to quit buddy, you can make it," he babbled under his breath, trying to get control of his racing heart. Sweat ran down his sides from his armpits and he prayed none of his fellow workers would notice his violent shaking.

August 19, 4:30 p.m.
Denver, Colorado

The psychiatrist leaned back in his expensive leather chair, hands steepled before his face, staring at the small black box resting on his desk. Why would someone send this to him? It must be a joke, he decided. He straightened the pen set on his desk and reread the letter to determine if he had possibly misunderstood it. Sterling Harrington was a careful man and he didn't want to make a mistake here.

The side of the box had, what appeared to be, a speaker. He turned it over and examined the back, or maybe the front, where he found a hinged door. It was fastened by some unknown method and fit snugly but there was a tiny crack around the perimeter. Other than these few features it was a plain black box weighing very little, perhaps a pound and similar in size to a paperback book.

He picked up a screwdriver he had procured from the garage and tried to insert it into the tiny crack, but it was way too big. Going to his study closet, he searched through a small toolbox until he found a tiny flat blade screwdriver, used to repair glasses, that he thought might fit. Going back to his desk, he made another attempt, inserting the screwdriver and applying as much pressure as possible, considering he was completely unfamiliar with the use of tools. He succeeded in making a small dent along one side of the panel. Inserting the larger screwdriver in the indentation and putting the box on the table to prevent stabbing himself, he pushed with all his might.

"Aha!" he cried as the lid of the box popped open. He had fortuitously placed the blade directly over the point where it latched on the inside.

"Ohhh, Shit," escaped from the lips of the usually reserved doctor. Inside the small compartment was a broken glass vial and burned remains of what appeared to be money and possibly a map.

Being careful not to touch the contents he dropped the remains into the wastebasket next to his desk. He certainly wasn't going to berate himself about it since, as a psychiatrist, he knew guilt was self-destructive. He shrugged and left the study to have an early dinner before attending the opera that evening.

August 19, 6:00 p.m.
Denver, Colorado

The screen door slammed behind them as Lori Arnaud, carrying a bag of groceries in her left arm, and pushing Ashley ahead of her with her foot, pulled Kevin into the house. "Hurry up guys, we're running late. Go watch T.V. while I get dinner going. Daddy will be home soon."

With everyone safely inside, she hurried to the kitchen to stash the groceries and get dinner started, thinking of the statement "the faster I go, the behinder I get." She hurried to finish her chores before her husband arrived home. The situation had been worse these last few days, since she'd been gone four days last week while attending her mother's funeral in New Mexico. John had been very angry. She told him originally she would only be gone three, but her father was so distraught she didn't want to leave him alone, and even now she wished she could be there to comfort him and keep him company during his bereavement.

Her girls' high school pre-season track meet had taken considerably longer than she'd anticipated and she'd picked the kids up from the day care facility at five-thirty, thirty minutes later than usual. The track meet was held after the summer session classes, and ran late into the afternoon, contributing to her being behind schedule.

Practice meets started in mid-August before the regular semester and the girls were making excellent progress toward getting in shape for the regular season. The girls did exceptionally well today and she'd felt obligated to treat them to McDonald's as a reward. Kimberly Seaver won the 5K cross-country for the third time this summer and, since Kim's a senior, several colleges were showing serious interest in recruiting her. Kim was Lori's first really good runner. Lori desperately wanted to coach at the community college level, and having coached a national class runner in high school would definitely increase her chances.

But now she was late, and if dinner wasn't ready when John got home there would be hell to pay. She carefully put away the groceries, "a place for everything, and everything in its place." John hated clutter and could be very unpleasant if he couldn't immediately find whatever he was looking for. She threw the pork roast in the pressure cooker and got out the potatoes. As much as she would have loved to fix something quick and easy, she didn't dare - John wouldn't allow her to use prepared foods. She loved to cook, but it would have been convenient to use prepared foods on occasion, especially on days like today.

She returned to the living room to check on the kids and found them watching a talk show host humiliate several groups of people on national television. Daughters were surprising their mothers with the revelation that they knew their mothers had been sleeping with the daughters' husbands. The husbands were waiting in the wings to be humiliated in turn.

"Ashley, you know you aren't allowed to watch those shows. Turn to the cartoon channel. I'll be checking on you in a minute and if it's not cartoons, it's the dungeon for you."

"Oh no, mommy, not the dungeon." Ashley laughed at her mother's fierce scowl. "Anything but the dungeon! Make Kevin go too. He's watching it with me."

"Am not! Please don't make me go to the dungeon!" he wailed. He tried to act frightened but couldn't hold back a giggle as his freckled face broke into a delighted smile.

Then, in a know-it-all tone, Ashley said, "Except he doesn't know what they're talking about."

Lori, en route to the kitchen, paused in mid-stride and raised her eyebrow at Ashley, "Do you know what they're talking about?"

"Of course. I'm six years old you know. I would be mad too, if you were sleeping in my bed with my husband. I would have to sleep on the couch and that wouldn't be fair." She gave her mother a what-else-could-it-be look.

Lori brushed back a long stray wisp of dishwater-blonde hair that escaped her hair clip, falling in front of her pale blue eyes and agreed it wouldn't be fair at all. She quickly returned to the kitchen, listening at the door for a moment until she heard the voice of Sponge Bob. She thought for the hundredth time how wonderful her children were, considering the difficult conditions they were growing up in.

The kitchen was cramped, and boasted few modern conveniences. She and John had purchased this house, a small, three bedroom, two bath, tract house, when they first moved to Denver nine years ago. John used one of the bedrooms as an office so the kids shared a bedroom.

The back yard was tiny but Lori had landscaped it whenever she could squeeze money from her meager allowance. It consisted of a play area with grass and the "dungeon," a playhouse that looked like a castle. Her small wooden shed contained her gardening supplies, her mountain bike, and a few hand tools. She had installed a drip system for a few plants and flowers.

John didn't allow her to use the garage. It was his "space" where he tinkered with his electronics. He owned every tool known to man but the majority of them had never been used. He bragged to his co-workers that he kept his house in terrific shape and that he seldom needed to pay for repairs. He was unaware that Lori fixed almost everything herself, or paid for repairs out of her allowance. She was painfully aware of how difficult it would be to live with him if anything went wrong and he had to deal with it himself.

They had planned to buy a larger, more modern home after having children but John's career had fizzled and their plans stagnated. John had earned Bachelor's and Master's degrees in electrical engineering and was pursuing his doctorate when they'd met at the University of Arizona. He was so handsome, with dark hair and eyes and he spoke with a slight French accent, left over from his early years in Quebec, which she had found irresistible.

Lori fell in love with him almost immediately. She was a PE major and he told her he liked women who were physically fit. Soon after they met, he insisted their relationship include frequent sex and she realized why he was interested in a physically fit woman.

She helped him in his studies by typing all his papers, wishing he would put more work into their relationship, but knowing he was completely involved in research for his thesis,

"The Effects of Ionizing Radiation on Electronic Equipment." It looked like he would go far as a scientist. He expected to quickly work his way up in a big company, supervising research and making tons of money.

Madison Electronic Supplies in Denver, Colorado manufactured motherboards and other components for sale to computer manufacturers and John had received an offer of employment right out of college. Companies were well aware of the fact that new graduates were willing to accept a much lower initial salary. Arnaud's credentials had been excellent and it appeared he had a future in the Research and Development Department. Although computers weren't exactly his area of expertise, he knew they were the wave of the future. He and Lori married and bought their small house in Denver to start their new life.

Nine years later he was still employed in the same job. Although an adequate researcher, he had significant problems with authority, was arrogant, and failed to put company interests ahead of his own. Twice he'd been passed over for promotion to Research Department Assistant Supervisor. He told Lori the first time that the individual promoted was a woman who was sleeping with the boss. Lori knew the woman, Jenny Harper, and she was extremely competent and happily married. The second time, the man promoted, according to John, was an ass-kisser.

Although she had obtained her degree in Physical Education, Lori hadn't worked until a year ago. John made decent money, but his habit of spending it on his hobbies, computers and electronic toys, had kept them financially strapped. He drove a BMW while Lori drove a Honda Civic. He finally agreed to let her work part-time, if it didn't interfere with her duties at home, and she obtained a part-time high school coaching job. After a year, she was offered and reluctantly accepted, a full-time position as track coach and PE teacher, not daring to tell John she had gone full-time. She rationalized that as long as she managed to accomplish her chores he wouldn't notice and everyone would be happy. Sometimes she was so tired she could barely function, but she loved coaching and she loved the girls, and helping Kimberly Seaver to obtain a track scholarship would make it all worthwhile.

Lori finished fixing dinner; pork roast with small red potatoes, string beans prepared by hand, and a fruit salad, and was setting the table when the phone rang.

"Lori? I have to finish some work on a project. I probably won't be home until around midnight." This was the third time in two weeks he'd worked late, which was unusual. She could only remember his working late one other time in nine years. "Make me a plate of whatever you prepared for dinner 'cause I'll be starved when I get home."

Suddenly Lori felt a distinct shock. She could hear a woman laughing in the background. This wasn't particularly unusual but somehow she realized why John would be late, knew it as clearly as if he'd said, "I'm going to screw my secretary and I'll be craving dinner when I get home."

"Lori? Did you hear me?" She realized she hadn't answered him.

"Yes John." Completely taken by surprise she hung up before he could say anything more. Although she'd thought of leaving him every day since their marriage, she never expected this.

"Mommy, what's wrong?"

"Nothing, honey." She quickly wiped tears from her cheeks as she turned to see Kevin standing in the doorway, big brown eyes close to tears. "Go wash up for dinner, sweetheart."

Kevin turned and ran for the bathroom. Something was wrong. Mommy usually only cried when daddy was home.

August 19, 7:35 p.m.
Ganado, Arizona

With one foot on a boulder, his arms resting across one thigh, Gregory Whitehorse leaned forward and squinted toward the setting sun. The giant yellow fireball, flattened on top and bottom, shimmered in the desert heat and slowly disappeared as it descended below the horizon. The red spires of Monument Valley, throwing lengthening shadows across the valley floor, reached up to kiss the brilliant crimson and gold clouds that glowed with a fiery radiance above the horizon. As the distance from the horizon increased, the clouds faded to silver and were laced by a cobalt blue and emerald green sky. As it always did, the beauty of the sunset choked him with emotion.

This was his favorite time of day at his favorite place on Earth. A light breeze fanned his straight black hair back from his shoulders and he gazed across the domain of his forefathers, this high desert region tucked in the northeast corner of Arizona. His tribe, the Navajo, had lived in this area for hundreds of years.

With a Ph.D. and a full professorship in geology at the University of Northern Arizona in Flagstaff, he spent considerable time there, but his real home, the home of his heart, was here in Ganado, a small town at the reservation's southern edge. He was Arizona's foremost geological expert on the land of his people, although Gregory looked at it with a different eye than most Navajo. He saw the history of the land, knew its foundations, its characteristics and its future. Gazing out across the Colorado Plateau he saw buttes and mesas formed by erosion of the horizontal layers of limestone, sandstone and shale. The brilliantly colored layers were the remains of ancient sea bottoms and sandy shores of a once great inland sea dating back over two billion years. This land, between 5000 and 8000 feet in elevation was cut by magnificent canyons, The Grand Canyon, Oak Creek Canyon and Canyon de Chelly, among others. The land had emerged and re-submerged repeatedly over the eons, creating metamorphic, sedimentary and igneous rock, the latter representing prehistoric volcanic activity in the region. Many of the mountains around Flagstaff and into Northwestern New Mexico, are all that remain of once mighty volcanic cones. The Painted Desert, with its kaleidoscope of color, alternating stripes of red, yellow, purple, blue, brown and gray, extends south from the Grand Canyon down to the Mogollon Rim. To the east, the Colorado Plateau butts up against the Southern Rocky Mountains in Northern New Mexico and against the Sangre de Cristo mountains just beyond them, a range that contains the highest peaks in that state.

As the evening wore on, the mountains faded to purple and the colors of the sky evolved through the spectrum, until, as the light diminished, the land and sky turned to shades of gray. Gregory sighed and reluctantly turned his back on the spectacle, winding his way down the steep, dirt trail, his heavy leather boots digging in for traction. He swung his leg over his Harley Davidson Dyna Low Rider and felt the rumble of its 1450 cc engine in his bones as he hit the starter and it roared to life. Swinging the Hog in a tight circle, he rode his modern steed down the road toward home. A small paper-wrapped package was tucked in the right saddlebag of the bike.

August 19, 7:40 p.m.
Newport Beach, California

It had been a very long day and Mark was relieved to be home. Will had received the call from Washington just before four a.m. that morning and had called Mark immediately. Since then Mark had flown to Washington, met with the President of the United States, waited at the airport for Miles and Heinrich, flown back to Los Angeles, gone to the plant for a couple of hours and finally returned home.

This afternoon's brief meeting seemed like a pronouncement of doom. Mark spent two hours at the plant putting things in motion and fretting over Will's indifference to the possibility of new contracts. Will hadn't stayed at the plant when they returned from D.C., but had left immediately after the Gulfstream landed. It reminded Mark of the "dark years" after Katherine's death when Will neglected his business and spent all of his time on "the project."

Closing the door behind him, he let out a sigh. The security system automatically slid the deadbolt and reactivated the silent alarms as he crossed the tiled entry, through an archway into the living room. Pulling off his already loosened tie, he threw it, and his coat, over the arm of the sofa and checked the answering machine for messages. There were two. The first was from the plant production manager asking for clarification on a job order and the other was from Chris Hargraves. She would be leaving town soon and "was dying to see him before she left." The latter invoked his lopsided boyish grin and his heart quickened in anticipation of seeing her tomorrow. He tried to return her call but Ernest, Will's butler, said she had gone out for the evening.

Shutters covered the wet bar in the room's far corner. He pulled them aside and selected an MGD from the under-counter refrigerator. Twisting the top off, he flopped down on the couch to consider the implications of today's astonishing events.

He sought a reason for Will's indifference to the job and the only explanation he could come up with caused his stomach to turn. Will didn't think the projects would ever be completed. He recalled the years Will relied on him to manage the company, essentially without his help, and Mark didn't recall them fondly. He'd been inexperienced, just out of graduate school with a Bachelor's degree in aeronautical engineering and a Master's in business. He was aware that Hargraves wouldn't have allowed him to embroil the company in any financial or legal trouble and Mark suspected that Miles Bannister was the real man in charge, reporting to Will on a regular basis. Mark had initially found it difficult to work with senior management. They resented his being placed in the CEO position with very little training or experience, but Will had faith in him and he learned quickly, soon gaining the respect of the rest of the management team by relying on them for their expertise.

Will had been distant, preoccupied, and absent for much of the time. He'd been involved in "The Project," a venture Mark knew very little about.

Hargraves had been a surrogate father to Mark since his own father had died, an alcoholic, over thirty years ago. Mark remembered very little of his dad, being only five years old at the time of his death. His mother Claire, had sold the business to Will shortly after her husband died. Mark's father, deeply in debt, had been drinking the profits for years and had Brad Teller not died of cirrhosis when he did, he soon would have become bankrupt. Will had been keeping the business afloat for the last few years anyway and Mark's mother knew selling out was the only way she would realize any profit.

Claire, also an alcoholic, had sent him and his older sister Jill to live with her brother. Mark was unaware, until Chris told him many years later, that Will had supported them after his mother squandered the profit from the business. When Mark was ten, his mother died and he was invited to spend the summer with Will's family at their home in Laguna. His sister, who was four years older than he, and closer to his aunt and uncle, chose to remain with them, never establishing a relationship with Will and Katherine.

Mark spent the next two summers with the Hargraves, and once he became a teenager lived with them full time. His uncle, a nice enough man, was basically uninvolved with either his own two daughters or with Mark and Jill. Mark was five years older than Chris and Chris followed him around like a puppy. They were best of friends.

Although a rich and powerful man, Will spent considerable time with Mark, functioning as his mentor and Mark had a serious case of hero worship for William Hargraves. Will had felt a great debt of gratitude to Mark's father for hiring him and giving him a position of responsibility with the company and Will always paid his debts.

Mark attended The University of Southern California, the total cost borne by Hargraves. Mark could have done anything with his life and career, Will had asked nothing in return for his support, but never considered doing anything other than working for Hargraves Aerospace Industries. Over the years as Mark grew older, his hero worship changed into a great respect and friendship, and even though he was almost thirty years younger than Will, he considered him his best friend.

Finishing the beer, Mark got up, went into the bedroom and slipped on a pair of running shorts, a T-shirt and a worn pair of Asics Gels. It was late but he needed to run to unwind from the day's exhausting events. He left the house, ran through his local streets, and exited the residential area, running at a moderate pace. He turned down Newport Drive toward the ocean, too tired to go all out but needing to push hard enough to clear his body of the stress chemicals that built up during the day. The sun had already sunk into the ocean, and as the evening shadows spread before him he was assailed by a sudden and deep melancholy that his world might not go on forever, as he'd always assumed it would.

TWO

August 20, 6:00 a.m.
Sangre de Cristo Mountains, New Mexico

Pete and Sandi, planning to hit the trail early, left Las Vegas at five o'clock in the morning. They drove north on Interstate twenty-five and turned left onto highway fifty-eight traveling from the plains toward the higher elevations. They drove through rolling hills until they reached, and drove through, the small town of Cimarron thirty minutes later. A faded sign on the outskirts of town announced "Where the Rockies Meet the Plains" and sure enough they began to climb shortly thereafter. Pete rolled down the window, allowing the mountain air to ruffle his hair as he breathed in the sweet taste of freedom, and reveled in the cooler temperatures as they ascended into the mountain range. Several miles later, they came over a hill and spotted a picturesque lake on their left, a small marina visible on the opposite shore.

"That's Eagle Nest Lake. I've camped there a few times. Caught some delicious Lake Trout and Flathead Cats." He licked his lips in an exaggerated manner, running his tongue over his lips. "I can't wait to have trout for dinner."

"You're pretty sure of yourself. We'll probably be eating dehydrated meatloaf."

"No way! You wait. I'm a good fisherman. Speaking of food, I'm starving and I need to buy a fishing license. We can have breakfast and I'll just get a five-day license in Eagle Nest. The turnoff to the trailhead is only a couple miles farther up the road."

He swung his Ford Ranger into a roadside diner's well-maintained parking lot in the tiny mountain town of Eagle Nest. The diner had a sign out front advertising "home cooked food" and

Sandi had to admit it was delicious. She ate sparingly, feeling slightly nauseated by the increasingly mountainous, winding road that had gained two thousand feet in elevation over the last few miles. She prayed her breakfast would at least partially digest before they started hiking. Pete stuffed himself with three eggs, bacon, and hash browns, along with a giant stack of hotcakes.

"I really liked your brother and his family," Sandi told Pete. "Are you sure he doesn't mind me borrowing his equipment?"

"Of course not. He just wishes he was going with us."

Jerry, Barbara and Jeremy had visited the night before, Jerry bringing his camping gear and backpack for Sandi to borrow. Usually shy around strangers, Sandi had, surprisingly, enjoyed their company immensely. She and Barbara, both education majors, found they had many things in common.

They finished breakfast and went next door to a sporting goods/tackle store to purchase Pete's fishing license. The place was crammed full of a variety of goods stacked clear to the ceiling. Hunting and fishing gear took up the left side of the store including a large display case with rifles attached to the wall behind a counter. Camouflage clothing was mixed in with orange vests on central racks. The entire right side of the store had shelves with toiletries and grocery items. Judging by the number of animal heads mounted on the walls the local taxidermist was a busy man.

They headed north again, this time on highway 38 and soon found the dirt road leading west into the mountains. Pete frowned when he saw the condition of the road. "Uh oh. It looks like they've quit maintaining the road and the sign's missing that used to indicate the trail. Oh well, I know where the trailhead is and the road can't be too bad."

"How long has it been since you were here?" she asked.

"Actually, it's been about three years. I've camped several times closer to home, but this area is gorgeous and the trail is flatter. No offense, but I thought it would be easier for you, since you're a flatlander and a wimp." He flinched as she punched his arm.

After bouncing along the rutted road for a quarter mile it unexpectedly widened and was graded smooth as it wound through tall, aromatic pines.

"That's weird. This part of the road's in excellent shape. Why would they leave the entrance such a mess? There are numerous cabins all through these mountains so you'd think they'd maintain the whole road."

After a few miles they passed a road leading off to their left, going south, that Pete knew led to a hunting lodge. They wound another mile and the road dead-ended in a huge graded dirt clearing, much larger than Pete remembered, large enough for at least a hundred cars. A sheer rock face, around one hundred fifty feet high loomed on the west side. Trees framed either side of the cliff and several massive boulders littered its base. The trail, barely visible on the cliff's right edge, lead northwest into the forest. The cliff face presented a barrier to the west and the trail made a huge loop to the north to get around the ridge. To the southeast the topography sloped gently away, creating a magnificent view out over the foothills. Pete parked his truck close to the trailhead, climbed out and took a deep breath inhaling the scent of the pines. The morning sun blazed in the eastern sky and the temperature was still cool but warming fast.

"This is absolutely great! Every time I come back to the wilderness I wonder why I stayed away so long."

"It really is beautiful. I'm so jazzed we came," she said.

He retrieved the packs from the truck bed, helped Sandi adjust her straps and held the pack up so she could slip it onto her shoulders. The pack extended above her head with the sleeping pad rolled and tucked under the top flap. Her stuffed mummy bag was strapped to the pack's bottom.

"Wow! It's heavy. How far are we hiking?"

"Don't worry, it'll lighten up when you fasten the belt." He helped her to fasten the waist belt.

"Oh man, how cool is that! What a difference. How does it do that?" She was pleasantly surprised at how the weight diminished once the belt was tightened.

"It lowers the center of gravity, redistributing the weight to your hips and legs. Your water bottle is in the outside pocket. There's plenty of water up here and I have purification tablets so don't get dehydrated."

They started up the seriously overgrown trail, Pete leading the way and trying not to set too fast a pace. Fortunately, sparse undergrowth in the forest made the going easier and Pete checked his topographic map frequently to avoid going in the wrong direction. He was familiar with the area and wasn't particularly worried about finding their way back, thinking more about the river and the trout they were going to have for dinner.

August 20, 7:00 a.m.
Durango, Colorado

The heavy steel door, clanking loudly, slid back to give access to the malodorous, cramped cell. Arby Clarke, his prominent heavy brows permanently furrowed in a scowl, was shackled securely with his handcuffs fastened to a metal waistband and with fetters that allowed him to only take short steps. A chain, dangling down the front, connected the cuffs and fetters. He wore the grungy, orange coveralls that made prisoners immediately identifiable. Arby's body filled the doorway as he exited the enclosed cell with its solid walls and solid door, broken only by a barred hole, ten by ten inches square.

An unarmed guard, Fred Harris, jerked Arby forward by the tether attached to his cuffs, eliciting a deadly glare from the giant prisoner. Harris and Arby both knew an inaccessible armed guard had them under surveillance and covered by a mini-14 rifle. Arby, totally silent, stared at him until Harris nervously averted his eyes. Arby had learned quickly that nothing could be done about these assholes, except to get yourself thrown in the hole, but he also knew that someday he would smash this dude's face in and grind it under his heel like a fat beetle. He didn't know when, or under what circumstances, but he knew his time would come. He hated these Detention Officers, these cop wanna-be's.

Other doors scraped open as he passed. Similarly attired, bound prisoners, hooked together by a chain that attached their cuffs at the wrists, joined the queue behind him. The line halted at another solid door. Harris spoke into an intercom and the door slowly drew back revealing a second, lighter hallway. Another armed guard, sitting behind bars in a small cubicle, kept his weapon trained on the men emerging from Death Row.

Prisoners jeered as Arby and the others walked down the narrow hallway between cells on one side and a crumbling brick wall on the other. Word had already spread that Arby Clarke was transferring out of Durango Territorial Prison.

"Hey, Clarke, you lucky bastard! I'll give you my entire fortune if you'll take me with you," a prisoner yelled as they passed, holding his crotch with both hands and thrusting his hips forward.

"Yo dude, I hope I never see your face again, or your dick either," another called. The inmate reached through the bars attempting to touch the men who, regardless of where they were going, were walking out of this hellhole.

An early morning chill permeated the corridors, creating condensation on the dank walls. The old prison stank of urine and even with new "no smoking" policies, cigarette smoke as well. Brick walls were covered by cracked and peeling plaster, leaving large areas of the brick exposed underneath. Although lighter than "Hell", the death row area, this section was still only dimly lighted, low-wattage bare bulbs hanging overhead giving off feeble illumination. Each cell contained a two-man bunk and a toilet.

Durango Territorial Prison was the oldest prison in Colorado, built in the late eighteen hundreds and updated very little during the last one hundred and twenty or more years. Exposed wires ran up the walls where intercom, telephone, data and electrical lines had been installed, and cameras, mounted in the corners of the hallway, recorded their passage down the corridor.

Lifers inhabited this portion of the facility. The men behind Arby now numbered fifteen, fifteen of the most dangerous men in the United States, all awaiting execution for murder, and/or repeated sex crimes. Five, including Arby Clarke, were serial killers. Three of the fifteen had been permanently incarcerated at Durango, while the others, brought from prisons throughout the Southwest, had been housed here overnight while awaiting transport this morning to the country's newest, state-of-the-art federal prison in Denver. There was one last prisoner to pick up from Santa Fe, before the trip's final leg.

The procession of inmates passed through a final automatic door to a processing area where small windows opened to the outside. The men had been locked in the bowels of the prison and they all squinted in the bright morning sunlight. Guards roughly pushed them onto a wooden bench along one wall and the chains that linked them together jerked the men at the end of the column down onto the bench.

"Keep your fucking hands off me," growled one of the prisoners, Jaime Ferrar, at Harris, the guard who'd pushed him. Ferrar tried to lunge toward the guard.

He backed off quickly, then grinned at Ferrar, "What you gonna do about it, asshole?" He jumped back as Ferrar aimed a kick in his direction, but the fetters limited Ferrar's movement and the heavy metal cut into his leg. The guard laughed as the prisoner next to Ferrar was jerked off the bench.

Another officer yelled at the guard, "Leave them alone, Harris. We don't want no trouble. My vacation starts two minutes after we deliver these ladies to Denver and you ain't gonna fuck it up for me." Jake Petersen, the federal Marshall in charge of the transport, wanted nothing more than to get these guys transferred to Denver without any problems, but upon examination of the transfer paperwork he noticed several pieces were missing. As usual, nothing was going according to protocol, and they were going to be stuck here for a while.

"Oh shit, can't anything go right? It's going to be one long fucking day."

Through a barred window, Arby saw the black and white transport bus pull up to the loading dock. He furtively glanced down the line of men seeing that they had noticed it also. No matter how dismal the situation appeared, being outside prison walls caused them to dream of freedom.

August 20, 7:30 a.m.
Long Beach, California

Mark strode down the center aisle of the enormous hangar, the roof over one hundred feet above his head, high enough to accommodate the giant aircraft being assembled there. He waved at familiar workers, some of whom he had known most of his life. Administrative offices, consisting of an entire two-story building, occupied the back corner of the cavernous space. Company policy dictated he wear a photo I.D. and it was visible on the lapel of his suit jacket, but the guard knew him well, and smiled, nodding as he entered the building. "Morning, Mr. Teller."

"Good Morning, Phil." Ignoring the elevator, he bounded up the stairs, taking advantage of every opportunity to exercise. Besides, the stairs were quicker. The building had been completely ripped out of the hangar and rebuilt three years ago in order to upgrade the wiring for the computers and telecommunications equipment. The job was completed using company equipment, supplies, and manpower, saving the corporation a significant amount of money. Will Hargraves hadn't become one of the country's wealthiest men by wasting it.

Mark entered his office and took off his coat, hanging it on the coat rack beside the door. As always, the first thing he did was flip a switch turning on a stereo system that played easy listening music. Mark preferred doing most things with music playing. One entire wall of the office, from the waist up, was glass, offering a view of the hangar's immense interior. The polarized glass could be changed from transparent to opaque at the touch of a button.

This was Mark's home away from home. The office was large with a mahogany desk on the left, angled to give him a view out the window. The wall behind the desk was lined floor to ceiling with bookshelves, crammed full of rolls of blueprints, bound financial volumes, aircraft magazines and thirty or forty books, including Mark's prized, original copy of "Stick and Rudder," by Wolfgang Langeweische. A Nordic Track exercise machine stood in the back left corner facing toward the window.

Carpeting covered the entire floor, and on the right, surrounded by four chairs, was a large, round conference table covered with schematics for a project Mark had been working on before the unexpected trip to Washington. Above a row of cabinets extending the width of the right wall were framed photos of vintage aircraft including one of Mark's favorites, his P-51 Mustang. Additional photos included several of space shuttle landings, including the first, Columbia in 1986, and a pictorial history of aircraft the Hargraves' plant had manufactured over the years. There was a picture of Mark and Will with Burt Rutan, and another showing Will shaking hands with President Bush. A concealed wet bar was built into the back wall to the right of the door.

He turned on his computer and immediately picked up the phone, "Hi Jenn. Could you please tell Miles I'm in? Thanks."

While waiting for Miles to appear he went to the bar where his secretary had prepared coffee. Carrying the steaming mug to his desk he checked his E-mail. One of these days, he promised himself for the hundredth time, he would get Jennifer Groves to screen his E-mail for him. There were over sixty messages and he'd only been gone one day. Miles arrived, rumpled clothing and eyelids drooping at half-mast attesting to the long hours he'd put in the day before. Mark poured him a cup of coffee. "You look like you can use this. How's the search going? Find what we need?" Mark had left at around 7:10 p.m. the previous evening, leaving Miles still sitting in front of his computer.

"I assigned Moore the task of pulling all the old paperwork, but quite frankly Chief, I think the stuff's just too old to use." He tossed a sheaf of papers on Mark's desk. "I took the liberty of having the new engineer, Ray Twohey, start working up some preliminary designs for a totally new concept. The kid has some fantastic ideas. Take a look at these."

Mark took a few minutes to look over the work in the folder. He was impressed. It reminded him of some of the imaginative ideas Will Hargraves came up with as a young engineer. Many of the patents Will owned, especially those on avionic equipment, had significantly advanced the safety of flight.

They called Ray in for a meeting and spent the rest of the morning going over the new concepts. Although it would take longer to develop totally new ideas it would be well worth it. The old projects were outdated and Mark laughed at what they considered advanced technology only eight years ago. To defeat today's modern weapons new technology would definitely be required.

"I need to go over some of these specifications with Mr. Hargraves. I'll get back to you this afternoon. Have the design department start getting some of this stuff into the computer. I'll want to see prelims tomorrow afternoon."

Ray threw a worried look at Miles, but Miles answered without hesitation, "Sure Mark, we'll have something for you." He knew you didn't tell Mark Teller something couldn't be accomplished.

August 20, 10:00 a.m.
Sangre de Cristo Mountains, New Mexico

The trail wove in and out through Ponderosa pines, following the natural contours of the mountain. First trending north, it eventually swung around to the west and passed over a saddle before descending again on the far side of the ridge. It alternately passed through shaded glens, and open areas bathed in sunlight and then gradually gained altitude, generally using gentle switchbacks, and occasionally steeper ones, but overall the increase in altitude was within Sandi's ability. After one and a half hours of hiking they stopped for a break alongside a gigantic ravine that dropped away precipitously to the right, and gratefully shedding their packs, sat propped against them on the ground while Pete carefully checked his topographic map and sipped from his plastic water bottle.

"There's a great little river in the bottom of this canyon but the trail down is rocky and could be dangerous. It's quite a long way from here. There's another stream with good fishing a few miles farther along this trail but at a higher elevation. What's your preference?"

"Well, let's see, if we go down into that canyon we have to come back up, right? That's pretty much of a no-brainer. I much prefer a gentle uphill now rather than having to climb out of that monster later."

"That's what I figured. I think we can reach the campsite in another hour or so. Ready?"

"Slave driver." She climbed to her feet, again needing his help to get the pack on. "I don't think I'll ever get the knack of slinging that thing around like you do."

Pete balanced the pack on his knee, held it by the straps and swung it around his shoulder, slipping his arm through the strap as it settled neatly onto his back, all in one efficient motion. "Sure you will, nothing to it."

In another half hour they came to a "y" in the trail, the right fork continuing along the edge of the abyss, the huge chasm curving away to the northwest. The left fork headed in a southward direction up a hill. They bore left and, using switchbacks, climbed to the top of a plateau. As they came over the edge of the plateau they saw an incredible range of mountains that rose toward the sky in the west.

Pete paused to allow Sandi to catch up, and pointed westward. "Aren't they beautiful? We're on the backside of the range that holds the Taos Ski Basin, and also Mt. Wheeler, the highest peak in New Mexico. It's something like 13,200 feet."

She nodded, breathing heavily, sweat dripping from her hair, "I'm glad I'm not hauling this pack up that monster!"

"No, don't worry. We're almost to the creek where we'll camp for the night. Those mountains are quite a distance from here."

The plateau, being much flatter than the forest they had passed through, was also more open, and a multitude of downed trees and large boulders littered the landscape. The day had become progressively warmer. They hiked through a wide meadow dotted with Pinyon pines and Juniper, and boasting a riot of color from purple lupine, blue columbine and yellow brittlebush. Pete breathed in the mountain air, enjoying the sweet smell of the yellow-flowered bushes. The trail wound through some large boulders and began a gentle descent that eventually brought them to a fast moving stream flowing out of the high country on their right and spilling into a small lake approximately a half-mile in the distance. Pete could see that the trail descended to the shoreline of the lake and continued along it until it disappeared in thickening vegetation along its banks.

"You know, it's funny," Pete said. "It's been a long time since I camped in this area but I don't remember this lake being here. I doubt if they stock it, although there's a fish hatchery not too far from here at Red River, but there's always been plenty of fish in this river."

"Are we stopping then?" Sandi was sweating even more, her cheeks flushed from almost three hours of arduous exercise.

"Yeah, we'll camp here but we need to stay back from the lake about a hundred feet." They selected a level campsite under a grove of pines and Sandi gratefully dropped the pack with a sigh of relief and collapsed on the ground. She watched Pete pitch the two-man backpacking tent. He explained that he preferred to sleep in the open, but at this high elevation the weather could turn cold at night, even in the summer. "We can always sleep outside if it's comfortable," he told her.

They would use Pete's white gas stove to cook dinner that evening, providing he caught some fish, but decided on a cold lunch. They ate sandwiches and Fig Newtons and laid down on their sleeping bags to take a well-deserved nap.

August 20, 1:00 p.m.
Los Alamos, New Mexico

The breathtaking view framed by the oversized picture window went unappreciated by the despondent man gazing out at the Sangre de Cristo Mountains. His reddened eyes, wet with tears, intellectually perceived their beauty, but he was emotionally numb, unable to savor it.

The view from his house also encompassed the town of Los Alamos, a view that in the past had always excited him and filled him with wonder. Los Alamos, the national laboratory where the first atomic bombs were developed during World War II, and that today boasts what is arguably the world's greatest concentration of computing power.

He was born several years after Los Alamos was established in 1943, and by the time he was 12 years old he had fallen in love with anything having to do with nuclear technology. As a teenager, with the cold war heating up, he studied and learned everything he could about physics, chemistry and astronomy. He decided in high school to become a nuclear physicist. While other boys' heroes were baseball and football stars, he idolized J. Robert Oppenheimer, Edward Teller and Enrico Fermi, physicists who had envisioned and constructed this scientific enclave out of a wilderness - to experiment and develop, against tremendous odds, weapons of unimaginable power... the power to end a war. At Los Alamos, owned by the department of Energy and managed by the University of California, they branched out from that original nuclear research to studies of the solar system, innovative biological research, and modeling of global climate.

The man had attended the University of California at Berkeley and actually took a course taught by Edward Teller, the "Father of the H-bomb." After the development of thermonuclear weapons, Edward Teller had left Los Alamos and became a professor of physics at U.C. Berkeley. The man remembered the course fondly. Along with his marriage to Marie, and the birth of their daughter Lori, it was one of the highlights of his life. He realized the culmination of his lifelong dream when, after obtaining his doctorate in nuclear physics, he went to work at Los Alamos, where regardless of the other technological research going on there, he still found atomic nuclei to be the most fascinating of all things God created.

The black box he'd received from a gentleman named Karl yesterday morning should have represented hope for the future but he was filled with the deepest despair. He'd buried his Marie just over a week ago and was now lost in a world without meaning. He was one of the most brilliant men of our time, an eminent nuclear scientist, but without Marie, life to him was not worth living.

His daughter had returned home to Denver following the funeral, after he'd assured her he was all right. He loved her and his grandchildren very much, but saw them infrequently and he knew his life would now be defined by a complete and abject loneliness. This morning he had packaged the box for shipping, affixed a label with his daughter's address and sent it Express Mail, next day delivery.

Working at the laboratory at Los Alamos he knew there was a substantial risk of nuclear war. The news media didn't know or report the entire story but the scientists at Los Alamos realized the significance of the Chinese hydrogen tests; the beginning of a new era of cold war tension, and a very real possibility it could escalate to a nuclear holocaust. He sincerely hoped the box wasn't a hoax and that his daughter, son-in-law and two grandchildren would be spared.

He turned from the window, walked in a daze to the couch and sat down. From the coffee table, he picked up the custom Colt revolver, a beautiful handgun with engraved scrollwork and scrimshaw handgrips that he had loaded with .45 caliber ammunition. He lay down on the couch, put the revolver in his mouth and pulled the trigger.

August 20, 1:30 p.m.
Laguna Beach, California

Warm breezes blew off the ocean, rustling the bougainvillea and honeysuckle draped from the second floor terrace of Hargrave's Laguna Beach estate. The ten thousand square foot, pure white mansion stood at the ocean's edge, close enough to catch the sea's salty fragrance, floating on the on-shore zephyr. Huge, west-facing windows furnished incredible views of the rolling ocean swells, crashing breakers and the deep blue Pacific.

Two men and a woman relaxed around a table, sheltered by a red tiled patio cover shading the large veranda that overlooked both the ocean to the west and, on the south side of the house, a magnificent black bottom pool in the yard below. Caterers bustled about preparing the terrace and the adjoining rooms for tonight's party.

Comparing the two men, one would never guess they were father and son. The handsome young man, a single diamond stud in his left ear and a small gold ring piercing his right eyebrow, had a brooding appearance; his goatee framed a mouth with pouting lips. Short cropped, brown hair was fashionably gelled to stick straight up and he was darkly tanned. His well-muscled, athletic body was the result of working out each day in the well-equipped spa in the home he shared with his father. He slouched in a patio chair dressed in baggy khakis and a black tank top.

The only things he and his father had in common were the unusual gray eyes and his father's money. He had an arrogant demeanor, a result of being rich without having worked a day in his life to earn it. Clay's father was William Hargraves.

Will was ignoring the conversation between his two grown children, his thoughts returning to the meeting with the President again and again. He had returned home from Washington the previous evening and had called Karl Dohner to check on his progress in delivering the signaling devices. He'd almost been embarrassed a few days ago when he instructed Karl to begin the distribution, but the situation with China indicated the time had come.

And he'd promised Katherine.

He stood and walked to the terrace's low perimeter wall, staring over the ocean. The sky was cloudless and the burning afternoon sun, glinting off the water, caused him to squint. As thoughts of his wife drifted through his memory, his face softened. He recalled her fear after they'd lost their daughter Laura many years ago, killed by a hit and run driver. All his money and power had been unable to discover, and bring to justice, whoever was responsible.

Laura was only ten years old when she died.

Five years later, when Katherine lay dying of ovarian cancer, she made Will promise that no matter what it took, whatever his money had to buy, he would ensure that nothing ever happened to Chris or Clay.

After her death, when newspaper headlines screamed of international problems and the United States became embroiled in small regional conflicts, he first considered building the shelter. But the Berlin wall had come down and the Soviet Union had collapsed and as the pain of Katherines' death had lessened he felt like a fool, and called a halt to the architectural planning. Much of the preliminary groundwork had already been completed at that time. The land had been purchased and excavation was already underway.

But the more things change, the more they stay the same, and the nuclear weapons once controlled by the old Soviet States began to show up in other countries, countries not limited by treaties or reason. And then, there was always China, lurking, a behemoth bulging with people and needing room to grow. September 11, 2001 started a new round of problems with the "War on Terrorism", 2 or 3 wars and the rise of radical Islam. He reconsidered his earlier decision to discontinue the project, resumed the environmental work and began actual construction of the facility.

He was asked by the government to join a civilian advisory group to keep the administration appraised of advances in aerospace technology and learned as part of this group that international tensions were always high and peace was never certain. On June 11, 1998, after India and Pakistan began their nuclear competition, the doomsday clock, an indicator of how close the world is to war, was moved ahead five minutes. On that date it stood at 11:51 p.m. Gazing out over the Pacific he wondered if the world would ever be safe, and what time the doomsday clock now read after China's unbelievable missile test. The closest it had ever been to midnight was two minutes before twelve, when Truman first authorized testing of the hydrogen bomb.

Hargraves continued building the shelter, but over time he put in less and less time there, eventually losing interest. It had consumed a large part of his energies for a long time, reminding him of Katherine and making him feel as if he were doing something to keep her memory alive. He hadn't been there as frequently in the last couple of years, and finally began to renew his interest in aviation and to concentrate more on his business.

He'd left the shelter in good hands, however. Glen Mitchell, a rather eccentric engineer and closet survivalist, had made it his passion. He worked for Hargraves Aerospace for years as an aeronautical engineer, but when he heard about the project he requested that Will let him participate in its planning and construction. It was now Glen's baby and even Hargraves had begun to think of it as "Will's Folly" as it was called by some of his peers in business and government.

Chris and Clay had been older than Laura. She was the baby of the family and her death had affected them differently. Chris felt a great loss, having always been protective of her baby sister, six years younger than she. Clay was closer in age, thirteen when Laura died, and seemed almost unaffected by her death. He and Laura had fought continually during their entire childhood. Will never understood Clay's attitude, not at the time, or since. When Katherine died five years later, though, it had been a different story, her death deeply affecting both his children. Chris was away at college when her mother died and flew home to be with her father, comforting him more than he comforted her, and it brought them closer together. Clay lost the one person in the world he felt loved him, his mother. He became even more withdrawn and distanced himself emotionally from his father and his sister.

Will's attention was brought back to the conversation behind him when he realized it was becoming another heated sibling argument. Clay raised his voice sarcastically, "You're wasting your time. Look at the general population. They're all overfed, as it is. Half the people out there are fat slobs! Where do you see all this hunger?"

Chris, usually adept at not being baited by her brother, felt compelled to defend her work. "Many poor people are overweight because they can't afford nutritious foods, not because they eat too much. If we can design inexpensive, nutritious foods we can ensure everyone has a healthy diet."

Will walked back to the others, still thinking of the past, as he fondly watched his daughter. She looked like a young Katherine, with dark auburn hair and hazel eyes, her complexion tanned from spending many hours a day outdoors. She, like her brother, was in excellent physical shape, with an athlete's body.

Six months ago she received her doctorate in marine biology, and she led an exciting and fulfilling life. Last semester, realizing a longtime goal, she obtained a teaching position at the University of California, San Diego, and was affiliated with The Scripps Institute of Oceanography through her research grant. As soon as she was certain of her income she purchased a small home in nearby La Jolla, feeling guilty about borrowing even the down payment from her father. Though she only lived seventy miles from her family, she didn't get to visit her father as often as she, or he, would have liked, traveling extensively with her colleagues in search of the perfect marine environment for experimentation. Dr. Tanner was a world-renowned oceanographer and she was one of his star assistants. Her flying skills were invaluable to the team, and they were all accomplished divers.

"Chris, you know Clay is just trying to annoy you." He glanced at Clay, whose scowl deepened.

"How surprising you'd take her side of the argument," Clay said.

"If I thought you were serious about the conversation I'd give more credence to your point-of-view. But you know as well as I that you only want to irritate your sister. When was the last time you thought seriously about the problem of world hunger?"

"Now that you mention it… never. I don't find it interesting at all." He leaned back in his chair; his fingers laced behind his head, and grinned. "There are already too many people on Earth. Why make it possible for the planet to support more?"

Will fought down an urge to once again defend his daughter. Clay was right; he did it too often. Instead, he changed the subject.

"How's the research going, Chris? Have you compiled enough data to renew your grant proposal?"

"It's going great, Dad!" She was relieved to terminate the conversation with her brother. Whenever they were together, he ridiculed her for working for a living, when she could follow his example and live a fun, exciting and totally unproductive life. She suspected he was jealous for having, so far, wasted his own life and because their father was proud of her accomplishments. "We're off on a new tack. Dr. Tanner is trying to develop a cold-water prawn that can be cultivated in areas now devoid of food fish. We're starting our research immediately upon our return from Mexico."

Her father looked troubled, "Babe, I wish I could convince you to postpone your trip for a while. Something's come up that I'm not at liberty to discuss just yet, but I'd really appreciate it if you could hang around a few days until we know how serious the problem is."

"I don't see how I can, Dad. Everything's been arranged and other people are involved." She hadn't seen him this disturbed since her mother's death and she was worried about him. "Anyway, we're not leaving for two more days. Why don't you tell me what's on your mind?"

Not wanting to alarm either of them unnecessarily, he told them, "I'm afraid I can't. It involves a government contract. That includes you too Clay. I want you to stay in contact."

"I'm taking the boat out this afternoon. I already promised a bunch of friends."

"Well, take your cell phone and monitor the ship's radio closely in case I have to reach you."

The maid brought another tray of iced tea and put it on the table. "Mr. Hargraves, Mr. Teller is here. Shall I show him in?"

"Of course, Helen, thank you."

Mark came through the patio door grinning, having seen Chris from inside the room. She jumped up and put her arms around his neck, giving him an exaggerated hug. "Mark, I thought I was going to miss you. Dad keeps you way too busy."

He flashed his crooked grin and held her at arm's length, "What a tan you have! You need to use more sunscreen. Melanoma and all that."

She grinned, "It's natural. Have a seat."

Mark greeted Will, nodded at Clay and took the fourth chair at the table. Clay ignored him, intentionally gazing toward the ocean.

"How are things going at the plant? Everything in progress?" Will questioned Mark.

"It's going fine but we need to discuss it when you have a minute."

"Let's have lunch and you can brief me afterwards. Chris, Clay, can you join us?"

"Sure. I'd love to," Chris said.

Clay stood to leave, "I'm going sailing, and I'll see you two later." He emphasized the word "two" and left abruptly, leaving Will unhappy with his rudeness to Mark.

Mark had never cared much for Clay, though he was always polite and had attempted, on many occasions, to be friends. He had such respect for Will Hargraves and it saddened him that Clay was so unlike his father and had caused him so much grief. For Clay's part, the feeling was mutual. Clay hated Mark's influence with his father and had been jealous of him for most of his life. It irritated him that Mark, only nine years older than he, was his father's friend and business partner.

Mark was extremely pleased that Chris was staying for lunch. He hadn't seen her in several weeks and thought she looked wonderful! They had 'dated' a couple times a few years ago, but the chemistry just wasn't there and Mark had the distinct impression she thought of him as a big brother. He very much wanted a second chance.

While Helen served lunch, Mark and Chris walked arm and arm to the edge of the terrace, looking down at the pool. A beautiful Bentley outdoor pool table stood sheltered under the ocean side Gazebo, its blue slate surface contrasting with the white marble railing. Covered with white linen tablecloths, a large number of tables were being set up around the pool with generous flower arrangements as centerpieces.

The large, irregularly shaped, black-bottomed pool was landscaped with black and gray rock that formed a small mountain as a backdrop. Fan palms, ferns, and flowering bushes were interspersed throughout the rock, and a slide, almost unnoticeable, wound down from the mountaintop into the pool. A waterfall of warm water cascaded into the pool from a hot tub, situated on a slightly higher level and partially hidden beneath the veranda they stood upon. A small bridge spanned the water and led to a path that extended around the back of the mountain giving access to the slide by a staircase cut into the rock surface.

"You're coming to the party tonight, right?" he asked her.

"Sure, I wouldn't miss one of Dad's parties. I'm bringing a co-worker. I think he'll enjoy it since he's never been around this kind of opulence," she said, only half kidding.

Mark's gut wrenched. He'd hoped to have her to himself this evening.

"I have some errands this afternoon but I'll be back for dinner at around seven," she told him.

Looking at the pool with Chris by his side he had a rush of memories from their childhood. "Do you remember the great times we had sluicing down that slide into the pool? We'd play "Marco Polo", with little Laura in her rubber floatie and Katherine watching over us all." He smiled at the memory.

"Yeah, we had good times growing up here," she agreed. "It all seemed so normal, although with Dad's money, I'm sure it wasn't. Mark, do you have any idea what has Dad so worried?"

"He's concerned about the international situation. In the past, during similar crises there's always been a period, a window of a few days, when the outcome was decided. He'd like you to hang around for a while to see what comes of this Chinese nuclear thing."

"Is the situation as serious as that?" She seemed surprised.

"The point is, your father thinks it is." He reached over and put his arm around her shoulders and she moved closer to him. He felt his heartbeat quicken with the movement. God, he wished she would stay a while longer. He desperately wanted to spend more time with her and was convinced if they just had enough time she would fall in love with him.

August 20, 2:00 p.m.
Sangre de Cristo Mountains, New Mexico

The bus followed the curvy mountain road, traveling too fast for the conditions, but U.S. Marshall Carlos Hernandez was in a hurry to deliver this bunch of *essos* to the federal prison in Denver. His boss, Jake Petersen, was really pissed off about the delay they'd experienced at Durango and had been pushing him all day for more speed. They picked up the last prisoner in Santa Fe around noon and drove north on highway eighty-four. Carlos had checked out the map while waiting in Santa Fe for the final prisoner and figured that if they stayed on interstate twenty-five it would add miles to the journey, dropping in a loop south before heading north again through Las Vegas, New Mexico and continuing on toward Colorado. According to the map, by going through Taos and then East to twenty-five they would slice substantial miles off the trip. Unfortunately, the map didn't show the mountainous terrain they would encounter by taking this alternate route or indicate that it would actually add time to the trip.

The bus was a standard Marshall's black and white transport vehicle with the driver's section segregated from the prisoners' compartment by a solid locked barrier broken only by a slit that allowed the driver and guards to communicate. Directly behind the solid barrier was the guards' section. It in turn was separated from the bus's main compartment by floor to ceiling bars. The main compartment contained school bus style, bench seats with a metal bar running along each side. Each prisoner was handcuffed to the bar in addition to being secured by his fetters, handcuffs and metal waistband. Additional bars blocked off another guard section in the rear of the bus and a cubicle containing a toilet.

Two armed guards accompanied Petersen, the supervising Marshall, in the front guards' area. Another guard, Jesse Carver, accompanied the driver up front and still another rode in the rear.

Video cameras sent pictures of the prisoner compartment to the driver's cubicle. They didn't take chances with murderers.

"So I told her to put out or shut up. The bitch led me on all night and I spent over fifty bucks for booze. It was bogus. She just said 'So long baby' and walked right out the motel door." Carver was narrating the unhappy ending to his frustrating date the previous evening. He had tried to score in every town they'd stayed overnight in.

They came around a curve into a small town, and Hernandez, laughing to himself about Carver's problems, bore to the left at the intersection of highway 38 and 84. He knew Carver never got lucky because, once he took his pants off, women found him lacking in appeal. Hernandez had seen him in the bathroom and had only seen a smaller organ on immature boys.

"That's too bad man. Next time turn off the lights." He grinned at Carver but Carver wasn't grinning back. He'd been ridiculed his entire adult life for his tiny member and didn't want hear it from Hernandez, whom he knew to be well endowed.

"Fuck you, Hernandez. I'm going to sleep and don't bug me till we get to Raton." He scrunched down in the seat, closed his eyes and was soon snoring.

He awoke to the sound of cursing. "Goddam it, look at that. Fucking sign says 'Red River'. We took a wrong turn somewhere. No wonder I haven't seen no cars for a while. Get out the map and see where we are."

Carver, still half asleep, grabbed a clipboard from the dash and flipped up some papers to reach the map. As he studied it, Hernandez leaned over to check it out as well. The road curved to the right and for a brief second Hernandez wasn't paying attention. Instinct warned him too late, and alarmed, he glanced up just as the road disappeared and all he could see was bright blue sky.

He jerked the wheel hard, but screeching tires protested as the bus, already across the left lane, skidded ahead and smashed through a protective barrier with ridiculous ease, plummeting over the edge. Hernandez screamed as Carver instinctively jammed his feet on nonexistent brakes and grabbed for a handhold. The nose of the bus angled down as the bus sailed through a deadly arc.

The cliff was almost perpendicular for twenty feet and then sloped at an approximately forty-five-degree angle to a gorge below. The front end smashed into a car-sized boulder and was completely crushed and shoved back into the middle compartment. Hernandez and Carver died instantly, Carver with the metal rod separating the front windows skewering his neck. Ironically, the prisoner compartment was reinforced and was the safest section on the transport.

Petersen, Ray Korinski and Harris were thrown against the bars as the cab collapsed at their back. Petersen's skull burst like a dropped, ripe watermelon. Korinski's ribs shattered, penetrating his lungs, as bright red, frothy blood gushed from his mouth, soaked his clothes, and spewed into the prisoners' section. Harris had stood with his back against the compartment barrier and the force, distributed evenly along his body, pinned him between the wall and the bars, his breath whooshing out like compressed bellows. The bus continued to bounce down the slope, dragging boulders and uprooting shrubs and trees with blinding dust clouds billowing around it and rising into the air.

Everyone was screaming, some in fear, others in pain. Several were thrown against the backs of the seats in front of them, others flung completely over them, handcuffs tearing flesh from their wrists. The windows burst, scattering gummy shards of safety glass throughout the compartment.

The bus careened down the slope, ricocheted off another boulder and flipped on its side as its momentum carried it further down slope. The sound of grinding metal and screaming men was deafening. The bus collapsed like an accordion and the bar along the side broke loose, the handcuffs on the high side slipping off the bar's loose end. The choking clouds of dust filled the bus as dirt and rocks were thrust up through the broken windows and through the ripped open side of the bus. Arby landed on someone who began to scream even louder, this time in excruciating pain as his leg slipped out the window and was amputated at the knee. The prisoners on the high side collapsed onto those beneath them who were still handcuffed to the side the bus now rested on.

The transport finally ground to a halt, coming to rest at the ravine's bottom, the screams even louder now that the vehicle had stopped. Metal groaned and creaked as it settled. Choking, and trying to see through the thick atmosphere, Arby untangled himself from the lump of flesh beneath him. The man had passed out or was dead for he was no longer screaming. Many of the prisoners were lying still, unconscious, but others began to move about as the shock wore off.

"Shit, man, what the hell happened?" Jaime could barely speak, his mouth stuffed full of dirt. He trembled uncontrollably. He screamed again as the bus shifted and settled further. "Let's get the hell out of this fucker!"

"Check the guards!" Arby yelled at him, with one overriding concern on his mind - he was alive and he wanted to be free. Stumbling to the front, where the dust was slightly thinner, he slipped on something and grabbed the bars to keep from falling. Thick, sticky blood coated the bars and ran down and pooled on the ground that protruded through the window. He wiped his hands on his pants.

Petersen and Korinski were obviously dead but Harris was moaning, still alive. He was squeezed against the bars with arms pinned at his sides, his head held sideways by bars indenting his cheeks and forcing his mouth wide open. He slowly opened his eyes, straining to look forward where he detected the sound of Arby approaching. The sight of Arby standing in front of him, grinning maliciously, caused him to panic, and although he struggled wildly like an animal in a trap, all he could manage to do was to wriggle in place.

"Hey, if it isn't asshole!" Arby slipped his hand through the bars grabbing Harris by the throat. Harris tried to scream, but as Arby squeezed tighter, the only sound that escaped through the distorted mouth was a tortured gurgle. Arby relished the bug-eyed look of panic on Harris's face as he steadily increased the pressure until he pulverized the larynx and felt the man suddenly go slack. Harris's body, completely limp, slid down until it was wedged tightly and could go no farther.

Jaime came up behind Arby, "The guy in back is dead. I tried to get the gun but I can't reach it. Let's get the hell out of here." He stepped up on the back of a seat that had partially ripped away from the floor and grabbed the edge of the window. The bars had been torn away from the outside and he easily pulled himself up and out through the opening, slicing his fingers on needles of glass still attached to the window. He didn't seem to notice.

Arby searched the bodies of the guards, locating several key rings. He unlocked the fetters and cuffs of the live prisoners and then followed Jaime through the window and out of the bus to freedom.

August 20, 2:30 p.m.
Marina Del Rey, California

"Why the hell did you mention the extra costs? Cost overruns are unavoidable on a project this complex, it's expected, but Parker can't ignore them when you blatantly itemize them for him. God, that was stupid!" The man was livid, his face red, as he gestured wildly at the woman walking beside him down the corridor. Others turned to stare as they passed, wondering what was going on. They all knew Ron Carlin and Jean Barnes were returning from an important sales meeting. Something had obviously gone wrong.

Jean kept her face down, lips pressed tightly together, and plowed straight ahead, trying to ignore the angry man screaming in her ear. Fortunately, her thick, brown hair hid her eyes for she was close to tears, and knew if she glanced in his direction she'd lose it completely. Absolutely hating any kind of confrontation, all she wanted was to escape to her office to compose herself and figure out where she went wrong. She realized she'd blown it big time when, after she innocently itemized possible cost overruns, the head of the Navy negotiating team suddenly called a halt to the meeting. He thanked them for their time, asked them to refigure the proposal's cost and resubmit it to the Pentagon. She knew there was no chance now of getting the Navy bid.

"Baby, you really blew it!" she thought to herself. *"It looks like another job change for you."* The corridor seemed three times as long as it had been on the way to the meeting. Ron ran out of things to scream at her about and he lapsed into an angry silence that left the only sound the clicking of her high heels on the tile floor.

The original proposal for the project was Jean's, and Ron had to admit it was very thorough. Of all the manufacturers submitting bids he was convinced they had the best shot at the contract. Up until this year, his negotiating team had always been composed of high-pressure, hard-driven males and he seriously resented it when Jean was assigned to his department, but her significant ability to accurately calculate project costs had won him over. He'd made a couple of half-hearted attempts to get her interested in him personally but soon desisted, worried about the company's sexual harassment policy. They had finally settled into a tolerable work relationship, until this colossal blunder! They'd rehearsed the meeting several times and he thought Jean knew exactly what to say but the problem was that this was her first experience with presenting proposals and he failed to brief her on what *not* to say.

They reached her office door with Ron arriving first, and opening it for her. She ducked in quickly and turned, blocking his path. "Ron, please let me collect my thoughts. I'll talk to you in a few minutes." She risked looking up and he saw tears beginning to form in her large green eyes. His anger abated somewhat and he relented.

"You have ten minutes and I want to see you in my office." He wheeled abruptly and stormed down the hallway toward his own office.

Jean paced in front of her desk, furious with herself for being a naive fool. She didn't think it was such a big deal to mention possible cost overruns, thinking by mentioning how minimal they would be; she would impress the Navy team. This was her first big sales meeting and now she felt sure it would be her last.

She'd joined the company, Advanced Communications, Inc., last January, starting out in the accounting department, but was quickly reassigned to Ron Carlin's team, the group that made the sales presentations to the defense department and other contractors. They were the ones responsible for ensuring the company made money . . . big money. Now it looked like she'd be sent back to the accounting department, or worse, looking for new employment.

"Well idiot, what's your next career going to be?" she mumbled. Jean Barnes hadn't been able to settle down in one job in all her thirty years. She originally graduated from college as a psychology major. Her mother, a clinical psychologist, had died when she was eleven and her father, Byron Barnes, encouraged her to pursue her degree in the same career field. Although she had never really been interested in psychology, she would have done anything Daddy wanted her to do. Since moving to the United States from Scotland as a young man, he had spent his life working in a backbreaking job as a longshoreman in Boston, and he believed a college degree would ensure Jean, like her mother, would never have to make a living performing manual labor as he did.

After her mother's death, her father had raised her as a single parent and it had been rough for both of them. Her opportunity to broaden her horizons came when she applied for college; it was her chance to get away. Wanting a completely different environment than Boston, she chose the state of Colorado and attended The University of Colorado in Denver. Daddy died of pneumonia when she was a sophomore and she had placed a huge guilt trip on herself for having been selfish and moving away. She knew he'd been lonely after she left Boston, though she visited as often as possible.

After college, with no reason for returning home to Boston, she stayed in Colorado and moved to Colorado Springs. Trying to work as a child protective worker for El Paso County didn't work out, as she died just a little inside with each child abuse case she investigated, so with Daddy gone, she decided to give up psychology and, again, try something different. She had no way of knowing that being a psychologist and living in Colorado had given her a ticket to salvation.

Jean quit pacing and sat in her comfortable desk chair, glancing around her office. She had finally earned her own office after years of working in various labor pools as she worked her way through college the second time as a secretary. Not having any idea what she wanted to do this time around, she took a variety of courses and discovered she had a talent for mathematics. Her second degree was in Accounting and once she'd completed her retraining she moved to California, searching once again for a change of scenery and lifestyle. She loved the ocean and settled in Los Angeles, hoping this time it was for good. At her first job, over thirty people worked in the same room, each with a tiny cubicle.

She went on to work as an accountant at the corporate headquarters of a national chain of athletic shoe stores.

Still looking for something more fulfilling, she worked at four more companies in the next five years. In January she landed the job with Advance Communications in Marina Del Rey. The accounting department was boring but she was soon transferred to the infinitely more interesting cost analysis department where she had an opportunity to utilize her research and math skills. She was given her own office, which meant to her that she was beginning to achieve some success. Daddy would have been proud.

And Ron? She had absolutely no interest in getting involved with her boss. He was nice enough looking, just under six feet tall with short-cropped light brown hair and an outstanding short beard, but she considered him shallow and self-centered and she had never been interested in his type. She had a problem with relationships, her standards eliminating most normal human males from consideration and she wasn't going to allow her personal life to interfere with her career.

Now it looked like, once again, she'd have to start over. She'd miss this office with its large desk and state-of-the-art computer system. There were three lateral file cabinets along one wall and low bookshelves, filled with accounting books, lining another. The room was carpeted, with an artificial tree in the corner. On the wall above the bookshelves were three recently purchased, framed photos, the three together creating a panorama of The Sangre De Cristo Mountains in northern New Mexico. They gave her a sense of comfort.

She wondered if it was possible to avoid talking to Ron. Ten minutes had already passed. Just as she screwed up her courage, and started for the door, the intercom crackled, the voice of the receptionist announcing that Federal Express had delivered a package for her. Greatly relieved, she called Ron explaining she would be late. "This package could be really important," she told him. Driving slowly, and killing as much time as possible, she retrieved the package from the Company's main office building. Although she was mildly curious about it, she was too concerned about confronting Ron Carlin and she stuffed the package in her oversized purse and drove back to the building housing the Cost Analysis Department.

Returning to her office she steeled herself, knowing that Ron would be waiting for her. She left the package, unopened, in her purse. She and Ron arrived at her office simultaneously.

"Ron, I'm so sorry about the meeting . . ."

He waved her off. "I'm too angry about the whole thing at this point," he said. "Why don't we go to dinner tonight and we'll discuss it in an informal atmosphere."

Being totally caught off guard by this turn of events, she agreed. "Ah… all right, that sounds like a good idea."

"Good, I'll pick you up tonight at six." He turned and left her office.

She plopped down in her chair. Maybe she could salvage this job after all.

August 20, 3:20 p.m.
Cheyenne Mountain, Colorado

Since the Defense Condition indicator had gone to Defcon 3 the previous day, the intensity of activity at NORAD Command Center had doubled, the noise level rising tremendously as the rate of incoming data increased. Personnel moved on the double going through a routine they'd rehearsed frequently during drills.

Leroy had trouble controlling his breathing and was sweating profusely. The walls were closing in. He closed his eyes, picturing himself standing outside the complex - above ground. There were only ten minutes left of his shift.

Data being received and analyzed from the Millstar Satellite Communications System indicated the system would be up and available in the event of hostilities. The multi-satellite system links command authorities with a wide variety of resources including ships, submarines, aircraft and ground stations. Each satellite serves as a smart switchboard in space by directing traffic from terminal to terminal anywhere on Earth and provides interoperable communications among the users of Army, Navy and Air Force Milstar terminals.

At that moment in time Leroy Jefferson had absolutely no interest in the Milstar Communications System. Nor did he care about the reports being received from the Space Control Center or from the "Theatre Ballistic Missile" warning system. This system gave warning of short-range missiles, such as SCUDS, being launched anywhere in the world. The ones Leroy worried about were the ones monitored by the "Strategic Ballistic Missile," the long-range ones, the ones that could reach this mountain and trap him here in this underground tomb.

He forced himself to open his eyes and look at his console.

"Jefferson! Get your ass moving!" He was staring at the indicator, barely able to function. With the admonition his eyes snapped to his monitor but he had difficulty interpreting the data. His fingers began to automatically speed across the keyboard, transferring data to the mainframe. NORAD, continuously monitoring for enemy activity from their base at Cheyenne Mountain in Colorado Springs, reported all clear.

His replacement stepped up on the dais. "Hey Leroy, what's up?"

"Defcon 3 status. No indications of incoming missiles." He reported automatically. "See you tomorrow." He hurried off the dais to the waiting vehicle that would deliver him from this smothering womb.

Unbeknownst to him, the minute he left his station the indicator went to Defcon 2. Had he known, he would have gone AWOL rather than return to this place tomorrow.

August 20, 3:30 p.m.
Albuquerque, New Mexico

Aaron Brown's six-foot frame barely fit; as he flopped down on the narrow bed and tore the wrapper from the package the man had given him earlier this morning. It was now late afternoon but he'd had so many surgeries he just hadn't had the time to get to it any sooner. As a third year surgical resident at University Hospital in Albuquerque, he was constantly running, with a demanding surgery schedule every morning, surgery clinic in the afternoons, and frequent on-call for the E.R. Aaron lived on-site in the residents' quarters, and spending most of his free time studying, he had almost no life outside medicine. But he loved the challenging practice of surgery and secretly dreaded the completion of his residency when he planned to return home to Atlanta, Georgia to practice surgery at Grady Memorial Hospital where his family had received their health care since he'd been a little boy. He would have to establish a private practice and fervently hoped it wouldn't bore him to death.

The package contained a radio device of some sort and a letter. As he read the letter he smiled at the joke one of the guys was playing on him.

YOU HAVE BEEN SELECTED TO SURVIVE THE COMING NUCLEAR HOLOCAUST. A BOMB SHELTER HAS BEEN CONSTRUCTED AND WILL BE AVAILABLE TO YOU IN THE EVENT OF A NUCLEAR WAR. ENCLOSED IS A SIGNALING DEVICE. YOU WILL NOTE IT IS SMALL ENOUGH TO CARRY IN YOUR POCKET OR PURSE. YOU ARE ADVISED TO KEEP IT ON YOUR PERSON AT ALL TIMES. THE BACK OF THE DEVICE IS LOCKED AND WILL REMAIN SO UNTIL IT IS ACTIVATED. IF YOU TRY TO TAMPER WITH IT IN ANY WAY IT WILL DESTROY ITSELF AND YOU

WILL LOSE THE OPPORTUNITY TO UTILIZE
IT. IF THE SIGNAL EVER GOES OFF YOU ARE
ADVISED TO FOLLOW THE DIRECTIONS IN
THE BACK OF THE DEVICE IMMEDIATELY.
THERE WILL BE NO TIME FOR DELAY. YOU
MAY BRING YOUR IMMEDIATE FAMILY IF
YOU CAN LOCATE THEM AT ONCE. KEEP IN
MIND THAT ANY DELAY MAY MEAN YOU
DO NOT SURVIVE. ACCESS TO THE
SHELTER WILL BE FOR A LIMITED TIME
ONLY. I HOPE THE DEVICE WILL NEVER BE
NEEDED. IF IT IS I PRAY YOU WILL HEED
IT'S WARNING. IF NOT, MAY GOD PROTECT
YOU.

It had to be Jenkins, the clown of the surgical residents. He'd played practical jokes on almost everyone else but had always left Aaron alone. There was a group of third year residents that didn't seem to take the work as seriously as Aaron but he had the distinct impression he was now accepted as one of the guys. He ran his hand over his shiny, shaved, dark brown scalp. He got up and opened the bottom desk drawer where he kept a few small tools and grabbed a screwdriver, wanting to figure out what was in the box before he ran into Jenkins. He placed the screwdriver blade in the crack and began applying pressure when he heard a page, "Dr. Brown, please report to the O.R."

"Aw hell!" He tossed the box on the closet shelf and headed for surgery.

August 20, 4:00 p.m.
Kirtland AFB, New Mexico

Karl Dohner was beginning to panic. Hired by Will Hargraves over three years ago, he'd worked at the shelter during the final construction phase and currently performed whatever duties Mr. Hargraves assigned him. He worked with Glen's crew, rotating food stores, performing general maintenance, helping to take care of the animals, and it was his responsibility to deliver the signaling devices to those selected to receive them. Karl got a call a few days ago from Hargraves, a call he never expected to receive, instructing him to begin delivery.

He had always had a problem with procrastination, a problem exacerbated by alcohol, and the call had frightened him. Drinking himself into a stupor, he awoke the next morning to find he had lost a full day. He immediately started sending them out by Federal Express, but hadn't mailed them all when he received a frantic call yesterday telling him to finish delivering them as soon as possible. Hargraves didn't tolerate mistakes. If he discovered that Karl hadn't promptly delivered them, he might not let him return to the shelter. According to Hargraves, the possibility had increased tremendously that the devices might be needed. Karl took the last of the receivers and started delivering them by hand. Most of those he had failed to mail had been destined for people in northern New Mexico down into Albuquerque. He drove like a madman and spent as little time as possible with each recipient and, by the afternoon of August 20, he'd delivered all but one.

Karl drove down a quiet street in base housing looking for the address on the list in his hand. Jason and Kristen Douglas were the last people who would receive packages. He'd gained access to the base by telling the guard he was visiting the Atomic Energy Museum, his visitor's pass visible on the dashboard as he cruised the quiet residential street nowhere near the base museum. As he listened to the news on his radio he was becoming alarmed. The shelter was 160 miles from his current location.

There it was, the address on the paper! Karl pulled up in front of the well-tended front yard and climbed quickly out of his car. He approached the front door and leaned heavily on the doorbell as he wiped perspiration from his brow and glanced at his watch. Shifting from one foot to the other, he checked his watch again and nervously pushed the button a second time. When no one came to the door, he rapped loudly on the jamb, listening for any indication that someone was home. He felt he had waited an eternity when in reality it had been less than a minute, and when no one answered immediately he hurried back to his car, jumped in, and drove away at a clip guaranteed to get him pulled over if he was unfortunate enough to be spotted by the Security Police. He glanced in the rearview mirror just as a pretty young woman walked out onto the porch, staring after him with a puzzled look.

He would never forget that face.

"Oh God, I'm so sorry but I just can't go back," he whispered as he sped away. He couldn't rip his eyes away from her face, as it grew smaller in the rearview mirror. The young woman watched as he disappeared with her and Jason's key to survival.

***

They were five hundred keys to survival. Some recipients laughed, others worried, and many thought it was a joke. But most people kept them just in case. Only a handful took a chance and destroyed the devices by trying to open them. The news from abroad was too frightening for that.

News of the devices leaked to the media, but just as Hargraves thought it would, created very little sensation. The story was buried on page twelve of the L.A. Times and was soon forgotten. It was thought to be the work of a lunatic, a clever hoax, not newsworthy beyond a minor curiosity.

Hargraves had considerable difficulty in selecting candidates to receive the devices. One major problem was he had no way of determining whom, or for that matter, if anybody, would heed the warning and attempt to get to the shelter. Should he then select back-up candidates for all the major occupations? Of course, proximity to the Sangre De Cristo range in New Mexico was of prime importance. Denver, two hundred eighty miles north, and Flagstaff, slightly farther than that to the west, were within four to seven hours of the shelter. Smaller towns such as Durango and Colorado Springs, in Colorado, and Las Vegas, Santa Fe and Los Alamos in New Mexico were also reachable by automobile in a reasonable period of time. Albuquerque, one hundred sixty miles away was the closest large city with an international airport. It was approximately three and a half hours away, taking into consideration the mountainous terrain at the end of the trip. No one would make it if they had to travel too far.

Doctors were among those he considered critical. He selected a general practitioner from a small town in the foothills; male, divorced, age 56, and a young surgical resident from Albuquerque, African-American, age 29. Also, an experienced internist from Santa Fe, age 41. He hoped one or more would make it and possibly bring other medical personnel. The internist was married to a former nurse. Other medical personnel included two nurses, a Clinical Lab Scientist, an E.M.T., a pharmacist, a dentist, and a psychologist.

Another critical individual was someone skilled with environmental equipment. He chose a man from Las Vegas, New Mexico who had been the chief of the Crafts Department at Los Alamos for many years and had extensive experience with sophisticated environmental systems similar to the one they had at the shelter. The man was around sixty years old, but had two sons, one of whom lived close by and was his partner in his air-conditioning and appliance repair business. They would back up the permanent staff member responsible for those systems. Hopefully, they would make it.

Hargraves estimated that approximately fifty percent of his selections living in northern New Mexico had an excellent chance of making it to the shelter if they heeded his warning in time. In some cases, even though qualified people lived closer, he chose individuals who were top experts in their fields who lived a little further away. The probability of them arriving on time was lower, unless he could provide them sufficient advanced warning. They included two world-renowned astronomers from Lowell Observatory in Arizona, a history professor from The University of Texas in El Paso, two Nobel prize winners from the faculty of the University of California at San Diego, and farmers from Imperial County in Southern California who were specialists in hydroponics gardening. If he could only allow them a head start!

His money helped considerably in investigating backgrounds and checking qualifications. He vetted over three thousand individuals. It all started out as a game and he had fun with it for a while but then the Gulf War, Iraq and Afghanistan and al-Qaeda convinced him he needed to take it more seriously. He compiled a list of people with the requisite qualifications, considered proximity to the shelter and finally considered age, sex, and marital status. Women of childbearing age with technical skills were especially desirable. Conceivably he could be choosing the beginnings of a new race of humans.

His list that started with three thousand candidates was eventually condensed to five hundred names. Hargraves hoped forty percent would make it and bring friends or family. The shelter had been built to support six hundred people.

Some people had moved and it was Karl's job to keep track and let Hargraves know so he could make adjustments. Actually, Karl did keep track of some of them but failed to inform Will. He just mailed the devices to their new addresses and hoped they could travel the necessary distance.

Others included teachers, an army chaplain, carpenters, a geologist that taught at the University of Northern Arizona in Flagstaff, a famous singer who maintained a residence in Santa Fe, a city manager of a small town in Utah, a writer, cooks, electricians, biologists, physicists and botanists. All received packages in the few days prior to August 21.

It was just in time.

August 20, 4:30 p.m.
Denver, Colorado

"Good Afternoon Denver! Welcome to the Johnny Jay Show. We have a wonderful afternoon of tunes and talk for all you commuters in beautiful Denver, Colorado." Johnny's voice had a staccato, singsong quality as he broadcast his afternoon talk-radio program, helping to alleviate the boredom of the homeward bound traffic. Johnny's show generated considerable controversy as he tried to imitate the style of the acerbic west coast hosts, and he was capable of insulting anyone, regardless of their opinion or the subject matter.

A diminutive man, Johnny was punier than his resonant voice would indicate and he used his on-the-air persona to enlarge his off-the-air image of himself. Wearing speakers that dwarfed his head, with the exception of a shock of blond hair sticking straight up, and speaking into a mike suspended from the ceiling he continued, "We have a rumor going around here in Denver of mysterious black boxes being distributed to some of our citizens. They come by mail, and even by personal delivery. No one has a clue what's in them, but the Johnny Jay show will be the first to provide you with this vital information." He lowered his voice conspiratorially, "We'd love to know who's getting them and why, but no one's talking. What could they be? I personally think they're from aliens, and the chosen few will be whisked away in the mother ship any minute now. What do you think, Denver?" He raise the volume of his voice as he went on, "I'll tell you what, the first person that brings one of these mysterious little boxes to our KDVR studios will receive two free, prime seat tickets to see Taylor Swift in concert, at McNichols Arena, on September twelfth. She's hot, Denver, and worth sacrificing your little box for."

He went on to introduce the news and traffic segments and flipped the switch to go off the air. Ripping off his headset - he hated that thing - he turned to the sound man in the next booth and demanded, "If anyone brings in any little black boxes let me know.

Don't anyone open it or they'll be toast. I want to check it out myself. You got that?"

"Yes sir. I'll bring it to you personally." Everyone on the set was deathly afraid of Johnny Jay. He had a nasty habit of firing people for the slightest infraction, real or imagined. Don Jerrold had kids to support. He would love to tell Mr. Jay where he could put his little black box but obediently kept his mouth shut and manipulated his dials.

August 20, 5:00 p.m.
Sangre de Cristo Mountains, New Mexico

Sandi had never seen any place so beautiful in her entire life. The higher mountains reached up to kiss the western sky, while the mountains to the south tapered downward to lower elevations and she imagined she could see forever to the deserts and plains beyond. She saw the ridge to the east that they had gone around by taking the trail north. There was a tall outcropping atop the ridge blocking her view to the east. Green pine forests and flower-filled meadows covered the mountains, while fluffy white clouds drifted through crystal blue afternoon skies.

She shot a few dozen digital photos and had circled the small lake to the opposite side when she stumbled across a small dam, with a spillway on either side that allowed the river to flow around the dam and continue downstream. Pete had said he didn't remember the lake and it appeared she had discovered the reason why - it had been artificially created. Exploring the area further, she found additional signs of man-made activity; evidence of a deserted road and a foundation for a small building long since removed. It had obviously been a while, since the brush had overgrown everything, and in another year or two all signs of man, with the exception of the dam and the lake, would be erased.

Excited about her discovery, Sandi retraced her path, and found Pete sitting cross-legged on a rock at the north end of the lake, his line dangling in the water. When she'd left him earlier he'd been fishing upstream in the river. Three fish were strung on a rope passing through their gills.

"Hey, Sandi. Check it out. Two Rainbows, and I even caught a Cutthroat Trout! We're going to eat well tonight. Ye of little faith!"

"Hey that's cool, but guess what? I found a dam creating this lake. You want to see?" After stashing his gear, and catch, at their camp they circled the lake to explore the southeast side. He was every bit as puzzled as she by the dam.

They followed what remained of the road, a few broken chunks of asphalt, until it ended at the edge of a precipice. Just to the south were jagged rock formations that blocked the view in that direction, but directly ahead, as they squinted into the afternoon sun, they looked out over a breathtakingly beautiful valley southwest of the plateau. They didn't want to get too close to the edge, although Pete could tell that it didn't fall straight off, but could discern forests and a meadow with a river flowing across it. They stood looking out over the valley for many minutes appreciating its beauty.

"I never came this far south before. It's beautiful, isn't it? You know, if we had more time there might be a way to climb down into it."

"Not a chance, Bud," she told him. "You can climb down into it next year. Just remind me not to accompany you." She walked over to the right side of the road. "This cleared off area looks like it was a helicopter pad. That's the only way you'd get me down there. Bring a chopper and I'm there." The cleared off spot did suggest the possibility of a helicopter pad but it was obviously abandoned. He gestured back toward the lake, "The Fish and Game department probably put this lake here to protect and preserve the native fish population. They work in mysterious ways." He took her hand and they started back toward the lake. Come on, let's get back to camp and have some fish for dinner."

"You're cleaning them," she told him.

"Of course."

"You're cooking them."

"Of course."

"OK, I'll do the dishes."

August 20, 5:30 p.m.
Denver, Colorado

"God Damned traffic." The cars crept along at between ten and fifteen miles per hour, freeway construction in Denver making the traffic unbearable at almost any time of the day or night. John Arnaud had a splitting headache; created by the ongoing stressful conditions he faced at work and this intolerable daily commute. He'd had a miserable day, getting his ass chewed because that bitch Denise turned his report in late. He'd left it on her desk when she wasn't there but she should have noticed it, and it was quite possible that she'd intentionally turned it in late to get him in trouble. He longed to be lounging in his recliner, a beer in hand, watching ESPN.

Johnny Jay, his favorite radio host, was talking to some imbecile on talk-radio. The man, calling from a cellular telephone, was complaining about the loss of civility in America, having been flipped off three times in twenty minutes while driving on the freeway. John glanced around but didn't see anyone with a cell phone. He'd flipped someone off only moments ago when the idiot had cut him off. The other driver had signaled, but John attempted to close the gap and the asshole squeezed in.

"Well, Denver, you did it!" exclaimed Johnny Jay. "That only took one hour from the time I requested one of the mysterious black boxes until a brave soul delivered it to the studio. Free concert tickets go to Sherman Moscowitz. He brought us our box and right after this commercial we'll find out exactly what it is."

John finally reached his freeway off-ramp and flicked off the radio. It would take him another ten minutes to reach home after exiting the freeway. As he drove down quiet suburban streets he passed tract houses with a wide variety of landscaping, some with well-kept yards and others with yards of dirt or overgrown with weeds. This particular residential area wasn't considered the high-rent district, but nevertheless, he insisted that Lori keep their own landscaping looking nicer than that of his neighbors. She only worked part-time, and he figured she had sufficient time to do it.

As he turned the corner onto his street his house came into view, third on the left, and he hit the garage door opener.

His mood had steadily darkened as the traffic and his job had combined in a conspiracy to make his life miserable. As he approached the house he noticed Lori's car was in the driveway and the garage door was still closed. He whipped into the driveway next to her car and, furious, flung the control on the car seat. He clutched his briefcase, jumped out of the car and slammed the door.

Lori heard it and realized he wasn't in the garage. "Oh no, I forgot about it," she moaned. She had tried the opener earlier when she and the kids had arrived home, but it had jammed. Intending to troubleshoot the mechanism before John got home, she got busy with preparing dinner and completely forgot about it.

"Ashley, Kevin, go to your rooms until dinner." She quickly called out. John would be angry and she didn't want him to take it out on the children. Lori quickly released her hair from the 'pony' allowing it to fall around her shoulders the way John liked it, hoping to distract him.

"Mommy, we're watching TV," Ashley protested.

"I know, baby, but Daddy's home and he might be mad. Go on okay? Take Kevin with you."

Ashley took Kevin's hand and half dragged him from the family room into their bedroom. She didn't want Daddy to hit him again.

John stormed into the house slamming the front door.

"What the hell's wrong with the garage door opener?" He yelled without so much as a "Hi, how the hell are you."

"I don't know, Honey" she lied. "Is something wrong with it?"

"No, you idiot, I just asked what's wrong with it to hear myself talk."

"I promise I'll have it fixed right away, John. Dinner's almost ready."

She quickly set the table while he went into his 'shop' in the garage. If she were lucky he would remain there long enough to calm down.

She called the kids, put dinner on the table, and went to the connecting garage door. Knocking timidly, she started turning the doorknob, when it was suddenly jerked from her grasp. She jumped, as if she'd been slapped, and John smiled, gratified by her fear.

"Di . . . dinner's ready." She lowered her eyes as he smirked at her. He brushed by, and with her trailing him, went into the dining room. She'd learned soon after their honeymoon that she could be neither too aggressive nor too submissive. If she tried too hard to be nice, it disgusted him and he verbally abused her. If she didn't act subservient enough, it became physical.

When he saw the children, he acted as if everything was fine. "Hey, how you guys doing?" He ruffled Kevin's hair and gave Ashley a big hug. "Let's have some dinner, okay?" He was in total control. He needed to be. It diverted attention from his working late last night as well as several other nights this month.

They ate dinner with John questioning the kids about daycare and carrying on what appeared to be a normal family conversation. The changing moods, not knowing whether things were okay or not, not knowing when, at any minute, the situation would change and become violent, these were the ways John kept her off-guard and the way he maintained total control. A short while after supper Lori put the children to bed, relieved the evening had gone better than she'd expected. She was more convinced than ever something was going on between John and his secretary. He was being purposely magnanimous.

She cleaned the kitchen, brought him a beer, and took her place beside him on the sofa to watch old reruns of "Baywatch Nights," his favorite program. She detested it but it gave her a chance to relax and dream of other things.

Like getting out.

She knew, though, she could never leave him. What would she and the children do? Where would they go? He would come after them and never, ever, let them escape.

"Is it okay if I make a phone call?" she asked. "I want to check on Dad." She started to get up.

He grabbed her arm, holding her down until he'd answered her. "Bring me another beer first." Then he released her arm.

She tried her dad's number but he wasn't home, an unusual circumstance since he seldom went out at night. Concerned about him, she left a message for him to return her call, if it wasn't past nine, John's curfew for her to receive calls.

Lori grabbed a beer from the refrigerator, and when she returned to the living room she knew immediately, by John's scowl, that she'd done something wrong.

"You Bitch! I told you to bring me the beer first!" he raged. "Are you purposely trying to piss me off?"

He jumped up from the couch and extended his right hand, but didn't move forward to accept the bottle.

"I know you're smarter than that, big college graduate, so you must have done it purposely just to piss me off!" He stood, his hand still out, not moving.

"No . . . honest, John, I'm just worried about Dad and I didn't think for a moment." She moved toward him like a moth to a flame, unable to stay away, but knowing she was going to get burned.

Just as the beer reached his outstretched fingers he reached out and viciously grabbed her wrist, twisting it slowly, and as the beer tilted, yellow liquid slowly moved toward the mouth of the bottle. "Lori," he said tauntingly. "Are you trying to spill my beer?" He grinned, squeezing tighter and twisting farther.

Her eyes widened, fixed on the beer as it continued inexorably toward the orifice.

"No John . . ." she said. The beer was closer to the opening. He twisted.

"I'm sorry . . ." she whispered. It was there. He grinned. His grip tightened like a vise, bruising her wrist.

"Please . . . John." She whimpered. The first drop of golden liquid overflowed the lip and dripped to the carpet.

It broke the spell, and she looked directly into his eyes, angry, crazed eyes. She didn't see the blow coming but knew it would nonetheless. His left hand came out of nowhere, catching her on the cheek, and carrying through to smack the bottle, the beer flying across the room, clunking against the wall and spraying droplets across the couch, carpets and furniture.

"Look at this mess, Lori!"

He looked toward the hall. "What the fuck are you two staring at?" He took a step in their direction.

Ashley and Kevin scurried back to their room, jumped on the bed and listened for footsteps, Ashley holding little Kevin in her arms as they huddled against the wall.

Lori sank to her knees, wrapping her arms around his legs, desperately trying to distract him.

"Please John. They're okay. They're gone." She rubbed his legs, pushing her head against his crotch.

"Please. You can hit me. Please, let's go to the bedroom." She kept talking, wheedling and rubbing her head against his legs, between his legs. She caressed his legs with both hands.

He grabbed her head with both hands and thrust his hips against her. Entwining his fingers in her hair, he pulled her to her feet and crushed his mouth against hers....hard... grinding her lips against his teeth. She tried to ignore the pain as he viciously took hold of her arm and lifted, pulled and shoved her into the bedroom.

August 20, 8:30 p.m.
Marina Del Rey, California

Thus far, the evening had been a total disaster. Jean realized this was a mistake the minute Ron picked her up. They'd attempted to carry on a conversation about various subjects en route to the restaurant, but each attempt had fizzled and even before dinner was served, she'd excused herself and escaped to the ladies' room. While washing her hands she spoke to her image in the mirror, "*Jean, sometimes you do the stupidest things. Here you are trying to save your job in the worst possible way, socializing with the boss. What's next, dessert and bed?*"

She returned to the table and again tried to start a conversation. Unfortunately, they just didn't have anything in common. She liked sports, he didn't, he liked television, she didn't, she liked books, he didn't, he liked business meetings, and she most definitely didn't. She got a short reprieve as dinner was served.

"So Ron, I heard you recently got divorced." She saw him wince and realized for the umpteenth time she had made a major blunder.

"Yeah, I just received my final decree, but I really don't like to talk about it." He looked down at his food and an awkward silence followed.

Jean absently glanced around the room. He'd brought her to a very nice restaurant, The Blue Lagoon, with a magnificent view of the bay and the yacht harbor. She'd heard of it, it had an excellent reputation, but had never eaten here, unable to afford expensive restaurants. She'd hoped they would get to know one another better and he would understand her motivation for yesterday's faux pas. But, so far, all that had happened was she had bored him to tears.

She decided it was too soon for personal conversation and changed the subject. Although she hadn't intended to tell anyone about the package she received today it seemed like a safer topic. She swallowed a bite of her Filet Mignon and sipped her wine.

"Did you see the article in the paper about the black boxes being delivered to people around the Southwestern United States?"

"No, but they were talking about them at lunch today. Some crackpot claims they're maps to a bomb shelter."

"Well, guess what? I got one." She paused to see if she'd piqued his interest.

"You're kidding. What is it really?" He was showing interest at last.

"Just what you said, a map to a bomb shelter. At least that's what the letter says."

"Yeah? Where's it supposed to be located?"

"I don't know. The letter says the box will open automatically if there's a war and the directions to the shelter are in the box. If you attempt to open it before then it self-destructs. At least that's what it says."

"Why did you get one?"

"I haven't the slightest idea. I can't imagine why anyone would want me in their bomb shelter. I haven't exactly made my mark in the world." She immediately regretted the statement but he didn't seem to notice. "I used to be a psychologist. But that hardly seems like a good reason."

"Really? You were a psychologist?"

"It was in a former life." She ended up discussing more of her personal life than she'd intended but at least they had something to talk about and, to her amazement, the rest of the evening went considerably better.

As they finished their meal the conversation again turned to the box. "Why don't you bring it to work tomorrow? I'd like to check out the mechanism," he asked.

"Sure, I'm kind of curious how it works myself."

One waiter took their plates and another offered a dessert tray, which they both declined, and their headwaiter brought the check.

After Ron took care of the check, the valet brought his Camry, and they drove to her house, still discussing the box. When they arrived there was another major moment of awkwardness as nothing had been resolved about work and Jean knew he expected her to invite him in.

"You know," he said, "we haven't discussed the problems at work. What do you want to do?" She was definitely on the spot.

"I don't know. Would you like to come in and we can discuss it?" 'God, what a pushover I am!' she thought. His attitude had seemed to change when he found out about the device, but that was ridiculous, of course. She wasn't even convinced it wasn't a hoax.

After he settled on the couch, and she brought him a bourbon and coke, he brought up the meeting, the moment she'd been dreading all evening.

"Jean, I've been thinking about this whole thing and I've decided it's probably my fault."

She almost dropped her wine. "In what way?" She asked as casually as possible, crossing and then re-crossing her legs.

"Well, we rehearsed the meeting but I didn't tell you what not to tell them. Next time I'll make sure you know what to present and when to keep quiet. I've really been very satisfied with your work. You have a wonderful talent when it comes to a project's accurate cost analysis. Next time warn me before the meeting what the cost overruns will be and keep quiet about them at the meeting. Okay?"

She was flabbergasted. This had been too easy. She hung on the words 'next time'. That meant she wasn't going to lose her job.

"Okay, I mean sure, that's great." 'You're babbling', she thought, and took a big draught of her wine. Her elation was short-lived, however, when she began to wonder what he wanted in return, knowing she wouldn't pay for any favors in that manner.

He downed the rest of his drink and stood. "Thanks for the drink. I had a really good time tonight. See you tomorrow and we'll start out fresh, alright?" He started for the door.

"Yeah Ron, that's great, thanks for dinner." She locked the front door after him and, extremely puzzled, said aloud "What the hell was that all about?"

She was slightly disappointed he hadn't even give her a chance to say "no", but then decided she should count her blessings and headed for bed alone.

August 20, 10:00 p.m.
Sangre de Cristo Mountains, New Mexico

The flame cast flickering shadows of leaping, dancing fire demons, on the trees and rocks around the campsite. Pete and Sandi sat on their sleeping bags and stared, hypnotized by the fire. Crickets were chirping around them and other sounds of the night, an owl hooting in the distance, reached their ears, giving them a peace unknown in the civilized world.

Their campsite under the pines was on the edge of a small clearing and would catch the sun's morning rays. If he'd been alone, Pete wouldn't have built a fire, but he thought Sandi would appreciate the warmth and security that only a campfire seems to bring. After dinner they hung their packs from a rope high in the trees. He didn't think bears would bother them but he'd seen a Golden Marmot in the meadow during their afternoon hike, and those pesky varmints could rip a pack apart looking for food.

The evening was warmer than he'd anticipated and they decided to sleep outside the tent. The stars shone with that special brilliance seen only at high altitude, twinkling with all the colors of the spectrum. The stream gurgled happily where, nearby, it flowed into the lake. Pete had fixed the trout for dinner and Sandi, on clean-up detail, had finished with the camp chores. They were enjoying the woods, the fire and each other.

The conversation drifted among a myriad of topics as they talked about school, their parents and their dreams for the future.

"I want to teach third grade. It's such an impressionable age with the children just beginning to develop into individuals, and they're still really excited about the new things they're learning. Of course, teaching's not a very glamorous vocation. My mother doesn't understand why I find it appealing." She smiled fondly, "My Dad keeps her off my case, though."

"You don't like your mother very much, do you?"

"Actually, I really do love my mother, but it's just that she doesn't like me very much. I was never pretty enough, or precocious enough, or anything else enough. I'm sure she dreamed of having a baby Shirley Temple or something. I think she was sorry she ever had a child since I never seemed to do anything that pleased her. I try not to let it bother me, though, and my father's always been a buffer zone between us. He and I are very much alike and we've both learned to live with Mother."

He leaned over and put another log on the fire, causing it to flare up brightly, spitting incandescent sparks, then after a moment it, and he, settled back down.

"Where will you go when your folks get back from Europe? Are you going to live at home?"

"I'm not sure. I don't know where home is. I grew up in Albuquerque and most of my friends are there. My credential will be in New Mexico, but my parents are in Arizona. I guess I'll make up my mind after I get my degree."

They were silent for a while, each thinking their private thoughts.

"Pete, why did you bring me along on this trip?" Sandi broke the spell of the fire.

"Because I needed someone to protect me from the wolves. Besides, I kinda like you even if you are a girl."

"Gee, thanks for the compliment, but I'm serious. What happened to Tricia?"

Pete had a girlfriend when he and Sandi met. The relationship had been stormy, using way too much of Pete's energy trying to maintain it. Trish demanded constant attention, or else. They broke up recently, and Pete was much relieved about being done with Tricia Wentworth.

"It's over. What about Tommy?"

Sandi didn't smile. "It's over too." She replied bitterly.

"You don't sound too convinced about that," Pete said, surprised at the sadness in her voice. Many of their conversations over the past summer were about their respective partners but Pete hadn't realized until now how important Sandi's relationship with Tommy had been.

"No, it's really over."

"I'm sorry Sandi. I hope it's okay." He reached over and wrapped his arms around her. She leaned into him and looked up at his face. Neither of them had intended it, but by the light of a campfire, on a beautiful summer evening in a New Mexico wilderness, their relationship moved to a new level.

August 20, 11:00 p.m.
Laguna Beach, California

The party, a fund raising affair for one of Katherine's favorite charities, was lasting longer than he had intended or desired. Will considered canceling it when the international situation deteriorated, but everything was arranged and Katherine's best friend, Lillie, had been in charge. He just couldn't say "no" to Lillie. She had been a great comfort to Will after Katherine's death.

Mark and Will were on the veranda, Mark looking through the terrace doors into the Great Room, still filled with guests in formal attire. The one-thousand-dollars-a-plate poolside dinner took place earlier in the evening, but more guests had arrived for the after dinner party, at two hundred-fifty dollars apiece. Guests danced to the music of a full orchestra while others held impromptu business meetings, taking advantage of having a great number of their counterparts in one location. The room, designed for entertaining a large number of people, had two immense crystal chandeliers hung overhead while the end had two sets of double doors opening onto the veranda.

Will detested these charity events, preferring to be with his flying buddies, talking aviation. Mark, on the other hand, enjoyed them immensely. He enjoyed fine clothes, fine food and the company of hard working, intelligent people who'd been successful in life. Most of Will's guests had made fortunes in business or in the entertainment industry, including a few who were writers, producers or actors, and there were a large number of highly prosperous business owners.

Although he came from an early background of substance abuse and bad business dealings, Mark had spent most of his formative years living with the Hargraves and the finer things in life seemed completely natural to him. Not that anything was given to him without tremendous effort on his part. Unlike Clay, Mark had worked hard to complete his education, and he worked extremely hard, often fourteen to sixteen hours a day, to earn his seven figure salary as CEO of a major Aerospace Company. He never took his wealth for granted.

Mark watched Will Hargraves pace on the terrace, the phone glued to his ear, nodding every so often, or murmuring into the receiver. His frown deepened, "I understand the situation is bad Chuck, can't you give me something a little more specific?" He stopped pacing; his eyes meeting Mark's, and he shook his head. "Okay, call me if he does."

"What did he say?" Mark asked.

"The President's taking a wait and see attitude which I think is very dangerous. He should be on the hotline, talking to various heads of state. He should be talking to China, for Christ's sake!"

Will was getting angrier as he spoke. "I don't think he understands how serious this thing is. He thinks war is impossible and he's counting on China to back off. Doesn't he realize this nuclear test represents a new political strategy for them? Doesn't he know they wouldn't have demonstrated their power unless they were prepared to use it?" He walked to the western wall of the terrace and gazed out at the dark ocean, moonlight flooding its surface with a ghostly radiance. "NORAD has gone to Defcon 2. I think you'd better call Jill, and without alarming her, convince her to get a reservation for a flight to Albuquerque tomorrow morning. If nothing comes of this you can surprise her with a Santa Fe vacation, or some other pretense. If we get through tomorrow we may have some breathing room." He handed Mark the phone.

A waiter came on to the terrace with a tray of after dinner drinks. "Mr. Hargraves, your guests are asking for you." The two men had excused themselves when the call came from the Secretary of State, but they'd been absent from the party for too long.

"I know you haven't wanted to talk about your shelter, Will, but I would like to know more about it."

Will had started back to the party but stopped and looked at Mark. He had a great affection for this young man. Mark had kept the business going after Katherine's death, when Will went off and buried himself in sorrow. By building the shelter for Katherine's children he felt as though he'd never let her go. He'd always been reticent about discussing it with anyone in his everyday life. Somehow, that would make it seem too real instead of something between him and Katherine.

But Mark had a right to know.

"Let's rejoin our guests and we'll talk about it in the morning. Can you spend the night?"

"Of course. You're even making me edgy. I'm not letting you out of my sight until you tell me all about your shelter, and until this crisis is behind us. I'll call Jill. Can you tell Chris I'll be right in? Wouldn't want her to take up with someone else."

"I think you're too late. She's been talking to that fellow she invited from Scripp's Institute."

"Yes, well, I think he's just a co-worker." Mark said to him as Will went back inside.

He started to call Jill, but remembered the hour, that it was two hours later in Dallas, and realizing she wouldn't be calling this late for a reservation anyway, he decided to contact her in the morning when, after talking to Will, he'd have more information. He re-entered the room, scanning it for Chris and accepting an after dinner drink from a waiter who immediately came by with a tray. He spotted her on the dance floor and, sipping the cognac, watched her swaying to the music. God she was beautiful!

She was radiant, in a black, form-fitting gown that accentuated her sleek athletic body. Her hair, caught back and pinned up with a banana clip, cascaded over the clip and down her back. She wore a diamond necklace and earrings, and a diamond bracelet. He thought she was the most beautiful woman in this room full of beautiful people.

Clay was also dancing, with a young actress who'd recently received her pilot's license. Almost everyone in the room, including the celebrities, was connected to aviation in some manner. Mark downed the last of his drink and ordered bourbon, straight up.

It was one o'clock in the morning before the last of the guests departed. Chris left with her friend, promising her father she wouldn't be gone long. Jealous, Mark retired for the night.

THREE

August 21, 5:00 a.m.
Laguna Beach, California

Mark wandered into Will's large, first floor study wearing pajamas and a robe, his hands wrapped around a steaming mug of coffee. He found Will sitting behind a huge cherry wood desk, intently watching a bank of six television monitors in a wall-to-wall, state-of-the art communications system that, tuned to news stations around the world, kept Will informed of global events.

Mark sleepily gazed out the east facing windows where the morning dew dripped from a huge, ancient fig tree onto the sill. The eastern sky was beginning to lighten, shades of pink and yellow visible above the horizon, with sunrise only minutes away. Mark rubbed his eyes, wondering how the older man looked so refreshed after last night's reveling, and after the paltry three and one-half hours sleep they'd managed since the last of the party-goers departed.

"What's going on? Any news?" As if on cue the phone rang. Will put it on speakerphone.

"Will, this is Chuck. We're in big trouble. The Russians have formally denounced the Chinese and China essentially told them to go to hell! You know what? I personally think China's been planning this for a long time. You should get airborne just in case you need to evacuate from the coast."

"I'll arrange for the plane to be readied immediately. What happened to your Moscow trip?"

"Can't make it now. Hell, this thing is escalating rapidly. We've received intelligence reports, with Lacrosse satellite verification, that the Chinese have apparently refitted their entire arsenal with the red mercury super warheads… and they're armed. The system is operational! How they've kept it secret from our intelligence community is the question of the century but there you have it. We've been too distracted by all the terrorism crap. Get in the air, I'll notify you of significant developments. Talk to you later."

Hargraves pushed the button disconnecting the phone, momentarily hesitated as he considered the options, then turned abruptly to Mark. "Call and have the jet prepared for immediate take-off. Run by your place and get your personal belongings together. We'll meet you at the plant by six-thirty. And Mark, take anything that's precious to you."

"My God Will, you're really serious, aren't you?"

"Yes. I honestly believe we won't be returning here. Did you call your sister?"

"No, I planned to contact her today."

"Well, this may be it. Tell her to wait by the phone for your call." Will was shifting into high gear, working best when decisions were needed and immediate action required. Mark didn't question him. As Will left to rouse the household, Mark called the plant, leaving instructions for the Gulfstream to be prepped for take-off, and then called his sister in Dallas.

"Jill, hi, this is Mark. Yeah, I know it's early. I want you to have Mike stay home from work today."

"Hi Mark. I can't do..."

"No, listen to me for a minute will you. Keep the kids around home too. You've heard of the nuclear test the Chinese conducted? Well, we have reason to believe they may attack the United States."

"That's ridiculous!"

"Dammit Jill, It's not ridiculous! Will has been communicating with the Secretary of State and he says there's a significant danger. Stay home by the phone and I'll get back to you the minute there are concrete developments. What can you lose? You promise?"

"Okay, I think it's silly but I'll talk to Mike."

"Great, I'll call you later." He hung up the phone, and wondering what was happening to his world, started upstairs to get dressed.

***

Hargraves went upstairs to Chris's room. He had been mildly annoyed the previous night when she went out with her friend after the party, wanting her to stay in closer contact. And he felt bad for Mark. He'd always hoped someday Chris and Mark would marry.

He rapped on her door. "Chris, I need to talk to you right away."

"Come in Dad, I'm awake," came the sleepy reply.

Entering the room, he found her just awake and stretching out. "Babe, I'm going to ask a serious favor of you. Would you go to Washington with me today?" He lied. "Pack a small bag and come downstairs as soon as possible, okay?" He had already turned to leave without waiting for a reply.

Wide-awake now, she could see her father was deadly serious. She remembered as a child how his eyes would shine when something important was happening. His eyes were shining now. She didn't question him, although she was certainly curious and just a little alarmed, and called out as he left, "Sure Dad, right away. I need to get back tomorrow though…"

Downstairs, Will asked Helen and Ernest to pack, and met Mark, dressed, coming from his room. "Helen's throwing a few things in a bag for me. We should be ready to leave as soon as Chris and Clay are downstairs."

Mark, reminiscing, glanced around the room. He had so many wonderful memories of growing up in this house and he sadly realized he might be leaving this part of his life forever. Will took a picture of Katherine, off the mantel and asked Mark if he would pack it for him. More than anything else, this caused Mark to understand the seriousness of the situation, and he felt an overwhelming compassion for the older man who'd lived in this house for thirty years, raised his children here, and lost his beloved wife years before. Feeling sure this was all a fantastic dream, Mark believed they would be back here for dinner and a few laughs.

The others soon joined them, Clay grousing about the hour. He hadn't packed a bag. "This is crazy, Dad. I don't want to go. What's the deal?"

Will swung on Clay with fire in his eyes. "You're going whether you like it or not. Now shut up and get in the car!"

Clay stood shocked for a moment then quickly slunk out the front door. Chris, her eyebrows raised, followed him, and the others went out to the cars in the drive.

"I'll see you at the airport." Mark waved and drove toward home, his thoughts a mixture of uncertainty and disbelief. He called several friends but most were out on their morning runs and none answered his calls. He left messages, telling them about the shelter and how to get there and hoped that some would believe him and at least attempt to make the trip.

As he drove through Laguna Beach, crowded with trendy craft shops, art galleries and pizza restaurants, he thought back to twenty years ago, when he first moved in with Will and Katherine. This had been a small, upscale coastal town, an artist's colony. A short, gated street off Pacific Coast Highway led to Will's driveway and at one time his was the only house on the block. Now, although Will's was still the only house on the ocean side, the street had other homes crammed together on every square foot as. Indeed, the hills overlooking the town had mansions built on almost every buildable lot.

Mark and Chris used to wander through town, window shopping and looking at the paintings the artists displayed along the sidewalks. She loved the galleries and he loved being with her, even then. He was sixteen and although she was only eleven years old, she was mature beyond her years. Although Pacific Coast Highway, lined with eucalyptus trees, was fairly empty at this early hour he knew that later, and especially on weekends, the traffic would become almost unbearable.

When he arrived at his home in Newport Beach, he quickly threw a few mementos of his life into a suitcase; a medium size leather bag that now contained a few papers written by his great-grandfather, his display case with finishers' medals from the past six Palos Verdes Marathons, a small photo album with the only known photo of his mother and father together, some pictures of Jill and her family, and a few of he and the Hargraves children. This is crazy, he thought. Convinced he'd be home later he filled the rest of the bag with running shoes and a few clothes and sped away for the plant.

***

The Gulfstream was cruising over the California-Arizona border, the Colorado River directly below, when the radio crackled to life. A Man's excited voice asked for Will Hargraves and Will, flying in the copilot's seat quickly grabbed the mike.

"This is Hargraves. What's up?"

"Will, it's Chuck. The situation has become critical. No sign of attack directed at us yet but we feel it's imminent. Conventional forces are attacking North Korea from China and a nuclear device has been detonated in Russia by God knows who. It wasn't a missile, so terrorists must have smuggled it in. Of course Russia immediately retaliated by launching missiles with trajectories targeting Beijing, Shanghai, and other major Chinese cities. We're fairly certain it's only a matter of hours until global escalation. None of the other countries are communicating, but the President is on the hotline to Moscow. The Russian president assures Rissman they won't attack us, but China undoubtedly will, after this attack on them by Russia. In fact I'm sure this is what China planned all along. I think they wanted the entire world to exhaust their arsenals of nuclear weapons on each other. Furthermore, I believe no matter what assurances Russia is giving, if they come under heavy attack, they'll respond with a global retaliatory response to keep from being threatened by conventional forces after the nuclear holocaust.

"What steps are being taken by the government?" Will asked.

"Executive operations will reside in the command plane until it's safe to move to the government shelter. I suggest you go underground soon or it may be too late. We'll try and maintain contact with you once we're in the shelter. Good luck, Old Friend."

The radio went dead before Will could answer and he knew the Secretary had barely had time to notify him before leaving Washington. Will glanced quickly over at Mark in the pilot's seat.

"I can't believe this, but I guess it's decision time." He reached for his briefcase, opened it and took out a small satellite, radio transmitter. He looked up at Mark, took a deep breath and pushed a button, activating the device.

August 21, 8:00 a.m.
Denver, CO

    Lori had requested a vacation day to catch up on her housework and her shopping. She'd neglected both while attending her mother's funeral in New Mexico and was convinced that if she would just perform her duties more efficiently, John would have no reason to find comfort with another woman. She worried that he'd somehow found out she was working full-time, or that maybe she wasn't getting everything accomplished, and he'd noticed. She couldn't imagine where she may have screwed up, but something was bothering him, and she was certain it was her fault.

    After John left for work and she'd put the kids on the bus for their summer day care, she'd scrubbed the beer off the carpet and was starting on the furniture when the doorbell rang, announcing Express mail bearing an overnight package from her father. Lori, puzzled and concerned, carried the package into the living room. She'd left him only four days before. Her mother had died unexpectedly after rupturing an aortic aneurysm, and her father, a nuclear scientist at Los Alamos National Laboratory in New Mexico, was devastated by her untimely death. Lori's mother, at fifty nine, had previously been in excellent health. Lori took the children and went to New Mexico to attend the funeral, staying a few days to ensure her father was recovering from the emotional trauma. She'd put her own grief on hold.

    Ripping open the package, she read the note… and became even more alarmed. She hurried to the phone and tried to reach him again, but as before, the answering machine picked up and she could only leave another message. She was so far behind in her work she just stuck the device in her purse to deal with later. What could he be thinking, sending her this thing? She worried he was having a nervous breakdown, and decided to call the lab when she returned home from grocery shopping to see if he'd cut his bereavement leave short and had returned to work. After finishing the cleaning, she grabbed her purse and headed to the grocery store.

Lori dodged other supermarket customers, as she pushed her cart through the aisle, shaking her head at the astronomical grocery prices. Even with her salary supplementing John's it was becoming increasingly difficult to provide a good home and nutritious meals for her family. Moving to the aisle's edge she picked up two cans of tomato sauce, her gaze switching back and forth to compare ingredients and prices. She stared at them, suddenly unseeing, the labels blurring as tears welled in her eyes, and she remembered the woman's laugh when John called home the night before last. She hadn't had the courage to ask him about his 'working late' when he arrived home after midnight that night, and she certainly hadn't wanted to confront him with her suspicions last night when he came home in one of his foul moods.

"What did I do wrong?" She whispered, wiping her tears on the sleeve of her t-shirt.

"Excuse me, please." Startled, Lori jumped and moved farther toward the side of aisle, out of the woman's way as she zoomed by with her cart. Lori dropped one can in the basket and returned the other to the shelf without making a conscious decision.

With sudden resolve she made a decision. She hurried to the checkout stand and waited impatiently as the checker ran the grocery items across the scanner. She would confront John with her suspicions! She would ask him for an explanation! Even though she'd kept herself up for him, he'd been showing less and less interest in her, and he'd paid very little attention to the children as well, except to yell at them or hit them. She was determined it was time to get some answers, but while waiting in line she began to waiver, reconsidering her rash decision.

"Will that be all ma'am?" The cashier had finished checking the groceries. "Paper or plastic?"

"Yes, that's all. Thank you. Plastic please."

Lori reached in her purse for the $72.46, but jerked her hand back as though a snake hiding in the pocket had bitten her. The signaling device she carried had suddenly begun to wail loudly. She almost dropped the purse and looked up quickly at the clerk who was staring at her with a surprised expression.

"What in the world is that caterwauling?" inquired the clerk, retrieving a box of cereal she'd dropped, and placing it in the bag.

"I... I have to go. I'm sorry, but I don't want the groceries." The color had drained from Lori's cheeks and she felt light-headed. "Please excuse me." She turned to leave the check stand.

"Hey, are you all right? I've already wrung these up." Lori didn't look back as she fled through the front doors into the Albertson's parking lot.

The siren still emitted an ear-piercing scream from the inside of her purse, and she grabbed the box, flipped it over, and tried to figure out how to silence it. She was surprised to find the back was open. There was a small toggle switch inside which she immediately flipped and the noise mercifully ceased. Reaching her car, she climbed inside and quickly read the message. Money and a map were included with the note.

"My God," she muttered, "Is this some kind of joke? Oh Dad..."

She quickly drove to the daycare and pulled into the parking lot, sitting stationary for a moment to collect her thoughts. With sudden inspiration, she reached over and turned on the radio tuning to an all-day news station. The announcer was reporting an emergency situation in Russia and China that sounded fairly serious, although there were no specific details and nothing was said about danger to the United States. She sat in the car biting her lip and trying to make a decision. Her thoughts raced between her Dad, her kids and husband, and the signal. She decided she'd pick up the kids and return home, then attempt to contact her Dad again, and if she couldn't get him, she'd call John and ask him what she to do. Leaving the device on the seat, she finally climbed from the car and entered the school office.

"I'm Mrs. Arnaud and I need to pick up Ashley and Kevin early today, please. We have a family emergency and have to leave town for a few days."

"My goodness, again? I'm sorry to hear that," replied the secretary. She checked Lori's I.D against the authorization on file and turned back to Lori, who was fidgeting with impatience. "I'll notify their teachers to release them." Two students were copying papers in the next room and she sent them to get the children. Lori watched them go, wondering if they would soon die, or was this all some crazy product of her father's dementia?

She signed the log and told the secretary, "I'll wait out front. Thank you," and exited into the sunlight, waiting until her children came running to her from their respective rooms.

"Hi, Mommy. Look what I made!" Her youngest flashed a picture at her.

"Come on, hurry and get in the car. We have to go for a little trip." She took his arm and, almost lifting him from the ground, she ushered them to the car, shushing their attempts to ask her where they were going. Driving home way too fast, she prayed she wouldn't be stopped.

They entered the house and she went straight for the phone. There was still no answer at her father's residence. She started to dial John's office when her hand froze over the phone, a visual image popping into her head unbidden, of him in bed with another woman. She bit her lip and slowly pulled her hand back. Whirling around, she headed for the bedroom, grabbed a suitcase off the closet shelf, and filled it with clothes. Lugging the suitcase, she went to the kid's room to find them dutifully changing their clothes.

"Leave your school clothes on, it's okay. Ashley, honey, go fix you guys a sandwich. I'll be there shortly."

"Mommy, where are we going? Grandpa's house again?"

"Just fix the sandwiches. We need to go now!"

"Don't forget my fire truck!" Kevin reminded her as they ran from the room.

She threw some of their favorite toys, including Ashley's Barbie and Kevin's little fire truck, into the bag and hurried to the kitchen where she discovered the kids had made a complete mess of the sandwiches. She instinctively started cleaning it up when she realized it wasn't important anymore. Grabbing their bags, she hustled the children out to the automobile, throwing the suitcases into one side of the back seat.

"Stay here and get your seat belts on. I'll be right back!"

She returned to the house and dialed the number of Madison Electronic Supplies. A woman answered John's extension.

"This is Mrs. Arnaud. Please tell my husband he deserves whatever happens to him and so does the slut he's been sleeping with." She heard a sharp intake of breath and knew absolutely her suspicions about the secretary were correct. Slamming down the receiver, she grabbed a pad of paper kept by the phone and, with complete satisfaction, quickly penned a note to John. She knew him... he would race home the minute he received her message, furious, ready to teach her a lesson. She ran through the door, jumped in the car, and removed the map from the glove compartment, comparing it with the one she'd removed from the device.

"Mommy, where's Daddy?" Kevin asked.

"He's not coming, Kev." She drove across town on Colorado Boulevard, turned south down the on-ramp and headed south on Interstate twenty-five.

August 21, 8:15 a.m.
Marina Del Rey, CA

The devices went off all over the Southwest, from the coast of Southern California, across Arizona and New Mexico into Texas, and as far north as Utah and Colorado. Only those within a radius of approximately three or four hundred miles could possibly expect to make it by automobile. The others would need to fly.

Most contactees were so startled they wasted precious time; not believing immediately that the signal meant the coming of Nuclear Armageddon. Then, after consideration, and listening to the T.V. or radio the majority decided it was worth a chance believing. They could always return to their jobs the next day if it proved to be a hoax, and the consequences of ignoring a legitimate warning were too horrendous to contemplate. This line of reasoning led numerous recipients to start on their journey toward the shelter. Approximately half the people lived within the radius necessary to make travel by car a possibility while the others had occupations best filled by people in the industrialized areas of Southern California or other major cities.

Jean Barnes was with Ron in his office at Advanced Communications in Marina Del Rey, California when one of the secretaries called to tell her a buzzer was going off in her office. Puzzled, she excused herself and went to check on it. *"This can't be happening,"* she thought and immediately returned to Ron's office with the device, her heart thumping in her chest. She had silenced the alarm and removed the message.

"Ron, I have to show you something. You know the box I received?" She was shaking as she handed him the device and the original note she'd received with the alarm. He quickly read the messages.

"It was going off?" He hit the toggle switch and the ear-splitting alarm was reactivated causing him to jump halfway out of his chair before he quickly clicked it back off.

"Well, you said you wanted to see it. What do you make of it?"

"The thing was going off?" He stammered again.

"Yes. I silenced it once already."

He turned it over and examined it. "It's a fairly sophisticated little gadget and must have quite a range. It probably uses satellite communications. I don't know what to make of it." He looked up at her, "My God, the implications are terrifying. What are you going to do?" He handed the device back to Jean.

"I'm going to take the rest of the day off, no one needs to know why, and follow the directions in the box. It's probably a hoax and I'll lose a day of work, but if it isn't can we take a chance?"

"What do you mean we?" He asked her.

"Please go with me Ron! I honestly don't think it's a joke. No one would go to that kind of trouble for a practical joke. It could be a mistake, of course, the thing going off, I mean, but I don't think so. To tell you the truth, when I received it yesterday I listened to the news and the international situation is very scary. Then I called the airlines to see about flights to Albuquerque. One leaves at 9:30. We could make it."

"But we can't just leave. Arrangements would have to be made at my apartment, people notified . . ."

"We don't have time! Don't you understand? If this thing isn't a gag nothing else matters! We have to go right away. Please Ron!" She stood up and tugged at his arm. "Please."

He looked thoughtful for a minute and then stood up with a smile on his face. "Sure, let's go. We can always explain a day's absence from work and this might be an adventure even if it's a joke. If there really is a shelter it could be quite interesting. Let me call the airline, see if we can get a reservation." He reached for the phone.

August 21, 9:30 a.m.
El Paso, TX

"After ascending the Throne in 521 B.C. Darius I, or Darius the Great as he later became known, extended the influence of the Persian Empire eastward as far as the Indus River." Herbert Laskey, professor of Ancient History 1A at the University of Texas, El Paso, was caught up in his material and paced before the class, gesturing emphatically. "Who can tell me where his great defeat came?"

"Dr. Laskey." One of the students, a chubby young man with pink cheeks, waved his hand vigorously from the third row of the theater style seats. "The Battle of Salamis in 480 B.C."

"No Mr. Howard, that was his son Xerxes. Darius' forces were disastrously defeated at the historic Battle of Marathon in..."

The scream of a loud siren, emanating from Dr. Laskey's briefcase, interrupted the discussion. He quickly looked in the direction of his desk. "Oh my," he said.

Walking over to his desk, he fumbled with the device, discovered the switch and terminated the raucous noise.

"Let's change the discussion for a minute, shall we? What do any of you know about the current crisis in China?"

There were murmurs around the room.

"Come, come, don't be shy, this is important."

A young woman raised her hand and was acknowledged by the professor. "Well, I know the Chinese tested an atomic bomb and we protested. I think it violated a treaty, or something."

"Young lady, it was a hydrogen bomb, much more powerful than an atomic bomb and it did, indeed, violate several test ban treaties. But following that test there have been other developments and the tension has increased dramatically. Do any of you feel the situation could become serious enough to start a war?"

The student who had made the error on an ancient war, scoffed, "Naw, we've had plenty of close calls before and nobody ever started shooting. Look at the Bay of Pigs, Kosovo, and the Gulf War. They never escalated."

"Actually, the public doesn't realize just how close we came to all-out war in those instances, especially the Bay of Pigs."

He glanced again at the briefcase and then back at the students who were staring at him and wondering what the god awful noise was.

"Well, ladies and gentlemen, that siren that went off in my briefcase? It's supposedly a warning to proceed to a bomb shelter."

The class laughed nervously, the students looking at each other to see if anyone believed him. He folded his arms, waiting until they quieted and then fetched and read both notes.

One of the young women began to cry, and picking up her notebook, ran from the room. This started an exodus and several other students slapped their books shut, gathered up their belongings and followed her up the aisle.

"Uh, Dr. Laskey, what are you going to do?" Four students, including Eric Howard, two other young men and a woman, crowded around him, looking very nervous.

"I believe I am going to pick up my daughter at her place of employment and drive to New Mexico. I'll probably return to class tomorrow, highly embarrassed. Anyone care to join me? I have a van." He zipped his briefcase and started up the aisle toward the door.

"I'll go," said one of the students, "I live in New York. No way I can go home. It'll be fun."

Laskey halted and turned, looking at him over his glasses. "Come along then, for whatever reasons you may have."

The other three students, who all lived in dorms and were from other parts of the country, decided to accompany them. None of them really believed there was a problem.

August 21, 10:05 a.m.
Red River, New Mexico

Sheri exited the motel room, squeezing to the side of the opening to get her bike out the door. The fully loaded panniers snagged on the door plate but she gave a tug and the bike glided out into the mid-morning sunshine. She leaned it against the wall next to the air conditioner and looked up at the warm sky, throwing her arms wide and soaking up the warmth. The morning was still cool but already warming up. It would be much hotter later and she wished she had gotten an earlier start. She arrived in town last evening after a grueling day of over one hundred miles, and instead of going to bed early she had found this cool little bar and stayed up way later than she should have. There were several men playing pool and when they found out she was an Olympian they had insisted she party with them until closing. She had a blast and after all the serious training of the past few days she had needed to just kick back and have some fun.

Her stomach rumbled. She grabbed the bike and headed for the office to check out of her room and have her free continental breakfast that was part of the room rate. Money was tight and she took advantage of every freebie she could find.

The young male clerk looked up as she entered the office. "Good morning. Checking out?"

"Hi. Yeah, room 112. Can I lock my bike over there in the corner while I eat?"

"Sure." He surreptitiously looked her up and down. She was dressed in full cycling gear with tight fitting cycling pants and jersey, bright blue and yellow, and she was carrying an aerodynamic helmet that swept back to a point at its rear.

"Thanks. Be back in a few. In fact if you don't mind, I'll leave it here while I go for a little run?"

"Ah, yeah, I guess. Have fun."

Out of necessity, she ate a light breakfast; an egg, some fruit and a piece of toast. More than that and she would feel it on the long climb out of Red River. The television in the motel café was tuned to a news station and there were stories of Russia and China threatening each other over the Chinese nuclear test that took place a couple of days before. She shook her head, and thought that there was always something going on. She was proud that the Olympics allowed the nations to compete in an intensely competitive, but friendly atmosphere.

The hill on highway 38 eastward out of town was steep and began immediately at the edge of town so she needed an easy run to warm up her muscles before she started spinning up that monster hill. She left the motel cafeteria and took the sidewalk south toward the river that ran along the edge of town. There was a bike path along the river, mostly in the open but occasionally winding through the trees that grew close to the bank. She jogged east for an easy mile breathing in the aroma of the pines and flowers that lined the bike path, and then at a bench with an older couple enjoying the day, she reversed her course and ran back to town.

As she walked back to the motel she glanced around the town. It was a cute little town. She could see a ski lift on the slope of the pine covered mountains to the south, the sun gleaming brightly off the support poles. She assumed the town was a ski resort and the alpine-looking buildings around her lent credence to that idea. There were more motels and coffee shops than in a regular town and remembering the fun she'd had the previous night she thought the town was probably a great place to be in the winter ski season.

She retrieved her bike, a Fuji SST 2.0 Ultegra Di2 Road Bike. It was the largest expenditure she'd ever made in her twenty-one years. She paid more for her bike than the car she'd left in Walsenburg when she started this training ride. Out of habit, she checked her supplies in the bright yellow panniers, making sure she had not only lunch, but emergency supplies as well, in case she got stuck between towns and had to spend the night.

She pulled her long, wavy brown hair back and tied it up with a hair tie, then slipped the helmet snuggly onto her head. With a last look around the town, she mounted the bike and headed east. She rode slowly through the rest of town and began to pick up speed. But almost immediately she started to climb and gearing the bike down she began the long, slow ascent out of the valley.

After a couple of hours of riding she was spinning easily along some rolling hills and realized she was getting hungry again. It seemed like she had just eaten but her body functioned on a pretty regular schedule and it was telling her it was time for lunch. There was a pull-off ahead and she came to a stop next to a picnic table at an overlook. She leaned the Fuji against the table and walked to the edge of the overlook. The view of the mountains to the southwest was magnificent. She went back to the table, dug her lunch out of the saddleback and kicked back on the picnic table as she ate her sandwich and apple. The sun beat down now and she gloried in the beautiful cloudless day.

Sheri could hear a car coming from the direction of Red river. It was traveling fast and it flew over the hill and continued down the mountain to the east at a dangerous speed. It was immediately followed by a couple of others. She wondered what was up and hoped there wasn't an accident up ahead. In a few more minutes another car shot over the hill. She finished her sandwich and her apple and got back on the bike hoping to see what was going on.

The highway began a gentle descent and she tucked her head for more speed. Her hands were on the forward handle grips with her forearms resting on the center bars. She picked up more speed and flew down the mountain at a terrific pace, faster than she normally rode but she was reveling in the perfect day and just felt the need to fly.

She came around a gentle curve and saw several cars ahead making a turn across her lane toward the west. She didn't think they would see her in time, and wouldn't stop to allow her to proceed, so she braked hard and came to a stop twenty yards before the turn. One of the drivers spotted her and drove past the turn and up to where she had stopped.

"Lady," he called out to her. "You need to follow us. The U.S. is going to be attacked by China or Russia and you need to get under cover!"

She couldn't quite absorb what he was telling her. "What are you talking about?" She asked. She thought about the cars she saw traveling at high speed back when she was having lunch. "How do you know?

"Listen to me!" he yelled. I was notified earlier this morning and now the President has made an announcement. The bombs are on the way. There's a bomb shelter. Follow me!" he insisted. He drove just past her and slung his vehicle around and onto the shoulder throwing up dirt and rocks as he accelerated in a curve and headed back south. He skidded around the corner onto the dirt road and sped off to the west.

Sheri was aghast. The day was so perfect. This just couldn't be happening. Pulling over to the shoulder, and coughing as the dust swirled around her, she pulled her emergency radio out of the pannier and clicked it on. There was nothing but static but she figured that that was because they were out of range of any stations. She thought she should be able to get something out of Red River. She wasn't that far away yet. She very slowly moved through the dial and caught a very faint signal. She couldn't make out what was being said but the voice sounded frantic.

Just then another car came flying up the hill from the direction of Eagle Nest. Sheri caught sight of the driver's face. She looked terrified! The car screeched to a halt. The driver looked at Sheri and then accelerated around the corner and sped up the road, a long trail of dust obscuring everything around her.

The dirt had mixed with the sweat Sheri had worked up and she felt filthy and scared. A beautiful day had just turned into a nightmare. She just stood next to her bike for a long time completely unsure of what to do. She looked over at the road and wondered where it led to. Where were they all going? Her bike wasn't an off-road bike but she thought she could travel on it if it wasn't too rough. She had her supplies and could camp for a couple of days without any problem. She didn't have any deadline for returning to the Olympic Training Complex in Colorado Springs. The weather was certainly warm enough.

She finally decided she would follow the road for a while to see where it led. She turned off the highway and started along the road to the west. Her bike jounced and slipped and she worried that this was a big mistake when she heard another car coming up behind her. She pulled off the side of the road and dismounted the bike, but got blanketed with dirt anyway as the car sped by.

"Damn these people! Why don't they slow down?" she muttered as she brushed the dirt off her sleeves. She got back on the bike and continued, her teeth chattering as she bounced along. She rounded a curve and saw that the road became smoother and she was able to make better time. Several more cars passed her and one stopped to see if she was okay. It had two men in it, a big guy and a smaller one.

"Hey, you want a ride?" The driver asked. "We need to get to the shelter. The bombs are on their way."

"Oh God, then it's real?"

"Looks that way. Are you coming?"

"No, please go on. I can't leave my bike."

The driver looked at the larger man and shrugged. They started back up the road but courteously drove slowly to limit the dust until they were well beyond her before speeding up.

Sheri Summerland was a very tough girl but she almost lost it that day on a lonely dirt road in the Sangre De Christo Mountains. She started to cry and then jerked herself up. The discipline of an Olympic athlete kicked in, she jumped back on the bike and started pumping furiously, propelling herself after the retreating car.

August 21, 11:30 a.m.
Albuquerque, NM

The majority of the world's population had no idea anything unusual or dangerous was transpiring. In previous crises, few except the governments involved realized how close we came to conflict until much later when the stories were turned into television movies. This crisis differed.

It didn't end.

People went to work that day just like any other day and life went on as usual. It was 7:30 a.m. Pacific time when the jet carrying the Hargraves party received news from the State Department that war was imminent. No attack on the United States had commenced, but Will knew by the time he received word of approaching missiles it would almost be too late. He made the decision to set off the signaling devices knowing if the attack never came, the lives of many people would be disrupted unnecessarily. But then, if we were attacked, at least people would stand a chance of getting to the shelter before transportation was disrupted and the situation deteriorated into chaos. Mark tried to call his sister from the plane, but she had disregarded his warning and was not at home.

Hargraves maintained an aircraft/helicopter flight school and an airframe and power plant shop at Albuquerque International Airport, so he would have a base of operations in the closest, large city to the shelter. One of the two choppers was away on a rental but the other was always reserved and maintained in readiness for his use.

The jet landed in Albuquerque and Mark taxied to the end of the airport where the flight school was located. They stored their luggage in the chopper before heading to the main terminal in the SUV that was kept in the hangar for that purpose. Mark immediately called Jill again and she answered on the third ring.

"Jill, where the hell have you been? I told you to stay home!"

150

"I went to get the kids at the neighbors. Why are you so upset?"

"You have to believe that what I told you this morning is true. The Secretary of State has warned Mr. Hargraves that the United States is about to be attacked by China. You need to . . ."

"Oh come on Mark. That can't . . ."

"Shut up and listen to me! Let me speak to Mike."

He heard her relating to Mike what he'd told her. After an eternity, she put her husband on the phone. "This is not a joke, Mike. You need to get your family to Albuquerque as soon as possible. According to the Secretary of State, attack by China is imminent, but Will has a bomb shelter north of Albuquerque that will provide protection. Get a flight now and I'll meet you at the airport. Write this down." He gave Mike directions to the shelter in case they didn't connect. Mike was disbelieving but Mark convinced him to leave for Albuquerque on the next flight. Family and friends hadn't received signaling devices because Will felt it would be better to call them directly if it became necessary, that it would be easier to convince them with direct communication. Mark was painfully aware that that reasoning wasn't necessarily true. He sure was having trouble convincing his own sister! Will had called the plant when they left that morning. He hoped Miles and the others could start for New Mexico.

Mark noticed a "Special News Bulletin" on an airport television. The media was becoming aware that something significant was happening overseas. They reported the invasion of North Korea by China but didn't mention the nuclear device being detonated in Russia. Mark was certain that the news was being manipulated from Washington. Washington correspondents, aware that government leaders were unexpectedly leaving for an unknown destination, were speculating about the reasons why, and getting perilously close to the truth. A second story reported that the stock market was down over 600 points and trading limits had been activated.

Mark stood outside Garduno's Chile Packing Company and Cantina where the others were having an early lunch. He needed to make some calls. There was no crew on the Gulfstream this trip and the galley hadn't been stocked so they'd had no breakfast. They were starved by the time they reached Albuquerque.

He called Steve in Fountain Valley, trying to convince him there was a serious problem, but Steve wasn't buying it any more than Jill had. Mark was furious that nobody was listening. "Damn it, Steve. I've never lied to you and I wouldn't lie to you about something like this. Get your butt on a plane to Albuquerque! You can go home tomorrow if everything's okay. I'm telling you, nuclear weapons have already exploded in Russia!"

"Man, I have a business meeting this afternoon and what about Lorraine?"

"Bring her with you if she's immediately available, but get here as quickly as you can. We didn't have as much warning as we thought we'd have. Mr. Hargraves has actually set off signaling devices telling people to come to the bomb shelter. That's how serious this is. We'll be here for an undetermined amount of time. If the U.S. comes under attack we'll be warned and we'll have to leave immediately. When you get here, if we've already gone you'll have to get to the shelter in a rental car. Please Steve, you've got to come. Write down these directions."

He gave him directions, extracting a promise he would come. Calling several other people, he did his best to talk his friends into starting for the shelter. It was all he could do. He wished for the hundredth time he had known in advance they would receive that call in the plane. He would have gone and picked Steve and Lorraine up and forced them into accompanying him. The problem was, he admitted, he really hadn't believed it himself. God, if he only had more time. He leaned against the wall and tried to think of whom else to contact.

He called Jill again and received no answer. Good, she must be on the way. He headed back for the restaurant where he joined the others, too nervous and impatient to order anything to eat. It wasn't in his nature to sit and wait for anything.

August 21, Noon
Sangre de Cristo Mountains, NM

"Back off you stupid fuck, or I'm gonna kill you!" As Ferrar lunged for Jones, Arby intercepted Ferrar and flung him aside, expending almost no effort in doing so even though Ferrar was a large man, standing 6'3" and weighing 210 pounds. Ferrar went down hard, grunting loudly.

"Leave him alone, Ferrar. We gotta get out of these mountains. Quit wasting time fighting." Arby was absolutely and completely pissed off. When the bus crashed it had careened so far downslope there was no way to climb back to the highway. They had plummeted over a sheer cliff that had run north and south along the highway. After several arguments that had briefly come to blows they had headed upstream, expecting the river would lead to a road, but it hadn't, and now they'd been wandering around these mountains for over twenty-four hours.

They'd slept alongside the stream, thirteen very hungry, very angry killers. Two of the criminals had died in the crash, the man whose leg was ripped off, and one who'd been killed when the compartment bars crushed him against his seat. Arby hadn't known either man and wouldn't have felt sorry even if he had. Most of those surviving had cuts, bruises, and abrasions, and several had sprained their wrists or knees. They'd found keys on the bodies of the dead guards and had unlocked their cuffs and released their leg irons and metal waistbands.

Arby had had trouble waking the men up this morning, and since the sun was overhead when they got moving, he suspected they had wasted a good portion of the day. He would have abandoned the bastards but figured he might need them if they ran into trouble. If necessary, in a confrontation with authorities, he would use the men as decoys, and slip safely away while they died or were captured.

"The asshole keeps walking on the back of my feet! Why don't he watch where the fuck he's going." Ferrar whined like a small child picking himself up off the ground. He knew better than to challenge Arby.

"You guys spread out and stay off each other. When we get back to a road you can all split and never have to see each other again. Hey, check this out! Come on." Arby had spotted a game trail leading from the streambed up the far side of the ravine. "It looks like a trail." He splashed through the small stream, taking a long draught of water, and started up the footpath. The others drank their fill and followed him, grumbling at the sudden increase in effort needed to trudge uphill. The day was hot and their calves burned with the increased exertion.

They climbed for over two hours, traversing a series of long switchbacks, before reaching the top of the ridge, their red faces streaked with mud and their greasy hair soaked, as each of them sweated profusely. The game trail, which had split several times, finally petered out altogether in a pine forest and the men disgustedly threw themselves on the ground under the trees, refusing to go farther.

"Arby, this is crazy." said Freddy "Butch" Cassidy. "We left the water behind and there ain't nothin' up here but trees. Now what the fuck are we going to do? I'm starving."

Arby walked farther across the ridge, winding through junipers and pine trees, and stared toward the south across another canyon, a monster canyon, even larger than the first. He shook his head, "Oh shit! These dudes are really gonna be pissed off now." He mumbled to himself.

August 21, 12:30 p.m.
Albuquerque, New Mexico

The bright yellow taxi pulled up in front of the hospital's main entrance and parked in the area designated for picking up patients. Janet Prince pushed a wheelchair along the sidewalk toward the waiting taxi with conflicting emotions; happiness that Faye Claret was alive and going home, and sadness that she wouldn't have this wonderful lady to talk to everyday in the GI bleeder ward.

She maneuvered the chair alongside the cab, and the driver, a young man wearing a red beret, held the door open while Janet assisted Mrs. Claret to stand. The driver took her arm and helped her into the back seat, folded up the wheelchair and stuffed it in the trunk, while Janet said goodbye to her favorite patient.

"You take good care of yourself, promise me?" is what she said to her, but what she meant with all her heart, but didn't expect Faye to comply with, was "Never, ever, pick up another drink of alcohol."

"I will, dear. This time it was just too close for comfort." She scooted over in the seat and took a plastic bag containing her purse and other belongings from the nurse, placing it on the seat beside her. She reached out and took Janet's hand. "You take care of yourself too, dear, and don't let anything get in the way of your dreams."

"I won't, Mrs. Claret. Good luck to you." Her voice trembled and she turned quickly so the sudden tears wouldn't be seen by Faye, and hustled back to her duties. Faye Claret had come along at a time when Janet was at a crossroads, trying to balance her boyfriend's needs against her nursing career. He was chronically unemployed and was interfering with her studies as she desperately tried to finish her nursing program and take her test for Registered Nurse. Her problems were not that unusual or complicated but Faye Claret had listened to her tale and by asking Janet pertinent questions had led Janet to understand exactly what it was she wanted, and how to get there. She had a gift, leading

Janet to her own solutions without lecturing or influencing her decisions in any way.

Faye had been admitted to the hospital over two weeks ago with a 5.3 gram hemoglobin and bleeding ulcers. She used nine units of blood before they got the bleeding stopped and just barely escaped her second surgery in three months. Even though the bleeding had stopped, and she had detoxed, she was still in danger of busting loose. Her physician didn't want to discharge her, knowing full well her condition was marginal, but the utilization review staff at her insurance company had insisted. Her hemoglobin was stable, they claimed, and she could convalesce just as well at home.

"Where to, Miss?" the cabby asked her with a Latino accent.

"Please take me to "The Dugout" on 12th street. Do you know where it is?"

"Yes Senora, but are you sure you want to go there? You just got out of the hospital!" He was incredulous that this lady wanted to visit a sports bar even before going home.

"Yes, I'm sure. What's your name young man?"

"I'm Freddie." He glanced in the rear view mirror and pulled from the curb.

"Do you have children Mr. Freddie?"

He laughed. "It's just Freddie, Ma'am. No, I'm not married."

"That's too bad Freddie, a nice looking man like you. How come you're not married?"

The conversation continued and within six blocks Freddie Hernandez had fallen in love with Faye Claret. "Mrs. Claret, you really need to go home. Let me take you there, and if you feel better later you just call me. I'll give you a free ride anywhere you want to go." He hoped she had someone at home who could restrain her from going to the bar. He didn't know why she'd been admitted to the hospital, but he'd taken a lot of drunks home and he recognized the emaciated look, the tiny red veins on her face, and the dullness of her eyes.

"Actually," she replied, "I do need to go home to get my ATM card. Silly me, I forgot it when the ambulance took me to the hospital. It's very close to "The Dugout.""

She gave him the address and, immensely relieved, he swung in the direction of her home.

They pulled up in front of her house and he opened the cab door, helping her to stand up. "Do you need the chair?" He was worried she would fall but she walked right up the sidewalk with no problem.

"No, but you can bring it inside, please. I may need it later."

He jumped to do her bidding. As he entered the small, untidy house he heard an awful wailing sound, a siren of some sort. "Mrs. Claret?" he called out. "Is everything alright?"

"Freddie, can you come here?" He found her in the kitchen looking at a large stack of mail on the kitchen table, which included a small package with Express Mail wrapping. Her neighbor had been picking up Faye's mail each day and had deposited it on the table. The noise was coming from the package. "What do you suppose it is?"

He shook his head. "Guess the only way to find out is to open it." He picked it up and tore off the wrapper. He read and handed her the first note and then turning the device over, discovered and flipped the toggle switch inside. Frowning, he read and handed her the second one. "Man, this is really weird. What do you make of it? Do you think it's real?"

She smiled at him, "Guess the only way to find out is to…" She went into the living room and turned on the television. The news was bad but there was no indication the U.S. was in any imminent danger. She and Freddie sat down on the sofa and watched several special news bulletins. Listening between the lines, Freddie suspected things were worse than they made out and, after all, the device was already ringing. He was beginning to get real spooked.

"What are you going to do about the notes?" he asked her.

"Well, I just got out of the hospital where they went to a lot of trouble to save my life and it would be a real shame to lose it now. I guess I need a taxi to take me to this shelter. Do you know of one I could use?"

"Yeah, let's get the hell out of here! I have a feeling that if this is real the traffic is going to get real bad, real fast. Let's beat it."

He helped her get some things together and they climbed in the cab and headed north. He left the meter off and called his company to tell them he was sick and going home. There wasn't anything he could think of at home that he couldn't live without and he assumed they would be returning soon.

"No offense, Mrs. Claret but can I ask you why you got this box?"

"I've been wondering about that myself, but I haven't always been an old drunk, you know."

"I'm sorry, I didn't mean to . . . "

"No, it's okay. I know you didn't. But that's what I am now. Until a year or so ago, though, I was a teacher at Sandia High School. I taught English and Literature."

As they continued north, Freddie heard the unbelievably tragic tale of a woman's descent from a highly respected teacher and genuinely beautiful person, into the depths of acute alcoholism. He watched her in his rear view mirror as she told of a marriage gone bad, of a husband, a once successful businessman whose business had failed and who turned to drugs and alcohol, dragging his wife down into the abyss of his personal hell. Of her husband's sexual affairs, loss of his company and eventual suicide, with his wife standing before him struggling to wrench the gun from his hand. She told of trying to hide her drinking from her colleagues and students, of missing more and more work, of her friends desperately trying to get her help. But outwitting them, she moved to the far side of town, and became a steady patron of "The Dugout," drinking prodigious amounts of alcohol to drown out the memories.

She lost her job. Since she lived within walking distance of the bar, and never needed to drive drunk, no one she knew noticed as she destroyed her internal organs and her esophagus. She ended up in the ICU with bleeding esophageal varices the first time and bleeding ulcers the second. She would not survive a third.

They drove north on Interstate 25 passing through Las Vegas and as she related her story to Freddie he saw her start to tremble. She asked him, begged him, to stop in town to buy a bottle. This time he refused to do her bidding.

August 21, 1:35 p.m.
Albuquerque, NM

Mark was still waiting, and it was driving him crazy. After lunch, the Hargraves party had adjourned to the "Route 66 Microbrewery" where they could wait in relative comfort. Will was frustrated too, trying to keep everyone together without revealing highly classified information, although he realized that if an attack came it wouldn't matter if he shouted the information from the rooftops. Mark had gone back to the phones on several occasions, the last time receiving information from the sales clerk that Steve had left the store and hadn't informed his employees where he was going. He considered it a good sign. Will hadn't received any additional calls from Chuck and the television news reports had useless, out-of-date information. Mark went back to the lounge to reconnoiter with his group, buying a beer at the bar before joining them. Chris, Clay, and Will were carrying on a conversation in low tones.

"Dad, this is ridiculous!" Clay refused to believe the situation was dangerous. "We all have to be crazy sitting in this lousy town waiting to see if a war's going to happen. Why don't we go back to L.A.? We can wait it out there just as well and there's a lot more action."

Will's face was inscrutable, his tone, annoyed. "Clay, don't you think I just might have some inside information to base my assumptions on?" Will had never liked Clay's know-it-all attitude and, although he generally ignored it, he had no patience for it now. Helen and Ernest were sitting together and Will knew they were confused and frightened. Clay's whining was upsetting them more.

"My information comes directly from the Secretary of State. We have to wait here in proximity to a certain location for approximately twenty-four hours. If nothing happens by then we can return to Los Angeles. In the meantime, just keep your mouth shut." He glared at Clay and Clay had sense enough to settle back in his chair, nurse his drink, and keep quiet. His father didn't get angry often and when he did it was better to back off.

Chris came to Clay's rescue, "Dad, if you could just give us some idea of what's going on we might be able to relax. I don't blame Clay, I'm a little antsy myself."

Will paused momentarily, rubbing his forehead. He sighed, hesitated and decided that the information about the shelter wasn't classified, and with the current developments, he supposed nothing else was either.

"Alright, I guess you both have a right to know. Several years ago I was approached to become part of a civilian group of advisors to the administration, a group comprised of owners and CEOs of major aerospace companies that did business with the government. We've been advisors to three presidents, their cabinets, and to the Department of Defense and we all have top-secret security clearances. We basically keep the government informed of advances in weapons technology, new developments in aviation, etc. Because of my presence in this group, and the fact that the Secretary of State is a lifelong friend, I am privy to certain information that isn't available to the general public. A lot of it's classified, and that's the reason I haven't been at liberty to discuss it. The more I learned of foreign affairs the more I realized how precarious our situation is in regard to the possibility of nuclear war. Well, your mother had recently died at that time and I felt a great responsibility to the two of you. I have more money than any man needs and decided to build a bomb shelter in case of war. It started out as a small scale thing, almost a hobby, but eventually it ended up a rather large project."

He paused and took a sip of his scotch, his eyes shining as he gazed out the window across the tarmac. He turned back to Chris and Clay. "There are numerous shelters throughout the country. There's a major one, actually more than one, available to the President and other government officials. Others include shelters in basements of public buildings, and they even have supplies in public caverns like Mitchell Caverns in the California desert. Mine is one of the largest civilian shelters in existence and was built entirely with private funds. Under the guise of a government project it was easier to keep secret. It took several years to complete and what started as a small project soon after your mother's death became a large-scale serious endeavor that has only been completed in the last year. The shelter is in the mountains north of here. That's why we're here now. It's almost unbelievable, but there's a possibility of war at this very moment. The President and other important government officials are in the Command Plane, I assume that's Air Force One, and will utilize their shelters when it's appropriate. I've alerted selected people by means of a radio device that they should start toward the shelter."

As the implications of Will's words struck home, Clay sat up straighter, his eyes getting wider.

"You mean the possibility of a war is so great the government has already gone to bomb shelters?" This statement was too loud and Will held up his hand to quiet Clay.

"Shh, It isn't general information yet. That is precisely why we're here in this 'lousy' town as you put it."

"Well let's go now. We could get caught here!" Panic was beginning to creep into his voice.

"Take it easy, Clay," Mark spoke for the first time. "We'll have plenty of warning. The government's been keeping us informed. After all, if anything happens they'll want as many of our citizens to be saved as possible."

"You shut up!" Clay turned on Mark. "You always know so much. If they don't have time to notify us we could die right here."

Will grabbed his son's arm.

"That's enough Clay! Keep your voice down. We have a lot of friends that may be en route to this airport, including Jill and her family. We're going to remain here until we hear of further developments." He looked quickly around the lounge. "Mark's right. They'll let us know if anything significant happens. In the meantime, be quiet, you're scaring Helen." He turned to Helen and smiled, "Everything's going to be fine Helen, don't worry."

Helen managed a weak smile. Whatever Mr. Hargraves said was all right with her. She had Ernest with her and that was all that was important to her in this world.

Chris said, "Dad, if the threat of a war is that great, shouldn't people be warned so they can take steps to protect themselves? You can't just sit back and let everyone die."

"The general population will be informed the minute it's confirmed that the U.S. is under attack. Some will have time to evacuate. You just can't make that kind of announcement on a large scale without concrete proof. Besides, in the event of a war there isn't much that most people can do. Some know where public shelters are, but the general public will be caught flatfooted." He glanced at his watch. It was 1:45 pm Albuquerque time. He finished his drink.

They talked, killing time, while Mark nervously checked his watch every couple of minutes. The microbrewery was a sports bar with televisions in every corner and they'd paid the bartender to leave one tuned to Fox News Channel and were following the media's account of the crisis.

The overhead speaker came on. "Ladies and gentlemen, now announcing the arrival of Delta Airlines flight 451 from Dallas, unloading at gate 7."

Mark stood up, turned to Will. "I hope to God they made that flight. I'll check it out and be right back."

"Okay. After you get your sister meet us back here as soon as you can." He walked with Mark a few feet from the table speaking in a whisper, "I need to make some more calls to find out what's happening overseas. It bothers me that we haven't heard any more news from Chuck."

"Okay, I'll hurry." Mark left the lounge and turned to the left toward gate 7 walking through the cool, pink adobe concourse. Sun and cloud symbols and artwork by local New Mexico artists decorated the wide corridor in a distinctive Southwest motif. Evenly spaced, large windows looked out on the runways and lent an airy, open feeling to the concourse.

He was passing a sandwich shop by the gate when the music coming from the overhead speaker stopped and the public address system crackled and then, louder than usual, blared out, "May I have your attention please? This is a special news bulletin from Washington, D.C. Ladies and Gentlemen, The President of the United States."

Mark stopped in his tracks. "Uh oh," he said out loud, knowing full well what was coming.

"My fellow citizens," the president began, "I have some disturbing news. Nuclear devices have been detonated in Russia and in China and the North Koreans have retaliated against China for this morning's attack on their country. My military advisors have warned that an attack on the U.S. is imminent although no incoming missiles have been detected at this time. Our administration is taking all steps possible to prevent escalation but we are issuing this warning to allow people time to proceed to shelters and evacuate major cities. In the event we are attacked, our armed forces will take all steps necessary to intercept incoming missiles. The American people have always shown immense courage in the face of danger. Please, I'm asking everyone to keep calm, return to your homes and prepare to evacuate if you live in a major metropolitan area or in proximity to military installations. If we are attacked it will be safer and your chances for survival increased if you are away from these probable targets. Proceed to your homes and begin evacuation. We will do whatever is necessary to protect our country and her citizens. Good luck and God bless you all and God bless the United States of America."

It took a moment for the message to penetrate. At first the crowd began to just move quickly through the corridor and then suddenly they panicked and masses of people were pushing and shoving toward the exits of the airport, leaving their luggage behind which further obstructed pedestrian traffic. Mark was momentarily carried along with the crowd, struggling against the flow, until he managed to duck into an alcove where the restrooms were located. The door burst open and a woman rushed past him into the walkway and was immediately swallowed by the crowd.

An elderly man was jostled and fell to the tiled concourse floor where he was trampled by frantic people attempting to get around him. His wife, tugging at his arm, was buffeted by the panicked hoard and knocked to her knees. Mark caught the sight of blood and clutched at the old man, heaving him upright and pulling him into the alcove. The man's wife, crying hysterically, managed to join them, though she was bleeding from a facial gash and limping badly.

Mark yelled above the screams of the crowd, "Stay here until the crowd thins out! Otherwise you'll be killed!" He started back toward gate 7. When he arrived at the point where you weren't supposed to be able to proceed to the gate he saw that the security personnel were gone so he kept going all the way to the arrival gate.

He fought against the crowd, which was beginning to thin as people headed for the intersection of Concourses A and B and descended the escalators in leaps and bounds. When he arrived at the gate, unscathed, the passengers had just started to disembark. He watched as each person entered the terminal and was informed about the President's address. They were immediately swept up in the panic. By now the crowd was thinned out and he could see the few remaining passengers exiting the jetway. As they entered the terminal he could see that Jill's family wasn't among them. Bitterly disappointed he ran to a stewardess coming off the plane. "Are there any passengers left on the plane?"

"No, that's everyone, what's happening?"

"The government's issued a warning of possible nuclear attack on the U.S.," he threw over his shoulder, as he immediately started back toward the bar, moving with the last of the crowd. He arrived back at the bar in a few minutes.

The bartender was gone and the lounge was empty with the exception of a longhaired young man behind the bar who was helping himself to the money in the register. He looked up at Mark, "Well hell, dude, this is it. You want a drink?"

"No. Have you seen some people; a bearded man in his sixties, a pretty woman around 30, a younger guy, an older couple? They were at that table by the window." He advanced toward the bar and the other man backed away, his hands extended in front of him. Paranoia was already running rampant.

"No, man. When the bulletin came everyone split."

Mark raced back into the corridor and ran for the central escalators. He flew down the moving staircase dangerously taking the steps two and three at a time, pushing by people that remained stationary. He hit the second level and continued down the next escalator to the lower level. He needed to get to the Fixed Based Operator hangar where the chopper was located. Running through the baggage claim area, pushing through the thinned out crowds, he came to a dead end where windows looked out on the runway. Looking in both directions, he couldn't see any exits.

"Damn!" He realized it would detour him if he attempted to re-enter the crowded corridors so, instead, he hurried to the huge windows overlooking the landing area. There was approximately a four-foot drop to the concrete tarmac. Shedding the trappings of civilization, he grabbed a luggage cart and heaved it against the glass, leaping backward as it bounced back...but the glass had cracked. He swung it again with all his strength. The safety glass shattered explosively and he threw his arm up to shield his eyes as pieces cascaded over him. He kicked at the edges of the window to break off the remainder of the glass, stepped out on the ledge, and jumped to the concrete below, taking care to avoid large sheets of broken glass. He knew the others would have taken the SUV so he started running toward the flight school at his best race pace cutting across the taxiways and keeping a look out for planes and vehicles.

***

As the President's announcement ended Chris jumped to her feet. "Dad, what happened? I thought we would be warned ahead of time!"

"I don't know Babe! They obviously had no time. Damn! We've got to get to the chopper. Mark will know to meet us there."

They plunged into the melee trying to locate an exit that lead in the direction they needed to go, across the airport at a distance of slightly over a mile. Ernest had hold of Helen's arm to steady her. They beat most of the crowd to the escalators and quickly reached the lower level. Will was familiar with the layout of the "Sunport" and he led them to an exit where they burst out onto the tarmac. There was no time to get to the SUV in the VIP parking area. A small ground cart, used for transporting luggage and driven by a young man, was just starting away from the terminal. Will waved him down and threw himself in front of the cart, holding his arms in the air.

"Look, I need to get these people to High Desert Flight School. I'll give you five hundred bucks for a ride."

"Hop on bud, I'm going that way anyway. Show me the money."

Will gestured for the others to jump on, reached in his pocket and drew out a money clip. He tossed it to the driver, who thumbed through it.

"There's more than five hundred here," he told Will.

"Keep it. Let's move."

They sped past the end of the terminal and in a couple of minutes had reached the area where the flight school was located. Will pointed out where he wanted to go and the young man swerved in that direction.

They jumped off the cart as it swung alongside the chopper, the young man continuing away from the airport. Will squinted, looking toward the terminal for signs of Mark.

"What the Hell are we standing here for? Let's get out of here! Didn't you here what the guy said? The missiles could be fired any minute." Clay was pleading with his father.

"We're waiting for Mark. I'm not leaving without him."

"We don't have time. We don't need him. You know how to fly this… "

Will turned on Clay, grabbed him by the arms and shook him. "I said we're not leaving without Mark. Now get in the chopper before I throw you in!" He shoved Clay against the side of the large Bell helicopter.

Chris took Clay's arm. "Come on Clay. You'd better get in." She swung the door open and helped Helen climb into the back. The Bell 407 carried six passengers in addition to the pilot. If Mark's sister and her family arrived it was going to be a tight fit. Ernest climbed aboard and Chris jumped up after him. Will opened the front, glared at Clay and pointed. Clay briefly hesitated, and then climbed in. Will turned back to the field and his heart leaped as he saw Mark sprinting from the terminal.

He was alone.

"Here he comes!" Will yelled to the others. Mark was gesturing toward the hangar and Will turned to see two men running toward them, one of them carrying what appeared to be a large wrench. Will jumped up behind the controls and fired the engines. It was a race between Mark and the other men. The engine started and the four-bladed rotor began to spin.

Mark won, but just barely. The man with the wrench threw it at Mark. It hit the ground and bounced up, smashing against his leg just as he reached the chopper door. His feet were knocked out from under him and he went down against the strut. One of the men caught up to him and kicked him hard in the gut. Mark groaned and curled up, grasping his abdomen. Will had slid over to allow Mark behind the controls but now scooted back and jumped out of the chopper.

The second man screamed at Will, above the roar of the whirling blades, "We want the bird! Get out of the way and you won't get . . ."

Before he could continue, Chris threw the back door open against his back. He stumbled forward and Will shoved him into his companion. He tripped and fell hard to the ground. Mark staggered to his feet, gasping for air, as Chris picked up the wrench and waved it at the man still standing. The other man climbed to his feet, and both men, putting their hands up in surrender, backed away staring at Will.

He had a Sig forty-five caliber pistol pointed directly at them.

"Get the hell away from us, NOW!" The men turned, and looking fearfully back over their shoulders, ran back toward the hangar.

Will helped Mark aboard the chopper as Chris jumped back inside and secured the rear door. Mark was gasping, bent double and still having considerable difficulty breathing. He pulled back on the stick, lifting the chopper off the ground. They gained altitude and swung over the four level parking structure where a crash on one of the circular ramps had completely stopped the flow of traffic trying to exit. They passed over the terminal where Mark could see the traffic below horribly snarled as the mob surged into the streets, blocking vehicles. He tried the radio but no one was directing air traffic and he became concerned they might run into military planes since ABQ shared its runways with Kirtland Air Force Base. He banked hard, swung the helicopter around and headed north.

He yelled to Will over the noise of the engine, "Jill wasn't on the flight. I hope to God they get here and can find a car." His voice showed his frustration. He stared straight ahead, tears blurring his vision. There was no going back to that place.

August 21, 2:45 p.m.
Cheyenne Mountain, Colorado

Leroy had attempted to call in sick that morning but his commanding officer informed him that unless he wanted to be transferred to Minot, North Dakota he'd better get his black ass to work. He was so distressed he seriously considered disobeying orders and staying home, but he knew a guy stationed in Minot and it was truly the last place on Earth he wanted to be. His friend had worked in a very deep, narrow missile silo and told Leroy he hadn't seen the light of day all winter. Leroy steeled himself and came to work.

When he left the day before it had been Defcon 3, and as he entered the NORAD Control Center from the access tunnel he automatically glanced over at the indicator on the wall. He immediately froze in sheer terror. His tongue thickened and he heard himself making a whining noise in the back of his throat. Struggling with himself, he gained sufficient control to get to his station but found himself completely unable to concentrate on his work.

Data was flowing in a steady stream; reports of U.S. troop movements, scrambling jets, ICBM preparations as nuclear warheads were armed, incoming reports from the DEW Line in Northern Canada, all requiring his attention. Sea Wolf Attack Subs were on their way toward the Far East and aircraft carriers, previously stationed in the Gulf of Oman were steaming across the Indian Ocean. Data was received from destroyers and frigates towing underwater sonar arrays trying to locate enemy submarines.

Using space-based infrared detectors, The "Theater Event System" of the MWC, Missile Warning Center, had detected the detonation of a nuclear device in Russia that morning and had since detected short-range missile firings from Russia toward China. So far, the "Strategic Ballistic Missile Warning system" hadn't detected any long–range missile launches.

The United States' fleet of over forty nuclear-powered submarines surrounded the East Asian continent, Long-range B-52 bombers, and more modern B1's were en route toward Asia, and the Seventh Fleet with its hundreds of aircraft and tactical weapons, some nuclear, was ready for battle. The United States was fully prepared with a devastating retaliatory response if attacked by any foreign country.

Leroy would have attempted escape during lunch break had it been possible, but the facility was locked down, no one allowed to the surface during a Defcon 2 stage. He was so preoccupied with his work he actually began to think he might make it.

But then came 2:45 p.m.

On August 21 at 2:45 p.m. a Quick-Alert is displayed on the video display screens of the NORAD Command Center, initiated by one of the Air Force Space Command's worldwide network of Space Warning Squadrons. Infrared sensors had detected an unidentified, rapidly moving source of energy, which could be an intercontinental ballistic missile. A "threat fan" is generated by the Cheyenne Mountain computers.

"Jefferson! What the Hell is your problem?" Leroy vaguely heard the voice as it barely penetrated his consciousness. In near catatonia, with his eyeballs fixed and his mouth drooling spittle down the front of his uniform, he pissed his pants, urine soaking through his uniform and forming a puddle at his feet. His body had finally ceased shaking as he stared at the vast room's huge central monitor.

"Oh my God!" was the last thing he ever heard before his mind shut down forever. The Lieutenant was also staring at the screen. Showing on the map, overlaid with a grid of lines representing longitude and latitude and depicting the United States, Canada, and the North Polar Region, were hundreds of lights, each one an incoming intercontinental ballistic missile with one or more nuclear warheads.

The indicator switched to Defcon 1.

August 21, 2:45 p.m.
Denver, CO

John Arnaud slammed on his brakes, bringing his car to a jerking stop in front of his house. He jumped from the vehicle even before it completely stopped moving and bolted through the unlocked front door. "The bitch is seriously going to pay for that fucking remark she made to Veronica!" He muttered as he stormed into the house. What was wrong with her? Even though the accusation was true, he was infuriated she would embarrass him in that manner. He'd returned from an early afternoon meeting and Ronny angrily informed him about the call. He was so furious he left work early to teach the bitch a lesson she would never forget.

He slammed the front door and looked hurriedly around the front room, noticing Lori's note propped against the radio on the kitchen pass-through counter. He snatched it up and read it.

"You arrogant asshole - You beat me, you beat our children, and you fucked your secretary. Now you deserve anything that happens to you when the world goes up in flames. Dad sent me a map to a bomb shelter and I've taken the kids. We'll be safe while you burn in Hell!"

He was temporarily shocked out of his fury. What in hell was she prattling about? He grabbed the remote and switched on the T.V. The cable was out.

"Fuck!" He slammed the remote controller across the room and turned on the radio, twirling the dial quickly as he had trouble locating a station. Most of them seemed to be off the air with loud static blaring from the speaker.

Suddenly, a clear signal came through, ". . . minutes to impact. We repeat, the first of hundreds of incoming missiles will strike in approximately ten minutes. It appears that major cities from coast to coast have been targeted. Get under cover and stay tuned to this emergency station. We will continue to broadcast for as long as we can."

He stood there totally dumbfounded. Then he realized the significance of her note and the radio message. Denver was certainly a major city. He balled up his fists, looked up at the ceiling and screamed with fury, his neck muscles distending and his veins pulsing. Crumpling the note, he flung it across the room. Going berserk, he knocked the radio off the counter with a backhand, then ran across the room and ripped the paintings off the walls, overturned furniture and kicked gaping holes in the drywall. Exhausted, he threw himself in a corner, arms across his head, and screamed and bawled in frustration. "You Bitch! YOU FUCKING BITCH!"

August 21, 2:58 p.m.
Sangre de Cristo Mountains, NM

Taking the curves too fast, Robert Crowder gripped the wheel with white knuckles and prayed he and Lisa would arrive on time. She had called him immediately when the device went off, but he foolishly finished his assignment before heading home! The assignment seemed so important at the time but now he realized how utterly stupid he had been. Lisa looked nauseated as he careened around mountain curves speeding south on highway 25 at 2:58 p.m. They were coming from the north, from Colorado Springs where he worked as a communications instructor at The United States Air Force Academy. The baby's infant carrier leaned sideways as he barreled around a curve at 75 miles per hour.

The radio was tuned to the emergency channel, since most others had ceased broadcasting, and they heard that incoming missiles had been detected. He suspected that Colorado Springs and possibly Denver might be targets, and wondered how far away he had to be to keep from getting hit with the blast or thermal effects. Dear God, he thought, what if they hit Los Alamos? He kept on praying.

***

Dr. Sterling Harrington wandered through the wide hallways of Denver's Cherry Creek Mall swearing over and over again to himself when he heard the news. Tears rolled down his cheeks but no one noticed. He'd had a key to life and he destroyed it. All his degrees, the papers he had published, "The Group Psychology of Confined Individuals," the new therapies he had developed, all were worthless now. Someone, he would never know whom, had found him worthy and had sent him a black box and he had destroyed it.

There were others running through the mall with merchandise in their arms. Maybe they thought it really wouldn't happen and they would make off with whatever they could carry.

There was evidence of the earlier panic, broken glass, and overturned benches, mannequins in grotesque positions knocked from their window displays. A group of looters came around the corner and ploughed into him. They all went sprawling. The looters quickly gathered up their stolen goods and disappeared, leaving him alone in the eerily empty mall. He stood and brushed off his clothes. He would meet his end with dignity. A few minutes ago Sterling had heard someone in the crowd screaming that missiles were detected en route for the United States and the crowds had departed, trying to get home to their loved ones, attempting to leave town before the bombs arrived and leaving the mall looking like the aftermath of the world's end. He righted an overturned bench and sat down realizing it was indeed the end of the world.

He was totally alone. It was 3:02 p.m. and he had one more minute to live.

August 21, 3:30 p.m.
Bering Strait

Captain Richard Dombrowski paced the bridge of the Ohio Class, nuclear powered submarine. It was gliding through the water south of the Aleutian chain off the coast of Alaska and he had just disobeyed direct orders from the United States Military Command.

"Sir," The Exec informed him again in his southern accent. "We have been ordered to fire our missiles."

"I'm aware of that Mr. Finney," he replied. "But the United States has already responded to the attack with a killing blow. I'm concerned about throwing everything we have at them and having nothing left in reserve." The Captain had always been a man that considered all options and wasn't afraid to put forth alternative courses of action.

"I don't think we are the ones to worry about that, Sir. We have received direct orders."

"Well Sir, there may not be any one left to answer to. I'm saying we need to think ahead. We are officers of the United States Navy. We are paid to think as well as to follow orders." He turned to the communications officer. "Are we picking up anything?"

"No Sir. It's dead. I think the EMP has knocked everything out."

"Well, gentlemen, we have a choice. We were at extreme depth, which seems to have protected us from the EMP. Our systems are all still operational. We can fire our missiles and slink back home to hope that China and Russia have nothing left as well, or we can go back to San Diego with a full complement of missiles and possibly be the only protection our country has if they try to attack us later."

There was silence on the bridge as the crew considered his words.

The Exec looked at Captain Dombrowski with a sheepish grin. "Sir, hopefully the targets we were to hit have been taken out by other missiles. I know there was redundancy for every target. I believe you're correct in that we may be all that's left to protect the West Coast. I'd sure rather still have some teeth if they try to hit us later."

The Captain stood immobile for a few seconds then ordered, "Bring us about and set course for San Diego. Stand down the launch."

He fervently hoped he had made the correct decision.

August 21, 9:00 p.m.
Sangre de Cristo Mountains, NM

Wincing with pain, Aaron Brown succeeded in turning his head enough to elevate his nose and mouth above the muddy water that chilled his face and saturated his clothes. He struggled to regain consciousness, desperately trying to remember the circumstances surrounding his current predicament.

This wasn't his life. He knew it wasn't his life. He was a doctor. What happened to put him in this dark place, barely able to breathe and in this intense pain? He vaguely recalled a journey through unimaginable hell. His head cleared slightly, his thoughts traveling back in time to this morning's first surgical case and the beginning of this nightmare.

Aaron's surgery schedule began daily at 7:00 a.m. University Hospital, a 384 bed tertiary hospital, was the primary teaching hospital for the University of New Mexico at Albuquerque. From the day he arrived as a first year resident he'd found a plethora of interesting cases on which to sharpen his skills. His first case this morning, a routine cholecystectomy, went well and the patient would recover uneventfully. The next case, an exploratory laparotomy, went sour soon after the surgeon made the opening incision. The patient was loaded with metastasized cancer and Dr. Mannix, the surgeon, while attempting to completely excise the largest tumor, nicked an artery. All hell broke loose. The customary blood order for an exploratory lap is a type and screen; no blood had been crossmatched.

"Brown! Why the hell didn't you keep the field clear? Get that cell-saver over here! Call the lab and get six units 'stat'!"

It took the lab twenty-five minutes to get blood crossmatched. They transfused four units, and an hour later than originally expected, they wheeled the patient into recovery. Aaron was confident he wasn't at fault and swore that when he became a practicing surgeon he would never blame a resident for his mistakes.

It was approaching eleven a.m. when they broke for lunch, the residents gathering in the doctors' lounge to discuss their cases. The first year surgical resident, David Garcia, was questioning Aaron and furiously scribbling notes when the phone rang. Garcia, low man on the totem pole, answered it, motioning to Aaron, "There's a God-awful racket coming from your room. Mrs. Newell says it sounds like an alarm or something and it's driving them nuts. Been ringing for over an hour."

"Alright, tell her I'll check it out." As Aaron left the lounge he told Garcia, "Finish reviewing those notes and get scrubbed for the next case. I'll be right back."

"Hey man, don't we get to eat lunch?" David, as usual had overslept and missed breakfast.

"You have ten minutes. Better grab something quick," Aaron was seldom able to get lunch himself until things slowed down around two in the afternoon.

The residential wing was on the ground floor of an older section of the hospital. He rounded the corner and went from the gleaming "Alvarez" wing to the 30 years older "Harper" wing. Proceeding down a corridor, a right turn brought him to the hallway where his room was located. He could already hear the jangling alarm and was puzzled about its origin. As he unlocked the door, and pushed into the room, his eyes immediately rested on the device he'd thrown on the closet shelf the previous day. He stood stunned for a moment, then glanced quickly at a nurse standing behind him, shrugged at her, and closed the door squarely in her face. He hurried across the room, grabbed the box, which was now partially opened and examined the back. The hinged compartment swung down, spilling the contents onto the floor. Aaron noticed a toggle switch in the compartment, flipped it and was rewarded with sudden silence. He reached down and retrieved a note, some money, and once he'd unfolded it, what appeared to be a map. He briefly glanced at the map and read the note,

SINCE YOU ARE READING THIS MESSAGE THE WORST HAS COME TO PASS. NUCLEAR WAR IS IMMINENT! YOU MUST LEAVE FOR

THE SHELTER IMMEDIATELY. I CANNOT OVEREMPHASIZE THE URGENCY OF THE SITUATION. YOUR ONLY CHANCE FOR SURVIVAL IS TO FOLLOW THESE DIRECTIONS WITHOUT DELAY. DON'T BOTHER TO BRING PROVISIONS WITH YOU, AS EVERYTHING WILL BE PROVIDED. BRING YOUR IMMEDIATE FAMILY AND ONLY THOSE POSSESSIONS THAT ARE PRECIOUS TO YOU AND CAN BE CARRIED ON YOUR PERSON. HURRY AND GOOD LUCK!

He stood there totally confused, unable to assimilate the contents of the message. There was no way he could just leave, not with another surgery in a few minutes. Of course, if this message weren't a classic Jenkins practical joke, the surgery wouldn't matter. He looked around the room he'd lived in for over three years, and would live in for another two if this wailing siren was a hoax and didn't signal the end of the world as he knew it. It was home.

His Levi's were tossed across the end of the bed and his closet door stood open, revealing a few clothes and his guitar, standing in the corner. An open textbook lay on the desk where he had been studying the night before and the bookshelf was bowed from the weight of every textbook he bought for medical school, and had been unable to get rid of. A stereo occupied the top of the tiny dresser, which also held a picture of his younger brother and sisters.

On impulse he crossed to the dresser and removed the picture from the frame, noticing that his fingers were shaking. When he went to replace the frame on the dresser it slipped from his fingers and shattered on the floor. The noise galvanized him into action, and he moved quickly around the room. He put the picture in the back pocket of his jeans but left them on the bed. Grabbing a small daypack out of the closet, he emptied the contents on the bed, an old Gameboy video game, a pocketknife, a small first aid kit and an unopened package of Gummy Bears. He stuffed the things back inside and went into the bathroom, adding his toothbrush, toothpaste, a washrag, a small bar of soap, and his razor. He returned to the room, tossing the bag on the bed, his mind a confused jumble of thoughts. How long, he wondered, before the bombs come, assuming they come at all. He stopped to reconsider his actions, needing to think through the facts before he made any rash decisions that could ruin his career.

He hurried back toward the surgical suites. Was this whole thing for real? Why wasn't it on the news? He detoured and went by the hospital gift shop to buy a paper, noticing that everything seemed so normal; the pink shop with its aroma of fresh flower arrangements in the cooler, stuffed animals on the shelves and magazine racks with People and The Enquirer. The cheerful volunteer, her smock identifying her as a member of the Hospital Auxiliary, smiled as he came in. He went to the newspaper rack and scanned the headlines, looking for evidence of a serious problem. "Secretary of State to go to Moscow", "China Tests Nuclear Weapons," They proclaimed. He knew events were transpiring that he wasn't aware of because of his isolation as a surgical resident. With a touch of guilt he realized he hadn't seen a paper or news broadcast in weeks but he did know he was late for his next case and he quickly headed for surgery.

"Where the hell have you been Brown, we're ready to start. Get scrubbed." Harold Ewing, the surgeon, looked irritated. He was an outside man and Aaron would be assisting on his private case. The patient on the operating table was already prepped and the surgeon had finished scrubbing. Aaron quickly scrubbed and entered the operating room to find Ewing briefing the surgical team as he took his place opposite the surgeon. The patient was anesthetized, the nurse anesthetist reporting blood pressure, temperature, and pulse were fine and he had control of the patient's breathing.

Ewing was in a foul mood, his usual state, and berated Aaron continually about minor details until Aaron was getting angry himself. "Brown, can't you clamp those bleeders any quicker than that? It's sloppier than hell in here."

"This sounds just like the last surgery." Aaron thought. *"What is this? Aaron Brown screw-up day?"* The surgery seemed to deteriorate into slow-motion, a horrid nightmare, as he first looked up from the patient to Ewing, and then glanced at the scrub nurse and the anesthesiologist. The awful clamor of the siren was ringing in his imagination. It suddenly occurred to him, "Oh my God!" that it could be real, and he was wasting time. He looked at the clock - 12:05 p.m. The second hand swept the dial and he stood transfixed unable to take his eyes off the inexorably advancing time.

"Brown! What the hell are you doing? Wake up and pay attention!"

Ewing was glaring at Aaron while a small amount of blood welled up into the incision. The nurse applied suction and the blood welled up again. Aaron stared at Dr. Ewing but looked down again and concentrated with all his energies until the surgeon had finished. He could never leave a patient in the middle of a surgery.

"Go ahead and close, Brown." Ewing instructed him, but as far as Aaron was concerned, the surgery was over, the patient in good hands. With sudden resolve he handed a hemostat to the nurse. "Here, Mrs. Stark." She stared at him in shocked amazement.

He looked back at the surgeon, his mind suddenly made up. "Screw you Ewing! You close it." He strode purposefully from the operating theatre.

As he hit the corridor outside the surgical suite he broke into a run. He rounded the corner to the Harper suite and bowled over a group of young nursing students, skidding to a halt to help them up. He muttered apologies and started down the hallway. Then he stopped, turned back, and said to them, "Did you know we're having a nuclear war and you're all going to die soon?"

They stared at him as though he were crazy. "Yeah, right… whatever! Let's get out of here." One directed this at the other students and they hurried around the corner glancing back at him with quizzical expressions, certain he was deranged.

Aaron ran to his room, entered and closed the door, leaning back against it and shutting his eyes. "Maybe I am crazy," he muttered. The phone rang and he crossed the room, grabbing the receiver.

"Brown? This is Dr. Garand . . ." the caller began. Without thinking Aaron slammed the phone down hard. Dr. Garand was the Chief of Surgery and was the last person Aaron wanted to talk with at this time. Dr. Marvin Garand had mentored him all through his residency and he was genuinely sorry he couldn't explain his actions.

The phone rang again but Aaron ignored it. Taking off his green scrubs he slipped on the Levis as the phone continued ringing. Exasperated, he steeled himself and reached over and picked it up.

"Aaron Brown," he answered.

"Aaron, don't hang up! What's going on? I got a call from Ewing and he's really pissed. Says you walked out in the middle of surgery. Are you sick? Is there something wrong?"

Aaron didn't answer right away trying to decide what to say. "The surgery was essentially finished, Dr. Garand, he just needed to close. I know you'll think I'm crazy, but we're about to have a nuclear war and I'm evacuating. I received an advance warning and I believe it. Check out the news."

The other man sounded incredulous, "Aaron, you're right, this is crazy. I know there's a lot of international tension but I'm sure there's no real danger. Walking out on surgery is a serious matter and we need to discuss it to see what action should be taken. Please come to my office before you ruin your career."

"I'm sorry, Dr. Garand. You've been very kind to me and I hope you survive. Good luck, sir." He hung up the phone before Garand could answer. He dialed his home in Atlanta but no one answered. "Damn, where is everyone?"

He threw on a t-shirt, pulled on his hiking boots and grabbed his bag. He wanted desperately to talk to his folks but he didn't have their work numbers, and his little brother and sisters would be at daycare. Hoping to get another chance, Aaron would have to try them later. He looked quickly around the room but couldn't think of anything else to take. While he was locking the door he heard footsteps running in the hospital corridor and he quickly headed the other direction to the stairwell leading to the basement. As he passed through the door he looked back to see two security guards approach the door of his erstwhile room, Doctor Guerrero, a psychiatric resident, accompanying them. He heard them banging on the door as he bolted down the staircase.

Dr. Garand obviously thought he'd flipped under the pressure and was trying to rescue him from himself. Emerging into the basement corridor, he quickly checked each direction for signs of security guards, believing that Garand undoubtedly would have alerted them to detain him. Aaron knew Dr. Garand had his best interests in mind and that he truly thought Aaron had a serious problem. Well, he did, they all did, but not what Dr. Garand imagined.

Aaron heard a door slam at the top of the stairwell and hurried toward the exit just beyond the kitchen, when another pair of guards came around that corner, effectively barring his advance. Worried, he ducked into the Pathology Department door midway between the stairwell and the kitchen. The secretary looked up from her transcribing. "Oh, Dr. Brown, I almost didn't recognize you in those clothes. May I help you?"

He walked past her desk. "I need to see Dr. Pathmarajah."

"He's doing a post in the autopsy room."

"Thanks, I'll find him." He passed through the Histology lab then heard voices behind him.

"Yes, he went to autopsy room."

They were too close! He panicked and hit the door at full speed. The diener and Dr. Path had just wheeled the body lift into position next to the autopsy table. They'd completed the post-mortem exam and were putting the straps around the cadaver to return it to the vault. Aaron smashed into the tech, who in turn crashed into the lift. The corpse was jerked off the table by the one strap they had secured and fell heavily to the floor. Blood was everywhere. Except for the body itself, the tech hadn't cleaned up yet, and in spite of the vented table, the room was filled with the overwhelming stench of death, layered over with formaldehyde. Aaron bashed his arm on the table and pain shot all the way to his shoulder. He caught his balance and continued across the room.

The tech, slipping on body fluids, tripped over the corpse and sprawled on the tiled floor, covered with gore.

Two security guards came through the door, one of them skidding to a halt, staring at the body on the floor. He turned away and began to wretch while the other continued chasing after Aaron. Aaron sprinted past the morgue boxes and out onto the loading dock running past a hearse parked at the dock, up the drive to the street level, and into the alley that ran behind the hospital.

He rounded the corner into the street and immediately slowed to a walk. He didn't think they would follow him out of the hospital since they had no criminal case against him and only wanted to stop him for his own good.

It would be foolish, though, to attempt to get his car from the garage. He looked at his watch - 12:55 p.m. He could have sworn he had spent hours trying to get away. The map showed the shelter's location in the mountains of northern New Mexico. He went into a diner, called a cab and had the cab drop him off at the bus depot. It was now 1:30. He checked the schedule on the monitors. One bus was leaving for Denver at 1:50 but it went through Santa Fe and then up highway twenty-five. That was out of the way. Another went to Taos, which was the right direction but not far enough. He began to wish he'd taken a chance on getting his car but decided he should at least get as far as Taos by bus. It was leaving at 1:40 so he bought his ticket, went to the lunch counter and got a plastic wrapped sandwich. He had never gotten to eat lunch. When was that? About a week ago? In a matter of two and a half hours his life had completely changed. What would his folks say?

One thing a resident learns is fast eating. Aaron gulped down the sandwich followed by a bottle of Snapple iced tea. He bought the afternoon paper to validate his reasons for ruining his career, to see if there was even the faintest hint of war.

Same headlines, same stories. The underlying tone of the paper, though, hinted the situation was becoming serious. The Secretary of State called off his trip to Moscow and the President and members of his cabinet had left Washington for places unknown.

"Now why would they do that if there's such a crisis?" Aaron wondered. *"Shouldn't they be making some phone calls?"*

After settling down on the bus he started thinking about the enormity of his actions, suddenly becoming anxious, worried this was an elaborate hoax and he'd destroyed his career for nothing.

But then, he wished he knew where the president had gone.

It was sixty miles to Santa Fe and another seventy to Taos. His arm ached where he'd smashed it on the autopsy table, but he finally relaxed somewhere between Albuquerque and Santa Fe, and drifted off to sleep.

August 21, 2:57 p.m.
Durango, CO

Jonathan Peters drove like a madman trying to get home to Mary and his children. "A matter of minutes... " the radio said. He sped through the streets of Durango remembering the warning that came with the box; "You are advised to keep it on your person at all times." He hadn't, and now it was too late. Tears streamed down his face as he swung into his driveway and climbed out to see Mary mowing the front yard, such a domestic scene, as if they weren't about to be incinerated or radiated. She couldn't hear the car but smiled broadly and waved when she turned and saw him approaching. The kids, their twin toddlers, played at her feet.

"Why Jonathan, what's wrong?" She signed, frowning and suddenly frightened when she saw his tears. He could hear the siren's wail coming faintly from somewhere inside. He signed that everything was fine, to come in the house and he would explain, as he scooped the boys up, one under each arm. It was 3:02 p.m.

He turned on the television but the cable was out and the static suddenly ceased as the power went out as well. He signed to her, asking where the portable radio was. After she located it he tuned it to the emergency broadcast station.

"... hit the west coast. We will try to keep you informed. If you are not in a major city it is extremely important that you get under cover and stay there as long as you can. Even if no missiles hit nearby, the radiation from fallout will be very dangerous for an extended period of time."

Jonathan explained to Mary what was happening. As she hugged her little boys and held her husband she was sorry for the first time in her life that she was hearing impaired. She started to cry quietly while signing to him for instructions.

The radio, filled with static, continued, "We are receiving reports from the west coast that several huge explosions have been spotted all over Southern California. The observers are located many miles from the blasts in smaller communities spared from direct hits. Communications are difficult with the radio signals disrupted by the nuclear energy. We repeat, if you are away from targeted sites you must get under cover."

Even the powerful emergency channel was faint and was being disrupted by EMP, electromagnetic pulse. An effect of atmospheric nuclear explosions, it is caused by an electrical charge collecting on wires, cables, antennas, etc, and produces very high voltage for a fraction of a second. This pulse can knock out all electrical devices, even those that are turned off as the pulse jumps across open circuits. Jonathan was surprised the radio was working at all but unless the nuclear explosions are at the proper altitude the EMP might not completely knock out everything.

Jonathan and Mary gathered all the provisions they had in the house and relocated them to the basement. She went below with the children while he walked outside to see if there was any evidence of the war. There wasn't. They lived in a quiet neighborhood where people minded their own business. Nobody was trying to evacuate since Durango wasn't likely to be a target, and the nearest city he could think of that might be was hundreds of miles away. Some of his neighbors stood on their lawns looking northeast toward Denver or South toward Albuquerque and Phoenix. Nothing unusual was visible from this beautiful, Rocky Mountain community in the southwest corner of Colorado.

He went back into the house and flicked the light switch.

Nothing.

Obviously the bombs, or EMP, had taken out the power grid. He wondered if anyone would be alive to get it working again, or was this the beginning of the end of all civilization? The air-conditioner was off and he realized with no electricity they would have no heating, lighting or air-conditioning. There was no bathroom in the basement and he doubted they would have water for long. Didn't that require pumps and power? It became painfully obvious how little he knew about these things, how dependent they were on others for the basic utilities and how totally unprepared he was for this kind of an emergency.

Even in the basement, how long before the radiation assaulted them? Would they become chronically sick, or die quickly? He didn't know the answers to these questions but, as he joined his family, he knew he had a loaded pistol and he wouldn't let his loved ones suffer.

August 21, 9:30 p.m.
Sangre de Cristo Mountains, NM

It was thirty minutes later than the last time he'd regained consciousness, and still soaking in the muddy puddle, Aaron could feel the temperature beginning to drop. Although summer, the weather at this high altitude was cold at night and lying still as he was, he could feel the chill seeping into his bones. A strong breeze blowing from the north to the south exacerbated the chill. Gathering his strength, he tried to shift position but cried out in pain when he dragged his injured arm through the mud. He almost blacked out, but the sharp pain helped to clear his head and he became slightly more alert. His skull rested against a jagged rock and he was concerned that he may have sustained a concussion. He vaguely remembered cracking his head against the rock when he catapulted over the handlebars of the ATV. ATV? What ATV? With a tremendous effort he dragged himself out of the small stream and rolled onto his back. Staring up through towering pines he struggled to recall more of the events that had brought him to this place and remembered having fallen asleep in the bus.

He'd been jolted awake by a blaring horn and by the bus driver who, cursing loudly, had slammed on his brakes, throwing Aaron forward in the seat. He sat up groggily, trying to see what was happening and noticed the road was choked with traffic. A glance at his watch, it was 2:20 p.m., indicated they must be getting close to Santa Fe. They shared the road with speeding cars, their drivers recklessly cutting in and out, seemingly without regard to safety. The bus driver continued to brake until the bus stopped completely as the surrounding traffic slowed to a crawl and then ground to a halt. Aaron grabbed his backpack and headed toward the front of the bus.

"Hey, what's going on?" he asked the driver.

"Don't know for sure, but it wouldn't surprise me a bit if it's a big accident, the way those idiots are driving out there." Opening the door, he and Aaron descended to the roadway, other passengers following behind them. The majority of the other cars had stopped, their drivers climbing out as well, although some attempted to proceed along the shoulder. Aaron could see cars stopped ahead for a half mile until they disappeared around a curve. There was no traffic on the other side of the freeway and cars were beginning to cross the median and were starting up the wrong side of the road. People whose cars were hemmed in started walking or running in the direction the traffic had been traveling, as others leaned on their horns. With sudden apprehension Aaron drew the driver back to the side of the bus. "Do you have a radio in this thing?" he asked.

"Yeah, but it's too soon to pick up news of this roadblock."

"Just turn the damn thing on. I have a feeling there's more to it than a traffic jam." Aaron shoved the driver up the stairs against the flow of passengers descending. The driver turned on the radio but received only loud static. He grunted and turned the dial until he finally picked up a faint, crackling signal that suddenly became loud enough to be heard in the first few rows of the bus.

"...the city. Don't panic. Take only what you need and try to stay away from major . . . ties. Drive carefully as . . . will make it difficult for anyone to evacuate. We repeat. Missiles have been detected en route for China apparently launched . . . Russia. The government expects China to retaliate, with a very real possibility they will launch missiles at the United States. It is believed Moscow has already been . . . nuclear devices from unknown sources. All major cities are now in the process of evacuation. This... gency radio network. Stay tuned for further details."

"Good God Almighty" the driver muttered. Someone behind Aaron, having caught the announcement, pushed him aside, and he stumbled into the terrified driver.

"Let me out, we can't get anywhere in this thing. We're trapped."

Aaron moved to let more passengers squeeze by. He could see panic in their eyes. Fortunately, he had received advanced warning, but these people were taken completely by surprise.

One passenger remaining on the bus shouted to the driver, "It's gotta be a joke, like *War of the Worlds*. Do your job and get us moving."

"You drive it, buddy. I'm outta here!" The driver jumped down the steps and joined the mass of people moving toward the front of the traffic jam.

Aaron decided he wouldn't get far in that direction and started back against the flow, jogging slowly to make better time, and eventually, after swinging around a wide curve, reached a point where the traffic thinned out. He tried unsuccessfully to flag down passing motorists who continued to speed along until they too, were mired in the traffic jam. Continuing back along the highway, he reached an intersecting road, and breathing hard from exertion stepped behind a row of bushes to try and catch his breath. He realized the traffic would soon be backed up to this intersection so he pushed through the bushes to a point where he could see cars coming down the side road, hoping to catch a ride. He heard a car approaching from the left and peered through the hedge to see a Toyota 4X4 containing three men as it sped by him and, never slowing down, pulled around the corner onto the main road, directly into the line of traffic. The surprised drivers of other vehicles slammed on their brakes and skidded sideways, as the Toyota sped away to the north. Traffic was starting to build up around the curve ahead and he knew he was almost out of time. When the jam reached the intersection, cars coming from the side road would be blocked.

He heard another car coming and moved forward through the bushes determined to get a ride. As the gray Chevy Cavalier slowed at the intersection Aaron leaped out of the bushes, grabbing for the door.

It was locked! The window was lowered about six inches and he tried to jam his arm through the window to unlock it. The single woman occupant screamed at him and started to move forward into traffic but instinctively slammed the brakes when on-coming cars honked and swerved around her. Aaron held his bag in his left hand, which also grasped the window's top edge, and in a last ditch effort, shoved his right arm farther into the window, taking a chance on serious injury as the woman slammed the car into reverse. His fingers slipped on the lock mechanism but he was strong enough to grasp it tightly and pull it up. He had to run alongside of the car until she swerved slightly and went off the side of the pavement. She slowed, corrected her direction and started to accelerate. He pulled his arm free and throwing open the door, jumped in just as the car picked up speed in reverse. He threw his bag over the seat and grabbed the woman's wrist. She was crying and screaming at him to get out.

"Shut up lady! Please. I'm not going to hurt you. We've got to get out of here, you're going the wrong way!"

He held her for a moment until she stopped struggling. He heard a car pass on the left, and a screech as a pickup skidded to a stop in front of the Cavalier. Two large, burly men threw open the doors of the pickup and started back toward the Chevy. Aaron, on his knees, was dragging the woman toward him.

"Move over now, or I'll throw you out!"

She slid over and he roughly scrambled across her and slipped behind the wheel. The automatic transmission was already in reverse and the car had continued to move backward, but the men were almost upon him.

"Leave her alone you Goddamn nigger!" one of the men yelled as he reached the front of the car, smashing his fist on the hood. Aaron stomped on the accelerator and the car jumped backward. He turned the wheel, backing completely off the road into thick brush and shoved the car into drive. With tires squealing and kicking up clouds of thick dust, and the rear end fishtailing, he sped back in the direction from which the woman had originally come. For a minute he drove without watching her, trying to regain control of the car, and his breathing, after the close call. When he was satisfied he wasn't being followed he slowed down and glanced over at the woman. She was younger than he originally thought, younger than his thirty years. She had stopped crying and was staring straight ahead murmuring something under her breath. She seemed to be praying.

"Look, ma'am, I did you a favor. There was a colossal traffic jam on the main highway and you would have been stuck for good. I needed a car to get around it. Now you can go with me, or I can drop you off, but I need this car. What do you want to do?"

She looked over at him. "Please take me home. I was going to pick up my kids."

"You wouldn't have gotten through anyway. Where's your husband?"

"He's on his way home from work. He called and told me to get the kids." She started to cry again.

His tone softened, "Look, I'll get you home and you can wait for him. Then you can try to get your children. But don't take the main road again or you'll get stuck. Where do you live?"

She directed him to turn ahead and pointed to a small isolated wood-frame house about a quarter mile away. He pulled into a dirt driveway in front of the house and she started to open the door. He reached over and took her arm, "Wait a minute. I know of a bomb shelter in the mountains north of here. If you get your family together you can try to make it there." He lifted his rear, pulling the map out of his back pocket. "Do you have a pen?"

She fished around in her purse and handed him a pen and a grocery receipt. He drew a quick sketch and handed it back to her. "Stay away from main roads and get there as quickly as possible. If the bombs are coming now there won't be much time. I'm a doctor and that's where I'm heading. Good luck lady, I'm sorry I had to take your car." She stepped back and slammed the door as he gunned the engine.

"My God," he thought, as he raced down the road. "I can't believe this thing is really happening."

FOUR

August 21, 1:30 p.m.
Sangre de Cristo Mountains, NM

Pete peeked through thick bushes that separated him from the magnificent buck on the far side of the clearing. He motioned to Sandi to approach quietly and when she reached his side he whispered to her, "Get a picture of this. It's a Rocky Mountain Mule Deer." He pointed to the clearing and heard her intake of breath as she saw the animal only thirty feet from her.

"It's beautiful", she whispered, as she brought up the camera for a shot. Suddenly the buck raised its head and gazed intently in their direction. It poised only a moment and then, as if they had shouted, leaped away so quickly Pete wasn't sure which way it had gone.

The camera clicked.

Pete laughed and grabbed Sandi from behind. "Oh, that should be a great shot! Rocky Mountain bushes."

"Pete let go of me!" She wriggled and turned in his arms, looking up into his eyes. They froze for a moment and he kissed her, a kiss that for him meant forever, as he became aware that his feelings for her had changed overnight.

"Hey, we'd better get back to camp," he told her. "If we don't start back before long we won't get to the car before dark."

They retraced the route they'd taken on the way from their camp. They'd been out all morning, carrying their lunch and supplies in a small daypack and Sandi had shot an unbelievable number of photos. She always took too many with the assumption that she would delete many of them when she downloaded them to her computer - but she never did.

They'd strayed a considerable distance from their campsite, traveling west into the high country and passing the trail leading down into the canyon. This portion of the footpath led along the southern edge of the colossal canyon. Pete looked across the abyss and pointed to the other side, "Hey Sandi, look over there. What a huge group of hunters." Although the rim of the canyon was quite distant Sandi could see a large group of people dressed in hunters' blaze orange. She waved at them.

"Hey, wait a minute." Pete said. "It's too early for hunting season. Large and small game seasons usually start in the fall, though sometimes bow and arrow hunts are held earlier. I wonder if they're poachers. It's probably better not to attract their attention."

He had no idea how lucky they were that there was a monster canyon between them and thirteen homicidal maniacs.

The trail veered away from the edge as they retraced their path, coming to the brook they crossed on the way out, six feet across, with several large rocks forming a natural bridge. Pete took Sandi's hand and stepped gingerly on a rock, damp and slick with algae. His foot slipped, and trying to catch himself, he threw out his other leg, landing on his butt in a foot of water. Sandi started to laugh, and then shrieked, as Pete jumped up and pulled her after him and they both toppled backward into the pool. She fell on top of him and they splashed around, getting completely soaked.

"Oh damn! Pete, you retard, look at me!" She jumped up and promptly slipped down again on the slick rocks. He managed to keep his footing and pulled her to her feet, both of them laughing so hard they hurt. Sloshing to the edge of the stream, he retrieved her camera where she had thrown it clear, and handed it to her.

"Sorry 'bout that," he said. But he wasn't. "Now that we're already soaked let's head downstream, it'll be quicker than taking the winding trail. Otherwise we'll get chilled before we can dry off."

They traveled downstream, crisscrossing it several more times, and finally reached camp and dry clothes. They'd only brought one extra set of clothing apiece so they hung the others on a tree limb to dry in the sun.

"We should let them dry a bit before we stuff them in our packs so they won't mildew. I guess we can wait a while before we head back since we saved some time by staying with the stream. Do you want a snack?" He pulled out a bag of dried fruit and tore off the top.

"I'm dying for McDonald's. How about a Quarter Pounder with cheese. And with onions. Can you arrange it?"

"This'll have to do." He handed the bag to her and flopped down on his sleeping bag. "We made good time. We don't need to start back for an hour. I don't know about you but I came up here for rest and relaxation so I'm going to take a nap."

"That sounds like a winner. Me too." She lay down beside him. He looked over at her, took her hand and pulled her closer. Just as they started to embrace there was a brilliant flash in the southern sky followed almost immediately by another and still another. The flash was so bright it temporarily blinded them as they jumped to their feet.

"What in the world was that?" asked Pete.

"I don't know. It almost looked like an explosion."

They watched as the light faded and suddenly noticed that there was a dead calm to the forest. The usual background noises, birds chirping, even leaves rustling had stopped. Deathly silence.

"Look!" he cried, pointing south in the direction the light had come from.

She looked up, already having a gut feeling what she would see. Rising above the trees in the far distance were three oddly shaped clouds, billowing mushrooms, one large and two smaller ones, as if they were at a greater distance, that were already spreading out in the stratosphere due to the extreme altitude they'd reached by the time the couple espied them above the trees.

"Oh my God!" moaned Pete, "My parents!" He grabbed at Sandi's hand. "Come on let's go!"

She snatched her hand away and held up both in front of her as she backed away. "Pete, don't be a fool! If that was a nuclear bomb we can't go back there. We have to stop and think a minute. It would be too dangerous with radiation or heat or something."

"But it looked like it came from the direction of Las Vegas," he pleaded. "I have to go. Sandi, Please!"

"No! Stop and think a minute, okay? If it was a bomb, we'd die, and if it wasn't, then there's no reason to go rushing back. Let's just keep our heads. I think we ought to take the equipment. We might need it if there's really something wrong. Then we should go back down to the highway and see if we can get some news. Let's stuff our bags. Come on." She grabbed the clothes off the tree limb and put them in her pack. Her actions calmed him slightly,

"You're right, I . . . I'm sorry. I'm just scared for my folks and my brother. If it's an atomic bomb they might all be dead." His heart was in his throat as he threw the other supplies in their packs, and then, with a renewed surge of panic, grabbed her hand and started on the return trip to the car.

The silence persisted as they hurried down the trail, Sandi almost having to run to keep up with the pace Pete was setting. Finally, regardless of what she'd said earlier, she dropped her pack and ran to catch him.

A few minutes later, they heard the noise. The most terrifying noise either of them had ever heard. She went to him and he held her.

A low rumble, it gained in volume until it was a steady roar even though the distance muted it. They held each other, imagining they could feel the sound vibrating in their bones, a death knell for civilization. She buried her head in his shoulder trying to block it out.

***

Sunlight reflected off something metallic across the canyon, catching Arby's eye. He detected movement and realized he was seeing people.

"Hey, dudes! Come here!" He yelled at the others. Three of the men joined him at the canyon's edge where he was pointing toward the south.

Moose shook his head, "So what? Look at the size of that fucking canyon. It would take us the rest of the day to cross it, even if we could find a way down. I say we go back the way we came. At least there's water in the bottom of that last canyon."

"There's water in the bottom of this one too," said Arby pointing down into the ravine. "Look, by the big rock, you can see it."

Bobby Bennett agreed. "Yeah, he's right. I can see it. Those dudes probably have food and they must have a car somewhere."

"We still don't know if we could find a road if we went back. I say let's go on." Anders said. Arby was surprised Anders agreed with him. He had bitched vehemently when they initially started up the game trail, having wrenched his knee badly in the bus crash.

They went back to the others and, with a lot of cursing and shouting, talked them into continuing.

They couldn't see a trail on their side but could see that the couple on the other side was obviously following one. They assumed the couple had to have backpacks and all thirteen of them became very excited at the prospect of acquiring them and the food they must contain. Just then the smaller of the two people waved in their direction and Arby could tell it was a woman. This excited him more than the prospect of getting his hands on the packs. "Come on!" he yelled. "Let's find the fucking trail!" The cliff before them was too steep to climb down so they crashed through the bushes along the precipice searching for a way down.

"Dude, check it out." Ramirez pointed to the other side at a faint line crisscrossing up the opposite canyon wall. "That's a trail. If it goes down it has to come back up this side. Come on you guys. Spread out" He hurried farther along to the west, looking for the trail down.

Twenty minutes later they found it. It led over the edge and began a series of long switchbacks. They were becoming weak from hunger but headed down the trail with renewed vigor. The switchbacks caused the trail to be much longer than they originally thought and by the time they'd descended to the bottom of the gorge they were exhausted, even though they'd been going downhill. Arby, Bennett, Ferrar and Ramirez arrived first, the rest of the band lagging behind. They threw themselves down beside the river to rest after slaking their thirst in a small pool with a huge overhanging rock. Ferrar, looking in the water upstream, slowly came to his feet, climbed the rock and crept stealthily toward the pool. He jumped in headfirst, surfacing in a spray of silver droplets with something wriggling in his hands and flinging water everywhere!

"I got the son-of-a-bitch!" He had a large Brown Trout held securely by the gills. The men came to their feet, gathering around him as he waded to shore. The other ex-prisoners arrived, grousing, but ran over when they saw the fish.

"How we gonna to eat it? We ain't got no knife," complained Ramirez.

"Don't need one." Ferrar said as he pulled with both hands, his biceps bulging. The fish split apart, red blood droplets splashing his face as the head of the fish snapped off in one hand.

Ferrar returned to the pool and washed the blood off the fish. Laying it on a large, flat rock he looked around for a smaller one with an edge. They all searched until Bennett came up with one that would suffice. Ferrar, wielding it like a crude knife, ripped the fish apart, pulled out the backbone and hacked the fish into pieces, skin still attached.

"I ain't gonna eat no raw fish." Ramirez said.

"Great, Asshole, that leaves more for the rest of us." Ferrar told him.

Each man ate a small portion including Ramirez whose hunger overcame his squeamishness. They were eating the fish right off the skin when the sky lit up with a strange radiance.

"Shit, what the hell was that?" Arby was holding his arm over his eyes as he looked up out of the canyon. The light faded slowly.

"Must have been the sun hitting a cloud or something. That was fucking weird." Bennett said.

"If we don't get out of this hole we'll never catch the bastards," said Arby. "Let's get moving. Come on, drink up." They all drank as much as they could and started following the trail along the river looking for a way out of the canyon.

"Shut up! Listen. Do you guys hear something?" asked Arby. They all shushed and listened expectantly. "I thought I heard an engine, but it's gone now." They listened, shrugged, and kept going, thinking of the food in the backpacks of the hikers.

As they trudged along the bottom of the canyon they missed the vegetation covered trail, and continued upstream along the river. Darkness came quickly in the depths of the canyon and when it became too dark to continue they settled down beside the river to spend another long, cold night.

August 21, 2:45 p.m.
Kirtland Air Force Base, Albuquerque, NM

Kristen had used an ovulation test kit and, smiling with anticipation, informed her husband Lieutenant Jason Douglas, it was time. She went back into the bathroom to freshen up.

Jason had taken the entire week off for them to enjoy a second honeymoon and had unplugged the home phones and turned off the cells that morning to ensure they wouldn't be disturbed.

After their marriage, they'd waited for two years to have a baby, while she finished her enlistment and he finished his Bachelor's degree. Discontinuing the pill six months ago, they'd been using condoms until the time was right.

She and Jason had met at Howard Air Force Base in Panama, where she worked as a secretary at the Tactical Air Command headquarters, and he worked as Security Police. At the time, Kristin still had a year left of her enlistment and intended to return to civilian life. Jason was a lifer.

After her discharge, Jason had been transferred to Kirtland Air Force Base in Albuquerque, New Mexico where they were married. He finished his degree at the University of New Mexico with a major in physics and applied for, and recently completed Officer Training School. Kristen had stayed in Albuquerque working in a lawyer's office as a legal secretary until he was commissioned and returned to Kirtland.

Now he worked at KUMSC, the Air force's nuclear weapons storage facility. He enjoyed the assignment. The facility was fairly modern and technologically advanced since the Air Force had transferred the weapons from Monzano Mountain within the last decade. Jason's passion was nuclear physics and he hoped to continue his education and earn an advanced degree that would enable him to become one of the military's greatest authorities on nuclear war. He was especially interested in the effects of nuclear radiation on military and civilian populations during a nuclear conflagration and had written several papers on the subject.

Jason had gone to Home Depot in the morning to buy supplies to repair the sprinkler system and, returning home after noon, they'd spent a leisurely couple of hours having lunch and just enjoying a rare day together. The last two years had been hectic, with him going to school and her working, earning enough money to afford a family. With the phone unplugged they had no idea Jason's commander had ordered him contacted to report for duty, or that the base had gone to ThreatCon Delta.

Standing at the bathroom sink Kristen heard a noise, and turned just as Jason swept her into his arms and carried her to the bed. Their lips met, tongues probing passionately. She pushed him away laughing.

"Jason, pull the drapes. Do you want the whole neighborhood to see us conceive our first child?"

"What the hell, this is a pretty boring street. We could liven it up a bit." He got up and pulled the heavy drapes shutting out most of the midday sunshine. She stood with him, hugging him from behind, swaying against him seductively as she reached around him, unbuttoning his pants as he took off his shirt. He turned around and continued to kiss her, with increasing passion, as he undressed her. Jason's twenty seven year old body was hard and well-muscled and he had obviously been thinking about this moment. She became excited looking at him, touching him, caressing him. He gently shoved her back on the bed.

"Jason, wait honey, slow down, okay? Let's make it last. I want it to be the best ever." That plan lasted only minutes as they explored each other's body with fingers and tongues.

Despite her best intentions she became inflamed under his caresses, pressing against him, breathing harder, making it obvious to him she had no desire to take it slow.

They'd waited so long and all she could think of, was they were going to have a baby. Almost blind with need she pulled him onto her, as their bodies joined. She moaned and started to move with him, slowly at first, then with increasing tempo. "Slow down, Honey, give me a minute." She whispered.

He knew what she needed, pushed hard and held it, letting her take the lead, as she moved against him, looking for that right spot.

She found it.

As she felt that unmistakable internal flutter signaling orgasm was imminent she slid her hand down his back and pressed. They'd been married long enough for him to know her signals and he began to move again, in that perfect primal rhythm that makes two people one. The flutter grew into a pulse as each stroke took it higher, then became a throb, then went higher, and she gasped as the orgasm engulfed her entire body, and she and Jason cried out together in ecstasy.

At the peak of the greatest orgasm she had ever experienced, the room lit up with a brilliance that penetrated the very walls, and she and Jason were vaporized by the blast of a thermonuclear explosion at ground zero.

August 21, 1:50 p.m.
Las Vegas, NV

Las Vegas, Nevada was sweltering, with the temperature over one hundred degrees and the air unusually humid. Gray cumulonimbus, or thunderclouds rose to a height of greater than two miles looking like giant anvils, billowing northeast of the city and threatening to release torrents of hot summertime rain. The storm clouds lent an eerie glow to the oppressive atmosphere, darkening the skies and creating a backdrop for the ever-blazing lights of this unique desert city.

Billy Gale and his new girlfriend Tawny cruised along Interstate Fifteen at a sedate eighty miles per hour, being passed, on both sides, by vehicles traveling much faster, vehicles filled with dreamers barreling their way to sin city to gamble away their hard-earned cash; at Blackjack tables, Roulette wheels or the Mega-Bucks slot machines. The license plates on Billy's Mustang convertible were Nevada plates. He was going home after spending three interminable days "meeting the family."

The traffic traveling south on Interstate Fifteen, away from Vegas, was unusually heavy for a weekday and he could see a wreck that appeared to have just happened and was obstructing the heavy flow. Cars were beginning to actually enter the median to get around the obstruction. He smiled. It was usually the northbound traffic that was in such a hurry.

Billy was a twenty nine year old croupier at the Golden Nugget. He'd only known Tawny for three weeks and already she was beginning to smother him. He was baffled that he'd agreed to this L.A. trip, but somehow her showgirl body and abundant blonde hair had convinced him it was the right thing to do.

He passed the Sloan turn-off, and a couple minutes later a small, view-obstructing hill on the right, and, as he came around the hill, there it was! He caught sight of the city he loved, to him, the world's most beautiful and exciting city. He caught his breath at the beauty of it, the colored lights against the angry dark clouds giving it the appearance of a scintillating jewel in the afternoon sky. The Mandalay Bay dwarfed the hotels behind it. The green light from the Luxor shone straight up toward the heavens through an increasingly misty atmosphere, moisture diffused the lavender glow from the Rio, and there was a brighter light farther to the left of that. Confused, he did a classic double take.

"What the hell is that?" He looked over at Tawny and she was looking at it also. Similar to the thundercloud ahead but in a state of motion, churning and growing, it climbed to a height as great as the anvil before them.

"I don't know, baby." Her voice was like that of a little girl. Billy always expected her to go, "boop... boop... a do."

"You don't think they're doing more of that testing do you? It looks like it's up at the Nevada Test Site."

Billy slowed, pulling over through the slow lane, and coasted to the freeway shoulder. A few other vehicles finally began to slow down when their drivers noticed the new and unusual cloud, but several of them dangerously careened into the median and, making U-turns, headed back out of town, even though they had seen the colossal traffic jam.

"What the hell's going on? Shit, if that's another storm we're going to get drenched." He pushed the button to raise the canvas roof and latched it shut. He pulled back into traffic and accelerated to match velocity with the flow, only a few miles from the beginning of the Strip and the behemoth hotels and casinos that line both sides for miles.

"I don't think it's a storm, Billy. It looks like an A bomb explosion. My boss says she used to live in Vegas when they tested bombs and she has a photograph with Las Vegas in the foreground and a mushroom cloud behind it. That's what it looks like to me."

"They're not supposed to be testing anymore. Besides, it looks a lot closer than the test site," he told her.

"Unless it's not a test."

He quickly looked at her and then back at the cloud. The top had begun to spread eastward taking on the same anvil shape as the thundercloud. He looked back at Vegas. "Oh shit."

Billy watched with growing comprehension and dread as a wall of dust burst through the gap in the low western mountain range where the freeway led to Reno. He couldn't drag his eyes away from the spectacle as the dust front initially swept across the desert, and then over the tracts of suburban homes that had sprouted up on the periphery of the city. The strange shimmering wall reached the giant edifices along the Strip and he saw the Mandalay Bay topple and the glass walls of the Luxor shatter and blow out toward the east, as Cleopatra's needle toppled over into the street. The towers and minarets of Excaliber tilted and collapsed like slow motion bowling pins and the MGM Grand and Tropicana Hotels literally exploded before his eyes.

He grasped the steering wheel and barreled straight ahead down the freeway. Other cars ran off the road or collided with one another. He was unable to speak as he watched his beautiful city disintegrate before his eyes. The strange wall appeared before him, snatched up the car, and heaved it hundreds of yards across the landscape to the far side of Las Vegas Boulevard, bouncing it end for end across the desert like a child's plaything.

August 21, 2:56 p.m.
Sangre de Cristo Mountains, NM

The chopper, traveling in a northeasterly direction, skimmed low over the trees, the landscape rushing by beneath them. More mountains loomed ahead. Ten minutes ago, Will had received an ominous radio message - missiles were on target for the United States. Until that very moment Mark had held out hope the U.S would be spared, the war confined to countries overseas. Until then, he had planned to deliver Will's family to the shelter and go back for Jill, or wait for Steve. Until ten minutes ago.

Up ahead the trees thinned out as they approached a large grass covered clearing filled with cars haphazardly parked. He swung the bird around, coming down to the meadow through towering trees on all sides, looking for an empty place to set down. It wasn't difficult to find since the meadow had been cleared with the intention of holding many more automobiles than were now located there.

People scurried away from the nearer cars as rocks were flung from the chopper. As the rotors slowed to a halt, the four men and two women climbed down and Will headed off in the direction of the towering cliff that bordered the meadow on the west. Some people were still in their cars and more were in small groups standing around, children staying close to their parents as though sensing their parent's fear. Many of the adults looked dazed, many had been or were crying, and all of them looked very, very tired and frightened. As the group from the chopper headed across the meadow they were met on all sides with questions.

"Please follow me and your questions will be answered," Hargraves told them raising his arms to quiet them. By the time they reached the rocks the majority of the people had gathered around them. Will climbed onto a large rock and faced a crowd he estimated to be approximately two or three hundred people. He didn't have to ask for their attention, no one made a sound except for a baby crying in the background.

"Ladies and Gentleman, my name is Will Hargraves. A few minutes ago I received a message that the U.S. is under attack. Missiles are on the way from China and possibly Russia. We have no idea yet what the extent of the damage will be, but I can tell you that it's liable to be extreme. You are here at my request. I'm the one who sent you the messages and devices to warn you of the impending attack. Inside this mountain at my back is a shelter with sufficient equipment and supplies to keep us going until it's safe to leave. Nobody has to go down but if you do you must agree to follow my instructions and to help us all to come through this terrible ordeal. Now the first thing we must do is to get under cover as quickly as we can. The elevator holds approximately fifty people at a time. It's a large freight elevator."

With this he turned and, climbing down from the rock, went to a smaller rock beside the cliff. He lifted a cover in the rock to reveal a phone. Pressing a button on the side he spoke into it, "Alright Glen, let us in."

There was a sound of rock scraping on rock and a portion of what had appeared to be the side of the cliff slid back and opened before them.

"Open sesame," Mark whispered. He could see a large cave inside with an elevator door at the rear.

"Please enter the elevator and when you get into the shelter, follow the instructions of the people inside. Don't push, please, there's still time."

As though the words were a signal, the sky lit up like a billion flashbulbs all going off at once. Everyone quickly glanced to the south and then just as quickly turned away as the light stabbed their eyes like white-hot knives. Arms were thrown up as everyone tried to shield their eyes. Someone screamed and the crowd surged forward toward the elevator door. Many people began to push to the front. Will pulled his forty-five and fired once into the air.

"I will shoot the first person that pushes or shoves another to get to the elevator! Do you hear me?" and he lowered the weapon and pointed it straight at the crowd. "The blast can't reach us here and it will be hours or longer before any radiation does.

The prevailing wind is out of the north. Now keep calm." He lowered the gun and people began to move forward in a more orderly fashion.

When most of the refugees had gone below, Mark heard the sound of a car. It raced up the road, turned into the lot and parked at the end of a line of vehicles. A woman quickly jumped out and helped two small children unfasten their seat belts. One of the other men went over and assisted her with their suitcases. The woman kept looking to the south where the mushrooms were now unrecognizable as high-altitude winds blew the effects of the blasts southward. Mark knew other refugees would soon be arriving, having seen from the chopper, a line of cars winding up the mountainous road.

August 21, 9:55 p.m.
Sangre de Cristo Mountains, NM

Aaron drifted in and out of consciousness. He shifted position and pain shot up his arm into his shoulder. His arm was splinted and wrapped with duct tape. What was with that? He managed to sit up and tried to recall additional details of his ordeal.

Using back roads and going in the general direction of Taos he'd managed to get around Santa Fe and by 2:45 p.m. was back on the main road. He wondered if there would be bombs and when. How far away did he have to be to survive? He had better than a half tank of gas but was now in unfamiliar territory having never been north of Santa Fe. He flew through the town of Espanola at 75 miles per hour, curves permitting, but the road was becoming increasingly mountainous and he reduced velocity to prevent crashing. His destination was another thirty-five miles beyond Taos in the highest mountains in New Mexico.

Traffic increased slightly as he approached Taos. He was unsure how to get around the town the way he had skirted Santa Fe. He decided to drive directly through and take his chances. He entered the outskirts and pulled over at a small convenience store. Looking quickly around he exited the vehicle and ran through the front door. Finding no one there, he went to the cold case and picked out two sandwiches and a six-pack of Coke. Finding it difficult to completely slough off the trappings of civilization, he called out, "Anybody here?"

No answer.

Where had everybody gone? He expected more traffic but there'd been very few cars since he'd circumvented Santa Fe. Of course, the traffic jams out of the city would prevent many cars from getting this far and most of the inhabitants of these northern cities seemed to be fleeing to the east. What were they running from?

Then he remembered Los Alamos. It was probably going to be a target and he was twenty miles away from it! He scooped up the items and glancing fearfully around, he raced out the front door.

As he pushed into the light he suddenly felt dizzy, the daylight becoming much brighter. He looked to the south and threw up his arm to shield his eyes from the blinding glare. Alamogordo, White Sands, Kirtland Air Force Base, all were probable targets of those miniature suns, but apparently not Los Alamos, at least not yet. He ran to the car, a sense of doom overtaking him, how long before Los Alamos was hit? When it was he knew he wouldn't have any time to worry about it since he'd probably be vaporized immediately. He wondered how long it would be before the radiation got this far north. The sound of the explosion reached him just as he jumped in the car; a deep, bone-jarring rumble, then two more, blending together like a devil's requiem. He revved up the engine, trying to drown out the noise, but he could still hear the sound in his imagination, blending with the screams of humankind.

He drove through town, recklessly now, seeing people on the street looking south. A few tried to flag him down and he was forced to swerve when someone jumped in front of his vehicle trying to force him to stop. He wished now that he'd tried to find an alternate route. Unfortunately, in these mountains there weren't too many options.

All of a sudden a group of men ran out of a garage directly into his path. Carrying tools in their hands, they chucked them at the Cavalier as Aaron swerved and accelerated in an attempt to avoid them. A wrench struck the hood and bounced into the windshield cracking it into a spider web of opacity. Instinctively, he stomped the brake as the windshield shattered completely, and a hydraulic jack came crashing through, showering him with dull shards of safety glass. The jack struck him solidly on the right shoulder, causing him to lose control of the car, which careened right and smashed into the brick garage front. His head smacked the steering wheel with a sickening crunch, temporarily dazing him, but he managed to unfasten his seat belt and groped for his bag, which he'd moved to the front seat, and pulled out his pocketknife. He fumbled with the large blade trying to get it open with numb fingers. Just as he managed to get it open someone threw the door open and rough hands grabbed his shirt, jerking him from the car.

"We needed that fucking car, asshole! Why'd you crash it?"

The man, a hulking six feet plus, slammed Aaron against the side of the car, holding him with his left hand as he struck him a vicious blow to the stomach. Aaron's breath whooshed out and he would have collapsed but the man held him up, drawing his fist back for another blow. Dazed, and trying to protect himself, Aaron brought up his hand with the knife. As the man lunged forward the knife sunk into a yielding body, something warm and slippery suddenly covering Aaron's hand. The knife, catching the man just below the bottom rib, penetrated upward through the diaphragm and he stumbled back, stupidly staring down at the blood soaking his blue flannel shirt. He gave Aaron a surprised look and dropped to his knees. Then he looked down at his hand covered with blood and slowly toppled over face first into the street. Aaron moved away from the vehicle into the street and whirled toward the other men.

"Son-of-a-bitch knifed Ron!" A tall, bearded man rushed at Aaron but he stopped when Aaron waved the knife in his direction.

Another of the men jumped in the car, which had stalled, and hit the starter.

"It still runs, come on you guys!" The Cavalier, with the front end crumpled, backed out of the hole, bricks cascading to the sidewalk. The others hesitated for only an instant, and then jumped into the car, which accelerated away toward the north.

Aaron stood swaying for a moment. He shook his head to clear it, staring down at the man's body. His first instinct was to see if he could help him, but although this morning he woke up as a skilled surgeon, this afternoon he was a scared survivor, he hoped, of a nuclear war. Nothing would ever be the same again.

He noticed other men down the street taking too much interest in him, but he had lost his main attraction, the car. He'd also lost his backpack and the sandwiches. Still clutching the knife, he stumbled forward into the garage. Looking around in the cluttered interior he spotted a grease covered sink behind a stack of tires. Washing the blood off his knife and hands he folded the knife and put it in his jeans. Some of the blood was his own; from numerous cuts on his face and arms that he'd received from the exploding glass. Lifting his hand to his forehead, with his shoulder screaming in protest, he felt a huge goose bump already forming there.

A swishing noise alerted him to danger and he spun to see a man swinging a jack handle at his head. Throwing up his left arm, he caught the blow directly on his wrist. Paralyzing pain shot up his arm and he felt the bone fracture under the considerable force. With all the strength left in him Aaron brought his foot up and kicked the man squarely between the legs. The man screamed, falling to the concrete in pain. Aaron started to kick him again, but the man was crying, writhing on the ground and holding his groin. "You killed my brother, you bastard," the man sobbed through clenched teeth.

Aaron glanced around the garage. It was full of tires and there were compressor-driven tools but the bays were empty and he saw nothing he could make use of. Holding his wrist and feeling sick Aaron went out into the street. There was a vacant lot across the street with open space beyond. He quickly crossed the road, passed through the lot and emerged onto a completely deserted dirt road. It was obvious that all the cars in town were gone. He had no transportation and radiation was undoubtedly spreading rapidly, although the wind was blowing toward the south. Hopefully that would delay exposure. He was very worried there would be additional explosions. He slumped onto a small brown patch of lawn in front of a tiny featureless house. The pain from his injuries nauseated him and he vomited on the lawn. He was trembling violently and having trouble staying upright. He just wanted to lie down and close his eyes.

He sat back on his knees and stared at the house. If only he'd heard the signaling device earlier or left right away when he did hear it, he may have beaten the news of the impending attack. But it was futile to speculate about that now.

His arm was partially numb. Feeling totally helpless and unable to think clearly he struggled to his feet, holding his injured arm against his side, and walked up to the front door. It was unlocked and he simply walked in. He searched the house, pulling open cupboards, trying to locate a splint for his arm. There were several large wooden spoons in a kitchen drawer, and in a cupboard over a washer and dryer in the laundry room, he found some small tools and a roll of duct tape. He held the tape between his legs, pulling up the edge with his good hand and unrolling a length measuring about a foot. He laid the tape on the washer and placed a spoon across it longwise. He gingerly laid his arm lengthwise along the spoon, laying a second spoon on top of his arm, which he noticed was already swelling and bruised. Fortunately, he couldn't see any protruding bones. Using his good hand and his teeth he managed to turn the roll of tape around his arm and the spoons several times. It felt loose but at the rate his arm was swelling it would tighten all too soon. If he didn't get to the shelter it wouldn't matter anyway as he doubted he could survive for long unprotected. Finding a medicine cabinet containing a bottle of Excedrin, he gulped down the only three tablets contained in the bottle. He looked through the broken crystal on his watch to check the time. It was 3:46.

His stomach had settled and he helped himself to food and milk from the refrigerator. Feeling slightly better he left the house through a back door and crossed an overgrown lawn. A small wooden garage with the door standing wide open, and a smaller shed, stood behind the house. The garage was empty, so he limped to the shed and looked through a small side window, his heart leaping when he spotted an all-terrain-vehicle parked inside. The door was held shut by a rope threaded through the hasp and tied in a knot. He tried to untie the knot but found it impossible with only one hand. He took the knife from his pocket, managed to get it open with his teeth and sawed at the rope until he cut through.

The ATV, a Yamaha 348 cc Warrior, appeared to be well maintained and started immediately when he hit the electric starter. A red gas can sat on a tool bench and he was relieved to find it almost full. Topping off the two and a half gallon tank with considerable difficulty he drove out of the shed and again headed north. Only thirty-five miles to go.

His arm hurt like hell and his kidneys and teeth were feeling the effects of the ATV's jouncing. Steering only with his right hand, his shoulder protesting every minute, he rode for almost two hours and was so completely exhausted he was in danger of falling off. At Taos he had headed east paralleling Highway 64. The dirt road he was following sometimes wound north or south but overall continued in a northeastern direction.

He was worried about running out of gas.

The sound of a blaring horn beyond trees to his right distracted Aaron and, losing his concentration, he failed to notice a large hole directly in front of the ATV. He saw it at the last minute, jerking hard to the right, but the ATVs front wheel caught the edge, dipped severely and it flipped into the air. Aaron, trying desperately to protect his injured arm, smacked his head against a jagged rock and the last thing he remembered was a feeling of wetness as he skidded into a roadside puddle.

August 21, 3:15 p.m.
Sangre de Cristo Mountains, NM

Mark accompanied the last group to descend in the elevator. The doors slid open and they stepped into a room that resembled an airlock, with a smaller door on the left and a large door directly before them. They waited while three men checked them with radiation detectors and, when no evidence of radiation was found, they passed through another airlock and finally stepped into a carpeted hallway. Turning left, they proceeded down the hall, turned right into an intersecting corridor and then left again into the back of a large auditorium where the other survivors had been led by Glen Mitchell. Mark gratefully sank into a seat toward the rear while Will strode to the front of the room and ascended some stairs to an angled podium on the side of a raised stage. Curtains were drawn back on either side of the stage.

"May I have your attention again, please," Will spoke into a microphone. "I know you're all bone tired so the primary objective this afternoon and evening is to get some food and rest. The gentleman who directed you here is Glen Mitchell, the caretaker of this facility. As soon as this meeting adjourns he'll show you the first floor mess hall. The complex is probably considerably larger than you expected and I assure you it's large enough to accommodate us all, in comfort, for a considerable length of time. We'll monitor the parking area above for stragglers. Those of you here now left well ahead of the actual attack and I thank you for having faith in my message. It must have been very difficult to leave your homes and come here not knowing for certain an attack was going to occur. There will be others who started the journey after the public evacuation orders were given and others who will begin only after the initial explosions. I fear that those who delayed that long may not make it. We can handle approximately five hundred people and it looks to me as though there are about two or three hundred here now.

Quarters will be assigned to you. I'll show you a schematic of the complex in just a minute. We have a complete

218

communications center and will attempt to get news about the outside as soon as possible."

He pressed a button on the podium and a large screen descended from the ceiling in the center of the stage. He flipped another switch and the lights dimmed in the room, another, and the screen showed a diagram. "The complex has three main levels, a control tower above and a couple of areas deeper in the mountain that house the reservoir and power plant. The computers in your quarters have this same diagram."

He gave a brief description of the shelter to the exhausted and shell-shocked crowd.

"There are only a few locked doors although your apartments have deadbolts inside to lock your doors for privacy. Anyone here who came with someone else and doesn't have an assigned room, see Glen. We will meet in this room again at 0900 in the morning for a more complete report. If you'll remain here, Glen will announce room assignments and show you to the mess hall. Is there a Mister Crowder or Lowell here?"

A slightly built young man, in his early twenties, with his brown hair trimmed in military style stood up about halfway back in the audience. "I'm Micah Lowell."

"Mr. Lowell, if you would be so kind, I would like you to come with me to the radio room after this meeting. I'll need you to try communicating with the outside."

"Sure thing." Lowell said. Mark was ready to follow him, interested in seeing what this control room consisted of.

Several hands shot up and questions were shouted from the crowd but Will held his hands up and said, "Please, I have much to do. All your questions will be answered at tomorrow's meeting. Be back at 0900."

Will stood surveying the little band of survivors. Everyone seemed to have calmed down although many faces were tear streaked and many dazed by the events of the day. He left them in Glen's care and he Micah and Mark headed out the door.

They returned to the corridor that lead to the freight elevator but, instead, turned right at the intersection. Elevator doors were located forty feet down the hall but Will passed by them, and stopping before a second door he pulled out a key and unlocked it.

"What's behind here that's so valuable?" Micah asked.

"The room at the top of these stairs is one of the most important rooms in the facility, our nerve center, and we certainly don't want it to be damaged by curiosity seekers." Will replied.

They climbed a narrow flight of circular stairs that seemed to Mark like it would go on forever. Finally he asked Will, "Where the Hell does this staircase go? I'm humming 'Stairway to Heaven'."

"There's an elevator, but I wanted you to be familiar with our little escape route and this gives you an idea of how far up the room is from the rest of the complex." They continued to climb and eventually came to a landing and a door. Entering an alcove with three other doors, Will opened one and they went up a much shorter flight to another room. This door was unlocked and they entered a room crammed from one end to the other with radio, radar and monitoring devices with a computer console occupying the middle of the room.

"Whoooee, this is beautiful! Man I've never seen such equipment and I've been around the best the Air Force has to offer." Micah was rushing about the room checking out the various instruments. "I mean this is fantastic! Space Shuttle? This is mission control."

"Mr. Lowell, as far I can tell you're the only communications expert who's made it here so far. Darryl Washington, our computer expert hasn't returned from town. I'm afraid that means you'll have to put in some long hours, at least to begin with."

Mark examined the readouts. "How come there's only one monitor on?"

"There's only one camera on. The other cameras and sensors are protected until I'm certain there won't be any additional blasts. The mountain has been turned into one big Faraday cage to protect our equipment from EMPs and there are smaller Faraday cages with electronic components stored in them in case something sneaks through and we have to replace parts.

The camera is focused on the parking area, Micah. When people show up you can contact Glen using his pager. If he doesn't answer right away, call my beeper or use the paging system by depressing this button and speaking into the mike. It can be heard in all common areas of the shelter. Mark and I will also take shifts at the radio. There are other people who may be able to help us although I don't know exactly who's here yet. I'm afraid our cell phones are useless. The pagers are actually walkie-talkies and will work throughout the facility."

"Do you really expect many more people to make it now that the fireworks have started?" Micah asked him.

"I really don't know. I hope to God more people make it."

"Won't we have to worry about them being contaminated?" Mark asked. "Yes, it may come to a point where we may not be able to let them know of our presence if they get here too late. I hope Darryl gets here before then." He went to a bookshelf and pointed out several notebooks. "The manuals are here for all the equipment and we'll have to improvise with some of it. They're all online as well. The main thing tonight is to try and make contact with authorities on the outside, or anybody for that matter. I'm going below to check on things."

Micah went around the room turning on radios and other equipment. He pulled down a manual as Will and Mark exited and started down the stairs to the alcove. This time they took the elevator to the level below.

Numerous people were wandering the halls when the two men left the elevator. A few asked if they had heard anything yet but most seemed to be more interested in exploring the complex. Will and Mark went to the mess hall where a large group had gathered and were drinking coffee.

Mark spotted Chris across the room and started in her direction while Will stopped to speak to a group of several people.

Chris reached out and took his hand. "I'm so sorry about Jill, Mark. Maybe they'll still get through." He was touched that her first concern was for his family.

"I'm still in such a state of disbelief about this whole thing that I can't really comprehend that she's in trouble." He poured himself a cup of coffee. "I wonder if Will stocked anything any stronger. I don't know about the rest of these people but I sure could use a drink." He smiled sadly at her.

Will walked over to them. "Have either of you seen Clay?"

Chris answered. "He was talking to some pretty young thing a few minutes ago. Said he was going to show her around, although I'll wager he's never been here before. Am I correct?"

"You're correct. You know I would have told you if I'd told him. Clay likes to talk too much, especially if he thinks it would impress someone."

"Come on Dad, don't be so hard on Clay, after all it probably hasn't been easy for him being your son."

"Has it been hard for you being my daughter?"

"That's different. People don't expect as much from a daughter as they do a man's son. I can't believe you had this place built and nobody knew about it."

"On the contrary, a lot of people knew. The government was fully aware of the shelter, in fact the land was purchased from them, and they fully supported and encouraged me. They especially supported the idea of it being built strictly with private funds. They know we're here and I hope they're trying to contact us. The majority of the construction people involved thought they were working on a military project and accepted the secrecy for that reason. None of them knew the exact location. Some of the construction workers who lived close by were chosen to come here. I don't know yet if any made it. We'll have a complete list of the people tomorrow. We also have a permanent staff of seven people. And Mark knew."

She glanced at Mark and he hoped she didn't take offense. After all, he didn't know much about it.

"Your quarters are next to mine but we can change that if you like." Her father smiled and winked at her. She felt relieved; her father seemed to smile too little anymore.

"I'm going to look around, see you guys later." She reached up and kissed Will on the cheek.

"O.K. Babe. If you need me my number's in the directory on the computer." There were two computer terminals in the room and Mark had seen some in alcoves in the hallway.

As Chris walked away, Mark's gaze following her, he knew she was the reason this shelter was built in the first place. He and Will walked over to the larger group that had gathered by the door.

One of the men, wearing a black suit, was addressing the others, "This was an opportunity to pick the very best of mankind, but it looks to me as though some rather undesirable types were selected. Oh, hello Hargraves," he greeted Will as they joined the group. "I was just mentioning to these folks that there seem to be some . . ." and he lowered his voice as he glanced around at the rather scruffy-looking group of survivors, ". . .undesirable people in the group. They must have come on their own."

Will bristled as he replied, "And just who do you consider to be undesirable, Mr. uh, I didn't catch your name."

"Richenour, Vernon Richenour. This is my wife Jennifer." He indicated a mousy woman standing beside him who blushed when Will looked at her. Richenour looked fairly scruffy himself, his once natty suit rumpled and covered with something greasy. He normally combed the long thin wisps of his hair completely across his bald pate but they now hung down in strings. He had red, soft appearing lips that lent the appearance of a perpetual sneer residing under an overlarge nose.

"Mrs. Richenour." Will nodded his head in acknowledgment. "Mr. Richenour, I don't seem to recall your name on my list. Exactly how did you know of this place? Or perhaps you came on your own?"

"Our daughter's husband received one of your little boxes and they invited us. But, you know whom I mean. You could have weeded out bad seed so to speak."

"Well, Richenour, you aren't seeing these people in their best light. They've had a terrible shock. Or are you referring to other characteristics?"

"No, of course not." He was intimidated by the terseness of Will's reply and now was sorry he had started the conversation.

"Would you please excuse us? I believe we'll find our quarters now. Good day."

The others in the group watched them leave and there was an embarrassed silence. "Will, I think I'll check and see if anyone new has arrived." Mark excused himself and left. As he ascended to the control tower he realized this wasn't going to be any picnic.

"Hi Chief, how are things below? Got the flock settled down?" Micah greeted him enthusiastically.

"Yeah, most of them are getting something to eat. Why don't you go on down. I can spell you here for a while. Have you picked up anything?"

"No sir, and I've tried every band. There's a tremendous amount of static. The blasts may have temporarily disrupted the ionosphere, sort of a super sunspot effect. It could take days before it settles down. There's been no sign of anyone on the monitor either. Wait a second!"

Mark quickly followed his gaze to the monitor and saw a swirl of dust enter the picture. A car sped into the lot and lurched to a stop. As a man jumped out, looking around frantically, a woman got out of the other side. She opened the back door and took a baby from a car seat all the while glancing fearfully to the south. Micah paged Glen and when he responded on the intercom Mark told him about the couple.

"How's the radiation level?" came the reply from below.

Mark checked the radiation indicator. "So far it's in the green."

"Great." They heard Glen's voice through a speaker as he acknowledged the couple's presence and opened the door. The man ran back to the car and grabbed a bag and the three of them entered the complex, the massive rock face sliding back into place after they'd passed.

Only twenty-five minutes had passed when Micah returned from dinner. Mark stayed in the control tower for two more hours, his eyes glued to the monitor, hoping against all odds that he would see Jill and her family enter the parking lot. A taxi had arrived bearing a slim older woman and she and the cab driver had entered the shelter together. Mark smiled, knowing the cab driver was one of those 'people without an invitation' Vernon Richenour was so worried about. Several other cars had arrived and the passengers had been admitted to the shelter.

Will joined them and offered to take a turn monitoring the instruments, but Micah protested he was fine and would notify them if he received anything. Will, checking the radiation monitoring devices, called Mark over and pointed at the readout.

"Mark, take a look at this. There's a slight increase in background radiation. It's not strong enough to worry about yet but we'll have to watch closely and check anyone else who arrives for radiation contamination." He walked back over to where Micah kept fiddling with the radio. "How about it Micah?"

This time Micah's enthusiasm seemed dampened, "Not a damn thing Sir, not a damn thing."

August 21, 6:10 p.m.
Sangre de Cristo Mountains

Pete and Sandi came crashing through the last foliage and stood momentarily disoriented by a jumble of cars parked in the clearing before them. Three other cars hemmed in Pete's truck but he thought he could get it out if he drove over some thick brush.

"What the Hell?" He stared at the cars and then turned to Sandi as if for an explanation. They advanced to the nearest car. It was unlocked but nobody was in sight. There was a bicycle laying on its side, the panniers lying next to it on the ground.

"Where is everybody?" She stared through weary eyes. Her face was streaked with dirt, and tears had made muddy tracks down her cheeks. Pete had traveled so fast in returning to the truck she'd had trouble keeping up with him. It took them over two hours to get back around the mountain, much less time than it had taken to hike out to their campsite in the first place, but the faster pace, even though she had dropped her pack, took its toll and her leg muscles ached from the exertion. The sun had gone behind the western cliff and the ghostly shapes of the cars gave an impression of loneliness that sent a shiver down Sandi's spine. There was a deadly silence pervading the clearing.

They moved among the cars disbelieving, both of them thinking this is just what the end of the world should look like. Sandi sank wearily onto a rock alongside the cars, too tired to continue, and Pete came over to put his arm around her. "Sandi, I don't know where all these came from but it doesn't look good. They must have been running from whatever happened. Maybe there's a hell of a lot more cabins up here than I thought. We could look for them if you feel like it."

"Oh Pete, I'm too tired, couldn't we just stay overnight in one of the cars? It's getting dark and it seems a lot colder."

"Alright, let's find a van. He looked down and gave her a wink. She looked exhausted and he realized he too was very tired. They had been so worried they had panicked, but they needed to think more clearly now and plan a sensible course of action. He still wanted to get to Las Vegas as soon as possible and figured they could take a nap and then he would get his truck out. Suddenly he heard a crackling sound that seemed to come from the rock itself as the speaker came to life.

"Please don't be frightened. There's a group of people in a bomb shelter underground here. If you'll follow my instructions we can let you in. There's been a nuclear war and it's dangerous for you to be exposed. The elevator will open and you can enter but you have to leave your equipment outside."

The side of the mountain grated and then slid aside revealing a large cave with an elevator at the rear. The weary twosome looked at each other, hesitated for a moment and then Pete helped Sandi to her feet as they walked, without Pete's pack, into the cave. He was worried about what lay ahead but knew there was no other reasonable choice. The man was obviously correct about the war. Pete had witnessed the evidence of that, although he didn't want to believe it, and he was worried about Sandi, concerned she couldn't go much farther.

They stepped into the huge elevator, which looked like it could carry a great number of people. Robes were hanging on pegs on the side of the elevator. "Please place your clothing in the hamper and put on the robes," the speaker instructed them. The outside door began to close and, for a brief moment, Pete considered fleeing before it was too late, but the door slid shut and he'd lost the opportunity. They stripped down, feeling uncomfortable and embarrassed, Pete turning his back to give Sandy some privacy. They put on the robes, plain knee length robes with no buttons, just ties. They felt the elevator begin to descend and Sandi shuddered in Pete's arms. It seemed to go down for miles, but in a few moments the door on the opposite wall opened and someone in a space suit motioned them into the next room.

"Hi, don't worry, I just need to check you for radiation." The man carried an instrument he extended to them, moving it from head to foot. "My name's Glen, welcome to our home. You go through this side door, and there's a shower that you exit on the other side where you'll find clothes. Leave the robes in the bin on this side of the shower and go through the next door. You seem to be clean. Did you come from down below?"

"No, we were camping in the mountains when we saw the flashes." Pete helped Sandi to the door the man indicated.

"That's good. It's why you haven't picked up any radiation."

"How many others are here?" Sandi asked him.

"You guys look beat. Go on through first. All your questions will be answered after you're decontaminated. I'm going a different way so I'll see you later."

They turned to the door Glen had indicated and pushed the button adjacent to it. It slid aside and they entered a small room with a hamper to one side and plastic curtains separating the room from the showers. A sign on the wall read,

> "LEAVE ALL CLOTHING IN THE BIN. SHOWER AND WASH YOUR HAIR. STEP THROUGH THE SHOWER TO THE OTHER SIDE WHERE YOU WILL FIND CLOTHING."

They slipped off their robes and dropped them into the bin, beginning to feel self-conscious with all this disrobing. They stepped into the same shower stall even though there were two. There were no controls for the shower, only a single button, so Pete pressed it and a stream of water at just the right temperature, and with considerable pressure, washed over them. In a few seconds it became warmer, until it was very hot, but bearable. They clung together for comfort in the strangeness of the environment. The water stopped suddenly and then started again, this time smelling of a strange odor and Pete suspected it was a disinfectant or decontaminant or both. It too stopped, and a second harder water rinse sprayed like needles against their skin. They waited a minute, but it appeared the shower sequence was over. Opening a solid door on the backside of the shower they stepped out onto a tile floor where they found shelves with folded clothing.

They selected their sizes and dressed in shorts, tee shirts and a soft pair of slip on shoes. The clothing fit them within reason. Sandi's was green and Pete's blue. "Welcome to the future my dear." Pete said.

She smiled and pushed a button that caused the door to slide aside and they stepped into still another large airlock. Two men were waiting for them. One looked like the face in the spacesuit.

"Hi, It's me again, Glen, and this is Doctor Jim. He just wants to give you a once over to see if you're alright and then, if you're hungry, we can get you something to eat."

"Hi, I'm Pete Thompson and this is Sandi Baker." He shook their hands.

"Gee, I'm sorry," Glen looked a little embarrassed, "I thought you were married or I would have sent you through decontamination separately."

"It's okay." Pete tried to alleviate the man's embarrassment as Sandi blushed. The strain of all that had happened struck her at that moment and she sagged against Pete. The movement was not lost on the doctor.

"Let's get to the infirmary so I can examine you two." The door opened to reveal a hallway and the doctor led them down a corridor and into a typical medical exam room. Let me check out the lady first son, she looks a little tired. You can wait over there." He pointed to a chair against the far wall. "Come here and have a seat young lady." He walked over and took her arm. She looked up at him gratefully. He was a large gentle looking man with soft brown eyes full of genuine concern. She started to tremble, close to tears, but maintained control as she sat on the edge of the exam table. The doctor pulled a curtain for privacy.

"You kids have been camping huh?" You look like you hiked a hundred miles." He told her.

"When we saw the flashes from the bombs we panicked and came back really fast. I guess I'm just a little tired." She was grateful to have a chance to relax for a minute before having to worry about the future.

The Doctor checked her eyes and throat, looked in her ears and listened to her heart and lungs, and then helped her to lay back. He was palpating her abdomen when he looked in her eyes. He started to speak but she shook her head almost imperceptibly. He helped her sit up.

"Young lady you seem to be fine but you need to get some rest. I want to see you in my office as soon as you're rested. Promise?"

She was looking at her hands folded in her lap. "Yes, I'll come see you." She slid off the table and he held the curtain for her. Pete looked concerned and came to help her to the bench.

"She's fine son, come hop up on this table."

An hour had passed since their arrival in the lot outside and Pete realized he was famished. They hadn't eaten since earlier in the day before the unbelievable flashes of light started them on their flight back to his truck. Glen directed them to the mess hall and then excused himself, needing to return to the entrance in the event other survivors arrived.

They entered the cafeteria, which was decorated with pictures of mountains, meadows and seascapes on pale yellow walls. The dining area was carpeted while the serving area had linoleum. Approximately a dozen other people occupied the room, some dressed in similar attire to theirs. The majority appeared to have finished their meals and groups were sitting or standing around talking.

"Good evening." Pete said to a woman sitting at the next table. "I don't have any money. How did you pay for the food?"

"You don't. Just help yourself." She said. There was a cafeteria-style food dispensing area along the right wall, but it was unused. Refrigerator/freezers with glass doors were along the back wall opposite the entry door. Pete selected a dinner of Roast beef, potatoes and a vegetable, and popped it into a microwave oven while Sandi took a salad over to a table and sank down gratefully. Pouring them both glasses of milk from a dispenser, Pete brought the glasses to the yellow plastic table with matching plastic chairs that gave it the appearance of a fast food restaurant. They ate most of their meal before they spoke, each lost in his own thoughts.

"I guess we're safe for the time being. I'm sure they'll let us leave if we want to." Pete said.

"Oh, Pete, I don't think I want to leave. It must be deadly out there. Where do you think we could go? I really don't have any place to go." She started to cry again.

He reached over and took her hand. "I know, Sandi. You should stay here but I have to find out if my family is dead or alive. I couldn't stay here without knowing for sure."

"Well, I have no way of knowing what's happened to my family, but I do know there's no way for me to find out."

"Okay listen, I'll tell you what. We'll stay here for a while and see what happens. I'm sure they're trying to find out what's going on outside. I don't want to leave you here with strangers." They finished their meal in silence and put their trays in the window provided.

Glen told them to look up Marilyn Simmons for room assignments, so they started down the corridor to find out where she was located, and coming to an intersection and turning right, Pete walked directly into someone. "Whoa, excuse me, I . . ." He looked up at the surprised man he'd bumped into and stood dumbfounded. Then his father grabbed him and they were hugging each other and pounding each other on the back until Pete could hardly breathe.

"Pete, oh my God, you're safe!" His mother was crying and then Pete was hugging her and they were all talking at once.

"Dad, Mom how did you know about this . . .?"

"Jerry and his family are here too!" his mother told him through tears.

"How did you find this place, Pete? I never told you about the box."

"What box?"

Then Pete noticed the look on his mother's face as she stared behind him. Pete remembered Sandi and turned to see her trying to smile through a steady stream of tears.

August 21, 9:50 p.m.
Sangre de Cristo Mountains, NM

Aaron regained consciousness and knew if he didn't get up immediately his life would end without him ever knowing what had happened. With a Herculean effort he pushed himself to his knees, his freezing joints and muscles protesting with pain, then climbed unsteadily to his feet and stood there swaying, with waves of nausea washing over him.

"We've got it clear!" A man cried triumphantly and cheers went up from half a dozen others.

Aaron thought he was dreaming. His bandaged arm, hanging limply, had gone numb again. He looked around, vaguely conscious of the ATV crumpled against a tree. He forced himself forward, creeping through thick pinyon pines to reach the edge of a road. Just ahead he saw a mass of cars and trucks, a jackknifed semi-truck blocking all the lanes. The other vehicles had ploughed into it. Two people lying by the side of the road appeared to be injured, but Aaron knew that he didn't dare try to help them even if he were in any condition to do so. Several men and women were bellowing orders, working to clear the vehicles from the road. The highway traveled through a long shallow depression at this point, a high bank along both sides just above the tops of the vehicles. Two more cars and a one and a half ton flatbed truck were stuck behind the crashed cars. Ropes had been attached to the jackknifed truck trailer and to the bumpers of two three quarter ton pickup trucks. They'd managed to pull the trailer around to clear a narrow passage between the trailer and the bank.

Aaron sneaked to a point opposite the flatbed truck and waited impatiently as the group split up and climbed into various vehicles. As cars started up and began maneuvering through the passageway he eased himself to the edge of the embankment. The last and largest pickup truck barely cleared and as the flat bed entered the narrow cleft Aaron eased himself over the edge of the embankment and slid down, jumping to the bed of the truck. He landed hard, twisting his ankle, but immediately flung himself forward under the small window in the back of the cab. The truck scraped against the side of the embankment, jamming momentarily, and Aaron held his breath as the driver gunned the engine and slammed it in gear.

"Please," Aaron whispered. "I need a break."

The tires squealed, rocks spitting backward as the tires spun, and the truck scraped forward as pieces of the embankment crumbled and fell onto the truck bed pummeling Aaron. The screeching sound of tearing metal reached him as the flat bed's front fender hooked the rear of the semi but, gears grinding, the flat bed jerked free and bounced onto the road with Aaron lying on the truck bed, curled into a tight ball.

As the truck sped up the road he tried desperately to stay awake, not knowing where the truck was going, or how he would know when to get off, but he drifted in and out of sleep, or possibly consciousness. The map in the signaling transmitter had indicated a roadside sign, an advertisement for a non-existent cigarette that was the code for the turn off. He needed to go north at Eagle Nest and knew if they hit the small town of Cimarron that they'd have gone way too far. He tried to stay alert but finally dozed off, until he was awakened with a start by the sound of voices. The truck wasn't moving and the driver, a short man with his belly hanging over his belt, was up ahead talking to the driver of one of the other vehicles. "I think we should just barrel on through town so we don't run into no trouble. There's probably no one there anyway and my brother's place is stocked so we don't need to stop and get any food or supplies. His cabin's just before Cimarron so bear right at the next intersection. Aaron peeked around the edge of the cab and saw the two men talking beside a battered road sign that said "Eagle Nest - 1 mile."

Not far now. "What the . . ." The fat man was returning to his truck and was staring malevolently at Aaron. "Get the hell off my truck you asshole!" His companion, a large woman dressed in coveralls, who looked like she could hold her own in a fight, jumped down from the passenger compartment.

"Wait, please, I'm injured. Just let me ride to Eagle Nest. I'm not hurting anything." He pleaded, holding out his good arm to the man.

"I said get off my fucking truck or we'll kick your ass off." The man signaled to his friend in the front vehicle.

"Okay, okay, I'm going." Aaron scooted to the rear to avoid either the man or the woman and as soon as he jumped off the back of the truck, with sharp pain shooting through his ankle, he immediately limped into the bushes to avoid inviting violence. He heard the engine fire and saw the cars speeding off down the road. Although physically hurting, he was mentally anguished as well; at the violence he had encountered, at the loss of civility, and especially at what atrocities he had been forced to commit in the space of a few hours. He waited until he was sure they were gone and struggled toward town.

The mile to town took forever, his ankle getting much worse as he progressed. His arm was throbbing painfully. Eagle Nest, not much more than a truck stop in these mountains, was deserted. He passed a diner that said "Open 24 Hours" but obviously, it wasn't. He came to a bait and tackle shop and realized he had come too far. A sign on the other side of the street indicated that he needed to backtrack and go right, or north, toward Red River. He almost cried at the realization. It was past 10:30 p.m. when he finally passed through town and continued up the road. Around a quarter of a mile beyond Eagle Nest he saw headlights appear and instinctively started to hide, but realized he was sick to death of running and hiding. He just stood in the center of the road until the headlights of the approaching car illuminated him.

The car slowed and came to a halt. Aaron muttered under his breath, "I'm a dead man," as a figure approached him through the glare. It was an old man.

"What're you doing out here this time of night, son? You look half dead. Can we give you a lift?"

Aaron couldn't believe his ears. He stumbled forward, the old man catching his outstretched right arm. "Please help me," he pleaded in a rough voice that the old man had trouble hearing. "I'm hurt and I need to get up this road." The old man helped him back to the car where Aaron saw that an elderly woman accompanied him. They helped him into the car.

"Don't you know what's happened? The United States has been attacked." Aaron told them.

"Yep, we heard it on the radio, before they all went dead. We live in a cabin a couple miles up the highway. We don't have anywhere to go so we'll just stay put. I've been living in this town all my life. Hell, I was just a boy but I lived here when the name was "Therma" back before they named it Eagle Nest. We're going to town to see if Jake Perkins wants to come back with us. He runs the diner and lives alone. Couldn't sleep since we saw the bombs this afternoon. Where you going looking like that?"

"There's a bomb shelter north of here. I was trying to get there but ran into trouble. You could go with me. I know how to get there but we have to go before the radiation gets here. The wind is blowing toward the south but there might already be some in this area. Besides, I just came from the diner and it's closed down." He looked at them hopefully.

"If the road's open to your shelter we'll take you there but we've lived here a long time and I don't know of any shelter around these parts." The old woman was nodding her head in agreement. The old man turned the car around and headed back up the hill and Aaron gratefully sunk back on the seat.

A short ride later he spotted the ad. It had a big arrow pointing to the left and said you should head straight for the cowboy's brand of tobacco. "There", he said excitedly. "That's the ad!"

The old man swung the car onto a narrow, poorly maintained, dirt road through a metal gate. "You sure this is the place?" asked the old man, skeptically.

"I hope to God it is," replied Aaron.

After a short distance the road improved, and they continued on for a couple of miles until suddenly they came across a downed tree that totally blocked the road. There was a group of cars lined up behind it that made further progress impossible but no one was around. The old man got out and looked to see if he could get around the blockade but there was no way, the trees growing too close together on either side. "Well, that's it son. You can go back with us if you like."

Aaron crawled stiffly out of the car. "No, I have to go on. It can't be far and I've been trying so hard to get there."

The old woman spoke for the first time, "You can't go off in the dark like that. Come back with us 'till you feel better."

Aaron was touched. He knew she was afraid of him. "No, I have to go. Thank you so much for helping me. You're the only ones who have. He grasped the old man's shoulder briefly and started off into the night. Being too sick to crawl over it, he circumvented the downed tree by going through the trees on the left. He saw the car backing down the road and almost called to them, suddenly lonelier than he had ever been in his entire life.

This morning he was a competent, respected surgeon in a modern world. Tonight he was a hurt, dirty, lonely man in the wildest of wilderness areas, stumbling through a pitch dark forest, not even sure if there really was a shelter at the end of this interminable road.

He was barely moving now, almost falling with every step. His shoulder ached from the blow he'd taken and his broken arm sent stabbing pains up his left side. Just put one foot in front of the other, keep moving, he thought. He was running a fever and dragging his right foot with every step. Although the dirt road was fairly smooth, it had an uphill grade that was inexorably wearing him down, slowing his pace until he barely moved forward. Onward through the darkness, he moved in a trance, unable to see where he was headed, frightened by phantoms, branches blowing in the frigid wind on both sides. He worried he may already be dead, was in a hell he never expected to end up in. He had tried so hard to be a good man.

He jumped as a shape loomed up in front of him, instinctively throwing his good arm in front of his face for protection. The shape didn't move. Reaching out with his good hand he approached the looming shape. It was a car.

Excited, he starting yelling, his voice weak and raspy, "Hello, is anybody here? Please, someone answer me!" He stood swaying in the middle of the clearing, convinced he had been pushed over the edge and had gone insane.

The rocks were talking to him.

A sudden, brilliant light blinded his dark-adapted eyes and a spaceman came to apprehend him. He chuckled, and gave up his tenuous attachment to consciousness as he pitched forward, the spaceman catching him and cushioning his fall. He was vaguely aware of a second spaceman, and the two carrying him toward the light. The movement caused him to be violently sick. Afterward, someone bathed his forehead with a cool rag, hurting his goose bump, but he was beyond caring. He saw an outline of big, smiling man who called himself Doctor Jim, and he remembered no more.

PART TWO

"And From the Ashes…"

238

FIVE

August 22, 5:00 a.m.

Dimly lit corridors lent the shelter a surrealistic appearance as Mark wandered around in search of the main dining room. Following directions posted on the wall, he walked down a quiet, empty hallway, and rounded a corner just in time to catch a glimpse of Will entering a doorway up ahead. They shared breakfast together that first morning of their new lives, lives forever altered by cataclysmic events beyond their control.

Mark had spent a restless night; worrying about his sister, her husband, his niece and nephew, and friends he knew he would never see again. He hadn't even bothered to examine his quarters; just went in, threw himself on the bed and worried away the remainder of the night. He was overcome with guilt as he reasoned, quite logically, that if Jill and her family had somehow managed to leave Dallas and had arrived in Albuquerque - he'd ordered them to their deaths. There was no way for him to know for sure whether or not Dallas had been a target, but it was indisputable that Albuquerque was. Before leaving his quarters for breakfast he had used the intercom to contact Micah and heard the heartbreaking news that they had never arrived.

The two men finished a simple meal of prepackaged, microwavable eggs and potatoes while discussing the incredible events of the previous day. Then, curious about the number of people who'd arrived during the night, they headed for the infirmary, knowing each individual had passed that portal on the way in. They entered an examining room to find Doctor Jim sitting on a stool, scribbling entries into a medical chart. He looked exhausted, having spent most of the night examining and treating people as they'd arrived at the shelter. Mark noticed a four- footed cane leaning against the wall in the corner.

"Good morning, Doctor. Do you have a few minutes?" Will asked.

The doctor stood and turned weary eyes toward them. "Call me Jim, please. Sure, come on in."

"Don't get up… Jim. You really look tired. Did you get any sleep?" Will asked him as he sat on a chair, while Mark crossed to the examining table and drew himself up on the edge.

"Yeah, I slept a couple of hours. We had a steady stream of people arriving until around two this morning. Many were injured, and those arriving after midnight received varying amounts of radiation as well. Ninety three people arrived after the bomb blasts started, most of them in the late afternoon." He shook his head, and then laughed, "A college professor with a van full of kids drove all the way from El Paso. He must have driven like a bat out of hell. Anyway, they passed through Albuquerque only an hour before the first explosions and one of his students says the bomb picked them up by the ass and wheel-barrowed them all the way up the mountain."

Mark smiled, visualizing the situation the boys and their professor had found themselves in and he was thankful they had managed to squeak through. "Do you have any help, Jim?" he asked the doctor. "Have any other medical personnel arrived?"

"I brought my nurse Carmen with me and there's a pharmacist, actually a biochemist, who worked for Pfizer Pharmaceutical Company. Another young man arrived during the night but he's in pretty bad shape. He only briefly regained consciousness, but says he's a doctor from Albuquerque. Guess he had trouble getting through. He started late and was slowed down, and even attacked, by mobs of people trying to evacuate the city. Somebody took his car from him and it appears he was in some sort of an accident. God, it must be hell out there." Jim, sitting on his stool, leaned back against the wall and closed his eyes, rubbing them with balled up fists. His clothes were rumpled and looked as though he'd slept in them, which, Mark realized, he probably had.

"Do you think he'll recover?" Mark asked.

"I think he'll be fine. I need to operate on his arm, do an open reduction, as soon as the swelling subsides. He'll be out of commission for a while though. You know, it's really difficult to comprehend what's happened out there. You sit around for years knowing nuclear warfare is a possibility, but you never really believe it'll happen. Tell me Hargraves, how did you happen to pick me? Or any of us for that matter."

"Well, it was a difficult selection process, believe me. I needed certain critical occupations; medicine was obviously one, and communications experts, scientists, teachers, craftsmen and the like. Proximity to the site was another major factor. Most of those receiving boxes lived in New Mexico, Arizona and Colorado, with a few from California. But that was a long shot. I called many of my friends and co-workers in California, but I don't believe any of them made it.

"You're a family practice physician, well known for keeping your knowledge and skills up to date, and you live in New Mexico. You also have a reputation for working hard and that will be a considerable asset around here in the coming months."

Jim chuckled, "Yeah, and I'm divorced. Not like I'm going to be spreading my genes around at my age, though."

Will grinned and stood up, "In a closed environment like this you never know what will happen. Right now though, you need to get some rest. We're going to be relying on you to be clear-headed and to help lead these people. Most of them are above average intelligence but they've had a terrible shock. There's no telling how they'll react when the reality of what's happened sinks in and they realize the world as they knew it is gone forever. Someone else, your nurse maybe, can monitor things and call you if there's anything obviously wrong. What's the extent of the other doctor's injuries?"

"Well, there's his broken arm where someone hit him with a very heavy object, and his right shoulder is one massive bruise. He has a nasty bump on his forehead, and probably a concussion, and he's covered with cuts and abrasions. His right ankle is sprained and badly swollen. He's lucky he made it here at all, but I believe he'll fully recover. He says he was on your list; uh, Aaron Brown?"

"Oh yes, I know who he is, a surgical resident, third year, I think. Go to bed and I'll look him up later. There's an alarm on your control console if you want to attend the 9:00 a.m. meeting. Otherwise, I can fill you in later."

The Doctor nodded, "Okay, see you later then." He opened the door and held it for them.

"It looks like Jim Wiggins was a wise choice." Mark commented to Will after they had exited the room and started down the hallway. "He's already assumed a tremendous amount of responsibility without being told to."

"Yes, he was one of the first people on my list." Will told him.

They separated, with Mark heading to the communications center to check on things prior to attending the morning meeting, and Will going to his room to prepare to face the survivors. Mark told Micah to go to bed. Although the young man seemed to have almost unlimited energy he was beginning to show the effects of pulling an all night shift following the longest day of any of their lives. Dark circles smudged the underside of his eyes. He pointed to the third man in the room, "Hey Mark, this is James Bascomb, another electronics guy." Mark shook hands with the tall, distinguished looking African-American.

"Nice to meet you. How's everything look?"

Bascomb was examining the equipment readings. "There's been no word from the outside and no refugees since about 2:00 a.m. this morning." He waved at Micah as he left the room. "Take a look at that radiation reading." James told him.

"Whew, it's completely through the red zone." Mark shook his head as the significance of the digital readout sank in. "No one else is going to make it through that." He finally accepted the reality that he would never see his sister or her family again.

Mark and James engaged in small talk for another few minutes and then, suddenly needing to be alone, Mark left the tower. Sickened, he paused in the alcove below the control room as emotion overwhelmed him. Leaning back against the wall, he slid down to sit on the floor and buried his head in his arms, where he remained for fifteen minutes more, trying to regain his composure, until he could trust himself to enter the elevator.

Mark arrived at the auditorium shortly before 9:00 a.m., joining a few other stragglers as they entered the room and moved down the aisles looking for seats. The majority of the attendees appeared little more rested than they had the night before, after finally comprehending the enormity of the previous day's events. Small knots of people were talking among themselves but most just took seats and waited for Will's arrival. Faces had been washed and hair was smoothed down but everyone looked as though they'd slept in their clothes and had gotten very little sleep. An occasional smile was seen, usually from one of the children, but generally faces were grim. Mark looked around. It seemed like there were between two and three hundred people. He waved at Helen and Ernest at the back of the room. Helen smiled briefly but she looked frightened.

Will entered from a hallway behind the auditorium, walked across the stage and approached the podium.

"May I have your attention please?" he asked, waiting a moment to allow the shuffling and noise to settle before continuing.

"I need a few volunteers to take the children to the child care area and to baby-sit. Glen will direct you. After the kids are settled most of you can return. There's a monitor in the day care center and those who remain with the children can watch the meeting from there."

Several people stood up and gathered the children together. A few parents, feelings of fear lingering from the previous day, were reluctant to allow their children out of their sight, but finally relented.

Glen was at the rear door of the room. "Bring the children this way, please." He ushered approximately 40 children, of whom a dozen or so were babies and toddlers out of the room. Most of the teenagers stayed to listen to the briefing but a few accompanied Glen and the women that went along to care for the children.

Will continued, "I know you all have a lot of questions, but please wait until I've finished the briefing and I'll attempt to answer them.

"First of all, we haven't been able to communicate with anyone from the outside."

There was a murmur from the crowd at this disappointing news, and tears sprang unbidden to the eyes of several men and women.

"The outside world is deaf and blind due to the EMP, or electromagnetic pulse, which is caused by high altitude detonation of nuclear devices. It causes the buildup of high voltage on all electronic devices and it even jumps across open circuits, burning out all communications and computerized devices. The equipment in this shelter was shielded from EMP so we will be able to re-establish communication when their systems are repaired. There's also a tremendous amount of static since the Earth's atmosphere has undoubtedly been disturbed by the nuclear blasts. As soon as we receive any messages at all we'll make an announcement. There's a public address system throughout the shelter and everyone has E-mail on their computer." He took a sip of water from a glass on the podium.

"Will the following people please stand up? Manny Boulder, Robert Crowder, and Farley Brand." He looked up from his list to find just one man standing. He was average looking, about 35 years old, with short sandy hair, and he repeatedly glanced down at the woman sitting beside him. She reached up and took his hand.

"What's your name, sir?" Will asked the man.

"I'm Robert Crowder. This is my wife, Lisa." He indicated the woman, a decent looking woman with shoulder length brown hair, about thirty years old.

"Welcome, I'm glad you two got through. We're going to need some help in the communications room. You're an Air Force communications officer, correct?" Crowder nodded.

"Good. I'd like to see you at the conclusion of this meeting and the facility tour." Crowder nodded and sat down.

Someone from the back spoke up. "Do you know how many of us there are? Or how many more might get here?"

"The level of radioactivity outside is extremely high so I'm afraid everyone that's coming is already here. It looks like around 250 people made it. That's fewer than I'd hoped. Many of the later arrivals were injured so you'll be glad to hear we have two physicians. Some of you have met Dr. Jim Wiggins. The other physician arrived early this morning and, although he's badly injured, I'm told he will recover."

"Mr. Hargraves," A woman called out, "Do you have medical supplies? I'm on regular medication."

"Yes, we have supplies, examining rooms, an operating room, and two hospital beds. We also have some lab and X-ray equipment and a well-equipped pharmacy. I'll conduct a tour of the entire complex when the meeting's over."

He took another drink and continued, "There's a child care center for preschool children and a regular school area for older kids. Please understand that education will be a top priority. There will be formal schooling for the children and vocational training for all the other residents, since each individual here has abilities and skills to pass along to others. When we return to the outside world we don't know what conditions we'll face or what shape civilization will be in, so it's imperative that each individual becomes as self-sufficient as possible.

"What good did our civilization do us?" a tall, well-muscled man called out. "Maybe we should go back to a simpler kind of life."

"Sir, we'll be forced to go back to a simpler kind of life, as you call it, whether we want to or not. Please understand, this shelter will care for us only for a limited period of time. We can't stay here forever and we'll live a much less technological existence when we leave."

A stunning woman in the front row, with raven hair and green eyes, spoke up softly, "Just how long will that be, when will it be safe to leave?" Many people started to talk at once.

"Wait a minute, please. I'll try and explain everything, but let me take it in order." He waited until the murmuring and shuffling ceased.

"Although it's only speculation, we estimate we should be able to live here for approximately a year and a half, if necessary. Theoretically, we should be able to leave here after only a couple of months and be safe from radioactivity, but as long as supplies hold out we should stay here to allow the social disruptions to subside and civilization to be re-established."

Mark, listening from the center of the auditorium, thought, *"If there's anyone left out there, that is."*

"How can you determine how long the radiation will last?" someone shouted out.

"We have monitoring equipment for that." Will continued. "Hydrogen bombs by themselves don't generate radiation because the fusion process, the thermonuclear reaction, creates non-radioactive particles. The problem is that it takes such a tremendous amount of energy to start the thermonuclear reaction that it requires an atomic bomb to detonate it. Atomic bombs utilize fission, the breaking apart of large molecules into smaller, radioactive elements, generating a considerable amount of radioactivity. In addition, they surround the casing of the bomb with additional fissionable material to create a larger explosion and even more radiation. It's called a fission-fusion-fission process. Unfortunately, the Chinese have recently complicated the situation by using a substance called Red Mercury in their nuclear warheads that, completely apart from the regular bomb, creates a tremendous amount of additional radiation. The half-life of this super radiation is very short, however, and it should deteriorate quickly. The scintillation devices we are using upstairs are indicating a condition in the highest area of the red zone. The radiation is deadly out there, and has been since around four this morning when a shift occurred in the prevailing wind. People who arrived around two a.m. had to undergo significant decontamination procedures and may still get sick. We'll be able to calculate the radiation's rate of deterioration as we collect data over the first few weeks."

"How about food? Will there be enough?" This question came from an obese individual who obviously placed a high priority on food. His jowls bounced as he talked.

"The types of meals you ate last night and this morning, the pre-packaged stuff and the fresh foods, are temporary. There's enough for about two weeks. That may stretch out, however, since fewer people arrived than I hoped. We have frozen, freeze-dried, cured, and dehydrated foods that will last a long time. There's a farm area where we will attempt to cultivate crops, using artificial means, of course. My daughter Chris has a graduate degree in organically grown foods. We also have quite a few animals: cattle, goats, pigs, and poultry, in a portion of the farm. Supplementing the fresh foods with frozen foods we may be able to extend the period of time we can exist underground. Again, you will see all these areas on the tour.

"We also have machine shops, laboratories, and manufacturing areas to produce many of the things we may need now and in the future. Hopefully, once we vacate the shelter we can continue to use it as a base of operations, depending, of course, on the conditions we encounter. Maybe the damage outside has been minimal and we can simply return to our old lives."

"Yeah, sure. What are the chances of that?" asked the big man.

"Probably not great, I'm afraid, but we can hope. We have a computerized library containing most of the material in the library of Congress. There are computers and microfiche readers in the library for retrieving and using this information and we also have a great variety of printed material. We actually have the resources to resurrect a semblance of civilization if one no longer exists on the outside."

His voice began to rise in volume as the pent-up emotion of the previous day was released. "If you think about the magnitude of our job here! This remnant may be all that's left of the human race and if we're not, we're certainly among the best equipped to continue on. When I speak of maintaining civilization, I don't mean to perpetuate our past mistakes. There's so much good that mankind has accomplished; our medical knowledge for instance, that we must educate ourselves and our children to carry on. We may have to combine a primitive lifestyle on the outside backed up by whatever technological knowledge we can save or develop on the inside. We've been given a reprieve so let's make the most of it."

He paused for a moment and someone clapped, the rest of the assemblage picking it up as the crowd stood and applauded him. As bad as their current situation seemed, they realized he had saved all their lives.

"I'm sorry," he said when the spontaneous display had quieted. "I didn't mean to preach. All of you will be asked to share your skills and knowledge and I'll need some administrative help to organize the work force. We have people from all walks of life here but many skills are not represented and we'll all have to learn new things. After the tour you can return here to view videos of the facility. We have a complete series showing each of the various areas and the supplies that are available. You can also view them on the computers in your rooms if you prefer. It will be a good way for each of you to decide where you can best function to help us all survive." He left the podium and walked to the edge of the stage.

A teenaged boy stood and waved his hand. "Mr. Hargraves? Is there someone who can take my braces off?" Mark was gratified to hear members of the audience laughing.

"Do we have any dentists here?" Will asked.

There was no answer. "Uh oh. Well don't worry son, we have plenty of teaching material and I'm sure the physicians can help you. Dentistry has become a very specialized profession and I'm sorry we don't have a dentist."

He waved at the audience, "If you'll follow me, I'll show you around your home."

As he came down the steps and proceeded up the aisle along the side of the auditorium the crowd fell in behind him. Just as they reached the door to the hallway, the room lurched violently to one side and then quickly slammed the other way. People were thrown to the floor and up against the wall. Mark fell into the seats, bashing his already bruised ribs.

"Let's get out of here!" Someone screamed as several people ran out the door into the hallway.

Others shouted and attempted to crouch against the walls and between the seats for cover. Will tried to keep order, "There's nowhere else to go!" he shouted. "Get down and stay where you are."

"Earthquake! It's an earthquake!" Someone yelled and others picked it up. But Mark didn't think it felt like an earthquake, the shaking was too abrupt, not persisting.

"What the hell happened?" He groaned through teeth clenched in pain. People were screaming as the room shuddered, the force diminishing quickly until eventually it was still. A woman ran into Mark and he turned quickly to take her by the shoulders. "Settle down! There's no need to panic." He stared into her eyes and she immediately quieted, calmed by his authoritative presence.

"Everybody be quiet!" Will's deep voice claimed their attention and the babble of voices quieted. "We'll find out what happened and let you know as soon as possible. I don't believe we're in serious danger. It may have been a hydrogen blast in fairly close proximity, maybe Los Alamos."

"Well hell, that's reassuring!" the big man murmured.

Most of the people had regained their feet and were calmed by the fact the shaking hadn't continued. "The shelter was constructed to survive if Los Alamos became a target. The worst should be over." Will told them.

"Mark, can you check with the tower and let us know what happened?" He turned to the others, "Come on now, calm down and we'll continue our tour."

August 22, 10:05 a.m.

Chris stood with her hands on her hips looking at the large cavernous space that was designed to hold "the farm." Following the briefing in the auditorium, and the unfortunate reminder of yesterday's events, she came directly here by following a map she discovered in the main hallway. She came alone to get a feel for the place, knowing in the immediate future a large portion of her time would be spent here, trying to produce fresh food for two or three hundred people. It was going to take a tremendous amount of space to grow food for that many, especially in an artificial environment, but she was amazed at the dimensions of the room and thought it might be possible. The banks of lights hanging from the low ceiling were level, even though the ceiling itself varied in height. It had obviously been hewn out of solid rock, leading her to believe a large underground cavern previously existed here before they enlarged it for their purposes. The ceiling above the lights showed evidence of stalactites although the cavern floor had been completely smoothed over.

This room's lighting, her father had told her, was superior to that anywhere else in the shelter, since the plants required it for growth. To her right was a control panel with several columns of switches. She started experimenting and found the illumination could be regulated independently in different areas of the room.

Directly in front of her were raised wooden benches, with arbors suspended above. Some were lattices, and others were open frames to allow light to penetrate to the plants after the boxes were planted. There was enough variety to allow for varying amounts of light. Wires or strings were suspended from the arbors to the interior of boxes allowing the shelter's hydroponics garden to grow plants supported by these wires, the roots of the plants suspended in a nutrient broth or artificial soil. As she walked slowly down the aisles between the rows of boxes she noticed some had pumice lining the bottom while others were filled with a liquid she could tell wasn't water. The rows, numbering a half dozen, were broken into sections to allow access in both directions but she estimated that the total length was at least a hundred yards long.

The metal entry door had reminded her of an elevator, opening down the middle when she pushed a button and closing automatically after she'd passed through. It seemed faster than most elevator doors, though, and made a whooshing sound as it opened. Because of the excellent lighting, she could see completely across the cave to the far side where she could see an identical door set in the rock wall. To her left was an area without hydroponics equipment, furrows had been gouged out of the cavern floor and it was obvious to her trained eye the soil had recently been brought in from the outside. This area had drip systems visible throughout.

All the way back to the right she discovered a small grassy area with three fruit trees growing in front of a row of offices built directly into the cavern wall. A row of windows looked out on this small lawn. She could see desks, computer equipment, and shelves full of books and manuals. In a separate area there appeared to be analyzers and lab equipment in what appeared to be a research lab to the right of the offices. Lights were on in all the offices and she wondered about the waste of electricity. The lawn butted up against the rock wall where the offices ended on the left and a small waterfall cascaded into a pool. She smiled at this seemingly unnecessary, but welcome, amenity. There was a small niche between the pool and the first office wall, which protruded slightly out into the cave. This tiny alcove was the only dark place she'd seen in the entire cave, shaded partially by the office wall. She walked into the niche and knelt down to touch the lawn, feeling a seam that indicated it was recently planted sod. Sinking down in the darkness, she leaned back against the rock wall, drew her knees up and put her head down on her crossed arms.

She let her thoughts drift to the events of yesterday, when her life was normal and she was preparing for the new project with Dr. Tanner, Jim Burlesen, Jackie Kwan, and Joyce Barnett. Where were they now? She had worked on two other experimental marine projects with Jackie and had known him during her entire post-graduate career.

She made love to him the night before they left. Following the charity ball, he had wanted to stay overnight with her, but she was embarrassed to take him to bed in her father's home, so they went to a motel, and afterwards, he left to drive home to San Diego. If she'd only let him stay the night he'd be with her now.

Voices woke her and she was surprised that she'd dozed off. Although yesterday's events had been exhausting she'd slept very little that first night. A large group of people was coming down the central aisle toward her. The woman whose voice she'd heard, a large, jovial woman about fifty years old, was gesturing at various areas and explaining their function to the others. Chris didn't remember having seeing her before. She stood and stepped out of the shadow.

"Oh, you startled me!" said the woman. "Where did you come from?"

"I'm sorry," Chris said, "I came to explore and fell asleep on the lawn. May I join your tour? I'm Chris Hargraves."

"Oh, Miss Hargraves, I'm so glad you're here. This entire area will be under your direction. I'm Kate Barkley, one of the members of your father's permanent staff, although, now I guess, you all are too." She giggled and extended her hand to Chris. "I'm the dietician, farmer, cook, and chief bottle washer." She giggled again.

Chris was surprised to hear she was in charge, even though this was her area of expertise. Surely there were other people more qualified than she to be in charge of food production. She decided to wait and ask her father about it when she could chase him down. Others in the group were introducing themselves to her and she fell in with Kate Barkley's entourage.

August 22, 10:15 a.m.

"Hey James, any information on the bomb blast or earthquake or whatever the hell it was?" Mark entered the tower and found a man he didn't know sitting at the computer, a small, maybe five-nine, black man wearing glasses. "Oops, hi, I'm Mark. Where's James?" He glanced around and nodded at Micah who was at one of the other computers.

"Hi. Mark Teller? Will has told me a lot about you. I'm Darryl Washington. I'm one of the permanent staff members. James went off to spend some time calming his wife down. She's still pretty hysterical." He stuck his hand out and Mark shook it.

"Does Will know you're here? He was very concerned that you wouldn't get back." Mark sat at the console next to Darryl.

"Yes, I called him. We arrived around midnight. Fortunately, for me, we went north to Colorado Springs rather than to Albuquerque. We brought back a truckload of supplies. Bobby and I had to winch a tree out of the way to get the truck to the entrance cave, otherwise I would have been here a lot sooner."

Micah entered the room and came over to look at the computer printouts. He had apparently already met Darryl.

Darryl pecked at the keyboard and brought up some data on the monitor directly in front of him. "The blast? Let's take a look."

"Wow, Los Alamos is definitely history." Micah said.

Darryl hit a few more keys and explained the readout to Mark, "Yesterday's blasts took out Albuquerque with one warhead - actually the targets were probably Kirtland Air Force Base and Sandia National Lab; Alamagordo and White Sands with a second warhead, and the third apparently targeted Roswell. I'm not sure why, unless the Chinese believe all that crap about flying saucers. Actually, I think it may have been targeted for Los Alamos and something went wrong with its guidance. I thought Los Alamos had been spared. That would have been good for us, because, if that were the case, the closest blast would then have been over one hundred fifty miles away.

"We're lucky, though, because today's blast was off target as well and seems to have hit a bit south of Los Alamos. Fortunately for us, it's more lousy targeting by the bad guys. Sensors put it about halfway between Albuquerque and us. Also, it was only about a five-megaton bomb, which is fairly small compared to the other Chinese super bombs. We will definitely get the radiation effects but it probably didn't do much damage to the surrounding countryside in this area." He frowned and leaned closer to the screen as the readouts changed. "This is weird. The blast was smaller but it is creating a tremendous amount of radiation. What's up with that?"

Mark realized he was seeing the effects of the weapon the Secretary of Defense had told them about in the meeting with the President. It seemed a lifetime ago. "The bomb that hit Los Alamos was probably a Neutron Bomb," he told them. "Is there any way to tell what type of radiation it's producing?"

Darryl pulled up another screen. "Wow, it looks like almost pure neutron radiation. That'll be a real killer. What caused that?"

Mark told them of the meeting with the President and explained the Chinese' use of Red Mercury on their warheads.

"Oh great!" said Micah. "Does anyone know what effects this damn Red Mercury is going to have? I'd never heard of the stuff until Mr. Hargraves just mentioned it at the meeting."

"I get the impression there hasn't been a whole lot of testing in that area," Mark told him.

Mark was examining the screen, trying to interpret the data he was seeing, "Where are you getting this information?"

"We have seismic sensors in the mountain and there are external sensors as well, but they haven't been extended yet. Good thing, too. This morning's blast would have taken them out if we'd deployed them too soon. There are other detectors that are giving us the info on the radiation. Our Cray supercomputer takes all the data and extrapolates the size and direction of the blasts. All the functions in the complex are monitored and regulated by this main computer. The server resides in a computer room on the third level next to the emergency generator room."

A console in the center of the room gave Darryl access as he monitored the shelter's vital signs. "How come this morning's was so much later than the others?" Mark asked.

Darryl clicked his mouse and updated figures appeared on the monitor. "I have a theory about that. The radiation from today's blast has a completely different signature than yesterday's."

"What do you mean, signature?"

"Different radiation pattern. One of yesterday's explosions, the one that hit Roswell, gave off what we would consider normal radiation, ionizing radiation consisting of alpha, beta and gamma rays, a normal pattern of fallout, and induced radioactivity in the soil by neutrons released from the fusion process. I think it was an old-fashioned Russian hydrogen bomb. Looks like everyone's throwing bombs at us. The other two were definitely the Chinese MIRVS coming in on one Intercontinental Ballistic Missile, but again, they are normal hydrogen blasts. The one that hit today has this Red Mercury residue, and extremely, highly penetrating gamma rays. I think it's part of a second wave. It would appear that the retaliatory response, or second strikes, has already or are currently taking place. Wish we could contact someone out there. I'd love to know what kind of damage has been done... or if there's anything left."

Mark asked Micah, "Is there some sort of damage control team that's checking out the shelter for any effects from the blast?"

"Yeah," Micah replied. "We've heard from the power plant, which was our main concern, the computer and generator rooms and the open caverns that house the farms. There was some minor damage from things being thrown around but there doesn't seem to be any structural damage. Hopefully that's the last of the bombs."

Mark looked around the room. "There may be no one left to launch them."

August 22, 11:35 a.m.

Later that morning Mark again wandered the hallways of the facility, this time exploring and looking for Chris. Everyone he encountered asked him questions about the shelter, naturally assuming that since he'd arrived in the helicopter with Will, he'd been here before. They didn't realize he was no more familiar with it than they were.

He started his exploration with the top level, poking his head into various rooms that opened off the hallway beyond the auditorium. The daycare center contained a large number of small children and three women who were sitting in tiny kid's chairs, their knees almost under their chins. One of them was crying and the other two were trying to comfort her. Mark quickly retreated, wanting to avoid serious conversations until he'd had an opportunity to sort through his own feelings. Was it only yesterday? It all still seemed so totally unreal.

The hallways were carpeted with hotel grade carpet, and the lighting, with the fixtures behind soffits along the ceiling, was subdued, emitting a soft diffused glow. Will had told him the lights were always on, controlled by the computer to increase in brightness during the day, decrease in the evening and diminish even further at night. This would help to maintain the circadian rhythm of the residents in a world without natural sunlight. According to what Will told him, the power plant, which he hadn't seen yet, supplied enough power for a small city. They wouldn't have to worry about conservation of electricity.

Continuing to explore this level, he passed a library and a classroom, some empty rooms, a large room with a stage at one end, and a music room. The latter contained chairs, music stands and shelves along one wall that were loaded with various musical instruments. Working his way around a large square, he rounded a corner and entered the same cafeteria where he'd met Chris the night before. There were two people at one of the tables talking in hushed tones as though the atmosphere of the shelter required it. They nodded at him as he entered.

Mark crossed the room to the glass front refrigerators that contained salads, sandwiches, an assortment of burritos and small pizzas, and rows of Cokes, Diet Pepsi's, and fruit juices. There was a counter with two microwave ovens, a commercial coffee setup, plastic tableware, condiments and napkins. There was still no one working at the service counter or grill and everything remained spotless, looking completely unused. Breakfast had been early and he realized how hungry he was when his stomach growled at the sight of food. After selecting a turkey sandwich and a pear, and heating the sandwich in the microwave oven, he sat at one of the tables facing the door.

He'd just started to eat when a woman entered the room. She was one of the ladies he had seen in the daycare center and he thought she might be the woman he'd witnessed arriving at the parking lot yesterday. She smiled shyly at him and immediately lowered her gaze, going quickly to the refrigerator. Mark noticed a bruise on her right cheek and wondered if she'd been injured while getting to the shelter. She had allowed her dark blonde hair to fall loosely about her face, possibly in an attempt to hide the bruise. When she finished heating her food and looked for a place to sit, Mark decided he didn't want to be alone after all.

"Hi, I'm Mark, would you care to join me?" he called out to her.

She glanced at the original table she had chosen, looking like a frightened animal ready to bolt, but then hesitantly walked over to his table. "Hi, I'm Lori Arnaud. Thank you." She looked down at her food and immediately began to eat.

Mark was a little confused by her withdrawn demeanor but realized everyone here was in a mild state of shock. He had no idea how long it would take for people to adjust to their new situation and return to a semblance of normality.

"I think I saw you arrive yesterday," he told her. "Were those your children?" He immediately regretted the question, realizing many of the people here had lost family and friends and polite conversation in their new environment would require a totally different set of rules.

Mark was relieved when she answered, "Yes, one of the other women is watching them while I eat. They already had breakfast in the daycare room while I was at Mr. Hargrave's meeting. Ashley is six and Kevin is four."

He noticed she didn't mention a husband and being a quick learner he didn't pry.

Hesitating, and not quite knowing what else to say, he finally came up with something he thought would be safe, "Where . . . where did you come from, I mean, before . . . you know, before the signal?" He finished lamely.

Grinning shyly, she glanced up from her food, seeming to find his discomfiture amusing. "We're all going to have to be careful about what we ask people, huh? It's okay, I'm not going to freak out on you."

He immediately relaxed, and chuckling, replied, "You're right, I was worried about what I could ask, not knowing what you may have been through in the last 24 hours. Well?"

"I came from Denver. My father sent me the signaling box by overnight mail, from Los Alamos. He's a nuclear scientist at the lab there and I'm quite sure Mr. Hargraves would rather have him here than me." She dropped her eyes again.

"I don't know," he said. "There are a lot of people here that didn't get boxes directly. They came with family or friends, or even obtained boxes by methods that I'm sure Will never dreamed of. Everyone's welcome." She seemed so frightened that he felt a need to reassure her. "Your father must have felt you should have the box."

"I guess so. Mr. Hargraves said he thought the explosion this morning came from the vicinity of Los Alamos. They have an old bomb shelter there from the Cold War, so I'm clinging to the hope that he's okay. Where did you come from?"

"I live . . . or lived rather, in California, working for Will Hargraves as the manager of his aerospace company. Now," he said, suddenly realizing it was true, "I guess I'm unemployed." He finished his sandwich and bit into his pear.

"What did you do for a living?" he asked, already learning to speak in the past tense.

"I taught P.E. in high school, and I was the girl's track coach."

"Hey, you must be a runner. Do you want to jog with me? I thought it might be interesting to take a running tour of the complex. I need to go check out some things in the control tower but we could go after that. Say about 1:00?" For a moment he thought she was going to decline, but after a brief hesitation in which she looked twice at the door, she agreed to have the kids stay at the daycare center so she could join him.

"Great!" he stood to dump his trash in the container. "Meet me at the gym, okay?"

She continued to look down at her plate but nodded briefly.

August 22, 12:10 p.m.

After the ride up the elevator and a climb of about twenty stairs, Mark re-entered the control tower. He saw Micah turn up the dial on the radio. There was a break in the static and Mark waited expectantly, hoping he would hear a signal from the outside. The static suddenly screeched loudly and Micah, wincing, tweaked the dial to a lower volume.

"I thought I sent you to bed this morning. How come you're back here already? It's only noon." Mark walked up behind him. Micah was so engrossed he hadn't noticed the stairwell door opening.

"Whoa, you scared me Boss. I slept for a little while but I didn't want to miss anything. Bob Crowder checked in but I told him to go be with his wife."

"Picking up anything yet?"

"Naw, I have a feeling the EMP knocked everything out, but I'm hoping some equipment was insulated from it. There hasn't been a peep from the outside but there've been a few breaks in the static, so I'm hoping it'll make it easier to receive something. We're scanning with long-wave, short-wave, medium-wave, very-high frequency, ultra-high frequency and the prayer hotline, hoping to pick up anything we can from anywhere in the world. We're transmitting too. With no Federal Communications Commission to worry about, we're using everything from three kilohertz to three hundred gigahertz." He pointed out instruments to Mark as he referred to them. "I'm also trying to use satellite communications, but I can't tell if the hydrogen blasts have damaged, disconnected or destroyed the little suckers."

"When will you know?"

"We don't have full capacity on the antennas yet, we only have the auxiliaries extended." He waved his hand at some of the other instruments. "We have internal sensors on-line for the door systems, the power plant, atmosphere, etc., but we didn't turn on the outside sensors because they're all buried inside the mountain for their protection. Mr. Hargraves said he'd let me know when we could fire them up." He examined a few more readouts while Mark sat down at the computer console, and started clicking on icons and exploring the directories.

Micah leaned back in his chair, his fingers entwined behind his head. "That Will Hargraves is something, huh? I guess you know him pretty well?"

"He's been like a father to me all my life. He knew my dad and helped raise me when my folks died. I have to admit though, I thought this shelter was a waste of time. Will had tremendous foresight and saved us all. What's that instrument over there? It looks like an oscilloscope." He indicated a monitor with a squiggly line on it.

"It is. Signals will show up on it before we're able to hear them."

Mark was accustomed to being in charge, being aware of everything that went on around him, so he asked Micah to explain how each device worked. He wanted to learn all there was to know about the shelter and about the way it functioned. Being a pilot, and being involved in the manufacture of aircraft and missile systems, he was extremely knowledgeable about communication devices, and he had Micah teach him about the ones they were currently using at the shelter. They pulled down the manuals and got to work.

In addition to the communication devices there were instruments for monitoring the outside temperature, wind velocity and direction, the radiation level and barometric pressure. The sensors, inside their protective bunkers, were located at various points on the mountain. Redundant systems existed in case the bombs had destroyed some of the primaries.

Mark wondered if the nuclear war had ended yet, or if there would be delayed reactions and more bombs to come. If their presence became known, and a war was still going on, the shelter could conceivably become a target. From what he understood from Will, however, they were buried deep inside this mountain and only a direct blast from a hydrogen bomb could affect them. Although, he remembered, they were bounced around pretty good by this morning's blast. The sensors would be at risk if they were exposed and Will had decided to keep them secure until later.

The control room was approximately thirty feet square. The left-hand wall had a sixty-inch monitor, blank until the sensors were activated. There were indicators on either side of the screen, some with meters, most with digital readouts. A few indicated the output of the power plant, the water level in the reservoir, the power levels in the auxiliary batteries, and the air pressure in the complex. There was a bank of lights showing the status of all the doors, red lights that indicated if one of the doors failed to operate or stayed open for longer than two minutes. Although that probably wouldn't cause a problem they didn't want to take a chance with air leakage or contamination.

The lights were all green.

This room, sixty feet above the top level of the shelter was the nerve center of the complex. The alcove ten feet below had an airlock leading to a tunnel that traveled a few hundred feet south to the outside, an escape hatch should anything happen to the shelter. Another door in the alcove opened on the continuation of the staircase dropping down over six stories to the top floor of the shelter. This staircase could be used in the event of an elevator malfunction or a serious loss of power. A solid metal door was set in another wall with the words "Weapons Locker" stenciled on it. Mark had wondered about that one and decided he would ask Will about it later.

The tower door swung open and Will came in, followed by Robert Crowder. Will waved toward the others and immediately scanned all the active readouts.

Micah inquired, "When can we open up the eyes and ears Chief?"

Will looked at his watch. "Maybe tomorrow, Micah."

August 22, 8:30 p.m.

Mark closed his door, turned the deadbolt and looked around, only now really noticing the room for the first time. The quarters for single persons were compact and efficient, reminding him more of a cruise ship cabin than a hotel room. There were two rooms; a living room and a bedroom connected by a short hallway. A tiny bathroom, where he had showered after jogging earlier in the afternoon, was off the connecting hallway. On the opposite side of the hall from the bathroom was a counter top with a heat plate and a small microwave just large enough for a frozen dinner. A small coffeemaker was suspended from an overhead cupboard and the counter contained a small sink. Drawers under the counter contained a few utensils, while a cupboard above had coffee. There was an empty under-the-counter refrigerator, but no other food or drinks anywhere in the "kitchen."

"Maybe I should have gone grocery shopping today," he thought. He had noticed people carrying items back to their quarters from the warehouse, but had been too busy to pick up supplies of his own.

The front room had a computer monitor/T.V. screen, approximately twenty-three inches, built into an entertainment center against the right hand wall with a desk chair in front of it. A computer keyboard rested on a pullout shelf beneath the screen, which was an all-in-one computer to save space. Recessed bookshelves, on either side of the screen, were empty except for the remote. A small couch sat against the left wall facing the computer and there was an end table, a tiny coffee table, a picture of a mountain range above the sofa, and an artificial plant in the corner. The living room wall just left of the hallway entrance held a consolidated instrument panel with a digital clock that indicated the time and date, a weather station and an intercom. The clock read 8:34 p.m. and the date showed August 22 – 1, day one after the end of civilization. No weather data was displayed.

The apartment was carpeted with a light gray carpet while the walls were off-white. He went into the bedroom where he had attempted to sleep the preceding night. The twin bed against the left wall spanned the entire width of the room. Sheets and blankets were stacked at the foot of the bed and he hadn't bothered to properly make it the night before. A recessed wall unit was built in directly ahead covered by a drape, which he brushed aside. There were several empty shelves, a set of three small drawers and a closet rod. He took his street clothes off the bed and hung them in the closet wondering what provisions there were for laundering or cleaning them. He'd checked out two pair of shorts and t-shirts this morning but hadn't taken the time to get any other supplies.

An overhead light fixture and a small reading light over the bed completed the furnishings. The bathroom had a toilet - fortunately someone had stocked toilet paper, and a shower opposite it. There was a small central sink with barely enough room to get around it. A recessed shelf unit, where he'd placed his razor and toiletries was above the sink. A full soap dispenser attached to the wall between the shower and the sink, was labeled soap/shampoo. It didn't appear there would be any fancy hair shampoos and conditioners.

Mark flopped down on the sofa using the remote control to snap on the television. It was menu-driven for selecting the program and he discovered there were only four channels. Channel one was labeled "movies" and when Mark used the remote to select the icon he saw there was an extensive listing of late run motion pictures. He sadly remembered there would be no new additions.

Channel two was an educational channel, a cursory examination revealing most of the selections were how-to programs, ranging from carpentry to farming to electronics. He marveled at the choices, hundreds of subjects, and from the first one or two he examined they were very detailed.

Operator's manuals for the shelter occupied channel three. The first screen brought up a map and when Mark clicked on any particular area it brought up a detailed description. Maps were included for the three main floors, the control tower, and several caves. The latter all opened off the third or bottom floor and contained the power plant, a reservoir, farm caves and one that was marked "sanitation."

The top floor had the infirmary, a small library, the auditorium, a music room, classrooms and daycare, some empty rooms, a multi-purpose room and a cafeteria. Level two was the location for the private quarters and a second dining area, and was at least twice the area of the top floor, and extended much farther back into the mountain. There were both individual and family apartments.

A larger library, the main kitchen, still another dining room, work areas such as wood and metal shops, the back-up generator room and computer room, a very large warehouse and a gymnasium were on the bottom floor. The levels were in the shape of a digital "eight" with hallways running around the outside and a central corridor down the middle. The bottom level had a second cross-corridor running perpendicular to the first. There were several dead-end corridors with doors labeled, "Beyond these doors there be dragons." He had examined many of these locations when he and Lori ran through the shelter earlier in the afternoon. They had jogged for over two hours; actually, they explored more and ran less. He was mildly concerned when they found that all the dragon doors led to unimproved caverns of varying sizes that were used for storage. Will assured him when he questioned him about it later that the caverns were all closed to the outside and the air would not be contaminated. Just in case, however, the doors were all monitored to ensure they didn't stay open long.

Having been to almost every part of the shelter including the power plant, the farm areas and every residential area, he figured he and Lori were probably more familiar with the facility than any but the permanent staff members. He had enjoyed Lori's company and wanted to spend more time with her but she was feeling guilty about leaving her children for too long, considering the trauma of the last two days, and left for her apartment right after the run.

The fourth channel was a tape of Will Hargraves welcoming the survivors to the shelter and explaining that although the apartments were empty, the residents could obtain supplies, additional linens, and clothing and furnishings from the warehouse. The message had to have been taped recently, obviously since they'd arrived, because he mentioned the events of yesterday and made reference to this morning's meeting. As Mark listened to the message the intercom came to life.

"Mark? Where are you? It's Chris. Come on over to Dad's place, we're having a get-together." He jumped up, looking frantically for a button to push. "Mark, if you're there, just talk, dummy."

Feeling foolish he replied, "Be right over. How do I find it?"

He heard Will's voice. "Bring up the map on your monitor. Down at the bottom are menu choices, one says 'directory'. It's not totally up to date yet; the data is still being entered in the computer because everyone is changing apartments. Click on it, choose my name from the directory and it will highlight my room. Your remote has buttons that allow you to navigate the menus and select icons."

"O.K., I'll be right there." As he exited and closed the door he remembered there was no way to lock it from the outside.

Mark was surprised to see how large Will's room was compared to his own. The main difference was a large living area with two sofas and two overstuffed chairs. He realized Will needed to have larger quarters for meetings or informal get-togethers.

Chris, Dr. Jim, another man, and two women Mark didn't know were spread out on the sofas. Will sat in one chair and offered the other to Mark.

"Mark, this is Kate Barkley, Marilyn Simmons, Walter Thompson, and you know Jim Wiggins. Kate and Marilyn are permanent staff and Walter came with the refugees."

They shook hands all around and Will handed Mark a glass of wine.

"Mark Teller is a friend and essentially the second in command of this facility, authorized to make any decision regarding the running of the shelter. He's worked for me forever and he's like a family member."

Mark was surprised to hear he was in a position of authority. The relationships and careers on the outside were going to be different from those on the inside and he felt ambivalent about the situation. As a natural leader he probably would have assumed some responsibility in time, but on the other hand, he had been in positions of responsibility all his life and would have liked to just worry about Mark Teller for a change.

Will continued, "Walter will assume responsibility for the environmental systems including the air filtering system, plumbing and waste management. Jake Cummings, the man in charge, was unfortunately on vacation when the attack came and didn't make it back to the shelter. This has been a blow for us but Walter should get up to speed fairly quickly."

"You said last night there were seven permanent staff members. What are their functions?" Mark asked.

"Glen is the manager, Kate's in charge of dietary and custodial, and Bud Nagle is our electrician and power man," He ticked them off on his fingers as he recalled the names, "Marilyn Simmons is logistics. She takes care of supplies, the warehouse and linen. Karl Dohner was in charge of maintaining our database of residents and delivering the signaling devices so he'll take on other duties since his job is over. Darryl Washington, who made it back last night much to my relief, is our computer expert and electronics wizard. Jake was the environmental expert. Chris is going to be in charge of food production although she's protesting."

Chris shrugged. "I'm sure there are others here more qualified than I to be in charge. I've always been a student following a professor's orders."

Mark had every confidence that Chris could do the job. He thought she could do anything.

Directing his question at Marilyn, a thin, no-nonsense woman in her forties, he asked, "How did you know when to bring in all the supplies? You must have cut it close."

"No, actually, it wasn't that much of a problem. Kate and I have a complete program for rotating stock and keeping everything in date. When Will first built the shelter, before my time, he hired a gentleman named Ralph Pierson to stock the warehouse and the storage caverns. Old Pierson, they called him, lived in Eagle Nest and he was something of an eccentric. He didn't keep very good records and God only knows where he put some of the stuff. This mountain has caves and tunnels all through it where we've discovered caches of supplies we don't have any record of." She shook her head, "I'm sure there are more that we'll never discover. Old Pierson apparently went into town one day and just disappeared, never coming back to work. Will hired me to replace him."

Kate Barkley giggled, "I came on board about the same time as Marilyn. It was a mess but we inventoried everything we could locate and set up an inventory system in the computer, which had just come on line."

Will said, "These ladies did a marvelous job."

Marilyn beamed at the compliment. "We have long-term food storage in the form of buckets that are packed in nitrogen, with a shelf life of over twenty years. There are years left before they expire. For the shorter term we have canned goods, frozen and freeze-dried food, dried fruits and smoked meats. We even have fresh produce to last for a couple of weeks. All this food was rotated on a regular basis and donated to the rescue missions around the state. There's a huge walk in freezer in the rear of the main kitchen."

During all those years he'd kept Will's business going Mark wasn't interested in the shelter, considering it a colossal waste of time. Now he was curious about everything. "How did you choose this site? It seems awfully close to places that would be primary targets for missiles, like Albuquerque and Los Alamos. Wouldn't the mountains in Colorado or Idaho have been safer?"

"This mountain range is in a national forest area that the government was willing to let me build in. Also, it's within a reasonable distance from major metropolitan areas like Albuquerque and Denver, which was necessary for access by the refugees. The range has some geological characteristics that made the construction easier as well, such as an extensive network of caverns, similar to Carlsbad, which made it easier to excavate and enabled us to enlarge it without too much damage to the exterior. Only the government knew of the caverns since there was only one small cave that gave access to the outside. I'm sure if others had known of the caverns there would have been considerable resistance to our project. Then there's the river in the forest above us that could be diverted for power and to fill the reservoir."

He hesitated in thought for a minute. "I don't want what I am about to tell you to go beyond this room."

He looked at each of them and they nodded. "There was another consideration. To the west of us is a valley with some unique qualities. The shelter has a back door, so to speak, an escape hatch that isn't shown on the maps. I don't want to inform the others of it until later, as they may pressure us to leave prematurely. A tunnel leads to this back door, which in turn opens on this special valley. Due to some freak meteorological quirks the valley is protected from prevailing winds and other weather phenomena, receiving much less snow in the winter than the surrounding mountains, and it's warmer overall. A river runs through it and it's surrounded on three sides by mountains with an opening to the southwest. My engineers were convinced this valley would receive far less radiation and fallout than other locations in the United States. From what I've seen on the sensors this may indeed, be true. We'll know for sure later but so far this location in The Sangre de Cristo Mountains has proved to be an excellent choice.

Innocently Mark asked, "What does Sangre de Cristo mean exactly?"

"It means, 'The Blood of Christ'."

August 23, 8:15 a.m.

Early the following morning, six men and women stood in the subdued lighting that illuminated a portion of a vast cave. The space, a combination of natural caverns and manmade excavations, extended beyond the feeble lighting as though there were no boundaries and they stared in awe at the unbelievable underground power plant that provided electricity to their new home. Some of those present would be working here and Bud Nagle conducted the tour to familiarize them with its features.

Mark had been through here yesterday but hadn't taken time to explore it thoroughly. He and Lori ran through the door from the lower level of the shelter, down a few stone steps to the rock floor of the cave, across to a larger, wider set of steps that ascended to the second level, turned and ran left on a ledge bordered by a railing, through another set of doors into downward slanting tunnels that led back to the farm cave.

The group stood on the recessed floor of the cave, Nagle speaking loudly to make himself heard above the sound of rushing water. "The penstocks bring in water from the storage lake we built outside and above this location. It's high enough above us to create sufficient head pressure to generate power for our entire shelter and then some." Bud explained. "The water's in a closed system and although it's undoubtedly contaminated it isn't exposed to our atmosphere. It enters the penstocks through the trashrack, which traps the debris, and then through wicket gates. After the water passes through the turbine the draft tube returns it to that enclosed underground river flowing away from the shelter beyond that wall to the west. The penstocks and as much of the other equipment as practical are lead lined."

Mark looked around at the cave, noting evidence that indicated this had been a natural cavern prior to the manmade excavation. To the right of the huge concrete covered aqueduct an asphalt path led into the darkness and he could see broken off stalagmites and jagged, pastel colored, limestone walls. The ceiling, almost lost in the darkness was tremendously uneven, long stalactites and grape-like clusters of smooth nodules barely visible in the dimness.

They walked up the staircase to the main, or middle floor and entered the plant through a large opening with no door. The space was large enough to drive a large truck into. Inside the plant, to the left, was an office filled with computers. "We control the level of the reservoir above by controlling the outlet of the retention dam. There are two more reservoirs in the higher mountains to the west, fed by glacial lakes, also controlled by these computers. The computers control the governor that regulates the amount of water entering the penstocks."

As they walked further into the plant the roar of the water and the whine of the turbine became louder. On this level they could see the generators at the top of the two story turbines. Cranes were suspended from the roof of the room for servicing the generators. The penstocks, six-foot diameter pipes, descended through the room carrying rushing water to the turbines below.

Mark reached up and touched the pipes. He could feel the vibration from the water, in fact, could feel the entire building vibrating.

They came to a staircase, a sign beside it reading, "Ear protection required past this point." Putting on earmuffs they descended the staircase to the lower level where they had an excellent view of the turbine, currently spinning at 240 revolutions per minute, although, as Nagle explained, the speed could be varied to regulate the amount of electricity generated. Only one turbine was spinning. Either turbine, Nagle explained, could power the entire shelter. They would be alternated by the month to allow for maintenance and repair. The wastewater cascaded into a covered ravine beyond the turbines.

"Mr. Nagle, what would happen if both turbines went down? With no power how would they be restarted?" The question came from a teenage boy, Tucker Smith, who had begged to be allowed to work at the plant.

"That's a good question, son. We have two banks of industrial batteries that are charged by the turbines for emergency power. We also have "blackstart" capability which uses water power rather than electricity to get the turbine going."

After touring the lower level they re-climbed the stairs to the mid-level. Going through a large open door to the backside of the plant and onto another ledge they saw a huge storage tank and stacks of fifty-five gallon drums containing the industrial oil used by the system. "The thrust bearings glide on the oil," he explained. "We use massive amounts of it. There are more barrels in storage tunnels beyond this ledge." Mark walked to the railing and looked over the edge. The concrete covered ravine was below and to his right, extending away from the building forty feet, then turning in an arc ninety degrees to the left, where it continued to the far western wall of the cave, lost in the darkness. He could imagine the wastewater rushing through that protective culvert. There was a dark space between the lower side of the plant and the aqueduct.

The top floor of the building contained the powerhouse and transmission lines disappearing through conduits into the complex. Each turbine was capable of generating 6.8 Megawatts; a step-down transformer supplying voltages at 110, 220, and 440 volts.

Mark and the others were thoroughly impressed with the power plant and the feat of engineering that allowed it to be built in this underground location. They finished the tour, with the others staying behind for more specific training.

Mark walked out the front door of the plant onto the ledge protected by a metal railing. He descended the staircase to the rock floor, three feet lower than the door that opened into the shelter. He stood at the door looking back into the cavern and was haunted by a sense of unreality. This gigantic power plant in the underground cave reminded him of the first computer game he'd ever played. He'd spent many hours adventuring in the "Great Underground Empire" instead of doing his homework.

He was haunted as well by the remembrance of a dream he'd had before he came to this place. A dream about "The blood of Christ", before he'd ever heard of the Sangre de Cristo Mountains - as if the dream were a premonition. If that was true then what about the rest of the dream, the horror of something unspeakable chasing him through absolute darkness? He shuddered as he recalled his terror.

August 23, 12:30 p.m.

Micah rapped his knuckles on the red light and chuckled when it turned green, indicating the protective sensor cover was operating properly. Mark stood with the others, holding his breath and waiting in anticipation as the covers slid back and the sensor arrays were extended into the atmosphere. Will, Mark, and Chris had just arrived, after having lunch together. Micah, Bob Crowder, and James Bascomb were already there, making preparations, and Will had invited Dr. Jim and Clay to join them. Clay declined, saying he was meeting someone after lunch. Darryl was in his favorite spot at the computer console.

Mark hoped Will wasn't being premature in activating the outside sensors. If additional bombs exploded close by, the sensors could be damaged and they would be blind. But twenty-four hours had passed since the Los Alamos blast and the instruments hadn't detected any other explosions within their range, so with everyone badgering him to determine what the conditions were on the outside, Will decided to take the chance.

The monitors blinked to life and the room took on a ruddy hue as images began to be transmitted to the monitors.

Red-orange . . . the world was dominated by a pervasive, dull orange radiance. The sun, directly above, was a molten fireball shimmering through the thick dust that appeared to cover the world, its image thrown on the large screen by a camera panning the sky. Two days had passed but the dust still dominated, reminding any creature fortunate enough to be alive that the effects of the nuclear holocaust still lingered.

A light breeze swirled the dust around, wouldn't let it lie as dust devils danced across the landscape. Digital readouts flashed on, revealing a sweltering temperature of one hundred-two degrees, heat seldom experienced at this altitude. The hi-lo thermometer indicated that it had been above normal since the bombs, but was beginning to drop rapidly as warming sunlight had trouble penetrating the thick haze. There was no way to determine whether any rain had fallen but now that the instruments were live, they would be monitoring for that as well.

The Earth had been torn and battered.

She hadn't known such torment since her youth. Oceans, blasted by errant missiles, overflowed and flooded the land that had kept them at bay for eons. The land, pummeled by giant fists of thermonuclear energy would be forever scarred by the massive explosions. Few areas had escaped.

Over a period of approximately twenty years the United States had detonated a grand total of three hundred thirty one atmospheric nuclear bombs, the largest around fifteen megatons. The Soviet Union had tested one or two that were larger. In the last two days literally thousands of warheads had shattered the earth, a huge number of them the sixty to one hundred megaton monster bombs and an equal number carrying their deadly cargoes of Red Mercury primed Neutron bombs.

Presidents and Prime Ministers ordered the buttons pushed, beginning a retaliatory response even before the other side struck the first blows. Intercontinental ballistic missiles had passed in mid-air; hurtling unmolested toward their targets as MIRVs, independently targeted re-entry vehicles with multiple warheads had spread the rain of death across vast areas. Each of the United States' forty nuclear powered submarines carried enough firepower to destroy one or more of the larger Chinese cities. Even the older subs, back when they carried the now obsolete Polaris missiles, had the power to destroy entire cities. Today, with their newer cargo of two parallel rows of eight, solid-fuel Poseidon Missiles they could inflict more damage than ever. The newer Ohio-class subs carried twenty four Trident missiles apiece, missiles targeted for Beijing and, just south of it, Tianjin. Others targeted Shanghai and Guangjhou on the coast, Kunming in the south, and Changchun, Harbin and Shenyang in the northern portion of the country. Additional warheads hit Lanzhou and Chengdu at China's heart, Wujan on the Yangtze River, and even the far west cities of Kashi, Shache, and Yumen.

It was determined by U.S. satellite surveillance, although the residents of the shelter were unaware of it, that Russia had launched a retaliatory response, including targets in the U.S. as well as China, on both days of the two-day Third World War. Not taking any chances, and although the U.S. didn't believe the war was instigated by Russia, the U.S. bombed many Russian cities, as well as Baghdad, Tehran, and Tripoli. Great Britain, France and Israel all launched in knee-jerk response. North Korea used their nuclear warheads on South Korea, blowing Seoul off the face of the earth, and missiles from the U.S. and China blasted Pyongyang in return. Bombers carried tactical warheads on a mission of revenge, and U.S. land-based missile silos disgorged their rockets toward previously selected targets. The United States had an arsenal of over twelve thousand warheads, enough to ensure complete destruction of all countries worldwide that could possibly be deemed a threat to reconstruction. That is, if anyone or anything survived the initial onslaught.

Humanity died - secure in the knowledge that the enemy was being taken with them.

Then came the deadly radiation . . . seeping into the soil, the air and the water and eventually into the very bones of exposed organisms. Genes, during the delicate process of reproducing lined up differently and mutation proceeded at a highly accelerated pace, the Red Mercury causing previously unknown and unanticipated types of mutations. Species reproducing the fastest would exhibit the effects soonest. No exposed organism had escaped the initial radiation that assaulted the Earth. Only those completely sheltered were free of the deadly effects.

Man wasn't the only casualty. Other forms of life on the planet were in a precarious ecological situation. Whole species became extinct overnight

Other digital readouts in the control tower flashed to life as they began to receive data from the sensors. Temperature, 102.6 degrees Fahrenheit; humidity, 78%; barometric pressure, 749 mm of mercury and fluctuating wildly; wind velocity, 17 knots from the northwest; radiation level, over 600 rads, more than enough to guarantee genetic and teratogenic consequences.

The wall directly across from the stairwell had an array of nine monitors attached to video cameras in various external locations. Only one had previously been turned on, the camera covering the parking lot. The other monitors were now coming to life.

Mark noticed one of the cameras showed the intersection of the shelter's access road with the main highway. Several cars had collided, bodies sprawled on the ground in grotesque positions.

"God, I wonder if there's any way to check on those people?" Chris said.

Dr. Jim shook his head. "They've been there for two days in this radiation soaked atmosphere. We can't do anything for them."

Another camera, aimed toward the southeast, was unable to penetrate the dust, and the visibility was barely beyond the edge of the parking lot. A third and fourth camera showed views south and north of the mountains, also blocked by dust. The western view was much better, showing portions of the protected valley Will had told them about. Mark noticed Will paying special attention to this monitor and the associated digital readouts. One camera panned the sky and two others appeared to be transmitting from remote locations. Again, the ever-present dust obscured the views from these cameras. Darryl had complete control of these myriad images and could send any of them to whichever monitor he chose including the large sixty-inch.

The data generated by the sensors and cameras was recorded, analyzed and evaluated by the computer. Changes over time would be measured, and the rate of radioactive decay would be calculated and extrapolated to predict when it would be safe to leave.

But the radios remained mute, picking up only pattern-less white noise.

Mark and the others became silent as the readouts and video pictures combined with the lack of communication hit them hard, like the thermonuclear blasts outside, and they realized that they could be the last humans on Earth.

August 23, 6:00 p.m.

A warm rain had started to fall, carrying lethal particles to earth from the radioactive, dust-laden atmosphere. Something was definitely wrong. Arby's group had become frightened by the sky's strange color. They had no idea what was happening, but the weird weather, the heat, the earthquake, and the rain falling in huge heavy drops, filled them with apprehension.

And they were starving.

Arby sat beside a stream that cascaded into a lake, thinking about the immediate past events and wondering what the hell was happening. They'd spent two days wandering aimlessly through the endless canyon they'd descended in their search for the couple they'd seen earlier. The first morning they were all jolted awake by a tremendous earthquake that shook the canyon, sending rocks and debris cascading down the sides of the cliffs and scattering the men from their sleeping places as they scurried to cover. The quake was followed by a strange blast of wind that roared up canyon and then just as quickly subsided. Arby had no trouble rousing them that morning as they all wanted nothing more than to get out of the deathtrap they'd been lost in since descending the day before. But the quake had partially covered and hidden the trail and, missing it, they had hiked miles up the river before realizing their mistake. Disgustedly refusing to go farther and, after spending all afternoon catching another fish, they decided to sleep right where they were.

The following morning they went back down river, fortuitously stumbled upon the trail, and made the long, very hot climb out of what they considered the depths of Hell, in search of the two people they'd seen from across the abyss two days before. They came to a fork in the trail and bore right, in the direction they had seen the couple travel. They had been in the bottom of the canyon when Pete and Sandi returned along this trail and had no idea the young couple had raced back in the opposite direction.

A small river flowed parallel to the trail until, a mile later, it emptied into a lake. Bennett, leading the group at the time, cried out and leaped forward. In the middle of the trail ahead lay a backpack. Several of the men grabbed at the pack and a scuffle ensued.

Arby waded in to the melee, flinging men aside and bellowing to get their attention. "Give the damned thing to me." He reached out and grabbed the pack. It contained three Powerbars, a bag of dried apricots, two packs of beef jerky, and a few Fig Newtons. Arby divided the food and distributed it to the men, who wolfed it down, barely chewing. The raw fish and these meager rations were all they'd consumed since the bus crashed three days before. Miller, a two hundred fifty pound serial killer, slumped to the ground and started to whimper. Several of the other ex-prisoners wandered over to drink from the river.

"This is bullshit!" Miller whined. "We better get out of these mountains fast or I'm going to eat one of these fuckers."

"How far can it be?" Arby asked. "We saw the hikers, so there has to be a road somewhere."

Arby sat down beside Miller and stared up at the polluted sky, rain hitting his face, falling harder than before. How had they managed to get in this predicament?

The first time Arby Clark was arrested he had only been fourteen. He was huge even at that age and had an unnatural hatred of all authority. Born in poverty to alcoholic parents he found himself, from a very early age, coveting the fruits of other men's labor. He drew an arbitrary line between himself and those he thought of as "men of privilege", feeling they unfairly possessed, by birth, something he didn't, and that it was his right and his destiny to take it from them. He raped and murdered his girlfriend's mother, after his girlfriend had refused his advances. His implausible story was that he tried to fight off her attackers but forensic evidence, blood and skin under his nails, had convicted him. Because of his age they put him in juvenile hall for rehabilitation, releasing him only two years later and sealing his records.

At the age of eighteen, Arby was sent to County Jail for armed robbery, serving another two years, during which time he learned the tricks of the trade from other inmates. Subsequently he had managed to pull off several robberies without being caught.

His probation officer was convinced Arby was a significant risk to the public and tried to watch him, but with an overwhelming caseload, he couldn't keep tabs on him as closely as was necessary.

In an attempted robbery of a small market an alarm unexpectedly went off and Arby, in a fit of rage, killed three men and a teenage girl. This time they put him away for good. He was sentenced to death and had resided on Death Row for ten years.

In prison they called him trigger. He loved guns with a passion and during the years when he'd committed his series of armed robberies he'd twice mowed down witnesses, but had never been connected to those murders. The night the alarm was accidentally activated, he became so furious he opened fire on everyone in sight and was so proficient with his favorite toy that not a single person survived. They arrested him immediately outside the store where he threw down his weapon and surrendered without a fight. Arby had an unnatural fear of dying and knew he could live for years, through several appeals, before his execution. That would give him time. Anything could happen if the process took long enough.

Now he was stuck in these mountains, and he was more worried about dying than he had ever been before in his life.

After they rested, the band of killers moved on, skirting the lake, passing a small dam and continuing down river. The mountains sloped away to the south, but the unusual atmosphere, thick with dust, limited visibility in that direction. The rain had become a steady downpour with streaks of lightning flashing in the darkening sky. The trail continued in a southeasterly direction, the vegetation thickening, and the trail entered another pine forest growing on the south slope of the mountain. Arby noticed there appeared to be a lot of newly downed trees in the area, older vegetation that had, perhaps, been destroyed by the freak weather, fresh soil still clinging to their root balls and fractured branches littering the ground and even spread on top of the ground cover. The sun squatted low on the horizon behind them when he spotted a flash of bright light directly ahead. He thought he was hallucinating; it appeared to be a reflection on glass. There it was again! He pointed it out to the others and they hurried along the path with renewed energy.

The trail emerged from the southern edge of the forest and directly ahead was a large two-story cabin with the forest looming closely at its back. A porch ran around three sides providing a magnificent view to the south. Even in their weakened condition they slowed and approached the cabin with caution. Arby motioned with his arm and the men fanned out, circling in from two sides, where they crouched, hiding in the forest, observing the cabin for a few minutes before making any advances. Arby picked up a thick branch for use as a club and stealthily worked his way forward using the trees and vegetation for cover.

The heavens opened and deluged them with buckets of the strange warm rain. Soaked, tired and hungry, and emboldened after seeing no signs of activity, they worked their way around to the eastern facing front of the building. There were no cars or other signs of inhabitants. Arby crept stealthily onto the porch and peeked in through a broken window. He tried the door, which was locked, and finally losing his patience he smashed through the remainder of the window glass with his makeshift club and climbed through into the darkened interior.

The others followed quickly, interested only in gaining protection from the rain and the fierce lightning which was now flashing steadily. The thunder was almost continual, crashing around them as they quickly entered the building. They stood poised in the cabin's interior, listening for evidence their forced entry had been noticed. There was none. Furniture was overturned and all the other windows had been broken.

"What the hell happened here?" Bennett asked.

"It was that earthquake we felt yesterday." Arby told him. "Everyone spread out and find some goddam food. There's no one here."

They began searching, Jaime calling out to the others when he'd found the kitchen. They stumbled over one another in their haste, spilling into the kitchen in seconds, to find the cupboards packed with food.

Insane with hunger, they tore open packages and stuffed crackers and cereal into their mouths. They pulled drawers onto the floor, located a can opener and ate cold beans directly from the cans. The refrigerator was full of cold cuts and beer. They gorged themselves until they were in a stupor of satiety.

Arby guzzled a beer and vaguely wondered about the whereabouts of the inhabitants since it was obvious the cabin was currently occupied. But he was too tired to worry about it. After all, who stood a chance against thirteen evil giants?

August 28, 4:00 p.m.

Sweat ran down Lori's cheeks and soaked her T-shirt as she furiously worked out, pumping her hands and feet in opposite directions on the mountain climber. She'd been going full blast for twenty-seven minutes, only three more to go. Her gym towel was slung over the bar but she couldn't retrieve it, being unwilling to let go of the handles. Chris Hargraves and Jean Barnes worked out on the other sections of the triangular climber, Chris grinning and pumping quickly, obviously loving every minute of it while Jean looked like she was dying, gasping for breath with every tiny step.

Most of the equipment in the gym was being used. Several men and two women walked or ran on treadmills, a half dozen Lifecycles had riders and most of the Nautilus equipment had someone pushing, pulling, pumping or pressing. The population of the shelter was determined to get in shape or stay that way and exercise helped relieve the stresses of the last week.

Mark looked around in amazement when he entered the room.

"Wow, this is a popular joint," he complained to Chris and Lori as he stood to wait for the mountain climber.

The timer dinged and Lori stepped down, wiping her forehead with the towel. "I came at three this morning and it was empty. Might be a good idea to skip the afternoons."

"What in the world were you doing here in the middle of the night?" He climbed up on the stepper and set the timer for thirty minutes.

"I haven't been able to sleep very well since we got here. My room's located beside the elevator, directly above the gym, so I wasn't worried about the kids. It's a quiet time of the day."

Mark called over to Chris. "Chris, how about meeting me for dinner? Say, in the main cafe at six?"

She answered through exhalations as she continued to pump, "Sorry, Mark but I'm meeting with Samuel this evening. We've done our research, and we're ready to make the nutrient broths for the hydroponics banks."

"Is no one going to keep regular hours around here?" he complained.

Mark glanced around at the other exercisers and, as he started to climb, Lori turned to walk away. "Lori, how about it? Are you free for dinner?" As she had on other occasions, she hesitated, looking as if she was ready to panic. Before she was forced to answer, he flashed his boyish grin, "Come on Lori, we'll go for a jog first when we finish with our gym workout. Meet me in an hour at the farm door?"

She nodded. "Okay, see you then." She turned to go to the abs machine and he couldn't see the shy grin on her face.

August 28, 5:00 p.m.

Lori was free. The world as she knew it had come to an end with everyone in the shelter, to some degree, suffering from the loss of loved ones. But Lori felt free. Occasionally, she felt a pang of guilt about John, but she would picture the beatings, and picture him with his secretary, and she felt free at last.

Before the brief war it was extremely difficult for a battered spouse to leave her abuser. He would stalk her, or sweet-talk her into returning with promises of change, and for a while change might even occur, but eventually the abuse would begin again. The bombs had altered that scenario for Lori. John was either dead or, at the very least, he would never, ever be able to find her.

She and the children had been assigned family quarters with two small bedrooms. Her room had a double bed, theirs, a bunk. The first day in the shelter, after she and Mark returned from their run, she went to the warehouse and picked up supplies and furnishings. A print of a seascape hung over the couch, a vase with artificial flowers sat on the coffee table and there were a few toys for the kids. Kevin's truck and Ashley's Barbie Doll were on their beds and lent a small hint of familiarity to their surroundings. She had stocked the kitchen with a few snacks and cereal but they would eat most of their meals in the mess hall.

She entered the apartment, thanking Cindy for watching the children, and changed into her running clothes.

"Mommy, where's Daddy?" Kevin asked for the umpteenth time since their arrival. The children didn't understand what had happened and, to them, the current situation was only a temporary separation from home and their father.

"He's at home, Kevin." she lied. "We'll see him when we go back in a few days. Come on, you guys are going to the daycare center for a while."

"Can I bring my truck?"

"Sure. But hurry, Mommy's going for a run." He ran to get his truck.

She didn't like to leave the children for too long a time but it was certainly nice having the daycare center staffed, as it was, for the entire day and most of the evening.

Faye Claret, a wonderful, grandmotherly woman, had stepped in and unofficially appointed herself social director, morale booster and childcare chief of the shelter. Lori liked her immensely. Mrs. Claret appeared to be close to sixty years old, was thin, almost scrawny, and seemed very cheerful. She had completely organized a rotation of babysitters the first day of their residence in the shelter.

"Look, dear. It's important for the adults to have time to get to know one another. This is not a time to be alone," she had explained to Lori. It was difficult for Lori to consider having a social life after having so recently left her husband behind to fry. She needed time.

Lori stood by the farm door, fidgeting. Her social skills had deteriorated during the time she had been married to John and she hoped Mark didn't find her completely boring. She'd convinced herself he wasn't coming when he ran around the corner and jogged up to her.

"I'm so sorry I'm late. Everyone keeps stopping me and asking me questions like I have the slightest idea how this place works. Why don't we stay on the third level, there aren't as many people down here?"

Mark pushed the button and the doors swished open. They decided to run through the cavern section of the shelter. Lori felt better down there where no one would see her with Mark.

As for Mark, there was always a chance he might run into Chris.

SIX

September 7, 11:20 a.m.

Aaron stuck his head into the hallway and glanced quickly in both directions for signs of Dr. Jim or Nurse Diaz. The movement caused his head to spin, a wave of nausea threatening to overwhelm him, but he was determined to escape, and started down the hallway with no clear-cut destination in mind. His only concern was to put as much distance as possible between himself and the infirmary, and Dr. Jim's overly solicitous attention.

Bored to tears, he had spent every day lying in bed doing absolutely nothing except thinking about his family. Jim had kept him informed with all the latest information, which at this time, added up to absolutely nothing. Over two weeks had passed since the war began, and according to what he'd been told, they had been unable to communicate with anyone on the outside.

The first few days he'd been heavily medicated and sleeping was the only activity he was interested in. Lately though, he had felt progressively better, and yearned for some exercise to speed his recovery. Taking advantage of brief absences by Dr. Jim he moved around the infirmary, gaining strength, until this morning he decided to take a chance and flee.

Aaron padded down a carpeted hallway. Up ahead someone rounded the corner, and ducking into an alcove, he discovered what appeared to be elevator doors. He jabbed at the button and was surprised to see when the doors opened that there was no elevator, only a set of stairs descending to a landing and then doubling back under him. Holding the rail for support, he crept carefully down the steps, chagrined to find he was so weak, while his left arm throbbed and itched continuously under his cast. He came to another set of doors but the staircase continued down. He decided he might as well keep going and get as far away from the infirmary as he could.

From the bottom of the stairwell he entered a hallway that differed from the previous one in that much of the walls and ceilings were uneven rock. The corridor had apparently been carved right out of the mountain. He found another set of doors, and deciding to explore what was on the other side, pushed a button and passed through the door to find he was in a huge cave. The immensity of the space and his weakened condition combined to disorient him and he was suddenly overwhelmed by a woozy sensation. Stumbling to the side of the door he collapsed, his back scraping against the wall as he slid down hard to a seated position. His breathing was fast, his pulse racing, and he thought he might become sick. Maybe this little excursion wasn't such a bright idea after all. If he'd insisted, Jim probably would have allowed him more freedom without risking his health.

"Hi, who are you and what are you doing here? You don't look so good."

Looking up, he saw a beautiful, very puzzled young woman standing over him, hands on her hips, concern written on her face.

He struggled to stand but she squatted beside him and placed her hand on his shoulder, indicating he should stay where he was.

"I'm Aaron, one of Jim's patients. I had this absolutely brilliant idea to do some exploring on my own. I think it turned out to be less than brilliant though, as I'm sitting here feeling pretty stupid." He smiled gamely and reached his arm out. This time she pulled him to his feet, supporting him by slinging his right arm across her shoulders.

"I'm Chris Hargraves. You've found the farm cave on your great expedition of discovery. Come on, I'll help you to the office so you can lie down." He gratefully accepted her assistance, and with him leaning against her, they slowly made their way to a building built into the cave's right wall. Inside the room, he sank onto a couch located against one wall, glad to relieve the weight from his bad ankle.

Even in pain, Aaron appreciatively watched her walk across the room. She went through a door into a second room that appeared to be a lab of some kind, where she opened a small refrigerator. He called to her, "Hargraves? I presume you're related to the man who built this place."

"He's my dad." She returned, carrying two diet Pepsis, and held one out to him. "How did you get all the way down here?" she inquired.

"I'm not sure," he admitted. "I found a staircase and just kept going down."

She plunked down in an armchair. "And exactly why were you doing this?"

He grinned wryly, "Well, as much as I like Dr. Jim, he was driving me crazy. I needed to escape and get some exercise but I overdid it big time. I'm feeling a little better now, though. This gives me a better appreciation of what my patients go through."

She smiled back knowingly. "Yeah, Jim's like an old mother hen. You're the other doctor then, aren't you?"

"Yes, I'm a surgeon... providing my arm heals properly."

"I'm sure it will. Dr. Jim seems very competent."

"So what goes on in this cave?"

Chris explained what they were trying to accomplish at the farm. Aaron wanted to know everything, and considering he was going to be partially responsible for the health of the residents, he needed to be concerned with their nutrition. He also immensely enjoyed being with this woman, the time going by far too quickly. He was reluctant to leave but knew he would be missed eventually.

They talked for perhaps thirty minutes more, when a page for Aaron Brown came over the intercom system.

"Oops, you're busted. Let's see what I can do to help."

She called a woman named Marilyn and obtained a room assignment. "Do you think you could make it upstairs? If so, I think I could convince Dr. Jim you're settled in and you're fine."

"Are you kidding? I'd do anything to avoid returning to that infirmary." He started to get up and sat back quickly.

"That is, of course, if you'll help me." He sat back up, waited for the nausea to pass and, with her help, struggled to his feet.

September 7, 3:45 p.m.

Mark, now thoroughly warmed up, finished his Lifecycle workout and yielded the equipment to the next person waiting. He looked around the gym trying to decide which exercise to tackle next. The entire left wall was covered with mirrors from floor to ceiling. The space between the wall and the center of the room was crammed with rows of equipment, some that utilized adjustable weights for resistance, a few benches for crunches, and several electronic exercise machines that monitored your progress on digital readouts. Aerobic equipment; treadmills, stair-climbers, mountain climbers, Lifecycles and rowers occupied the other half of the room. The back of the room was partitioned off, with free weights behind the low barrier. An open space led down the center of the gym to a second room.

Mark walked through the door into another large area. The left side had a hardwood floor for aerobic exercise classes and the right, separated by a waist-high wall, had red mats for martial arts training. Several men and women, just beginning a new class, occupied the room when Mark entered. Two men stood at the head of the class facing the students.

Hargraves had sent a signaling device to Lenny Ralston, a military survival teacher, and Lenny had brought along a friend and co-worker, David Cunningham. Will's plan was for everyone to learn primitive survival skills in the event civilization had been destroyed. These guys knew everything there was to know about survival skills, from starting a fire, to finding water in a wilderness. They were experts in to hand-to-hand combat and the use of all manner of weapons.

Although Lenny was average height and had an average build, he had a fourth-degree black belt in Karate. In contrast, David stood six feet-four inches tall and had a massive build. In spite of his size advantage he had never bested Lenny in sparring.

Everyone in the room was wearing a white gi. Lenny and Dave wore black belts, two people wore blue and all the others wore the white belt that denoted beginners. The two with blue belts had taken previous martial arts instruction and verified their training by demonstrating their skills to Lenny. One of the women in attendance had been an Olympic cyclist. Mark had been introduced to her a few days before in the gym.

He selected a karate gi from a shelf, went into a small dressing room and changed quickly. When he rejoined the group he noticed, surprisingly, that Lori was there. She seemed such a shy, frightened person, but here she was in a kick-ass karate class.

Lenny bowed toward Mark as he entered the dojo, "Hi Mark, we were just discussing a little contest. You want to be in it?" Mark got in line with the others. "David here, was a member of the U.S. Orienteering Federation. He's organizing an orienteering contest around the shelter that involves running through the caves, following a map, and checking in at checkpoints. Unfortunately, there won't be any use for compasses like orienteering events on the outside, but we can still make it interesting. What do you say?"

Mark had always wanted to participate in an orienteering event and found it ironic he would finally have an opportunity to do so under these strange circumstances. "Yeah, sounds like fun. When's it going to be?"

"We need to finish planning and sign everyone up but I'd say about a week."

"Sure, count me in," he said.

Their workout started with warm up calisthenics and 15 minutes of stretching. Mark was paired off with Lori. One of them would lie on the floor with his or her leg in the air and the other would apply steady pressure to stretch the hamstring.

After sufficiently warming up and stretching they worked on elementary katas; structured routines that use punches, kicks, and blocks in pre-designed patterns that were used repetitiously until they became automatic. Mark appreciated the discipline involved in learning to perform the katas perfectly.

Having only been taking lessons for a week the group was completely uncoordinated and kept bumping into one another. In performing her kata, Lori turned, punched and tripped over her own feet. She fell toward Mark and he reached out to catch her, but before he could grab hold, she flinched and pulled back, throwing her arm in front her face as though he were threatening to hit her.

"Wow, Lori. I'm sorry. I was trying to catch you."

"It's okay, Mark. I was just startled," she responded and self-consciously continued her routine.

Mark, thinking there was more to it than that, really wished he knew her story.

September 9

Jaime Ferrar leaned over the cabin's porch railing and puked his guts out. Arby, turning in disgust from the sight, ran his fingers through his hair and tried to keep from gagging. He'd been violently ill himself earlier this morning, as had all the others in the last few days. Looking down at his hand he noticed a clump of hair intertwined in his fingers. He grunted and shook his hand wildly, flicking the hair into the air, where the wind picked it up and sent it flying on the currents. Every bone is his body ached like he'd been in the street fight of his life.

Bennett, tossing restlessly in a lounge chair, moaned and grabbed his abdomen, rolling over on his side. "Shit, Arby, we got to get a doctor. We're gonna die out here. Look... my fucking nose is bleeding." He held his nostrils closed after he noticed blood dripping onto his filthy shirt.

"We're not going to die. We just have the flu. That's why we hurt so much. You want to hike your ass to the nearest town?"

There were no vehicles at the lodge and though there was a road, they had no idea how far it was to a main highway or to civilization.

"Somebody should do something. We can't just wait around here until we all croak."

After their initial engorgement when they had first discovered Wheeler lodge, they had completely lost their appetites. Two and a half weeks had passed, and they'd been suffering with various symptoms of what Arby initially assumed was food poisoning, but this was lasting way too long and he was getting worried.

They'd explored the lodge and, besides a fully stocked kitchen, they'd discovered a basement crammed full with boxes of canned goods, sacks of flour and sugar, apples and pears in bushel baskets and cured meats. Jarrod Garner, who had worked as a cook before he killed his wife and children in a custody dispute, took over the cooking duties. He was adamant that the food wasn't the problem.

Preparing for the eventuality of people returning to the lodge they'd barricaded the front door and the broken windows, and posted sentries, but no one ever came. After the first week they had discontinued the guards, but still had no idea what kept the hunters away. There was no television, and for some unaccountable reason the phone wouldn't produce a dial tone. They were completely isolated which, considering their circumstances, served their purpose for the time being.

Jaime wiped his mouth with the back of his hand and stumbled across the porch and through the front door, now no longer barricaded.

"I need a fucking beer. If I'm going to die at least I can die shit-faced."

Arby remained on the porch looking out over the mountains. The rain, which had been falling almost continually since they'd occupied the lodge, cleansing the air of the omnipresent dust, had finally taken a brief respite. Violent bolts of lightning pierced the clouds, and the closeness of the crashing thunder indicated to Arby the lightning was perilously close. He saw smoke a few miles away and assumed the lightning had started a fire.

The atmosphere had eventually lost the eerie orange glow they'd become accustomed to in the first few days. Dull yellow-smudged gray and black clouds lowered again and the torrential rain began anew, coming down so hard the visibility was cut to the nearer trees by the lodge's eastern access road. Rivulets merged into streams that swept past the cabin carrying small branches and rocks toward the south. With the rain came a chill and Arby shivered, reaching up to feel his brow with the back of his hand. He realized he was feverish.

As he brought his hand down he found his eyebrow smeared on the back of his thumb.

"Shit!" He jumped to his feet, spasmodically rubbing his hand on his filthy pants.

"*God, what the fuck is happening to us?*" he thought.

September 15

Mark tried to read his orienteering map as he sprinted down the corridor, coming to a set of doors where he impatiently shifted his feet while waiting for them to open. He'd cleared six "controls" with four more to go. The guys did a terrific job of laying out the course, leading him from the top floor to the lower level several times, through the dim eerie power plant cavern, then re-entering the shelter and down the corridor into the farm cave, where he found an orange and white recently sown windsock. He grabbed the small hole-punch and punched his card for the sixth time, indicating he'd managed to follow the course.

He had encountered other runners at various stages of the race but they all had slightly different routes making it impossible to tell who was leading.

Sprinting through the animal compound, he again had to wait for doors to open, this time into the "chicken ranch." When they did, he jumped back as Tucker Smith, gangly, all arms and legs, came flying out the door heading in the opposite direction. Mark's map flipped out of his hands and wafted to the floor.

"Scuse me!" Tucker yelled as he disappeared around the end of a corral and turned toward the farm.

Mark laughed, retrieved the map, and scurried into the next cave where he encountered three Dragon Doors. He knew the middle one led to the apparently bottomless chasm where they dumped the surplus animal waste they didn't need for the compost pile. Examining his map he selected the left door, pushed the button and sprinted into the adjacent storage area. He passed stacks of hay and bags of chicken feed and went through another set of doors partially hidden by the haystacks.

Sprinting about forty feet through the cave he became confused and skidded to a halt, glancing around as the tunnel quickly narrowed to become impassable. He had no recollection of ever being in this cave. He expected to see additional food and supplies for chickens and hogs but the cave was crammed full of boxes and large silver barrels. It was actually quite a large cave extending around to the left in a manner that would put it behind the animal compound. The floor was uneven and covered with piles of dirt and various sized rocks and, showing less signs of construction than other caves, it slanted downward slightly toward the far wall. There were a few small tunnels leading deeper into the mountain with crates stacked along these secondary tunnels.

He wondered if this could be one of the forgotten caves Kate Barkley had mentioned, one stocked by the first warehouse person before he disappeared, Old Pierson she had called him. He looked at his map and realized he held it upside down and had inadvertently entered the left door instead of the right one.

The race forgotten, he started examining the boxes. Many were unlabeled, but he became excited when he found Anheueser-Busch stamped on a huge number of cartons and he spied beer bottles through hand holes in their sides. He looked at the silver barrels more closely. They were full kegs of beer! There were cartons of Scotch and other types of liquor and stacked along another tunnel he found supplies for a bar, keg tappers and a box of chrome pour spouts.

"Now you're talking," he muttered.

To his amazement, he discovered supplies for brewing beer, what appeared to be supplies for making a still, and fifteen padded bar stools as well. It was obvious old Pierson thought any remnant of civilization would need a friendly pub to help them cope. He found himself praising and thanking old Pierson.

And then he found old Pierson.

He rounded a pile of crates and jumped back, his heart leaping into his throat as he espied a skeleton, clothed in ragged cloth, and curled in a fetal position, its clawed, bony fingers clutching the front of his shirt. Mark guessed that Pierson had had a sudden and massive heart attack. Quickly losing his appetite for exploration or orienteering he returned through the lost cave to inform the others of his grim discovery.

September 17

"Put it over here." Mark instructed. He spread the tape measure along the empty room's left wall. A row of rooms on the topmost floor consisted of the large multi-purpose room, with its stage at the far end, two unused rooms to its left and a single room to the right. Brian Morrison, a lay preacher, had already confiscated the room to the right for a non-denominational church. Mark designated the room immediately to the left of the MP room as "Pierson's Pub." Roughly thirty feet deep by forty wide, it was perfect for their purposes and he'd wasted no time in making use of the treasures he'd found two days before during the orienteering run.

Yesterday they'd buried Old Pierson in an unused cave off the reservoir, a cave so far back in the mountain Mark figured it might even be beyond the power plant. It contained another of the deep chasms they had found in a few of the other caves. The body had been wrapped in a sheet of canvas and secured with ropes. It was slowly lowered into the narrow crack by letting out about twenty feet of line until they hit bottom, or possibly a ledge and the ropes went slack. Bud Nagle shined a light into the four foot crevice but, due to a curvature of the chasm wall, visibility was limited to about ten feet and they could no longer see the body. The ropes had been tied with special slip knots such that a pull on a second rope untied them and the ropes were then pulled up from the chasm. Had they not hit bottom they could have released the ropes anyway and allowed the body to plummet to the depths of the cavern.

Brian had conducted a brief service that was attended by Will, Bud, Darryl and Glen, the only people who had known Pierson, and perhaps a dozen others including Mark. Their first tragedy had occurred even before the war, and Mark wondered if they would be burying others in this underground mausoleum.

Two men hauled a stack of lumber into the pub and began laying out baseboards for the bar where Mark had indicated. A speaker was blaring out "Brothers in Arms", by Dire Straits, one of

Mark's favorite groups. All the common rooms in the shelter had controls for accessing the computerized digital library with its thousands of songs.

The atmosphere was festive. A roll of carpeting stretched across the center of the room where everyone had to straddle it to accomplish anything, but no one minded. A product of the woodshop, four round, wooden tables and accompanying chairs were across the room from the work site, three already occupied. Chris Hargraves, Lori Arnaud, Jean Barnes, and Aaron Brown sat at one, with Bud Nagle, Walter Thompson and Kate Barkley at another. Sandi and Pete were at a third conversing in low tones. Kevin and Ashley Arnaud and Jeremy Thompson played by the door with two other children Mark didn't recognize. Jeremy was usually found in the company of his grandfather, whom he worshipped. Several empty beer bottles littered the three tables and everyone but Kate and Sandi had a partially consumed brew in front of them.

More workers, loaded down with building materials, entered the room and the self-appointed group of supervisors shouted instructions, all completely ignored, of course.

Mark marveled at the assortment of supplies Marilyn and Kate had tucked away. He and several others, having stayed up half the night planning the pub, had approached Marilyn in the morning to discover she had something they could use for every purpose including wallpaper, carpeting, building supplies and even a roll of padding and vinyl to cover the edge of the bar. A large mirror leaned against the wall outside the pub and a group of men had fetched the bar stools, lining them up in the corridor.

A new group of workers entered the room. Two men tilted another table to get it through the door, put it down in the center of the room and unrolled rough, hastily drawn plans. An unusual work group, it consisted of Jack Harmon, a former contractor, Manny Hernandez, the man that helped him with the table, three teenaged boys and two teenaged girls. All of them wore tool belts. Jack and Manny began to issue orders and the kids went to work.

"Hey Mark," Chris called out from the corner table, "It's getting crowded in here. You realize this room is right next to the multipurpose room?"

Mark walked over to the wall separating the rooms. He rapped on the wall in several places and yelled to the work group, "Hey Gorbachev, take down this wall!"

Chris laughed and pushed him out of the way. "Hey Guys. How about just a door?"

"Put a door through here!" Mark corrected himself. Jack walked over and immediately started measuring for a door.

"You got a permit for that door?" Mark asked him.

"If there wasn't children in this room, I'd tell you what you could do with your permit."

A group of young men, led by Clay Hargraves, entered the room. Clay looked around, his entourage waiting for his direction. Chris called out to him, knowing full well what his answer would be, "Hey Little brother, did you come to help with the work?"

"No, I'll leave that up to the grunts." he replied. "We came to sample some of the long lost brew." Clay sauntered over to the table occupied by Sandi and Pete followed by the other three young men.

"Mind if we join you?" He sat down before Pete had a chance to respond.

A large glass front refrigerator, confiscated from the cafeteria, was stuffed full of beer bottles. One of Clay's followers went to the box and returned with four bottles of Budweiser. He dragged over a chair from the empty table and Sandi wondered why they didn't just sit there and leave her and Pete alone.

"So Sandi, how have you been?" Clay looked directly at Sandi ignoring Pete as if he weren't there. Sandi knew Pete and Clay didn't like each other and they'd had an unpleasant encounter a couple of weeks ago. Angry words had been exchanged but it had gone no further. In a closed society with everyone crammed into a small space it was inevitable that sooner or later, there would be confrontations. She knew Pete was becoming angry but tried to make small talk to keep the situation under control.

"I've been fine Clay. Keeping busy. How about you?"

"I'm good but I'd be better if you'd have dinner with me tonight."

Feeling Pete begin to bristle next to her she stood up, "Pete and I were just leaving, Clay. I have lesson plans to work on."

"Petey's beer is still full. Come on, chill, hang out for a while."

Pete scowled, "My name's Pete, Clay, and we really have to go." He stood up, taking Sandi's arm and they hurriedly left the room.

Clay watched them go, a smirk on his face and the others at Clay's table chuckled.

Throughout the day people visited the pub, helped themselves to beer, and checked on the progress. The kids were learning fast and with instruction from the men the bar was going up smoothly. Mark helped out, trying to learn something without impeding the progress. Satisfied all was going well he turned to ask Chris to go to the gym but found she was gone. He hadn't heard her say goodbye.

"Lori, did Chris say where she was going?"

"No, but she and Aaron were talking about showing him what progress they'd made at the farm. They may have gone to check it out."

"Well, do you want to drop off the kids at daycare and go exploring? Maybe we can find some more treasure."

She dropped her eyes, nervously wringing her hands, but finally looked up and met his gaze. "Okay, Mark. Let's go."

September 29

Loud speakers blared forth with the sound of square dancing as the "caller" Jack Iverson sang, "Swing your partners round and round, allemande left to a Right and Left Grand." The set ended and Mark and Chris embraced in a final swing and headed for the dinner table. Square dancing was a lot of fun but had been largely abandoned in the world before the war.

When the survivors arrived at the shelter, those that got there before the bombs fell wore their street clothes into the elevator. If they arrived later, they had to be decontaminated and instead of their street clothes they were issued the "shelter scrubs" – lightweight cotton shorts or pants and a tee shirt and sandals. There were regular clothes in the storeroom but few people had checked them out. Two couples wore western square dance outfits that one of the women had made and the other dancers wore either the scrubs or regular clothing. It made for an interesting group of dancers.

A few tables had been loaded down with the traditional foods of a summer hoedown.

Several of the men had barbequed beef on portable barbeques, while other residents had prepared all the trimmings; salad, mashed potatoes and gravy, baked beans, a few raw vegetables, corn-on-the-cob, and apple pie. Beans were one commodity they had plenty of, every variety, in cans and bags. They used the last of the frozen corn. There was a small amount of lettuce and tomatoes for a salad, and they seemingly had a lifetime supply of dehydrated potatoes in #10 cans in several dragon caves. Preparing meals for over two hundred people each day was a major job. Everyone took fairly small portions to ensure they all got their share.

Two of the cattle were sacrificed for the occasion. They were the only two young males old enough to slaughter. That left their small herd at three pregnant cows in various stages of gestation, two lactating cows with calves that produced milk for the survivors, five cows they were preparing to artificially inseminate and two bulls. Beth Wright was concerned about the small gene pool with only two bulls but as Will pointed out they weren't planning on living here longer than two years at the most. The two calves were male. One would be consumed when older and one would eventually replace a breeding bull.

Mark was concerned about the smoke, but it disappeared through holes and tunnels in the natural ceiling of the cave. He wondered where it went since the caverns were supposedly closed off from the exterior. "Hey Gregory, do you think there's any danger from all this smoke?"

"There are miles and miles of fissures throughout this mountain creating a natural draft." Whitehorse explained. "I suppose if we did this often enough we could create some problems in the future. Of course, it's a different story if we were doing this inside the shelter."

They took their plates with them and went over to sit on bales of hay; joining Kate, Lori, Chris, Aaron and Ted Wright, who worked with his wife Beth taking care of the animals. A group of musicians played country music and Karen and Jeana, sisters from Albuquerque, taught everyone line dancing.

Mark danced with Lori and found that he enjoyed all this country-western music and dancing. He had never been exposed to it before but it was a lot of fun.

After the line dancing, Candy Pitowski played a mean fiddle backed up by two guitars and an electric keyboard as Micah belted out "Thank God I'm a Country Boy."

Several children were playing tag, chasing each other around the hay bales and generally getting underfoot. Everyone seemed relaxed and for a while they were able to forget their troubles. Mark was sorry Will had skipped the party.

"I wonder if it was such a good idea to eat the cattle. Don't we need them to breed?" Chris asked Ted. "We have other bulls for breeding stock. These were meant to be food, although we were a little concerned about slaughtering them this soon. We've only been here a little over a month."

"Wow," said Lori. "Those speakers are really vibrating this place. Did you feel that vibration?"

"It must have been the bass." Mark responded. "Either that or you're imagining things."

"No, I felt it too, Mark," Chris said. Could we be having some kind of aftershocks from the blast we took when we first got here?"

Gregory looked around the cavern, "I don't think so. This part of New Mexico isn't known for instability, although a hydrogen blast changes the situation somewhat."

"It changes a lot of things," Chris said. "What do you suppose is going on out there? We still haven't heard from anyone that I know of. Do you think anyone else survived this thing?"

Mark put his empty paper plate down on the bale beside him, "There are hundreds of shelters around the country and I'm certain that many people made it to them. This EMP thing knocked out the communications. Once everyone is able to leave the shelters we should be able to hook up with others."

They heard voices raised in anger on the other side of the cavern where the younger people were congregated and they saw Pete and Clay nose to nose in what appeared to be a confrontation. Mark and the others jumped up and ran toward the two when some of Clay's friends grabbed his arms to pull him from Pete. Clay pulled loose and threw a punch, connecting with the side of Pete's face. Pete went down hard and Mark jumped in to separate the two.

"Clay! Stop it!" He shoved Clay backwards and the others again grabbed him from behind. "What the hell is going on here?" Mark demanded.

"He won't leave us alone!" Sandi complained, through tears. "He follows us and provokes Pete wherever we go. We just want him to leave us alone."

Chris stepped in front of her brother and said something to him in a low voice. Mark didn't know what she said but he shrugged off the grasp of the others and stormed across and out of the cavern.

"Are you alright?" Mark asked Pete. A welt had appeared on his cheek underneath his left eye. "Maybe you should let Aaron look at that."

Aaron came over to check the injury but Pete shook his head. "I'm fine, but he had better leave me and Sandi alone." He took Sandi's arm and they left by the dragon door that led to the animal farm.

The rest of the people dispersed, with Clay's friends leaving the cavern and the others trying to resume the party, but the atmosphere had been ruined.

"I'm surprised there hasn't been more of this kind of thing," Mark told Lori. "But then we've only been down here a just over a month. The younger people are feeling the confinement more than the others. We may need to come up with more activities for them to do."

Chris frowned at him. "I don't think we can find enough for Clay to do. Everyone else spends a lot of their time working or learning new skills, but he doesn't want to do any work so he just hangs out and causes trouble. Dad is worried about him and so am I."

Mark started to put his arm around her but she walked over to Aaron and the two of them went to finish their meal. Mark felt a strange sense of ill ease. Could he be jealous of the time Aaron was spending with Chris? He knew they had to work together and wondered if there was some way he could volunteer in the farm to be with Chris more. Unfortunately he didn't have an awful lot of interest in that area.

He noticed Lori had finished her dinner and was staying behind to help clean up. He went over and started disassembling the speaker towers.

October 3

Samuel held the test tube of nutrient broth up to the light as if he could visibly determine what the problem was. "You would get better answers if you took it to the lab and ran it through the analyzer." Chris said.

"I don't know that that's true, young lady. I been growing things all my life without your fancy, shmancy equipment."

"Yes, but you weren't trying to grow them without soil in a dark, dank, underground cavern."

"You think the problem's the light?" he asked.

"Maybe. I think we need to talk to Bud about changing the wavelength. I don't know if it's possible but I know that florescent light is a different wavelength than incandescent or natural sunlight. Maybe one of the machine shops can make us new lights."

She was using small clips to anchor the new plants to support wires. The glass wool and peat the plants were anchored in didn't supply enough support on their own. Three weeks after planting they'd produced their first crop, with a yield far less than expected, and she was convinced the nutrient content was wrong. Of course, light was needed for photosynthesis but all plants also require carbon, nitrogen, hydrogen, oxygen, phosphorus, potassium, magnesium and several other essential minerals. Carbon, hydrogen and oxygen are no problem, obtained easily and in large quantities from water and from carbon dioxide in air. The other nutrients are usually supplied by salts in the soil. Here, however, since there was no soil, it was up to her to determine the proper percentages of mineral salts to add to the distilled water. Iron, manganese, boron, zinc, copper and molybdenum also presented no problem, being needed in minute quantities. These trace minerals were added, along with a fungicide, after the final nutrient broth was prepared.

It was painfully obvious to Chris that the original mixture was incorrect. Using computer modeling, she created a theoretical mixture, fed the data to the analyzers and created a new, and she hoped, optimal nutrient solution. She had changed the percentages of potassium nitrate, calcium nitrate, potassium acid phosphate, and magnesium sulfate. After dissociating in solution, these salts supplied necessary ions for growth, such as K^+ and NO_3^-.

These new plants were being fed the re-configured mixture utilizing the sub-irrigation method of hydroponic gardening. The solution was flooded through the peat or glass wool and allowed to drain periodically. There was no danger of depleting the salt solution since the plants extracted a fairly small amount of minerals from the solution, which would then be replenished and reused. Working her way back and forth through the hydroponic beds, she babied the young crop, coaxing them to flourish.

She was thoroughly satisfied with the crew assigned to assist her. Sam had proven to be a gem and although, as he pointed out every day, he had spent his entire life farming by "time-tested methods" he had surprised her with his feel for growing things in an artificial environment. Several teenagers were currently cultivating the open in-ground growing areas that would be planted next.

Theresa West, a botanist, provided valuable assistance. Chris believed Terry should have been in charge but she'd brought her family with her, and was able to spend far less time at the farm than Chris. Satarana Patel, a nutritionist, assisted Kate in the kitchen but spent considerable time working with Chris as well. Rana and Candy Pitowski, an entomologist were becoming good friends. Savannah Strahan, who owned an organic produce store helped out as well. Candy had worked for a farming co-op researching agents for exterminating insects that attack food crops. Samuel referred to these women as his harem and had been warned by Chris she was going to report him to the government for sexual harassment. All in all it was a talented and hard working group.

Ted and Beth Wright, a married team of veterinarians, had responsibility for the animals penned behind the doors in the farm's back wall. Their cave was slightly smaller than the food production cave and was filled with corrals holding several each of cattle, goats, sheep, and hogs. Many were pregnant, having been part of an on-going animal husbandry program. The Wrights enjoyed more volunteer assistance than any other work area, many of the residents, including quite a few teenagers, wanting to work with the animals.

A third, even smaller cave, which they referred to as the "Chicken Ranch," was accessible through more doors to the side of the animal cavern and contained chickens, turkeys and game birds. Tunnels led from this area and eventually wound their way to the power plant.

There were several Dragon Doors off the farm and animal caves leading to storage areas, some of the larger ones used for storing animal food, another used for disposal of their waste and, of course, the cave where Mark had found Old Pierson's body.

Chris didn't have a lot of experience with hydroponic gardening but knew it was only a matter of time until she discovered the optimal mixture of soil substitute, nutrient broth and lighting. The computer had an extensive collection of material on gardening in artificial environments and she was learning as quickly as possible.

The last of the original fresh produce had been consumed at the barbeque a few days before. They had been able to produce fast growing romaine, cucumbers, tomatoes and zucchini but with the low yield it would never be enough. Chris was using her new recipe for the broth trying to increase the yield for the next harvest period. She smiled as she saw Sam sneaking off to the lab with tubes of the nutrient. He would never admit to using the lab's computer but she had seen him with Darryl Washington on several occasions and knew he had been trained on it.

Someone grabbed her from behind and she jumped, whirling to find Aaron laughing at her. "You work entirely too hard, my dear. How about some dinner?"

She swatted him on the shoulder and immediately apologized when he winced. "Oh Aaron, I'm sorry, but you started it. Okay, good idea. I'm starved. I just can't seem to be able to produce a decent yield and it concerns me to death."

"You're worrying about it too much," Aaron told her. "Many of the residents have come in for physicals and although some have other problems no one is suffering from malnutrition."

She was touched by his support but knew the food stores wouldn't last forever and if they were forced to live underground for an extended period of time people would eventually be relying on her to provide necessary provisions. "I know we still have plenty of food but it'll be different now that the fresh food is gone. People will get tired of not having produce. What bothers me is that the science is right."

She walked beside him, checking the new plants. "I can't figure out why we can't get a decent yield. It's not that we aren't getting growth, it's just that the yield is too low. If we had more area we could provide enough food at this yield."

"Why don't we use some of the dragon areas? We could rig more lights and dig furrows in the dirt floors."

"That might be worth investigating. I'll discuss it with Dad. Thanks, Aaron." She turned and took his hand. "Keep the ideas coming, I need all the help I can get."

There was an awkward moment where neither spoke. Then Aaron leaned down and kissed her on the cheek. "At least I'm good for something. Until my arm is back to full strength I feel useless."

His cast had been removed but his wasted left arm was a reminder of two months of inactivity. Gradually beginning to exercise it, he was regaining strength in his arm as well as in his overall conditioning. It started that wonderful day he had stumbled, literally, upon Chris in the farm cave. She introduced him to the gym and had proven to be a stern taskmaster. During all the years as a medical student, an intern and a resident he had gotten out of the habit of regular exercise. There was never enough time. Fortunately he possessed good genes and hadn't turned into a complete cream puff.

Chris saw Rana Patel approaching from behind Aaron, appearing distressed.

"I want to know why these fellows tease me and call me "Frog face," Rana asked without preamble.

"Hi Rana, who calls you this?" Chris asked her as she elbowed Aaron, who was trying to suppress laughter.

"All those small boys. They hide behind the boxes and when I walk by they call me "frog face" and then they run. What does this mean?"

"Come on Rana, we're going to eat. Why don't you come with us? You're going to have to get used to that sort of thing, these kids don't have enough to keep them busy and I'm afraid they're getting too good an education. They must have learned that *Rana pipiens* is a species of frog.

Rana looked momentarily blank and then suddenly said with a completely straight face, "Oh, that's very funny. I like that." And they all headed off for dinner.

October 26, 12:30 p.m.

Walter checked the gauges in the environmental system control room. One of the readouts was swinging wildly, indicating the unit being monitored was malfunctioning.

"What do you think's the matter with it, Dad?" Jerry asked him. The gauge fell to zero, indicating the carbon dioxide scrubber had suddenly quit working completely, leaving five others in this part of the shelter to carry the load. Walter tapped on the glass and frowned. These scrubbers were similar to those used on Mir, the Russian space station. Funny, Walter thought, those had malfunctioned all the time too.

"I don't know, son. The others are fine but we'll have to adjust them to keep the CO_2 and nitrogen levels optimized."

The outside air was still contaminated, and although the radiation was beginning to drop rapidly, there was no way to make it safe with any amount of filtering. One of the dragon caves was used for storage of compressed air tanks large enough to supply air for the shelter for approximately two weeks if the main and backup oxygen generators should all fail, an extremely unlikely event. They still had plenty of capacity on the remaining generators and there were three additional banks in other areas. Walter didn't think they would need to utilize this equipment for much longer.

Pete leaned over his dad's shoulder. In addition to working in one of the machine shops he'd been trying to help his father and brother by learning about the environmental systems. "What about the air temp, Dad? Seems a little cool in here."

Jerry, thoroughly enjoying having knowledge about something his little brother didn't, jumped in to answer him.

"It's a cave Pete. It's always cold down here. The air temp is steady 64° on the top level and gets colder as you descend. The shelter doesn't even have any air conditioning. We've been heating the air although it's warming up on it's own with all these bodies down here."

"How do you keep the temp from getting too high on the upper levels?" Pete was examining the gauges on the equipment.

"The plenums are all baffled. The computer controls the degree to which they open and close to stabilize the temp on the upper two levels. We maintain it slightly lower on the bottom level since the machine shops, gym and farms are down here. The whole shelter is allowed to cool down to 68 degrees at night."

Walter pulled the cover off the generator and he and Jerry were examining the unit's innards. Pete took this as his cue to escape while he could. "I gotta go, see you two later." Walter and Jerry were so engrossed they didn't even notice him leave.

Pete took the stairs to level one and headed for the school to see if Sandi was ready for lunch. She had just dismissed the combined Kindergarten through third grade kids and they pushed through the door, almost running him over in their haste to get to lunch.

"Whoa, slow down kids." He pressed his back against the jamb until the final kid raced past and grinning at Sandi he reached for her hand.

"You interested in having some lunch?"

"You know, Pete, I'm not really very hungry." She turned away and went to erase the marker board covered with math problems.

"Come on Sandi, Chris told me they're having some problems getting the yield up on the crops. You need to eat your share of the produce. Did you have breakfast?"

She admitted that she hadn't which concerned him even more.

"Are you feeling okay? What's the matter?" He turned her around and hugged her. He was aware she was depressed about her family and felt guilty she hadn't gone home before the war. "You know, we're all having some problems adjusting. What can I do to help? Do you need to see Dr. Jim?"

"No Pete, I'm fine, really. I just need some time. She turned away and resumed erasing.

"Okay. If you want to talk later I'll be in the pub."

He left her, not knowing what else to do. They had spent a lot of time together and he was concerned that her depression was getting worse. Her smile was absent and she had become withdrawn.

Although it was only noon several others were sitting at the bar or at tables. Johnny Jay saw him come in and had a Bud open before he even reached the bar.

"Hey, Pete, you look like hell. What's up?" The phrase "You look like you've lost your best friend" was never used in the shelter.

Almost everyone had.

"Aw, I'm just worried about Sandi. Can't seem to cheer her up." He downed half the beer in one gulp.

"Hey Dude, most of the folks are having a tough time. She'll be okay. She just needs some time."

"That seems to be the consensus. Everyone just says they need more time. It looks like that's all we've got right now."

He glanced around the room, noticing with displeasure that Clay Hargraves and his three friends were there. Clay's friends were all in their late teens or early twenties. Clay seemed to fit in better with younger men than with men his own age. Pete didn't care for Clay's arrogance or his attitude. Clay intimated he had authority over others since his father was the owner but Pete didn't buy it and he didn't think Will Hargraves intended it either. He noticed that whenever Clay's father was around Clay backed off and didn't exhibit any authority at all. Clay's sister Chris had taken on a tremendous responsibility with the hydroponic farming, but as far as Pete could tell, Clay hadn't made an effort to perform any work at all, spending his time with his buddies in the pub or gym, or hanging out with the younger women.

As Pete gazed at the group Clay looked over at him, raising his hand in a gesture of greeting. Pete nodded and quickly looked away.

Elsewhere in the room people were talking and enjoying the company of others. Very few people liked being alone, and humans seemed to become more gregarious when cataclysmic events affected their lives. Karl Dohner was one exception, a solitary figure at the end of the bar, drinking scotch and spending hours staring into his drink. Johnny had the good sense to surreptitiously water down his booze but even though it was just past noon it looked like Karl was already drunk.

Doctor Laskey was interviewing a couple at one of the tables. He decided that in addition to being an educator, he would act as the shelter's historian by documenting the survivors' experiences. Being determined to write this history from a more personal perspective than most, he spent considerable time talking to people and questioning them about their feelings.

Pete got another beer and wandered over to a table where two of his friends, Tom Jenkins and Paul Brady were sitting with Vernon Richenour. "Hi guys, what's going on?"

Vernon leaned forward, speaking in a conspiratorial manner, almost a whisper. "We were talking about when we can get out of here."

"What are you talking about? Who in their right mind would want to leave?" Pete asked.

"I don't think Hargraves is leveling with us about the outside. There's no way everyone could have been killed. Surely we should be able to contact others by now."

"Well, I don't know much about it but I don't think the radiation is gone yet. My dad has monitors on the outside air and he says it's so radioactive out there we can't even filter it enough to use it. We're still using oxygen generators."

"That could be a ruse. How do we even know for certain there was even a war?" His gaze shifted between the young men.

Paul Brady shrugged his shoulders, "Duh . . . I saw the blast. It couldn't be anything else. It was too bright, and I'll never forget that noise." He visibly shuddered at the memory.

"Well, I just think we need more information. Hargraves should communicate better."

"No offense Mr. Richenour, but why would the man spend hundreds of millions of dollars to build this place to save our sorry asses and then keep us prisoner? I'll bet he'll let you leave anytime you want." Pete said.

"Don't get testy, young man. I just think we need some answers. I'm going to talk to Hargraves about it." He got up and left.

"That guy's a troublemaker," said Tom. "He goes around all the time stirring people up about non-existent problems. Why doesn't he just split if he hates it here so much?"

Pete looked toward the door. "Some people would complain if you saved their life in a nuclear war and didn't thank them for giving you the privilege." As he imbibed another beer he kept looking toward the door, hoping to see Sandi enter. But she never did.

Johnny went over to see if Dr. Laskey wanted a drink. He seldom did, but Johnny took his job as bartender very seriously and was determined that no one should go without. As soon as Johnny left the bar Karl reached for the bottle of scotch and filled his glass, tucking the half empty fifth up under his shirt. He glanced nervously at Johnny with bleary eyes and stood unsteadily to leave the room. Johnny returned to the bar and was relieved to see Karl's back disappear around the corner toward the elevator that would take him to his second floor apartment. He noticed that Karl had taken his drink with him.

Karl made it to the elevator and managed to punch the proper button for the second floor. He was intermittently blacking out and regaining consciousness as he bounced off the walls on his way to his room. He opened the door and entered an apartment, stumbling forward to the hallway where he put his drink, and the bottle, on the counter before falling to his knees in front of the john and retching violently. Sweating profusely, he leaned against the toilet for a while, with his head resting on the seat. When he thought he could manage it he climbed to his feet and staggered back to the living area.

Through bleary eyes he glanced around the room. "Goddamn forest isn't mine." He stood swaying, squinting at the print over the couch. His alcohol soaked brain realized he was in the wrong apartment and he re-entered the hallway, careening down the hall in search of home.

October 26, 2:30 p.m.

Mark and Lori perched on a rock in a dimly lit cave that overlooked a reservoir of black water. The cave was sufficiently illuminated to keep anyone from accidentally stumbling into the survivor's source of drinking water, but the far reaches were lost in shadow. The reservoir, slightly irregular in shape and approximately one hundred feet on each side, extended into the mountain on the third, or bottom, level of the shelter. Across the water on the left side of the cave, Mark barely made out the hulking outline of the filtering equipment, which wouldn't be used until the radioactivity diminished. He could just make out the pump for the well, which would be used if necessary, when the level of water in the reservoir dropped below a predetermined volume. Theoretically the water in the underground water table wouldn't be contaminated by ground water for months. The reservoir was ten feet deep and held close to seven hundred and fifty thousand gallons of chlorinated water, enough to provide 25 gallons per person, including the animals, per day for at least two months. A secondary reservoir just off the top level, the only cave accessible from the top two floors, contained non-chlorinated water for the hydroponic banks and cultivated areas, and a second tank where water was pumped from the main reservoir to allow for gravity distribution to the shelter.

The temperature at this level was much cooler than the main shelter and even though Mark and Lori were still warm from their run, he knew they would get chilled if they remained immobile for too long. They sat huddled together on the flat rock they had shared on numerous other occasions.

He'd come to treasure these moments he spent with Lori, talking about absolutely everything, reminiscing about the old days and speculating what the world outside might be like now, and in the future. Usually they steered their conversation away from personal topics, but today Mark could no longer contain the pain of losing his sister. He explained to Lori about the phone call, how he begged Jill to come to Albuquerque and only now, in opening his heart about that horrible day, did he realize how the guilt had tortured him for leaving the airport without her. From the very beginning, he felt he should have waited for them, even if it meant his own death. Everything had just happened so quickly.

"Mark, you have to think about the fact that you gave them a chance to be saved. It wasn't your fault they didn't make it in time. From what you've told me you never would have found them in that mob and you would have died too." She reached over and gently laid her arm across his shoulder. Although she too had left someone behind she understood that the situation and the feelings were entirely different.

Lori sensed that although Mark seemed to have it totally together, he was in reality a very lonely man. He'd spent his entire adult life in one meaningless relationship after another, always waiting for Chris to come to her senses and realize they were meant to be together forever. She wondered how long he was willing to wait.

He leaned his head over against hers, his eyes closed. "I thought I had time to go back. I just didn't believe the bombs were really coming." He could feel the tears on his cheeks but this time he wasn't embarrassed.

Trying to comfort him she said, "If they had stayed in Dallas they would have been exposed to the tremendous radiation we've registered on the instruments. In Albuquerque, at least it was quick."

She slipped her arms around him and held him tightly in this dark private place, the only signs of his grief, wet tears against her neck.

October 26, 4:20 p.m.

"Hi, Sandi, come on in." Dr. Jim was frowning over a tabletop chemistry analyzer wondering why his results weren't in control. "Damn thing! Wish we had a Med Tech so I could be sure these results are accurate." He glanced up, "It's about time you came to see me young lady. I've been expecting you for two months. I was getting ready to come drag you in. Let's go in here." He indicated an examining room down a short hallway.

He patted an exam table and she perched on the end. "How far along do you think you are?" He asked.

"My last period was mid-July so I guess about three months." She seemed very nervous. Jim thought there was more to this story than a pregnancy. He sat on a stool next to her.

"Have you told Pete?"

"No." She started to cry and he handed her a tissue. "The baby isn't his. I got pregnant by my old boyfriend just after I met Pete. I know when he finds out he won't want anything more to do with me. He's been hanging around with some of the other girls. Please don't say anything to anybody, okay? I need time to decide how to tell him."

Jim had seen the young adults all hanging around together. These were unusual circumstances and people had a need to be together. He didn't think Pete was being overly attentive to these other women and Jim had seen the way Pete looked at Sandi.

"I promise, but I think you need to tell him so you both can decide what to do. I honestly don't think you have anything to worry about. Pete's a very fine young man with his head screwed on straight. I could be wrong, but I think he'll be just fine about it. He cares about you a lot". He stood and fetched a gown, "Here, put this on and I'll check you out."

He went back to his analyzer and got out the manual to see if he could troubleshoot it. Checking the expiration dates of the reagents, he realized that some of them were becoming short-dated. He knew manufacturers made the dates shorter than necessary to be on the safe side, nevertheless, they would be running out of some of materials in a few weeks.

The population of the shelter had been in fairly good shape physically and the overall health status was improving. Most of the overweight residents had lost a few pounds and it was amazing how many people were using the gym. It had become one of the social spots of the shelter, along with the pub, the church and the multipurpose room. Of course, everyone had to give up smoking immediately upon descending into the shelter two months ago. He and Aaron had done physicals on about half of the residents including most of the children and had brought the kids' immunizations up to date. Three of the residents were diabetic, but only one, Jack Iverson, needed insulin. He had come to the shelter with someone else. They had enough insulin for about a year. After that, if they didn't find more supplies or learn how to synthesize it, Jack would be in trouble. Jim often wondered if Will had evaluated the individuals for chronic diseases before sending them devices since there seemed to be so few with chronic problems. A dozen residents had hypertension but since many of them had been overweight they were getting better with diet and exercise.

Vernon Richenour had come to him a month ago and asked him to put out a bulletin telling everyone to come have a physical and insisting that they be tested for infectious diseases, especially HIV. Jim had laughed at him. He made it clear to Vernon that he took his orders from Will Hargraves and he would never force anyone to have testing they didn't want. Vernon had been furious and left Jim's office insisting that he would ensure that it got done. He hadn't been back and was distant whenever they'd met, which was often. With a small population in a confined space individuals ran into each other almost daily.

He went back to the examining room to check on his first pre-natal patient since they'd entered their new home.

October 26, 8:40 p.m.

"What was your alternative, dear?" Mrs. Claret hugged Kevin as she prepared to leave Lori's apartment after babysitting the children, allowing Lori to attend the concert.

"I've asked myself that same question a thousand times." Lori replied. "You kids go play in your room." She patted Kevin's butt as he ran by.

"I honestly don't miss him much. Sometimes I think I should have told him about the device and brought him with us, but life would have been just as miserable as it was before the war. I don't think I could have endured the abuse any longer."

"Was the device sent to you or to him?" Mrs. Claret sat down on the sofa, realizing Lori finally needed to discuss this situation further. She had been reticent to talk about it ever since they'd arrived in the shelter. When she returned to the apartment after spending the evening with Mark, and Kevin had mentioned his daddy, she seemed to need to explain to Faye what had happened that fateful day.

"My father sent it to me. I only received it the morning before it was activated. John never knew about it." Lori had had an emotional day, comforting Mark earlier in the afternoon, as he poured out his feelings in the semi-darkness of the reservoir cave. Then they attended a moving performance by the Cavern String Quartet. She started to cry, finally relieving the tension of the past two months. "Oh Mrs. Claret, you have no concept of how difficult life has been living with someone like him. The worst part was never knowing what kind of mood he would be in, how he would react to what you said or what you did. One minute he would be nice, and the next, he would turn into a veritable monster. I still can't get over the guilty feeling, though, of leaving him to die."

"You didn't do anything to him, dear. Are you responsible for the war?"

"Of course not, but I left him there."

"Precisely. What you did was leave your husband. It sounds to me that you would have done it eventually. It just happened that after you left him there was a nuclear war and I don't see how you can blame yourself for that. I know you feel, that as spouses, it was your responsibility to care for each other, but it sounds to me that he failed in that responsibility long before you did. The device was yours. Your obligation was to your wonderful little ones. None of us knows exactly what the future will bring, dear, but at least they, and you, will now have the opportunity to find out." Lori was sobbing now and Mrs. Claret intuitively knew it was time to leave and let her finish working it out on her own. "You go ahead and cry it out, dear, I'll see you tomorrow. Goodnight."

"Goodnight, Mrs. Claret," Lori managed through her tears.

As Faye walked down the hallway, Karl Dohner stumbled toward her, staggering from one side to the other. As he approached, he became aware of her and swung wide to avoid a physical confrontation, managing a feeble wave in her direction as he looked down at her with his bloodshot eyes. He smelled of sour whiskey and vomit. She considered helping him to his room but reconsidered. After all, there really wasn't much chance of his getting lost. She turned down the corridor leading to her room.

The minute she entered the apartment the smell of vomit assailed her and she immediately realized Karl must have entered the wrong apartment on his way home. Maybe she should have helped him after all. She started to go back out the door when she froze, her eyes resting on a dark shape sitting on the counter across from the bathroom.

"Oh God. No." She murmured aloud, her voice cracking, her stomach lurching at the sight of the bottle of whiskey beckoning her, enticing her. She wanted to flee, tried to force herself to turn and run from that place, from the demon that threatened to drag her back into the hell she had emerged from when nuclear warheads scoured the earth and cleansed her soul. She put her hand on the doorknob, tried to turn it, but her gaze never left the bottle. As if in a trance, she released the knob and took a step toward the bottle, tried to stop, fought the craving, the yearning, but was drawn inexorably forward.

"Maybe I can have just one tiny sip," she murmured hoarsely.

October 27, 7:50 p.m.

"Everybody pays!" Chris yelled, spreading three eights out in front of her.

"Damn!" Mark said, throwing his cards on the table. "I had twenty nine, and was going to knock this round." The other five tables of card players, engrossed with playing their own hands and hoping to win more chips for the final round, ignored them completely. The other players at their table tossed their cards down and Mark gathered them up, his turn to deal.

"I hate to deal," he muttered as he shuffled the cards. "I always lose when I deal." The weekly meeting of the "31" club was an extremely popular social event. It was week four of the five preliminary rounds and Mark had only accumulated four chips. Chris had eleven. This was the first time the random drawing had placed them at the same table and to his embarrassment she was thoroughly kicking his butt.

"So Chris, are we going to have fresh vegetables for the Oktoberfest?" he asked as he dealt, hoping to distract her.

"I think so. This crop is doing better than the previous one and we have some produce from the in-ground planting. The kids have worked really hard."

Faye scheduled special occasions approximately bi-monthly, an excuse to get everyone together for a good time. September was the summer barbeque, although that didn't turn out so well, and October would be the Oktoberfest. Mark knew they were trying to kid themselves to a certain degree with these artificial "good times." Nothing was ever going to be the same but at least they could try to keep their spirits up as they prepared themselves physically and mentally for their return to the real world. "*What was it going to be like?*" he wondered.

A surprising number of residents played musical instruments, two were professional musicians and one had formerly taught music at the high school level. They'd put together a small orchestra that presented concerts weekly and provided music for the play the "Cavern Theatre Group" was putting on.

Herbert Laskey, who'd been involved with his community's performing arts center and also, passably, played the cello in his previous life, conducted the orchestra. At least twenty adults and most of the children were taking lessons. The music room was stocked with huge numbers of clarinets, saxophones, flutes, violins and other stringed instruments, percussion instruments and even electronic keyboards. A grand piano occupied the corner of the stage in the auditorium and could be moved to the center for recitals. Individuals who'd always wanted to play instruments but had been too busy were availing themselves of the opportunity.

Faye had recruited several people to assist her in making costumes and decorations for the upcoming Oktoberfest on the thirtieth for the adults, and on Halloween, the thirty-first for the children. Mark knew one thing for sure, they had plenty of beer.

Chris drew a card from the deck. "Everybody pays!" She threw down an ace, queen and ten of hearts.

"I'm out," Mark said disgustedly. "How can anybody be that lucky?" He tossed his last chip in the general direction of the basket, Bob Crowder catching it in mid-air and directing it into the basket with the rest of the lost chips.

Mark walked through the room weaving his way past the other tables where players were laughing and enjoying the game. People were trying hard to cope but even with the myriad activities designed to keep them occupied and to assist them in retaining their culture, Mark knew they hadn't recovered from the trauma they had lived through. Two months wasn't nearly enough time.

October 28, morning

It was apparent to Lori that Jean's physical condition was considerably improved in just the two months since the survivors had left their old world behind and entered the artificial environment they now inhabited. She no longer labored when using the workout equipment, her breathing was rapid but steady, and her face no longer turned beet red with exertion. Jean wasn't a natural athlete like Chris or Lori, but like the other residents, had been encouraged by Will to get in shape for the day they would abandon the shelter and re-emerge into the light of day, and so she visited the gym daily. Lori glanced around as she pedaled, hoping Mark would arrive for his workout. She knew she couldn't get interested in another man this soon, and she was aware Mark wasn't available but she felt exhilarated when she was around him.

"What were you and Ron arguing about this time?" Chris asked Jean. The three women were side-by-side, lined up on Lifecycles, and pedaling at rates sufficient to keep their heart rates in the training zone. Chris was not one to mince words or shy away from delving into another's personal business.

Jean didn't seem to take offense as these three women spent a lot of time together and had become good friends. "Oh, you know him. He was arrogant enough before we came here, but now that he's been working out with Big Rambo and Little Rambo, learning martial arts, he's insufferable. Thinks he's Mr. Macho."

"Why, what's he doing?" Chris asked.

"He keeps telling me what he thinks I should be doing, what I should learn while we're in here, who I should hang out with, where I should go. I just get tired of him telling me what to do, and that's why we were fighting. He really annoys me."

"Well, it seems to me that he really likes you. Maybe it's just his way."

"I don't think that's possible but let's face it, it's not as though this place is crawling with eligible bachelors. And look who's talking. What's with you and Aaron Brown?" Lori had been barely listening to the girl talk up to now, but her interest was piqued by Jean's question. She wondered what Jean was referring to, considering Mark's relationship with Chris.

"I'm not sure how he feels, but I really like him. He's a little moody but he's gorgeous and we have wonderful conversations. He's been coming around the farm quite often and I don't think it's just the plants he's attracted to."

Lori, who normally listened more than she talked, asked Chris, "What about Mark? I thought you guys were together."

"My Bro? I love Mark. He's my buddy and we've been best of friends forever. That's all. God, it would be like being with a brother. What made you ask that?"

"Oh, I just knew you weren't really siblings and since you've known each other for so long I guess I just assumed."

Chris laughed and the three kept on pedaling.

But Lori wasn't laughing, remembering how Mark had poured his heart out to her and thinking about how hurt he was going to be when he found out that Chris didn't return his love in the same way he loved her.

October 28, afternoon

The usual group was clustered around the radio, heads cocked, hoping for a repeat of the faint sound that penetrated the static for a brief moment. Micah swore it sounded like a frantic human voice. He twiddled dials and, using the computer, tried to clean up the signal. After tense minutes of silence they acknowledged they weren't going to get a repeat. Mark looked up and his eyes met Will's. Will shook his head, "This is much worse than I ever expected. I thought we'd be able to contact others fairly soon after the war. The government shelter has the best equipment possible and it should have been sheltered from the EMP. They should be putting out a very strong signal." He walked over to the monitor wall and examined each transmission looking for a change from the monotonous pictures they had become used to.

"Could they have taken a direct hit that managed to destroy their shelter?" Mark asked.

"Anything is possible. There are other shelters around the country as. . ."

The intercom interrupted him, "Mr. Hargraves? This is Vernon Richenour. I'm with a group of concerned citizens at the door to your tower. We need to meet with you on some important matters."

"Certainly, hang on a minute." Will answered. He hit the mute button by the door. "What the hell does he want?"

Chris said, "I hear he's been complaining ever since we got here. He goes around stirring up trouble."

"Is anyone listening to him?"

Mark shrugged, "I think a few people have been taken in by him. I don't think it's serious."

"What do you know about him Jim?" Will hadn't paid much attention to the social life of the shelter.

"He's annoyed me more than once. He thinks you should be a dictator and tell everyone what to do. He especially wants you to dictate that things should be done the way he wants."

"I'm going to invite him up here so he'll be on my turf. You all can stay. Let's find out what he wants." He hit the mute button again and simultaneously pushed the button that unlocked the door in the hallway below. "Please come up Mr. Richenour."

The elevator door slid aside and Vernon, followed by a woman and three other men entered the elevator. When they arrived at the alcove Vernon was shocked to see the large cabinet labeled "weapons locker" built into the left side of the rock wall.

"Oh my, this is a serious development. Did Hargraves tell any of you about these weapons?" They all shook their heads. "Well, its time he started telling us a lot of things," he huffed. "And I wonder where this other door leads."

The group entered the control room and was disconcerted to find several others in attendance besides Hargraves. In fact, they were outnumbered. Mark liked most of the other residents of the shelter but he had no use for Richenour.

"Come in Richenour." Will acknowledged the others as they introduced themselves. Mark hadn't had much contact with any of them and had never known the woman's name, Rona Jenson.

Will offered her a chair but the others remained standing. They seemed quite interested in the equipment, especially the video screens, and one of them started to ask a question about the pictures. Vernon cut him off, "We came here to discuss some other matters. Hargraves, all the residents of the shelter feel you have been withholding information." He looked to the others for support and two of the men nodded.

"Excuse me, Vernon." Mark couldn't let that go, "you don't represent the residents and from what I've seen, very few of them feel as you do."

"That's not true, I've spoken with many people who would like to know when we can leave."

Will folded his arms and stared directly at Richenour. "You are welcome to leave anytime you want. There's a door in the alcove below here that leads through a series of positive pressure airlocks to the south side of the mountain so when you're ready just let me know and I will personally usher you out."

"Well. . ." He stammered, "I . . . I didn't mean I want to leave. I just want to know when we'll be able to. But there are other concerns. We want to know why some people aren't working, including your own son, and they hang around the bar all day but get as much food as everyone else, and some people are even hoarding food."

Will turned to Chris, "Is this true?"

"The food is placed in the coolers and anyone can help themselves but I haven't noticed anyone taking food they don't eat in a day or two. At this time there's still plenty of frozen and dehydrated foods. Kate has a rationing plan she will put into effect if she feels it's necessary. Fresh foods are at a premium and I had the impression everyone was getting their fair share but perhaps we should invent some kind of coupon to ensure that they do."

"Discuss it with Kate and see what you can come up with." Will told her. He turned back to Richenour. "Any other concerns?"

One of the men tapped Vernon on the shoulder and whispered in his ear. "Oh yes, we also believe all the residents should be made to go to the doctor and be checked out for infectious diseases before he runs out of medicines or testing material. Oh, and another thing Hargraves, I just saw an arms locker down stairs. You never said you had guns here. That rather makes this a police state."

Will laughed, and Mark could tell he was genuinely amused. "In case you've failed to notice, Richenour, this shelter belongs to me and that puts me in charge. The weapons are mine and are intended for use only on the outside when we're able to leave. I don't anticipate having to use them before then but that's my prerogative. If you had brought weapons to the shelter I wouldn't confiscate them, they're yours. On the one hand you accuse me of running a police state and then complain that I'm not forcing the residents to undergo mandatory medical testing. That's contradictory."

Richenour was beginning to squirm as Will's amusement was turning to anger. "I provided this shelter to give a small group of Human's a chance for survival and I really don't give a damn what anyone does now that we're here. Every person in this facility is free to live their life as they see fit. Even though I own the shelter and I have suggested that people prepare for their future, I have no right to tell anyone what to do unless they hurt others, and if I choose to give away the supplies and provisions that's up to me.

"The only real freedom humans have is the right to property and your right to use the fruits of your own labor as you see fit. No one, especially not a government of other individuals should ever have the right to take your property by force. Individuals, however, have every right to form a body, call it what you will, to pay voluntarily to accomplish common goals. If the residents want to invent some form of exchange to place a value on their labor, that's up to them but since they don't have to buy provisions it may be fruitless. If they want to set up a quasi-government to handle other issues that's fine too. Just don't try to impose your will on others."

Will had advanced as he spoke, until he was directly in front of Richenour who took a step backward and cleared his throat before responding. "Well, we certainly will form a committee to address those issues but I… rather, we, must insist that you keep us better informed about your progress in contacting survivors on the outside."

"As soon as we manage to contact anyone," Will said, "you all will be informed. Until then everyone should continue to prepare for life on the outside. Now get out of my control room," He told them, placing the emphasis on "My."

330

October 29, evening

Swigging down a shot of watered down whisky, Karl Dohner gazed with blood shot eyes at his disheveled image in the mirror behind the bar, an image that mocked him, reminding him he still lived... and she was dead. He'd spent several hours a day at the pub since its completion a month ago, drowning the memories that tormented him. Johnny Jay and the other men and women that alternated as bartenders grew tired of Karl's incessant self-flagellation over past sins, real or imagined. Karl never confessed to anyone the real reason he drank himself into a stupor on a daily basis, visions of Kristen Douglas haunting him as he lived over and over again the view from his side-view mirror the day he panicked and drove off without delivering the last of the communication devices. She was young and very beautiful, her beauty increasing each time his tortured mind pictured her standing in her doorway looking at him with a puzzled expression as he drove off with her salvation.

Mark stuck his head in the pub and looked around for Lori. He spotted Karl at the bar and it was immediately apparent he was drunk as his head bobbed low almost hitting his glass. Mark looked at Johnny who just shook his head, came over to Mark, and remarked in a low tone, "He's been like this for weeks. I've even been missing booze and I'm sure he's the one stealing it. Who else would it be?"

Mark took Karl by the arm, "Come on Karl, you need a nap. I'm on my way to the daycare center and I'll drop you off on my way."

Once he'd left Karl in his apartment he went back upstairs in search of Lori. "Hey sport, hold up there." Mark reached out and swept Kevin off his feet as he ran by chasing his sister.

"I'm gonna be a monster for Halloween. Then I'll get her!" Kevin promised.

"Well, she might be something even worse," said Mark. "And she's bigger than you. Maybe you better stick to Trick-or-Treating."

Kevin thought about it for a second. "Well, maybe." He started to wriggle, "Put me down, I gotta get her!"

Mark set him down and Kevin took off, emitting a shriek the instant his feet touched the floor. Mark smiled as Kevin disappeared into the other room of the daycare center in pursuit of his sister.

He had come to know these children pretty well the last few weeks. He'd never been around kids much and didn't know how he'd like it but these children were a complete delight. Of course, it was probably completely different when the total responsibility for their care was on you.

He and Chris had never discussed children and he didn't even know if she liked kids. He realized there were many things he didn't know about her even after knowing her almost all his life. When they were together it seemed as if someone else was always there or, if they were alone, they just made small talk. Much of the time Chris was engrossed in her work with Sam or Aaron and he ended up spending his time with others. He suddenly realized how much time he was spending with Lori, that he talked more with her, and about more serious matters, than he ever did with Chris. He knew he was lucky to have as good a friend as Lori.

Mark went over to the bench along the wall and plopped down beside Lori. "Does he ever run down?"

"Not often." She leaned back against the wall. "Sometimes it can be exhausting. I don't know what I'd do without Faye Claret's babysitting service."

"Why don't you leave them here and we'll get some dinner?"

"Sure, I'm famished. I forgot to eat lunch."

"How come?"

"There's been a steady stream of instructors speaking with the kids lately. I do a lot of conventional teaching, of course, the kids still need to learn to read and write. But we're spending more time teaching them skills." They walked down the hallway to the cafeteria.

"What kind of skills?"

"Even the little ones are learning to make things, how to use tools, and are learning how things work. Dr. Whitehorse tells them how his people survived all these years, how they lived off the land, farmed, and raised animals. He's also teaching them geology, so they know how we use the things that come from the earth."

They selected frozen dinners and popped them into the microwave. Occasionally the refrigerators had some fresh vegetables but there weren't any today.

"Steffie Childress is teaching them all, including the boys, to sew using natural materials. They're all learning how to create clothes without the fabrics we take for granted every day. We've also had lessons in plumbing and carpentry."

"We?"

"Yeah, it's unbelievable how little I know about how things work or how to accomplish simple tasks. I'm learning as much as the kids." They took their meals to a table and began to eat.

"I know what you mean. In our modern world, we don't need to know how things work. If something breaks we call a repairman, or we buy a new one, or hire someone when something needs to be done."

In her former life Lori had never used frozen dinners, it wasn't allowed. She scowled at the barely recognizable food in front of her, poking it with her fork. "I wonder how much more food there is. Has Mr. Hargraves told you?" she asked.

"We're having some problems growing fresh food but I know there's a huge store of frozen foods. There's also nitrogen packed food if everything else runs out. I don't know how long it will last. We should have some more fresh meat before long, too. Some of the pigs are almost big enough to slaughter. Mrs. Claret is planning a thanksgiving feast and we should have fresh vegetables and meat for that. I like that they're supplementing the meals we're eating with some of the dehydrated foods so the good stuff will last longer."

"It's kind of scary, really. If we can't increase our food stores we may have to leave before it's safe. I don't know what I would do."

He reached over and touched her arm. "I don't think we need to worry about that and no matter what, I hope we'd all stick together." He knew she was worried about the children. "Lori, Kevin asked me why his Daddy isn't here. He said Daddy wasn't home when you left. Now, I know it's not polite to ask about former friends and family but do you want to tell me what happened?"

She wasn't quite finished with her meal but she dropped her fork. "No Mark, please, I don't think I want to talk about it." She abruptly stood and left the table.

He didn't try to follow her. He watched her go and was sorry he'd brought it up. Dropping the trash into the container by the door he dejectedly headed for home.

334

SEVEN

November 21

Halloween had come and gone and Thanksgiving was fast approaching. The remnant, as they now referred to themselves, had settled into a routine of working, learning, playing and coping. Vernon Richenour continued to complain about almost everything, but no one listened seriously to his chronic bitching after Harry Jackson reported the gist of the conversation with Will Hargraves. There was some minor concern about the weapon's locker, but the survivors trusted William Hargraves with their lives, indeed, had trusted him with their lives, and it was apparent to everyone they all would have perished, either from the nuclear blasts or the radiation, if not for him.

Thanksgiving dinner was much anticipated by the residents. The menu had been planned by Rana Patel to include turkey, dressing, yams, mashed potatoes and gravy, and fresh greens. Chris had timed a harvest perfectly, and the turkeys had matured just in time for the holiday.

The remnant was beginning to pull together into a cohesive unit after the first three months underground, but not as completely as Mark would have liked. The divisions, though, were along natural lines, with age, interests and functions dictating whom people associated with. The younger residents hung out together, spending a lot of time in the multipurpose room listening to music and talking about the things teens have always talked about, and there was the cadre of leaders that Mark spent much of his time with.

Unfortunately, a small minority of the residents didn't participate in the educational efforts of the population and failed to contribute in any meaningful way to their welfare. Mark was chagrined to discover that one of these deadbeats was Clay. He knew Will was embarrassed by Clay's behavior and he tried to suggest ways for Clay to become involved in the life of the shelter. He mentioned to Clay that he might conduct fitness classes or work in one of the machine shops but, as usual, Clay resented anything Mark suggested and refused to cooperate. He hung with his buddies at the pub or in the multipurpose room.

Mark walked through the gym into the dojo and suited up for a workout. As usual, Lori was already there. She spent a great deal of time training, had already earned her blue belt and was becoming quite skilled. Their friendship had grown and Mark found himself spending much more time with Lori than he did with Chris. It surprised him, considering his love for Chris.

He joined Lori in the workout line and they began with stretching. "Are the kids excited about Christmas?" he asked her.

"They're very excited. They're making gifts in school and practicing for the Christmas pageant the teenaged girls are putting on. Candy's organizing it." She took hold of his ankles for sit-ups. "I'm more excited, though, about the upcoming wedding. Did you hear that Jean and Ron are getting married?"

"You're kidding!" He paused in his sit-ups. "They're always arguing."

"Yes, but it's mostly good natured. I think it's super." She released his ankles as he started to sit up again and he fell over backwards.

"Hey, don't let go!" he laughed.

"Well, don't stop in the middle of your workout then." She reached for his ankles again but he seized her, pulled her onto him and they wrestled good-naturedly. She sprang to her feet, took on a fighting stance and he accepted her challenge. They circled warily and before he could respond she slipped under his guard, grabbed his gi and quickly flipped him onto his back, completely amazing him with her quickness and power. It was obvious she'd pulled up at the last minute, throwing him much more gently than she could have.

"Wow, that was great!" he told her as he climbed to his feet and the others in the room applauded enthusiastically.

"Come on folks," David scolded, "more fun later. Keep your discipline and go through your katas. After that, Mark, you can have another shot at her."

"I'm not sure I want one." He grinned at Lori and she looked directly at him, smiling back.

During the warm ups and katas Mark thought about their experiences in the shelter to date and admitted things seemed to be going pretty well. People were learning things they would need on the outside, they were safe and fairly comfortable and there really hadn't been any serious problems. He had no idea how quickly things could deteriorate.

December 4

Arby screamed through gritted teeth, his insides tortured as if something were attempting to break out through his flesh, like the creature in Alien that devoured its way through the astronaut's chest. Burning up and soaked with perspiration, he tossed back and forth on the bed. He was delirious, hallucinating about a long, burning tunnel, and running through a cave, crashing off walls as though trying to escape the bowels of Hell, pursued by his own demons while pursuing, in turn, something hateful. Pain shot through his shoulders, hips and joints as his body underwent the first "growing pains" since he'd been an adolescent. He felt pain orders of magnitude worse than that experienced by individuals with the most painful forms of rheumatoid arthritis. He screamed again and heard it answered from the room on the other side of the wall.

Arby was growing and changing. He'd noticed with horror his fingers lengthening, the knuckles growing thick, the backs of his hands becoming coated with thick, coarse hair. He almost didn't recognize his own image in the mirror, his face coarser, heavier, more animal-like. His clothing no longer fit him and he had stripped to his underwear, as had the others as they too devolved into an evolutionary precursor of human beings.

And the radiation continued to assault them.

One of the men died during this transformation. He'd been a murderer but felt remorse for his heinous crime, twice trying to take his own life while in prison. Unlike the others, he wasn't a personification of pure evil. Their malevolent nature kept them alive as the radiation tortured them, assaulted their DNA and changed them into creatures that surely had ascended from the hell Arby saw in his never-ending nightmare. The previously unimaginable effects of Red Mercury were apparent in these hapless creatures, mutation proceeding at a heretofore unknown pace. Mutation and devolution without death.

They now numbered a dozen.

December 13

Faye Claret clutched her abdomen and doubled over in pain. She groaned softly as she stumbled from her bathroom, where her mirror had reflected a pale and wane visage, down the short hallway to collapse onto her bed. Perspiration beaded her brow and she gasped, so short of breath she almost passed out. This was the third attack in as many days and having been vomiting bright red blood she was beginning to think the problem was serious. She didn't have time to be sick, she reasoned, having a responsibility to the remnant as self-appointed morale officer to ensure all holidays were suitably recognized. She was planning a Christmas celebration to lift everyone's spirits and worried that if she went to see Dr. Jim he might incarcerate her and she wouldn't get the party planned. Still, the pain was worse than it had ever been, even worse than her last visit to the emergency room. She didn't want to acknowledge that resuming her alcohol consumption had plunged her back into a medical crisis.

She thrashed from side to side, trying to find a comfortable position and suddenly found she couldn't move at all without tremendous pain. A sharp intake of breath and then a scream escaped her lips as white-hot pain stabbed through her gut. She struggled to get up, but discovered she was unable to rise from the bed. She was beginning to panic, which only increased her difficulty in breathing. With a great effort she rolled from the bed to her knees and crawled into the living area, unable even to reach her feet. She grasped the doorknob and, using all her strength, jerked the door open and crawled into the hallway.

***

Chris stood in her characteristic pose, hands on hips, staring at the pathetic crop before her. The overhead lights had been changed again and it didn't seem to improve the yield. They had harvested the "C" crop for the Thanksgiving dinner and after the feast the remainder had lasted only two weeks. At this rate they would fall behind approximately one day every three weeks, until five months from now they would completely exhaust their supply of fresh food. Possibly, it could be stretched with rationing, and by supplementing their diets with the emergency stores of dehydrated food, but Chris didn't want to utilize their emergency supplies unless it was absolutely necessary.

The tomato plants in the hydroponics section were actually doing slightly better and she gained some encouragement from that. She saw Samuel two rows over picking dead leaves off shoots that climbed up the wire supports, babying the crops, pruning and feeding, and trying to maintain the highest yield possible.

The doors swooshed open and Aaron entered, a smile lighting his face as he spotted her. He waved and started in her direction when the intercom came on, halting him in his tracks.

"Aaron Brown, please report to the infirmary 'stat'." The intercom seemed louder than usual.

"Aaron, what's going on?" Chris asked, trotting over as he reversed direction and quickly headed back the way he had come.

"I don't know. We don't have any in-patients." He grabbed her hand as they ran down the corridor and took the stairs two at a time, retracing the path he took the very first time he ventured forth from the infirmary and met Chris.

They reached the top floor, rounded the corner and encountered a large crowd outside the infirmary.

"What's going on?" he asked.

"Mrs. Claret's real sick." he was told.

The crowd parted to allow him and Chris access to the infirmary. Jim was examining Faye in the next room and Mark and Jerry Thompson were waiting outside the examining room door. They had been going in opposite directions outside her room when she crawled out directly in front of them. Mark had sprinted to the infirmary to retrieve a gurney while a panicked Jerry Thompson tried to comfort Faye.

Chris remained outside with the others while Aaron hurried in.

"What's wrong with her?" she asked Mark.

"I haven't a clue. We found her outside her door. She's in tremendous pain." He felt completely helpless.

They'd waited only a few minutes when Aaron came out, "We think she has a GI bleed and she needs immediate surgery. Mark, grab the gurney in the other room. Has anyone seen Nurse Diaz?" No one had. She hadn't answered her page.

They filed into the room, maneuvering the gurney alongside the exam table. Faye was moaning softly, her eyes glazed over with pain. It took four of them to transfer her to the gurney and Aaron wheeled his patient into the small operating suite.

He was extremely nervous. In his entire career he had never performed this type of surgery as primary surgeon. Dr. Jim would assist him but he wasn't a surgeon and Aaron had performed almost no surgeries for almost four months, the most complicated being when Paul Frazier cracked his head open and needed sutures. "Damn, where's Carmen?" he asked Jim.

"I don't know. We'll have to get started without her." He was getting out supplies, a sterile wrapped pack of instruments, medications and antiseptics. The anesthesiology machine was ready. Jim had used this particular machine before and despite Faye having lapsed into unconsciousness he would use it to keep control of her vital functions. Having had little else to do prior to this emergency, both doctors and Nurse Diaz had kept the instruments well maintained and they had all practiced with the various pieces of equipment.

Just as they were prepping the patient Nurse Diaz hurried through the door. "I'm sorry," she explained, "I was taking a nap and didn't hear the page."

She quickly took over the prep so Jim and Aaron could scrub.

"Carmen, please get the two units of O neg from the blood bank and have Mark check with the residents to see if anyone knows they are O neg besides the two who donated those units."

She hurried out and gave Mark instructions. He used the intercom to put out a call for donors. If they needed more units they would have to settle for O positive and hope she wasn't Rh negative with antibodies to the D antigen. They had no typing sera to type Mrs. Claret's blood.

Freddie Hernandez appeared in the doorway, looking scared and inquiring about Faye's condition.

"She's in a lot of pain." Mark told him. "They think she's bleeding internally."

"She's been drinking, I know it." Freddie said. "When I met her she was just out of the hospital for a drinking problem. I hoped she was better. I don't know what my blood type is but they can have it." There were tears in his eyes.

Mark was pacing the floor of the room outside the surgical suite. The time seemed interminable. He felt responsible for the remnant, their lives, their futures and many of the residents looked to him for leadership even though he had never asked for any authority. Will simply wasn't very involved in the everyday life of the shelter. He spent most of his time in the control room, which they now referred to as the Crow's Nest, or in his room. Mark was much more accessible.

He looked at his watch but only thirty minutes had passed. Lori came into the room and came over to take his hand. She didn't say a word. Mark thought about what Freddie had said and about Johnny Jay telling him that someone had been stealing liquor. It could have been Faye. No one locked up anything and the bar was untended much of the time.

The door opened and the small group knew immediately that something had gone horribly wrong. Aaron looked stricken, his brown face ashen and tears welling in his dark eyes. "I...I couldn't save her. She's gone. I'm so sorry."

Chris went to him and he hugged her. Mark felt a slight pang of jealousy but dismissed it quickly, laying his hand on Aaron's shoulder. He could see into the room beyond Aaron. So much blood! He saw Jim strip off gloves and lean heavily against the side of the operating table looking down at Faye. They had sewn her up out of respect for the patient and the non-professional people that would have to deal with the body. There were no mortuary workers here.

Jim came to the door. "Chris, take Aaron home. Carmen and I will take care of this. Go on. Aaron, you did a good job. There was nothing you could do."

He told Mark, "She had old ulcers and esophageal varices. She was bleeding from everywhere. She never told us but I suspect she had a severe drinking problem before coming here and there was evidence of a previous surgery. She had to have been drinking although I've never seen her."

Freddie left the room quickly, having heard all he needed to hear.

"Is there anything I can do to help?" Mark asked.

"You can make an announcement. Let everyone know. Thanks."

Mark knew he was the logical person to do it, it was his responsibility, but it was the last thing he wanted to do at this moment. Judging from the look on Jerry's face, Lori's tears, and Freddie's reaction, he knew everyone would take the news hard. Faye was unquestionably the most popular person in their sequestered world. Aaron and Chris had gone out through the exam room so Mark, considering his comments carefully, opened the door, glanced down at Lori and walked out into the hallway to make the announcement.

December 14

This was the second funeral held in this cavern. In contrast to the first, however, the huge crowd of people threatened to precipitate live persons into the chasm. Faye's body was wrapped in a linen shroud and was lying in the same canvas sling they used for Old Pierson. A prayer was said and several people wanted to say something about how Faye had affected their lives. Lori gave a moving, heartfelt eulogy but no one could imagine the true extent of the impact Faye had had on her. Freddie talked about his friendship with this special woman.

Will was here, and Helen and Ernest. Helen and Faye had become friends during the almost four months they had been in the shelter.

Aaron and Chris stood toward the back of the crowd. Aaron was still tortured about the loss, and telling Chris he would be right back he approached Will with a question. "Why me Mr. Hargraves? Why did you send me the box? There were so many doctors with more training and experience."

"I invited several physicians," Will told him quietly. "They included experienced internists and surgeons. I had hoped that you would finish your surgical training under them, while learning primitive medicine from the homeopathic doctor I invited that was so close... she lived in Taos. You're young and had very good references. And I knew your father. He and I were in basic training together in the Air Force. He was a fine man."

Aaron looked shocked at this, as a vision of his Dad came to mind.

"Aaron, I'm so sorry you have been put in this position, that none of the others made it. But you need to suck it up and learn as much as you can from Jim. Faye had apparently been sick a long time. No one could have saved her even in a modern, well-equipped hospital. We need your skills." He turned back to the funeral as Aaron moved back through the crowd to where Chris waited for him.

Mark and two others jumped across the narrow end of the crevasse to the other side. He was puzzled; it seemed slightly wider than it was when they were previously here for Old Pierson's funeral. That time they had easily stepped across.

The caves were part of a cavern system that extended from the southern end of the Rockies down into the Los Alamos area. The caverns lacked the beauty and the larger open caverns that were found at Carlsbad. Nevertheless, the cave system had made the excavation of the shelter measurably easier and had provided the remnant with this unlikely burial chamber.

The service ended, and after the crowd had left the cave, six men, three on either side of the chasm, lowered the body into the abyss to the end of the ropes. As they pulled the release, the weight on the bearing ropes ceased and Faye Claret was laid to rest, 11 days before Christmas.

January 5

It was one o'clock in the morning and the two people sitting by the waterfall in the farm cave conversed in low tones, although they thought nobody else was around to hear them. Three weeks had passed and Aaron was still tortured over Faye Claret's death. He knew there was nothing he could have done but he was painfully aware his surgical skills had greatly diminished during their four months underground.

Mark Teller stood in the shadows behind a row of hydroponics boxes. He and Chris had worked out together at the gym and she had finished her workout before him, leaving to go home and shower. He had entered the cave looking for her, when he suddenly realized she wasn't alone, and now he stood immobile not wanting to interrupt but not quite knowing how to make an unobtrusive exit.

"The main problem, besides the fact that I was unable to finish my medical education, is that we don't do any surgeries here. How do you keep current with your knowledge and skills if you don't use them?"

"You're still thinking of medicine in terms of your high-tech modern style of practicing. You need to lower your expectations, learn simpler, more primitive techniques."

"But we have a lot of good equipment here. We have to take advantage of it and try to maintain our skills for the future."

"That may be true for now, but we won't be in the shelter forever. When we get out of here you'll have to learn a whole new style of medicine, maybe even returning to the hands on medicine of many years ago. You may have to think more along the lines of internal medicine, rather than surgery, for treating your patients. I mean, what kind of conditions do you think we'll find out there?" She asked him.

"I have no idea. Are we supposed to return to our former lives and hope civilization has somehow survived? I suspect that very little of the infrastructure is still standing. How does a modern man, a doctor, react to having to step back in time? I don't know if I can do that."

"Maybe it's only the major cities that have been destroyed. I'm hoping that rural areas were spared. There could be a large number of small towns and cities with houses, schools, even hospitals still standing. Once the radiation has deteriorated we may be able to find a suitable place to live." She said

"You know what? In the entire time we've been here, I haven't even thought about what we'll do after we leave here. I guess I just didn't want to think about it. Do you think there will be people alive to start over with?"

"God, I hope so. If they were protected from the radiation, there should be many survivors including other doctors who can help you reestablish a medical community and raise the level of care."

"That's probably true. Others may not be in as good a condition as we are. We've been fortunate to be sheltered from the effects of the radiation."

"And we've been well nourished and even exercised ourselves into pretty good shape. We just need to persevere until the conditions are right for us to leave and then we'll see what awaits us out there. We'll just have to do our best."

"I'm not so sure how good our best will be." He said.

"Come on Aaron, you and Jim have taken excellent care of everyone. What happened to Mrs. Claret wasn't your fault."

He turned to her, anxious for her to understand, "Chris, I'm scared. I don't know if I should be a doctor here, be responsible for the health of these people when I don't have the skills."

"Please don't start questioning your abilities or your worth to the remnant. You just need to approach it from a different perspective, learn old fashioned methods."

"Yeah, just call me Marcus Welby."

She put her hand on his cheek. "You're not going to be able to save every person in every situation, but we need you." She paused. "I need you."

He looked at her blankly, and what she said finally penetrated. He leaned over and kissed her, and they moved farther back into the shadows.

Mark stood for another minute; his heart breaking as he finally realized that Chris and Aaron were about to become lovers. Gaining control of his emotions enough to escape, he quickly took the opportunity while the other two were preoccupied.

January 23, 2:20 p.m.

      "Turn on the flashlight you dork!" Garrett chided him. The door closed before Jeremy could turn the light on and they were plunged into darkness. He heard the other children suck in their breath as he fumbled nervously with the switch and finally clicked it on. A circle of light spread out into the cave and illuminated the nearer wall on the left.

      "Gimme the light, Jeremy." Garrett grabbed the flashlight from him and moved further into the cave, urging the younger children to follow. "Come on you guys, you chicken?" They followed him to avoid being left in the dark. Jeremy marveled at the natural strata of the rock, ancient rough limestone, never worn by water in this underground cavern. He wished that Dr. Whitehorse were here to tell him about the rocks. He had listened with rapt attention to all of the lectures about the geography of their home. To the right of the door behind them, boxes were stacked three or four high and stretched beyond the light's range. They were in one of the many storage areas in the shelter that had been left in their natural state except for a door installed to allow access.

      The children were both frightened and excited by the prospect of exploring these areas. Garrett had been bugging Jeremy and the other kids for two months before he convinced them to go with him. Besides Jeremy, Ashley and Kevin Arnaud, Tucker's little brother Sean Price, Darian Spears and Kelley Barkley had taken the challenge. They agreed to go when Jeremy's Uncle Pete gave him a flashlight for Christmas. Armed with the light they decided to try the door in the back of the animal cave since it was the most remote. They sneaked through the farm and animal caves undetected and rushed through the door before anyone discovered them. There was a light switch next to the door but they left it off, fearing the crow's nest would monitor it and find out they were beyond the boundary. They were unaware that the light on Micah's panel had blinked red momentarily and returned to green when the door closed but no one had noticed. Besides, the overhead light would only illuminate this immediate room and they wanted to go farther into the labyrinth. Garrett took out a marker pen and removed the cap. He made a small arrow on the wall where a tunnel led off to the left. "If we get separated, follow the arrows back to the door," he told the others.

"Wha... what do you mean. We're going to stay together aren't we?" asked Darian. "You said we would go together." Darian was ten years old, two years younger than Garrett, but a full head smaller. His mother hadn't encouraged independence in him and he hung back as though he would bolt for the door with the slightest provocation.

"It's just in case. We don't wanna get lost. We'd be in big trouble." He went around the corner into the tunnel and the others followed closely. The ceiling of the passageway hung low over their heads, varying in height as they progressed. In places they were forced to stoop or to squeeze through narrow passages to continue forward.

Each time they approached a side tunnel Garrett made an arrow on the wall. Jeremy figured Garrett was the one that would be punished if anyone found out what they were doing. He was the oldest.

This part of the shelter was far to the rear of the entrance. As they went farther into the cave Jeremy could feel a tiny vibration from the water in the penstocks that fed the power plant turbines. Kelley tripped and fell against Garrett causing him to drop the light and little Kevin, who clung tightly to Ashley, started to whimper. "I wanna go back."

"Don't be a baby," Garrett told him as he retrieved the light. "Watch where you're going, Kelley." He swung the light around to see what tripped her. There was a pile of rocks and dirt that appeared to have fallen from the ceiling. He swung the light around and noticed several other areas where debris had fallen from the ceiling or the sidewalls of the tunnel. One of the small side tunnels had caved in almost entirely. They heard a rumbling sound behind them and swung around just as some more rocks fell from the ceiling, several of them hitting Kelley.

"Let's get outta here!" yelled Darian. "This place is falling apart. Come on, Garrett, I don't wanna stay here. We've seen enough."

Jeremy didn't want to appear scared but he was worried that the tunnel behind them would cave in. "Come on Garrett, let's go back aways and take another tunnel. This one's boring anyway." Garrett smirked at him but he pushed through the others and started back.

They had retraced their steps approximately half way when a large section of the tunnel wall suddenly gave way. Garrett was thrown forward by the rocks hitting him in the back and the flashlight smashed against the side of the tunnel. Plunged into darkness, the other children panicked and screamed. The tunnel filled with choking dust. Darian was more directly in the path of the rockslide and was partially buried with only his left arm and head uncovered. He had been pushed to the left side of the tunnel and a larger rock that had fallen directly in front of him had kept the others from crushing him completely. Panting and barely able to breathe, he began to whimper softly, being unable to cry for lack of air. Ashley and Kevin, following behind had escaped injury but were sitting on the ground holding each other and crying in shear terror.

Jeremy climbed to his feet with his hand against the wall to get his bearings. He heard Darian wheezing just behind him and went to his knees. "Darian, can you hear me? It'll be alright." He felt for Darian, and feeling his arm sticking out of the debris he realized how completely he was buried.

"Garrett," he called out, "Darian's buried in the rocks. I think he's hurt!"

Garrett bumped into Jeremy in the dark, "Darian, don't worry, I'll get help. Hang on, okay? I'll be back. Hey you guys!" He tried to quiet the other children. "I'm going to get help. Everybody just stay here and I'll be right back." He felt for the wall and slowly crept through the dust and the darkness toward rescue.

Jeremy heard him shuffle down the tunnel and he heard Darian's strained breathing. He started shoving the rocks aside, to the other side of the tunnel. The other children had stopped crying and Jeremy sensed another person along side of him in the dark, helping to clear the rocks.

"Don't get too close to him." The other child was Sean Price. "We might cause the rocks to crunch him." They passed the rocks to Kelley, Ashley and Kevin and they in turn pushed them toward the rear of the tunnel. When they had cleared the lighter rocks Jeremy inched toward Darian.

"Darian? If the rocks move or it hurts you, tell me, okay?"

Darian moaned softly. Jeremy took it as a yes and very carefully began to move some of the dirt clods and rocks covering the boy.

They worked in the dark for an eternity, until they had cleared all but the larger stones around Darian. Jeremy was afraid to try and move them fearing the others would shift and crush him. Darian's breathing seemed a little easier so they decided to leave the others alone and wait for help. Occasionally there was the sound of minor cave-ins mixed with the sounds of children whimpering in the dark. This would cause new anxiety but the utter darkness had created a dreamlike atmosphere and they sat in the passageway hoping that Garrett could find his way in the dark.

January 23, 3:00 p.m.

"Come on Sandi, you could be a little friendlier. I just want to talk to you." Clay followed Sandi into one of the tunnels that dead-ended in a dragon door. She had left the multi-purpose room heading for the machine shop, looking for Pete to tell him she had won the dart tournament. When she left the stairwell on the third floor she noticed Clay following her. Slightly unsettled, she'd turned into the side corridor and stopped against the dragon door.

"I'm sorry Clay, I didn't see you. I'm kind of busy. Could we talk later?" She started to walk past him to regain the main corridor but he took her arm, "No, I'd like to talk to you now. You've been avoiding me for weeks."

Clay put his hands on the wall on either side of Sandi's shoulders.

"You know what? I'm getting tired of you ignoring me. Do you think you're better than me or my friends?"

She tried to duck under his arm but he pressed his body against her. That's when, feeling his hardness, she realized this was becoming a serious problem.

"Clay, I like everyone living here but I'm involved with someone. Let me go, okay?" She put her hands on his chest and pushed gently at first but more insistently when he didn't budge.

Her resistance seemed to excite him. He reached over with his left hand and slapped the button that opened the dragon door behind her. She stumbled as the door slid aside and Clay reached out, grabbed her arm, and pulled her to him as he forced her through the open door into the dimly lit cave.

"You're going to get in trouble. You can't just push people around."

"I can do anything I want. My dad owns this place, remember? Besides who's going to stop me? Your Petey boy?"

She tried to shrug off his hand but he had an iron grip that hurt when she tried to pull loose.

She was losing her temper. "Get off me! You're hurting me Clay! You don't seem to understand. I want nothing to do with you. Now, let go of me." Her voice was rising as she became angry and more than a little frightened. She found it hard to believe he would actually assault her.

The lightweight, cotton clothing they wore in the shelter ripped easily as Clay tore open the front of the blouse and began to grope her. Definitely scared now she pleaded, "Clay, please. Leave me alone, please don't do this, I'm pregnant."

He paused, "No wonder the little bitch is getting heavy. I thought you were just getting fat. Well, Petey boy's been busy, the little prick." He put his foot behind her and tripped her landing half on top when she fell heavily to the ground.

She struggled futilely, his weight pinning her down and both her wrists held above her head in his one hand, while he jerked her shorts down with the other.

"Clay, stop it! Somebody help me!" But she knew no one could hear her. With a final effort she tried to roll him off her, bringing her knee up in an attempt to catch him off guard, but he was far too strong.

As her shorts were jerked down around her knees she tried again to convince him to stop, struggling, she began to cry, her voice becoming hysterical, "I'll tell them you did this, they'll believe me. You'll be punished."

He pushed the shorts to her ankles and slid over her forcing her knees apart. "No, you got it wrong. I'm gonna do you, and no one will even believe it happened, you little slut, with you being pregnant and all. According to several of my friends I'm at the pub right this minute. There isn't any DNA testing in this place."

She screamed at him, struggling to throw him off, felt him slip his shorts down, felt him about to enter, when suddenly his weight was completely gone. Instinctively she pulled her shorts up as she heard a furious, booming voice, "God damn you, you fucking son of a bitch!"

She scooted back against the wall clutching the edges of her torn shirt together. She couldn't believe her eyes when she saw Walter Thompson heave Clay heavily against the wall. Clay pumped iron every day and was extremely well muscled but the blow against the wall disabled him and he was no match for the raging man Sandi previously thought was the gentlest person she'd ever known. She had never even heard him swear.

"You fucking asshole, think you can get away with anything you want?" He backhanded Clay full across the mouth sending him flying back into the wall. Clay fell forward to his knees, barely conscious, and Walter hit him again. "Think you're a big man, do you? If that little girl's hurt I'll personally kill you, after I rip your cock off!"

"Mr. Thompson, please stop! If you hurt him you'll be the one to get in trouble. Please don't." She came to his side and grasped his arm.

She was worried about Walter after Clay slumped to the floor unconscious. Walter was starting to kick him, fury in his eyes, when her tugging at his arm caused him to regain control. He turned and gathered her into a bear hug. "It's okay honey. He's the one in serious trouble. If you hadn't yelled at me just then I would've killed him right here and now." He let her go. "I was getting supplies from farther back in the cave and heard the noise." He held her at arm's length. "I heard Clay say you were pregnant. Is it true?"

She leaned against him, nodding her head. "These baggy shirts hide it well."

"Let's get you to the doctor then. He could have hurt you."

They entered the hallway where there was an intercom terminal on the wall. Walter pushed the button and it patched him in to the crow's nest.

"This is Walter Thompson. Send a medical team and some security folks to the dragon cave by the machine shop. The one on the other side from the farm."

"Uh, Mr. Thompson?" came the reply. "I don't think we have any security people but I'll notify the infirmary."

"Call Mark or Will then, but tell them to bring two or three big guys. I need them to keep me from committing murder." He smiled at Sandi and she smiled back, the first time he had seen her smile in a long time.

January 23, 3:20 p.m.

Mark watched Terry Berkowitz pipetting various liquids into test tubes as he worked on synthesizing one of the drugs needed by the residents. Terry, a biochemist and a registered pharmacist had been working for Pfizer, a pharmaceutical company, when his device had gone off. He wasted no time leaving for the shelter and brought his wife, two daughters and son with him.

Since their arrival he'd diligently studied everything he could get his hands on to try and learn to make simple drugs. Unfortunately, they didn't have the equipment or supplies to do anything complicated. Many modern drugs were made using complex manufacturing techniques or even biological methods that utilized genetically altered bacteria, things the shelter lacked. On the other end of the spectrum, he couldn't use old-fashioned methods since they usually made use of natural plants that weren't available to him either! He referred to himself as the apothecary and joked that he was practicing pharmacy, circa 1910.

Mark found he had an interest in Terry's work and helped out every morning. Not much use in the shelter for an old pilot he reasoned.

"How's our supply of prepackaged drugs holding out?" Mark asked Terry.

"We'll be okay for a while." Terry said. "Someone did a pretty good job of selecting the antibiotics and other drugs with longer outdates. Fortunately we haven't had a big need for most of our formulary. We have one person taking insulin and when it's gone he'll have to start on the oral glycemics and really watch his diet. Once they're gone, he's in trouble."

"Is there anything we can synthesize?"

"When we leave here I should be able to use plants to synthesize some of the drugs we'll need. Didn't you read *Clan of the Cave Bear*?" Terry said everything with an absolutely straight face and Mark never knew when he was kidding.

The intercom crackled and announced, "Mark Teller, are you out there?"

"Yeah, what's up?" he yelled back. He always yelled even though the intercom had a very good pick-up.

"Report to the dragon door by the machine shop. Walter says it's a security thing and to bring some big guys. I don't have any details but he sounded pretty upset."

"I'm on my way." He turned to Terry, "Sorry, can you take over here?"

"Are you kidding? Micah said to bring along some big guys. I'm going with." Terry was all of 5' 8".

The machine shop was across the hall from the chem lab. Mark stuck his head inside, recruited some big guys and went around the corner into the next hall. The dragon door was off the corridor in a dead-end side tunnel. Turning into the side hall he spotted Walter Thompson and Sandi Baker, Sandi holding the front of her shirt together where it appeared to be torn.

Walter said, "Glad to see you Mark. Can one of these guys escort Sandi to the infirmary? I couldn't leave, I have a rat cornered in the cave."

"What's the trouble?" Mark motioned to one of the men and he led Sandi away.

"We've got an attempted rape here." Before Mark could hit the button on the door Walter took his arm. "Mark, hold on. The guy is Clay Hargraves."

Terry asked, "You said attempted. How do you know he was going to rape her?"

"The son of a bitch ripped her clothes off, was on top of her and was getting his dick out, that's how I know!" Walter said angrily. "I was in the back of the cave. The bastard didn't know I was there. I heard him tell her he was going to do it."

"Oh Jesus," Mark said. "This is going to kill Will. Come on."

He hit the button.

***

The two biggest guys, David Cunningham and Tom Galloway hustled Clay along the hallway almost lifting his feet off the floor. He initially resisted but realized they were totally pissed off, and unless he wanted to get seriously injured, he'd better cooperate. Walter had messed him up pretty good, his left cheek and eye were bruised and swollen, and a good sized goose bump was rising through the hair and blood on the back of his head.

"You guys need to get me to the doctor. I could have a concussion," he told them.

"Shut up or you'll have more than that," Walter said.

"We are taking you to the doctor," Mark told him. "We'll page your father from there and see…"

They had almost reached the stairwell when the door burst open and Aaron, along with several others, all carrying flashlights, barreled out and turned toward the farm cave. Two of the men carried stretchers.

"Whoa, what's up?" Mark yelled at Aaron.

"There's been a cave-in. Some of the kids may be hurt. Come on."

Mark instructed the men holding Clay to take him to the infirmary and then to his quarters. "We'll deal with him later. There's no place for him to go." He ran off after the other group.

Garrett told them which cave the children were in and Aaron insisted someone take the boy to Dr. Jim rather than allow him to accompany them. He was scratched and bleeding although it didn't look serious.

They ran through the caves and passed through the door Aaron indicated. Mark flipped the light on.

"Garrett said to follow the arrows," Aaron said, his flashlight shining ahead of him as he turned left and slowed down to enter the tunnel. The air was filled with thick dust making it difficult to see ahead.

They hadn't gone far when it became hard to climb over the debris. Mark was disturbed at the extent of the cave-ins, remembering the rock falls in the reservoir and power caves he'd seen recently during his runs. He thought he'd felt minor tremors but assumed they were vibrations from the power plant.

They became aware of soft crying up ahead and soon came upon the children; the lights showing filthy tear streaked faces. The rescuers carefully approached Darian to avoid causing shifting of the rocks. Mark slid by to check out the other children, all of whom were in the tunnel beyond Darian with the exception of Jeremy and Sean. None of them appeared to be seriously injured so he handed each of them to men standing beyond Darian. Ashley, the last one, held tightly to his neck not wanting to let him go.

"Come on sweetheart, it's alright. You'll all be fine now."

"We tried to help him," she said, sniffling and wiping dirty tears on his neck. "We moved all the rocks we could but we were afraid we'd crush him. Is he okay?"

"He'll be fine. You guys did great." He handed her to Brian.

Aaron was examining the boy. He moved a large rock lying partially against Darian's leg and he cried out in pain. The dirt and rocks around his legs were soaked in blood.

"I think his leg's broken." Aaron said. He handed Mark some rocks and Mark put them further back in the cave, not throwing them for fear of causing additional cave-ins. As they moved the weight from his chest he wailed more loudly creating a din in the confined tunnel. Once they had him clear, Aaron stabilized his leg by tying it to one of the larger flashlights and he examined him as best he could for other injuries, especially his neck. When satisfied he wouldn't hurt him further he slipped a stretcher alongside and he and Mark lifted the injured boy on to it. The dust made it hard for any of them to breathe.

"Let's get the hell out of here." Mark said.

***

Once again, Mark paced the waiting room while someone underwent surgery, this time with Darien's parents. Everything had been going so well, he thought. Now it seemed like one crisis after another. He hated it when children were hurt, but he could understand why they had wanted some excitement. They were just kids and the shelter was beginning to seem very confining.

For the first time he began to seriously consider leaving the shelter and wondering what they would do on the outside, where they would go or whether they would all stick together. He glanced up quickly as the door opened.

Unlike the last time, when Aaron exited the surgical suite, he had a big smile on his face. "The surgery went well and I think his leg is going to heal up just fine," he told Albert and Janet Spears. "He's a lucky kid. Initially we thought the leg had been crushed but it turned out to be an uncomplicated compound fracture. He should have a full recovery and use of his leg."

Mark listened to the good news and left to spread the word to the rest of the shelter's residents.

January 23, 5:40 p.m.

"Sandi, why didn't you just tell me? Did you think we needed to keep secrets from each other?" Pete and Sandi were in her room sitting on the sofa. He held her hands in his.

"I'm sorry, I should have let you know, but I was so scared you wouldn't want to be with me anymore if you knew I was pregnant and it wasn't yours."

"Well you should have had more confidence in me than that. Remember me? The guy that helped you get over old whats-his name?"

"I know, I really should have told you." She picked up a tissue and dabbed her eyes.

"Are you sure you're okay? If that bastard hurt you they'll be looking for a way to punish me for murder." He angrily rose and started pacing the room. "I've disliked that slimeball from the moment we arrived here."

"Dr. Jim said I'm alright. Please, Pete, don't do anything to get yourself in trouble. We don't want to make it all worse. I'm going to have a hard enough time raising a baby in the world we'll have left." She started to cry again and he went back to her side, taking her hands in his again.

"What do you mean 'I'? We're in this together Sandi. You, me, and the baby." He tilted her head up to look in her eyes. "Will you marry me?"

She was completely shocked by this sudden proposal. The remnant had almost forgotten about institutions, including marriage, from their previous existence. He leaned forward and gathered her into his arms as she whispered "yes" into his ear.

January 23, 6:30 p.m.

Mark had never in his entire life seen Will Hargraves so angry, not over work related issues or personal matters, a cold furious anger that more than frightened Clay, it scared him to the core of his being. He had never seen his father this angry either. Clay sat in his father's room, cowering on one of the couches, soaked in perspiration, as his father paced back and forth, his face red, unable to speak. Mark sat on the other couch with Chris while Walter Thompson was in a chair. Walter had explained exactly what he'd heard and seen, including Sandi's confession of pregnancy.

Then Clay made a big mistake. He opened his mouth. "Dad, I screwed up and I'm sorry. I wasn't going to do anything. It won't happen again."

Will turned on him pointing to the door. "Get out! Get out of here this minute! Confine yourself to your quarters. If you think because you're my son you can get away with anything you please, you can think again. I'm convening a panel to consider these charges against you. I'll decide what to do with you based on their findings. Get out!"

Clay looked at his sister for support but she averted her eyes so he slunk out while he could.

"Dad, what are you going to do?" she asked.

"I have no idea. I never considered anything like this would ever happen. My God, my own son." He sank down in the other chair. "I need to think this over. Would you all please excuse me?"

The others left the apartment with Mark wishing Will would let him stay to discuss the situation. He was beginning to worry about him. They had always been able to talk about anything, any problem, but during the last couple of months Will had become withdrawn, didn't participate in the social life of the remnant, and had cut himself off from Mark.

Excusing himself from the others he went for a beer. The bottles were gone but the kegs were holding out and Johnny had the beer brewer in full operation. They may run out of food but the brewery was producing enough alcohol to last a lifetime.

Sitting at a table, nursing his beer and thinking about the problems they'd had lately, he was completely engrossed when a voice brought him back to the present. He looked up to find Chris standing over him.

"Oh, I'm sorry, didn't see you come in. Sit. It's a real bitch, huh?"

"Yeah, I always knew my brother was self-centered and didn't really care about anyone else's feelings or needs, but I never expected he would do something this stupid, if only for his own self-preservation. Did he really think he could get away with this?"

"He's an intelligent man. He must have genuinely believed he would be believed over her, especially if his friends lied for him."

"Mark, I'm so worried about Dad. He was depressed enough but this is just the worst thing that could happen. I don't understand why he's so withdrawn lately. Has he confided anything to you?"

"No, but I think he just feels that his job is done. After all, he's not a young man and his whole world has ended. Maybe he feels at his age that it's going to be too hard to start over in a new world. His entire life the last few years was tied up in providing this shelter against the possibility of nuclear war and now that it's happened he may feel he's accomplished what he needed to accomplish. You're safe, after all."

"It sounds like you think he's given up and doesn't want to go on, that he's lost interest."

"Maybe he has."

They drank a few beers and listened to the conversation of the clientele as they discussed the current problem. Will had never considered a brig would be necessary so one wasn't included in the plans when the shelter was built. There were as many different opinions about what they should do about Clay as there were people in the bar. Needing to relieve his bladder, Mark excused himself and walked through the door into the multipurpose room toward the men's room located in the rear corner. Several young people sat on the edge of the stage while others danced to loud music. Clay's name was mentioned and he knew the young people were as concerned about the recent events as the adults. They nodded to him as he walked by.

Mark opened the door and froze, then leaped forward, screaming for help, as he grabbed Karl Dohner's legs and tried to relieve the rope around his neck of the weight. "Oh God, somebody get the doctor!" he yelled at the youths that jammed into the room. Karl's complexion was ashen, his lips tinged with blue and Mark prayed they weren't too late. The rope was knotted around the bar over the stall door. He must have jumped off the toilet. His feet barely cleared the floor, but it was enough.

"How long since he came in here?"

"Just a few minutes ago," someone replied.

"Hold his legs so I can untie him!" Two of the boys wrapped their arms around Karl's legs and lifted.

Mark fumbled with the tightened knot, finally worrying it loose and they lowered him to the floor as Mark immediately began resuscitation efforts. He instructed one of the adolescents in the proper technique for compressing the chest while he cleared the airway, tilted the head back and breathed into Karl's mouth. Several people from the pub tried to push into the restroom.

"Everybody get back and give us some room!" Mark yelled.

They continued their efforts until Dr. Jim shoved his way through the mob with a small portable defibrillator and a medical kit.

"Keep doing what you're doing until I'm ready," he instructed them. He felt for a pulse, then tore open Karl's shirt and placed the paddles. The monitor indicated chaotic heart activity. "Ok, clear." When they moved back he hit the button and the body jerked off the floor.

They continued their efforts to resuscitate him, Jim using drugs injected into his heart and repeated attempts with the defibrillator, but they were unsuccessful. Although his neck hadn't broken in the fall, he'd tied the rope tightly and sufficient time had passed to finish the job before he was discovered.

"Oh hell," Mark said dejectedly. "Another damn funeral. What else can go wrong?"

February 2

"He didn't actually rape her. It's only attempted rape." Vernon reasoned.

"That's bullshit and you know it! If Walter hadn't been there he certainly would have raped her." Jean answered.

"But he didn't. You can't punish him for rape, only attempted rape."

She sneered at him. "That may have worked on the outside but we don't have any of that legal ambiguity here and we're not going to screw around with technicalities. We know an immoral act when we see one and this guy is an evil man who deserves to be punished!" Several voices were raised in agreement.

Will held up his hand, "Ladies and gentlemen, let's have some order." Jean Barnes was acting as prosecutor and Vernon Richenour was the only person willing to serve in Clay's defense. There were no lawyers among the remnant.

Most of the shelter's residents were in attendance at the hearing being conducted in the auditorium. Chairs were brought in and arranged to face the permanent seats. Clay, facing the audience, had regained some of his composure but was careful not to exhibit any arrogance. He was a skilled actor, used to manipulating people, and was acutely aware that he needed to be very careful if he wanted to avoid being alone in his room for the remainder of his time in this hellhole. There was no place else to put him.

This was an unusual hearing. Anyone with something to say had been allowed to state their opinion after Sandi, Walter and Clay each told their side of the story.

Clay's version shocked Sandi and infuriated Walter and Pete. She broke down in tears and Lori took her into the "green" room alongside the stage. Clay claimed Sandi had been coming on to him for weeks, that she'd led him to the dragon door, teased him, invited sex in the cavern and then changed her mind.

"I'm really sorry. She had me so hot I just got carried away and couldn't stop. I'll be more careful and not allow myself to be put in that position again. I swear," he innocently told the assemblage.

Walter roared to his feet. "You're a God damned liar too! I heard you tell her that the guys in the pub would lie for you, tell everyone you were there when the rape occurred. I heard you ridicule her and Pete, calling them names. She was begging you to stop, you . . ."

"Walter, take it easy and sit down." Will interrupted him. You told your story already. Does anyone else have anything to say?" He paused for comments but everyone had already contributed their statements.

Will stood and faced Clay.

"I don't think there's any question of what you did. You violated another member of our community, violently. You've never shown any regard for the people here and it's up to them to decide your innocence or guilt." He turned to the crowd.

"Raise your hand if you think he's guilty."

Hands shot up indicating guilty verdicts from almost everyone in the auditorium. Only a few of Clay's friends kept their hands down, but when Will asked for a show of hands for 'not guilty' they still did not raise them.

Clay's eyes widened and he visibly gulped. He looked at Chris but she stared straight ahead, tears in her eyes. She had not raised her hand for either verdict but in her heart she knew her brother was guilty of more than attempted rape. He would never fit in here.

"Now we need to decide what to do with him." Will said.

One of Clay's friends finally spoke up. "Put him in house arrest. Make him stay in his room."

"That's not good enough!" Walter was back on his feet.

Bob Crowder stood. "We could turn one of the rooms into a jail cell. We could take out the T.V., make it so it's more like punishment." A lot of people nodded their heads.

Gregory Whitehorse stood and looked directly at Will. "Jail is modern society's equivalent of banishment from the tribe, since there's nowhere else to send them. In the old days when someone was judged unfit to live in our society they were sent away, to live separately from my people. We still have that option here." He sat down and not a sound could be heard in the room.

"Hey, Dad." Clay murmured softly. He hadn't even thought of that possibility. "Come on, Dad, you can't even be thinking about that." He stood up.

"Come on you guys. I didn't kill somebody!" He turned to Chris "Chris, shit, say something. Please!"

No one moved. Clay bolted for the door but several people moved to block each of the exits.

"Let's get this over with." Will walked toward Clay and Clay swung wildly at the men blocking the door. He connected with someone's chin and the man went down but several others grabbed his arms and threw him against the wall.

The people in the crowd all began to talk at once as they realized Will was going to put Clay outside.

Will motioned to the door.

"You can't do that, Hargraves." Vernon yelled out. "We should vote on it. You can't put someone out there to die for attempted rape! That's capital punishment!"

"No it isn't." Will argued. "He's being banished, having proven he can't live peacefully in our society. The fact that it's dangerous out there is not the issue. The radiation has lessened. He'll probably be able to survive." Will motioned to the door a second time and the men holding Clay pushed him through the door and turned toward the elevator.

Clay was babbling, "Dad, please, I'll be good. Please. Mark, stop them, please, you're like a brother to me!"

They went through the two airlocks and pushed him into the elevator. No one got in with him. It hadn't been used since they lowered the supplies Darryl brought with him when he returned from Colorado Springs the first day of the war. The outside door was closed and the radiation monitor indicated there wasn't any radiation in the large entrance cave.

"I want you to think about what you've done." Will told him coldly, no emotion, whatsoever, in his voice. "I'm not putting you outside. You can remain in the entrance cave, safe from any radiation, and we'll send you food, water and supplies in the elevator. You'll be completely isolated from us for an undetermined time. Dig a latrine in the floor in the far corner. If you get tired of the cave and decide to go outside, let us know. There's an airlock located to the side of the main door that will allow you to leave without contaminating the main cave. There's a camera in the elevator. If you stay in it we won't be able to send you food." He reached over and hit the button on the intercom. "Micah, send the elevator to the surface and open the door. Leave it there until he exits."

The door slid closed. Will turned and without a word walked toward his apartment.

March 12

Chris and Lori sniffed, each of them pressing a handkerchief to her eyes as Ron and Jean said their "I do's" followed by Pete and Sandi's. Mark found it amusing. Why, he wondered, do women cry at weddings?

Everyone dressed in their street clothes for the double ceremony taking place in the auditorium. After all, this was a formal occasion.

Mark was very happy for the two couples, but the wedding caused him to reflect on the unexpected turn in his life, the knowledge that he and Chris would never be together. He tried to imagine what had gone wrong, but realized truthfully, that their union was highly unlikely from the beginning. As much as he loved Chris, she thought of him as a family member, and their relationship had always been more like that of siblings rather than lovers. It was obvious that Chris and Aaron cared a lot for each other and Mark tried to be happy for them too.

As he watched the couples binding their lives and futures together, he became aware of a slight trembling. No one else seemed to notice it, though, and he wasn't too concerned, intending to check on it later.

After the wedding, Mark promised Lori he'd be along shortly and ascended to the Crow's nest to obtain information about the tremor. Micah, being something of a party animal, was attending the wedding, so James was pulling a shift upstairs. He sat in a chair with his feet propped on a counter and the chair tilted so far back, Mark thought he would surely fall over. He was reading one of the many technical manuals.

"Hey James, any info on the tremor I felt about fifteen minutes ago?" Mark asked as he entered the room.

"No, I didn't even feel it. We really don't have any external readouts for seismic activity. Apparently it was fairly unknown in this corner of New Mexico, and Mr. Hargraves, or the designers, didn't think it was necessary to have readouts or printouts."

"Yeah, but we monitored for hydrogen blasts. Can't we use the same sensors and data?" Mark walked over to the computer, where the screen depicted the main menu, wanting to begin his search for the data, but he knew Lori expected him at the wedding reception.

James nodded, "That's a distinct possibility. I'll ask Darryl about it. How'd the wedding go?"

"It was great, all the women were blubbering. I'm heading back there now so I'll see you later."

Before he reached the door the intercom came on and Clay asked to speak to his father. "He isn't here, Clay. Do you need me to get him?" Mark asked.

"No, you speak for him anyway. I've been locked in this hole for over a month and I want out. It's obvious you aren't going to let me back in the shelter. Open the damn door. I'm going back to civilization to see what's happening. You can all stay in your underground warren and suffocate for all I care."

James looked to Mark for direction.

"Your father said you could leave anytime you want, so go ahead. And Clay," he added, almost reluctantly, "...good luck." Mark had known Clay all Clay's life and, although they had never cared for each other he still thought of him as a family member, even an errant little brother. He motioned to James and the airlock to the outside was activated, the inside door opening first, and then closing before the outside door opened.

Mark and James both glanced at the screen showing the image from the camera monitoring the parking area. They saw Clay enter the picture where he turned and looked back toward the camera mounted under a protruding rock above the shelter's entry door.

He started across the parking area, and turning again, he flipped them off. After trying to start a few of the cars and finding their batteries dead he left the camera's range and disappeared from view heading in the direction of the road.

Mark told James, "I'm going back to the party but I'll stop and tell Will about Clay."

He left reluctantly, having a feeling he should be paying more attention to the tiny earthquakes that appeared to have been gaining in strength and frequency over the past few weeks. Maybe they could alter the sensors to monitor them and evaluate whether they were indeed getting worse.

Stopping by Will's room on the way back to the party, he informed Will that Clay had left the entrance cave.

"The radiation monitor shows that it's fairly safe. Maybe there's even less radiation at the lower elevations." Mark told him. "He'll be okay."

"Mark, I had to do it. He's never cared for anyone after his mother died. I had always hoped he'd grow out of it but it's obvious he never will. May God forgive me."

The latter surprised Mark as he had never heard Will refer to anything religious. "I'm going back to the wedding reception. Are you sure you won't join us?"

"No. You go on."

As he left he heard Will whisper, "Oh Katherine, what have I done?"

The festivities had moved from the auditorium to the multipurpose room where a reception was already underway by the time he arrived, but somehow he had lost his desire to celebrate.

March 13

The world was wrapped in a glittering, white shroud, from the several feet of snow covering the frozen ground to the flocked tips of the ponderosa pines growing in profusion around the cabin. Huge cottony flakes of snow drifted down from a gray sky that had become progressively darker for hours making visibility extremely poor. The nearer trees looked like specters approaching through the swirling snow, and the air temperature was colder than this part of the country had ever known this late in the season.

They'd burned the first two cords of firewood and were half way through the second, a few logs burning in the fireplace now as the creatures, retaining few characteristics of men, jostled one another in an attempt to get closer to the warmth. When the firewood was gone they would have to resort to tearing apart the furniture and staircase railings to burn, or face interment in a frozen tomb. The stored food was three quarters gone but the creatures had lost the ability to plan for the eventuality of depleted supplies. They retained enough knowledge to open the cans but hadn't cooked anything for weeks. The staples had been consumed long ago and jerky, dried fruits and canned goods were all that remained. Arby, the only one left with any capacity for reasoning, could barely keep the others from eating the remainder of the food at one sitting.

The pain of their transformation continued unabated and they fidgeted, rubbed their shoulders and occasionally moaned, screamed or growled. The neutron radiation had targeted osteoclasts, the cells that reabsorbed bone, and destroyed them. It sent osteoblasts, cells that deposit bone, into a cancerous frenzy. Bone was being created at a tremendous rate and other tissues reproduced wildly to keep up with the organisms overall growth.

The changes were a combination of mutation and devolution. They were simultaneously becoming primitive precursors of *Homo sapiens* and genetically altered, otherworldly beasts.

Arby grunted at one of the changelings and motioned toward the door. The creature that had previously been Butch Cassidy growled at him but when Arby stretched to his full height the other beast climbed to his feet and shuffled toward the front entrance to fetch more firewood. When he opened the door, gusts of freezing wind blew snow and ice into the interior of the cabin, causing the other creatures to stir, moving closer to the warmth of the fire and whining their displeasure. He returned in minutes with an arm full of logs, his pelt covered with snow, and maneuvered his way through the others to pitch the wood on the fire. He shook himself like an animal and the others growled as the snow was flung in all directions.

The Arby thing descended the staircase to the basement and brought up a small box of dried food to distribute among the others. He had difficulty remembering what he was doing and had already satisfied his hunger before returning to the others. His only concern for his fellow creatures was motivated by self-interest; if he allowed them to die he would be alone in this white, cold, barren world that he had forgotten would someday be warm again. Though he had no love or caring for the other creatures, they provided companionship and did whatever he forced them to do, like fetching firewood so he didn't have to venture forth into the frigid outdoors. He would only allow them to starve if the food ran low and he needed it for his own nourishment alone.

March 30

    "In the still of the night..." The smooth tones of the Five Satins drifted through the room as dancers swayed together. Mark had suggested to Lori that the remnant have a dance to take their minds off the enormous problems they'd been facing lately. With Faye Claret gone they hadn't had as many celebrations as in the past. They decided on an old fashioned "sock hop" format since some of the survivors were in their sixties and had been teens during the "oldie but goodie" era. Others had known it through "Happy Days," a T.V. series that reprised the era. That period of time represented nostalgia to most of the inhabitants, even the younger people. The multi-purpose room had been cleared of furniture and the basketball hoops had been shoved to the back of the room. Only couches were left along the walls for people to sit on. Surprisingly, almost everyone was dancing, as if clinging to each other for strength and comfort, their sanctuary all that separated them from the hostile world outside.

    Johnnie Jay, being the natural selection for disc jockey, was programming the digital player to access the hundreds of songs that were stored in memory. He was alternating the fast and slow hits of the fifties and sixties with the more modern music the younger people enjoyed. For once the baby boomers, the generation X'ers and the millennials all seemed to be getting along, the music bringing them together where other attempts had failed. Decorations were barely visible along the walls of the darkened room and on the stage. Stores had only a few supplies for this sort of a party. White and pink crepe paper drooped along the walls with large red paper hearts, intended for a Valentines party, at the nadir of the loops. Crepe balls were strung from the ceiling at intervals, drooping so low they almost touched the heads of the taller men. In the tradition of sock hops "before," they had shed their shoes at the door, a large pile attesting to the number of people who had chosen to attend this affair.

    The past seven months had been tremendously difficult for the remnant. They had endured the worst catastrophe to ever befall mankind, had found security in the shelter, and subsequently had that security shaken with the tragedies that struck their little group. Although on an infinitely smaller scale, the events of the last few weeks had affected them all as personally as the nuclear war had done.

Mark stood in the doorway, looking around the room. It took a minute for his eyes to adjust to the darkness. He saw Chris in the corner with Aaron Brown and started in their direction, but saw Aaron reach his hand over to hers and hold it tenderly. She was smiling at him, tilted her face up, and he kissed her. Mark decided to leave them alone and temporarily felt unsure of what to do. He felt someone at his side. "They've been getting pretty close these past couple of months, Mark. I'm sorry."

In a daze he glanced to see Lori standing at his elbow. "I know. I was aware of it,...it's okay."

The song ended and Johnny Jay pushed buttons to select another song and the music filled the room with the voice of Rosie and the Originals singing "Angel Baby."

"Mark, let's dance." Lori took his hand and pulled him out on the dance floor where they were joined by at least half of the assembled participants. He held her formally, a space between their bodies, staring into the corner. Lori pulled him closer, and surprised, he held her tight.

His mind was a jumble of thoughts. Rosie sang on in that high voice, "Don't ever leave me, blue and alone . . ." He knew they had never really had a relationship; she wasn't leaving him in any sense. She had never led him to believe they would be together, he had just assumed all these years that they were meant for each other. Mark realized that he wasn't as upset as he thought he should be.

"Why not?" he wondered. He found himself actually happy for Chris, that she had someone to be with in this incredibly stressful period in all their lives. He held Lori close, swaying to the music. When the song ended he stepped back looking down at Lori and smiled. "I'm okay, really. Let's get something to eat."

Another song started and they snaked their way through dancers to the side of the room where the food was spread out on a long table pushed back against the wall. They had splurged for the party, but the selection reflected the lack of fresh supplies. They selected a small amount of food and made their way back to a sofa in the back corner.

The room had grown more crowded as additional people arrived late. At least three-fourths of the population of the shelter was at the party. Mark and Lori talked in hushed tones enjoying the fact that the others seemed to be having a good time for the first time in weeks. They listened to The Mamas and Papas singing about "California Dreamin," when Mark heard a sound, a heart wrenching sob that drew the attention of the others in the room.

"I want to go home!" someone wailed. The dancers spread apart and a woman backed away from her partner, bent over as if in pain. He reached for her hand and tried to pull her back.

"Come on, honey, it's okay"

"It's not okay!" She was crying loudly. "It's never going to be okay. We're buried in this underground hole with no place to go. I want to go home!" She repeated.

"If we were home, we'd be dead. This won't last forever, we'll get out of here when it's safe." He pulled her back to him but she pushed him away, threw out her arms and addressed the others.

"Are we sure we can't leave? How do we know what it's like out there? Maybe there wasn't even a war and we're in some kind of experiment. I want to go home to California, no matter what it's like."

Many of the remnant looked to Mark since Will wasn't at the party.

He stood and walked over to her, reached out both his hands and took hers. He smiled, "You know what? I miss California too. I miss the Dodgers and Dodger Stadium on a warm summer night in September with the Dodgers heading for the playoffs. The crowd doing the wave, dancing to music between innings and batting around beach balls until the ushers snag them."

She smiled back at him. "I miss Dodger dogs." She laughed through tears.

"And I miss concerts at The Hollywood Bowl and The Greek Theater" He backed slowly pulling her over toward the sofa.

"I miss Monday Night Football." Her husband added. "We used to go to a little sports bar with a big screen TV and dollar beer and hotdogs."

Mark and the woman sat on the couch and several people sat on the carpet in front of them. Lori came and sat by Mark.

Doug Harkens, an ex-lifeguard, sitting on a chair next to the sofa choked on his words as he said, "I miss the beach. We used to walk along the bluffs at Santa Monica and watch the sun set almost every night." Doug's wife hadn't made it to the shelter. He talked with her before he left and she told him she was on her way to the airport. He never knew what happened to her.

Greg Whitehorse added, "Yes, like the sunset over the spires in Monument Valley. The brilliant colors are unlike anywhere else on Earth. I miss the eagle soaring above the canyons."

Chris and Aaron pushed the sofa they had been sitting on across the room, ending up behind a growing number of people in the corner. Someone sat on the back of the sofa. "I sure would like to see a new movie. I miss seeing the previews for all the new ones. There won't be any new movies."

This caused another woman to begin to weep. "I love Harrison Ford. I wonder what happened to him?"

"I miss Keira Knightly and Adele," said one man with a grin.

By now all the others had crowded around in the corner, dragging chairs and sofas or sitting cross-legged on the carpet. Johnny Jay programmed the CD player for continuous, random play, turned the volume down and joined the throng. The teens sat at the edge of the adults. One of the girls shouted out, "I miss Justin Bieber," and then giggled self-consciously.

" . . . and after thoroughly chewing me out, Daddy hugged me and said he would always love me," one of the women finished as she told of the time, when she was sixteen, that her parents came home unexpectedly and found her and a boyfriend involved in a wild sexual encounter. Her husband of twenty years, the same boyfriend in the story, chuckled along with her.

They all agreed they missed old musicals, dining out at nice restaurants, New Year's Eve parties and family campouts. They missed fresh air and the sun, and especially the moon at night, and "moonlight walks on the beach." They missed the ability to instantly communicate with or get news from anyone around the world. Some missed mountains and rivers, others missed deserts and still others missed New York City. Summer concerts in the park, doing yard work and gardening, professional and recreational sports, dogs and cats and even T.V.

The kids opened up and reluctantly admitted to missing many of the same things the adults had. Most of them missed school and their friends. Skateboards, Malls, MTV and concerts, and especially junk food.

They all missed everyday pursuits, like going to work and wishing for the weekends, going to Little League and soccer games with their children, eating ice cream, skiing, riding horses and surfing the internet.

Many of these things they hoped to see again, the natural phenomena at least, but the cultural aspects of their previous lives, the things created by man, the things that had made it America were probably gone forever. All the denial, all the pretending that life would be the same when they left this place, all the wishing that it would be so, ended that evening.

They talked into the night, for hours, each person telling of something personal that was gone forever, talking of loved ones lost, of experiences they would never have again, of places that, if they ever saw them again, would not be the same. They were conversations and tears that cleansed wounds, a catharsis drawing them together, knitting their group closer and helping to alleviate the pain of the recent tragedies that had affected them all.

380

<u>EIGHT</u>

May 6, 8:30 a.m.

Sandi laughed and reached out to catch Jeremy as he circled her, Ashley in hot pursuit, but seizing him in her present condition proved impossible. She placed her hands on hips, leaning slightly backward, attempting to relieve the strain on her back caused by her bulging nine months pregnant abdomen. She had temporarily relinquished her teaching responsibilities, and although chronically tired as a result of her pregnancy, she continued to supervise the children at daycare, trying to stay busy and get some much needed exercise.

"It would be so wonderful to just stay in bed until this child decides to make its grand entrance," she had told Pete and Jim at her prenatal appointment three days ago.

It was already early May. Dr. Jim calculated she was full-term but the baby still hadn't dropped. She'd experienced some minor contractions, at times thinking she was beginning labor, but they'd ceased, leaving her bitterly disappointed.

"Don't worry," Jim had explained to them, "This often happens with a first pregnancy. You'll go into labor in due time."

"I just never considered I'd be overdue." And she had burst into tears leaving Pete feeling powerless to console her.

***

Sniffing the morning air, the creature that at one time had been Arby Clark ran, hunched over, up the trail following the scent of its prey. The others trailed behind, their insides twisting in agony, needing food to absorb the acid in their bellies. They had consumed the food in the cabin two days before and were starving.

The creatures were quick but there was still no chance of their catching the deer, though it was sickly and weak. Not realizing the need for stealth they pushed and shoved each other, crashing through the underbrush, each trying to be the first to sink his teeth into the yielding flesh of the deer. Snow still lay about in large patches but some had melted leaving new, green growth straining up through the wet earth to seek the warmth and light of the sun.

The harsh winter, with heavy unremitting snowfall and months without sun, had kept the pack inside the lodge until, finishing the food, hunger drove them from their lair to seek sustenance. Although the air was bitter cold at this early morning hour, the creatures didn't notice. Hairy rugs blanketed much of their bodies that were growing at an unprecedented rate as other changes continued to take place in them. But the hair had begun to fall out in chunks.

Radiation had altered the balance of their endocrine systems. Production of Growth Hormone had resumed and all twelve of the creatures exhibited unheard of degrees of acromegaly, gaining several inches to almost two feet in height as growth plates on the long bones of the legs were reactivated, their spinal columns curving as their bodies became almost serpentine. Foreheads thickened, bulging outward, cheekbones became prominent and hands and feet became oversized for their bodies. Their hair continued to fall out in clumps leaving raw reddened patches of skin. Most of the men were bald due to an overproduction of hormones from their stimulated pituitaries and, in turn, testes. Two of the smaller men had borne the brunt of the hormone changes being raped repeatedly whenever the urge struck one of the larger creatures. Stringy, long hair hung from fringes around some of their skulls and the skin on their heads, mottled with various shades of pink and gray, had thickened perceptibly, rough like that of an elephant but shedding in peeling patches of putrid flesh. Their teeth, especially the canines, had lengthened and sharpened, their thick, heavy lips unable to close over them completely and their nails had thickened, grown longer and became claws as lethal as any grizzly bear's. Exposed skin was blistered and oozed a serous fluid that smeared and matted their hair. Huge brow ridges protruded over their eyes giving them a sunken appearance, with brows bushy enough to interfere with vision.

And the eyes - deep set, beady, the irises glowing red.

The trail swerved right, around a small dam, but the deer scampered left, the pack following it around the dam and climbing slightly to the south side of a lake. On the left the land dropped off precipitously.

Bennett, or what had once been Bennett, crossed a patch of icy snow, excited by the sight of the receding deer. His foot slipped on the ice. He lost his footing, and flailing his arms to regain his balance, disappeared over the edge. He slid and cart wheeled twenty feet down the slope, striking a tree trunk that had lodged against a large boulder. The trunk was covered with protruding branches, one catching him on the inside of the left leg and lodging in his groin after it ripped through the femoral artery. A bright red gusher of blood spurted onto filthy, matted hair and covered the tree and the ground beneath him. Bennett screamed, his voice echoing through the canyon to the south, and grabbed his exposed genitals, attempting to staunch the flow of slippery blood from the jagged wound.

Several of the others slid down the slope scattering rocks and dirt before them. Bennett's screams were already diminishing as his heart rhythmically pumped his life out through the gash in his leg. Arby reached out and punched Bennett on the shoulder; jarring him, as if to say, "Get up. What's wrong with you?"

Bennett screamed again and the others jumped back becoming increasingly agitated and excited at the noise. One of them touched the blood and brought his hand up in front of his face, staring at it stupidly. He licked it. His eyes widened and he plunged his hand into the wound and, cupping it, brought hot, fresh blood hungrily to his mouth. Another, larger creature pushed him aside and grabbing the edge of the wound he savagely bit into it, tearing the wound open, shaking his head to tear off a piece of the flesh. Bennett's screams had mercifully ended.

Pandemonium broke out as the beasts jerked the body from the tree limb and tore it to pieces, fighting for a share of the meal. The creatures that originally stayed at the top of the slope plummeted downward, catching themselves on the fallen tree and joining in the feeding frenzy.

Covered with blood, leaves and dirt adhering to the sticky coating, they climbed back up the hill to the lake, some still carrying bones, tearing the remaining flesh with their teeth. A few waded into the frigid water rinsing themselves off. The others didn't even bother. They all drank their fill of water, washing down the remains of the meal.

Now that they had ventured forth from the lodge they felt compelled to stay free. They followed the lake's shore around toward the west. The sun rose higher in the sky and warmed them after their plunge into the frigid lake. The Arby creature followed the deer tracks where they veered from the west end of the lake, through a thin stand of Ponderosa Pines until they disappeared over the side of the plateau. He could see the leaves disturbed where the animal had gone down the slope past junipers and scrub oaks.

He grunted, disappointed, and turned to go back to the others but stopped when something caught his eye. Approximately ten feet below his position was a flattened area. From the angle he could barely see a portion of a metal grate in the side of the hill. Carefully slipping over the side he slid down the slope, reaching the flat area where a grate in the vertical wall closed off a small cave. The grate had two hinges on one side and was padlocked on the other. With the curiosity of an animal he considered the grate.

He cocked his head and grunted again. Taking hold of the bars he rattled them, tentatively at first and then more violently when it didn't budge with his efforts. Two of the others descended to his side. Arby put a large hairy foot on the rock beside the grate, took hold of the bars and bent his back into the task. The others jerked on the bars and, with dirt and rocks showering them, the hinge attached to iron rods driven deep into the rock pulled loose. They renewed their efforts and soon had the lower hinge pulled out of the rock as well. The grate was now swinging loose, held only by the hasp and lock.

The creatures looked at one another, trying to decide what to do next. Arby crouched down and stuck his head into the cave, sniffing the air. He crawled forward slowly, his eyes adapting quickly to the dark. The opening immediately widened and he had room to stand up within six feet of the entrance. The others were bending over looking into the opening. Unable to recall how to articulate words the beast gestured a "come on" to them and they went down on all fours and slipped through the entrance into the cave.

The area wasn't large, approximately an irregular dozen feet long by ten wide but had three other tunnels leading deeper into the mountain, each blocked by a wooden door. A few tools were discarded at the side of the cave; a shovel, two wrenches, a pick and some wire. Although the creatures poked at the tools they no longer were capable of identifying them. The Jaime creature approached the larger of the tunnels leading off the cave and poked at the door. He kicked it and Arby joined in until they had battered it down. Jaime grunted and disappeared into it. Arby listened intently, hearing Jaime's shuffling growing fainter. Other creatures were entering the cave and before it became too crowded Arby followed Jaime into the darkness.

May 6, 9:30 a.m.

Mark searched through computer directories trying to locate any evidence of monitoring for seismic activity in the Sangre de Cristo Mountains. Earthquake activity was unusual in this area so the designers of the complex hadn't provided external readouts for these parameters, nevertheless, the computer monitored and recorded a considerable amount of data and he fervently hoped it could give him what he needed. Staring at the screen, he suddenly realized he'd discovered what he sought. Seismographs, installed to monitor the effects of hydrogen blasts, were still sending data to the computer and Mark was shocked and dismayed at the graphical representation on his screen.

Mark turned to Micah, "Wait until you see what I've got! Page Will and Gregory. They need to see this."

A few minutes later the four of them gathered around the screen. Dr. Whitehorse examined the data displayed on the computer monitor, very concerned about the implications. The graphs indicated a small cluster of earthquakes that occurred soon after their arrival, some major chicken scratches off the chart, probably a result of the Los Alamos blast, and additional clusters at approximate intervals of one month. Rather than decreasing in intensity, each succeeding wave of tremors increased in strength until, only recently, they had become noticeable to the residents.

"We've seen increasing amounts of debris in the tunnels when we're out jogging." Mark told him. "And when we buried Faye, the fissure was wider than it had been when we buried Pierson. There's a previously unknown crack in the reservoir cave, too."

"Maybe we better have a look." Gregory said. "I might be able to ascertain how serious these geological changes are." Micah stayed behind while the others went to the lower level of the shelter. They entered the cave and Mark showed them the area with the new crack just beyond the reservoir.

Gregory examined the crevasse extending clear to the rear wall explaining the significance of the recent tremors to Mark and

Will. "Small earthquakes, gaining in intensity and occurring in clusters, like the ones we've been experiencing, often precede a larger quake. This area isn't known for seismic activity so I don't know why it's happening but it's possible the blast at Los Alamos destabilized existing faults."

"You think we might get a larger quake? How bad do you think it might be?" Will asked. Mark noticed additional debris had fallen from the ceiling since the last time he ran through this area including rocks considerably larger than before.

Gregory shook his head, "There's no way to predict it."

Concerned, Mark asked Will, "Has the shelter been designed to withstand a major earthquake?"

"The constructed portion of the shelter was designed to withstand the force of a hydrogen bomb exploding in close proximity but we always knew the natural caves could collapse if the hit was close enough. We didn't anticipate earthquake activity but the same thing probably holds true."

"We've already used a large portion of the supplies," Mark said. "And there are extra rooms for storage. Maybe we should move everything from the natural tunnels to the shelter."

"That's a good idea. We need to make a general announcement that everyone's to stay away from the dragons caves once we relocate the supplies."

Mark left the others to their inspection and reentered the shelter to assemble a work party.

May 6, 5:45 p.m.

Jerry Thompson and Richard Krieg loaded boxes on a hand truck, preparing to relocate them to empty apartments within the shelter proper. Both men were exhausted, having worked all day into late afternoon. This particular storage area was one of the most remote, leading off the back of the reservoir cave and extending approximately one hundred feet into the mountain. Typically, in most of the caves, side passages existed but most were not high enough to stand upright. Many of the boxes were too large to take on the hand truck and they had already loaded most of the smaller boxes they could locate. This cave had minimal lighting, a single bulb by the door and Rick was having to use a small flashlight to examine the boxes further back in the tunnels.

"Hey Rick," called Jerry, stacking the last of the boxes on top the others. "I'm ready to take this load. You coming?" He pushed the button and the door swished open.

"Yeah, I'll be there in a minute. Some of the labels indicate these boxes farther back have electronic gear in them. I'm going to check them out. We may be able to transport some of them directly to the electronics lab."

"Okay, I'll take these boxes to the same apartment we dropped the last load."

"I'll be there in a..." The room shook with a small tremor, dust drifting down from the ceiling. It lasted only a few seconds before settling down but both men, jittery from the last quake, ducked down and covered their heads with their arms.

"Shit!" Jerry knelt down alongside the dolly. "Rick, don't stay outside the shelter any longer than necessary. The place might collapse on you."

Once the tremor stopped Rick got off his knees. "Oh, you can count on that. I'll be there in a minute to help you unload."

The door slid shut and Rick moved farther back into the cave, shining the light overhead to see if the ceiling looked stable. He hated caves. Tomorrow they would bring the shelter's only forklift and get the rest of the supplies. Most of them had already been moved from the caves that were closer to the living quarters and it was their turn for the forklift.

He shined the light on the crates toward the back of the cave, amazed at some of the stuff he discovered, things they had needed, that they had built from scratch, not knowing these boxes existed. Damn Old Pierson anyway.

The tunnel turned left around a corner with more crates farther back. Rick went around the corner and his light dimmed perceptibly. "Damn, now what." he murmured, banging it against his left hand. It brightened.

Suddenly he froze. He had heard a noise farther back in the cave. He immediately aimed the light down the tunnel, but it curved and he couldn't see anything moving. More dust and small rocks fell from the ceiling and he chuckled, whispering, "You chicken, afraid of your own shadow."

Squatting down alongside a row of boxes, he was examining the labels when the light winked out completely. "Damn it to hell!" He again hit it against his palm but this time it didn't revive. Disgusted, he stood and turned toward the exit when he again froze, hearing a noise that sounded like something shuffling in the loose dirt of the cave floor. Frozen in place, afraid to turn around, he listened intently. He heard another scraping sound and whirled quickly, squinting, trying to see into the dimness beyond the crates. He saw an enormous darker splotch against the wall and bright red eyes glowing through the dust-laden air. Irrational fear grabbed hold of him, his pulse quickening. He suddenly smelled something God-awful! A stench of death and putrefaction.

He panicked and, with all his strength, launched the useless flashlight toward the eyes, simultaneously breaking for the door. A crashing sound behind him as boxes were scattered about, and a thunderous roar caused him to accelerate in fear. He rounded the corner and reached the door and the lighted area in seconds but the thing was incredibly quick. As he hit the button to actuate the door, he swung around, eyes bulging, breath coming in gasps. An incarnation of his worst nightmare loomed above as hairy arms enveloped him. Long incisors sank into his jugular vein, ripping his neck open and cutting off his impending scream. Rick's head was ripped from his shoulders and flung aside as giant sinews snapped the spinal column. The thing carried Rick's body, bright red, arterial blood spurting onto the ground, to the cave's far recesses, to feed in the semi-darkness. Rick's head had rolled into the doorway, preventing it from closing, the doors hitting it and reopening, closing and opening, again and again.

Once the Jaime-thing had satisfied his hunger he noticed the door's rhythmic thumping. Casting the remainder of the body aside he moved through the tunnel, cocking his head and studying the door. The creature slunk over to Rick's head and reaching out tentatively, he kicked it, causing the head to roll toward the reservoir with the Jaime-thing following behind. The door finally closed one last time.

Arby had followed Jaime but ended up in a different tunnel, losing his way. Eventually, following the spoor and noise of his fellow creatures he returned to the tunnel Jaime had taken. As they progressed, the smell of blood wafted to his nostrils. Excited, his stomach lurching, he hurried through the blackness, until he reached the remains of Jaime's kill. He and the others, still famished after sharing the hapless creature aboveground, fell upon the partially eaten body, ripping it to pieces and consuming it.

Arby's red eyes, which could see in almost absolute darkness, noticed dim illumination coming from around the bend ahead. He and the others crept through the tunnel emerging into the barely lighted room. Arby crossed to the front of the cave, his head held high, sniffing the air. He concluded Jaime came this way but their passage was blocked. Frustrated, he commenced throwing boxes around the room, bouncing them against the corridor walls, delighting in the sound of delicate electronic equipment shattering to pieces.

May 6, 6:20 p.m.

"Hey, Mark, take a look at this." Micah tapped on one of the indicators. "This is weird. It's blinking red and green, red and green, like the door's opening and closing." As soon as Mark glanced at the board it quit blinking and remained green.

"Ok, I guess I'm seeing things. It appears to be alright now." Micah went back to munching his reconstituted beef stew dinner.

Mark continued to examine the readouts. New tremors were occurring with greater frequency. The radioactivity outside had diminished rapidly as the effects of the red mercury had dissipated, whatever radiation remaining, resulting from the thermonuclear explosions themselves and that too was very low. The sensors indicated lingering radiation surrounding them but considerably less in the western valley.

"Uh, Mark, I hate to bug you again but you need to see this."

Mark looked where Micah indicated. Although, on the outside, the radiation had been dropping steadily, the sensors now picked up low levels in certain dragon caves. "It's funny, there's some radiation in the cave where the door malfunctioned." Micah said. "It's not a huge amount but there shouldn't be any radiation in that area.

Mark went to the intercom and called Will's room.

"Will, we need you in the Crow's Nest. There's something else you need to see."

"I'm on my way." Will said.

Will arrived within minutes. He checked the readings on the screens. "The tremors we've been experiencing may have created cracks around the barriers that close off the Dragon Caves from the outside." Will told them. "Several of the tunnels leading to the outside were utilized to bring in supplies since it was closer than using the main elevator and trying to bring them through the shelter. This was especially true of those leading to the rear caves."

Micah interrupted him. "Hey Boss, I'm getting a radiation warning in the power plant now. It's barely detectable. Do you think these sensors are failing?"

"No. If there's a leak to the outside it could be affecting much of the lower level since so many of the caves are interconnected. We need to have someone, protected by an environmental suit, of course, go check . . ."

". . . in. Please answer me!" The radio crackled to life, the signal fighting its way through screeching static.

Micah leaped to the controls, isolating the signal and flipping the toggle to allow him to reply. "Hello. We hear you! Keep broadcasting!"

Mark rushed to the computer, turning on the recorder and attempting to isolate the frequency of the broadcast, jubilant at the prospect of contact with others.

"Who are you, where are you located?" Micah responded.

More ear-piercing static emitted from the speakers, ". . . AD . . . vernment faci. . . . ado" the signal continued, extremely broken up and hard to understand, although Mark was filtering the signal, attempting to cancel the interference. "I hear you. Where are..." Frustrated Mark hit the console with his fist, "Damn, I can't get it any better."

"Keep trying, I think it's improving!" Will encouraged him.

" . . . trying to contact ... months. Where are you located?"

"This is Will Hargrave's shelter in New Mexico." Micah replied and listened for an indication the message had been received.

"Thank God. . . . ment was damaged. . . . cently repaired. How . . . " Screeching static interrupted the signal.

They waited in anticipation for several more minutes but were unable to pick up additional messages.

"It's okay," Will told them, "It sounded like he said they had recently repaired their equipment. I'm sure we'll hear from him again."

"At least we know we're not alone." Mark was grinning broadly. He had noticed that Will sounded happier than he had in months, perhaps at the prospect of contacting others.

"Micah, stay with the radio, I'll get you some help. We want to monitor it continuously." Will said walking to the intercom and patching it in for a general announcement. "Attention, all residents, this is Will Hargraves. Please meet in the auditorium in fifteen minutes for a general meeting."

May 6, 7:00 p.m.

As usual, every time Will held a general meeting a large majority of the population was in attendance. Jerry Thompson searched the sea of faces looking for Rick, since the turkey had never showed up this afternoon to help him unload the supplies. He must have found some really interesting stuff and transported it to the electronics lab but Jerry still assumed Rick would have attended the meeting.

"Ladies and Gentlemen we've just received a message from the outside." The absolute silence that followed the announcement surprised Mark until he realized the remnant was completely shocked. Then all hell broke loose, people jumped to their feet cheering, pounding each other on the back and shouting questions at Will.

He held up his hands for quiet. "The message was garbled and we lost the signal but they indicated their equipment had been damaged and only recently repaired. We know the frequency and will be monitoring it continuously."

"Where'd it come from?" someone called from the audience.

"I believe it's from the NORAD base in Colorado. If so, that's a fairly large facility and holds a great number of personnel. We'll let you know the minute we receive additional broadcasts," he promised.

"Now, on a separate subject. As you know, we've been experiencing small earthquakes over the last couple of weeks. By examining data from the seismographs it appears the tremors have been increasing in intensity and have only recently become strong enough for us to feel. The shelter is built to withstand even a very large earthquake but the tunnels may be unsafe. We've moved most of the supplies from the storage areas into the shelter and I would caution each of you to stay out of the Dragon Caves until further notice. We'll continue to monitor the situation and will keep you informed."

This concerned Jerry and he stood, "Mr. Hargraves? I was working with Richard Krieg and he was supposed to help me unload supplies a while ago. He never showed up. You don't think he was injured in an earthquake, do you?"

"Has anyone seen Richard this evening?" Will asked. No one spoke up.

"Where were you guys working?" Mark asked Jerry.

"The tunnel behind the reservoir." Jerry said. Mark recalled the radiation leak in that tunnel. Maybe a cave-in had opened a gap to the outside air and trapped Rick.

Will went to the intercom and pushed the button for general announcements. "Richard Krieg, please report to the auditorium."

"I need some volunteers for a search party," Mark called out.

Almost everyone in the audience raised their hands. He chose several and motioned them to approach him.

"We've detected some very low level radiation coming from that same dragon cave," he explained. "You and you," he pointed to two men, "Get environmental suits from Glen and meet us by the reservoir."

Will stayed behind to answer questions for the remnant while the search party went to look for Rick. Jerry explained to Mark about Rick staying behind to examine the boxes of equipment, as he, Mark and two others left the auditorium and started down the stairs. "How long ago did you leave him?" Mark asked.

"About an hour and a half ago. When he didn't show up I just assumed he took stuff to the lab. Until he wasn't at the meeting, that is."

They arrived at the door to the reservoir cave and waited for the two men who went for suits. "What happens to our water supply if this cave collapses?" one of the others asked Mark.

"We have a small backup supply inside the shelter proper and there's a second reservoir in a cave off the top floor. The water is pumped from this reservoir to the upper one so we get water pressure caused by gravity. We would have to clean out the reservoir cave and get the filtering equipment working. Will says they reinforced the caves containing the power plant and reservoir so they should be okay." Mark said.

The two men, Matt and Warren, arrived looking like spacemen. Mark pushed the button and walked into the dimly lighted space.

"What's that smell?" Matt asked. "Smells like something died."

"It didn't smell like this a while ago." Jerry said.

Skirting the edge of the dark water they reached the far back of the cave where Mark, spotting something shiny on the uneven cavern floor stopped and knelt down. He noticed a dark substance pooled on the ground, stuck his finger in it and brought it to his nose. "Oh God, it smells like blood."

"There's more over here." Jerry told him from next to the door.

Mark stood and looked around the immense cavern. "That's a lot of blood. If it caved in on him he may have come through here and be hurt somewhere in the shelter. We should still check out the tunnel." He addressed the men in the environmental suits.

"Guys, make sure he's not in there. We'll wait here and then start a general search throughout the shelter when you're back." Jerry hit the button opening the door.

"The light's burned out, it's darker than Hades in there," Jerry said. The two suited men flicked on their helmet lights, went through and the door slid shut behind them.

They had been gone only a couple of minutes when something thunked against the door on the other side. It slid open and both men spilled out into the cave, one desperately trying to get his helmet off. Mark grabbed him, helping to unhook the fasteners that secured the helmet to the suit. The helmet was flung aside as the man spewed vomit in an arc, coughing and choking, the bile coating the inside of his helmet and dripping down the front of the suit. The other suited figure had gone to his knees.

"Christ! He's in there all right! What's left of him. It's gotta be him. His body's torn apart and most of him's missing!" The man was wiping his mouth with the back of his sleeve. "Every box in the place is torn apart, everything smashed. It's a Goddamn mess!"

The man was starting to cry. "His head's gone!"

"Hey, calm down." Mark told him. He turned to the man with his helmet still on. "Let me have your suit, I'll check it out." The guy pulled off the helmet.

"No man, you don't want to go in there. It smells horrible! There's something in that cave, man, that's fucking dangerous. I say we bolt the door so it can't get out. Rick wasn't hurt by no cave-in, something tore him to fucking pieces!"

"Okay... Alright, let's get out of here." Mark helped the man to his feet. All six men were glancing fearfully at the door and quickly made their way to the front entrance of the cave.

"What the hell?" Mark jumped back in horror. Rick's head, lying on the cave's floor next to the door they had entered through, stared up at them with milky eyes. Mark whirled around, glancing behind them, the others doing likewise, forming a circle with their backs together. Nothing moved in the inky shadows surrounding the reservoir. Mark shivered, remembering the wonderful moments he and Lori had spent in this cave before it turned deadly. Mark reached out and hit the button for the door and they all bolted from the cave.

A half dozen, wild-eyed, extremely frightened men sat in Will's room trying to all talk at once. "Hold it!" Will yelled. "One at a time. Mark, what the hell happened down there?"

Even Mark was unnerved "We found Rick's body in the tunnel, torn apart and . . . and his head was across the cave, by the door. Blood was everywhere!"

"How did his head get across the cave from his body?" Will asked trying to make some sense of their story.

The men all looked at each other for help with the explanation. "That's a helluva good question." Mark said softly.

They all sat in silence for a moment. "His body was in the tunnel but his head was by the door leading into the shelter." Mark repeated. "Shit, that means something moved it from the tunnel into the reservoir cave. Oh my God! The warning lights were blinking in the crow's nest a while ago like the door was opening and closing. Something may have gotten in!"

"It could have been in the cave with us when we were there!" said Matt. "Shit, it could even be in the shelter!"

"I don't think so," said Mark. "Remember the smell? We didn't smell anything in the shelter. I'll bet it's the thing that smells."

"Yeah, I bet it fucking is!" said Warren.

Will stood and went to the entertainment center.

"We'll monitor the doors. Bob and Washington are with Micah and can help him keep an eye on things. You gentlemen get some sleep. It has to be a large animal that's somehow broken in from the outside and we're going to have to hunt it."

"You sure it can't be inside?" he asked Mark.

"No, we'd know it by now, it must be huge!" Mark said.

"Okay, I'll announce Rick's death in the morning. He has no family. No use upsetting everyone tonight. Tomorrow we'll break out some weapons and start training people to use them, just in case." He held up a key he had taken from the shelf.

May 6, 9:10 p.m.

The band of creatures left very little of Rick's body in the back of the storage tunnel, but they were still hungry. The Arby creature was furious he had been unable to follow Jaime. Seeking another passage that would lead to more food they reentered the tunnels.

Jaime was trapped. Hiding beside the pumps and the unused filtering equipment, behind a mound of fallen rocks, he watched the strange appearing creatures who had just entered the cave, the spacesuits and the number of individuals keeping him from attacking. Once they left he circumnavigated the lake looking for a way out and becoming increasingly frustrated and angry.

Pacing from the front of the cave to the back, over and over, becoming more agitated with each journey, he wondered how the others managed to get out. He returned to the door he initially entered through, raising hairy, muscular arms over his head and banging until his arms ached, first growling and then roaring in frustration.

Still he was trapped. His red, too deep-set eyes swept the room, looking for escape. He ran to the front door, smashed it with his huge fists then, spotting the decapitated head, he kicked it furiously sending it rolling through the filtering equipment where it disappeared. Angrily, he followed it, peering behind the tanks and jumping as the pump suddenly came to life. He backed off and waited to see what it would do. Then, emboldened, he edged forward, crouched over and squeezed under and behind the equipment to the back wall, looking for the head. There he discovered a niche and thinking it may be another tunnel he crept within. It proved to be a short dead-end cave. Like a lair.

The meal and the hour combined to make him sleepy, and after convincing himself he couldn't get through the tiny cave, he curled up and fell asleep, lulled by a rumbling sound on the other side of the wall.

May 7, 9:00 a.m.

At nine o'clock the next morning Mark rode the elevator to the Crow's Nest alcove and was completely blown away when Will unlocked the cabinet door and swung it wide to reveal what lay inside. Mark assumed there would be a few weapons in a cabinet, but instead an opening lead into a vault filled along one wall with every conceivable kind of gun, and hundreds of boxes of ammunition lining the other side.

"Good God, Will, this is unbelievable! What could you possibly imagine we would run up against?"

Will actually seemed embarrassed. "Guns have been a secret hobby of mine for years. I wanted to be prepared for every eventuality."

"Well, it looks like you accomplished that goal. I'm not very knowledgeable about guns but after what happened to Rick, I'm certainly ready to learn."

A hand cart occupied the far corner of the hidden room. Will loaded it with guns, placing ammunition on a shelf underneath and he and Mark transported the weapons to the multipurpose room. Lenny and David took possession of the arsenal and would begin immediate distribution and training. Mark and Will went to the Crow's nest to see if they had received additional messages from the outside.

"Hi, bosses." Micah was back on duty after Robert had pulled the graveyard shift. "We've been getting faint signals but they seem to be having trouble on their end. Nothing we do seems to clear it up. Hopefully they'll get it fixed soon."

"Are we able to get through to them?" Will asked him.

"Don't know for sure but just try to shut me up. I've told 'em who we are, how many of us there are, what we've been doing for eight months and I've asked them if they've heard from the rest of the world. No response. I'd sure like to know if we've become Chinese citizens!"

"How about activity in the reservoir cave?"

"I've been monitoring the alarms to tell us if any of the doors, anywhere in the shelter are opened. So far none has gone off. I hope the damned bear, or whatever it is, doesn't have the faintest idea how to open a door."

Mark had been examining the sensor readings, only vaguely listening to Micah's narrative. "The radiation in that Dragon cave is very low. Do you think it's possible the radiation level in the western valley is also that low?"

"I don't know," Will said "But if the cave is open to the outside it's certainly encouraging."

"As soon as we can I'd like to retrieve Rick's body for burial. Doesn't seem right to leave him like that," Mark said.

"I'll hold another meeting to announce Rick's death and let everyone who wants to, get started on training." Will told him. "As soon as we're ready we'll go after the animal in the cave. Then we'll retrieve Rick's body." Will activated the intercom and announced the meeting. He turned and left the Crow's Nest.

Mark checked the sensors for radiation and tremors. There were more tremors and less radiation.

"Micah, can you let me know if you get any news? I'm going to weapons class."

"Sure Boss Two." Micah answered.

Mark headed below.

May 7, 9:10 a.m.

     The cave he slumbered in was dark but Jaime awoke when his body told him it was morning. He was hungry and the sound behind the back wall of his lair interested him. He scraped at the wall and the soft dirt crumbled easily beneath his claw-like fingers. He continued to dig, faster and faster, his two inch long sharp nails serving as tools to speed the job to its conclusion, a gap in the wall leading into a similar tunnel on the other side. He widened the gap and pushed his massive body into the opening until he succeeded in wedging through to the next tunnel. Even in almost absolute darkness he could see enough to move around in the tunnel, past a few boxes, to a crack of light at the end.

     Frustrated at this barrier he went back to the reservoir cave and quenched his thirst. He pounded on the entrance to the tunnel holding his grisly kill not knowing his old comrades had eaten the remains. Throughout the morning he prowled the cave and the new tunnel he'd discovered. Late that afternoon, and entirely by accident, while punching at and around the crack of light in the door, he hit the button. The roaring noise becoming a crescendo, and he entered the next cave immediately in front of the covered waterfall exiting the power plant.

     His elongated, hairy feet stood in an inch of water covering the bare rock floor. He followed the path to the left, drawn to the brighter lighting in that direction, around the end of the wall that isolated the contaminated waste water from the power plant. Water flowed from a crack in the concrete wall, flowing over debris to the floor. Movement upstairs in the second story of the plant drew his attention and Jaime slipped up the steps, saliva drooling over his pendulous lips at the prospect of making a kill.

May 7, 11:00 a.m.

"You pull back on the slide to cock the weapon, let it loose and you're ready to fire." Lenny had his arm around Lori explaining the procedure for cocking and firing a handgun. Approximately twenty people were in attendance with Lori being among the first to arrive. She showed an interest in the more exotic weapons and Lenny was instructing her in the care and use of an automatic Uzi in addition to a .45 caliber semi-automatic pistol. The Uzi was a fully automatic weapon that was banned in the United States. Lenny wondered where Will had gotten some of these guns. They had disassembled the weapons for cleaning.

"After you're each comfortable with handling your weapon you can move to the machine shop," Lenny told them as he moved to the next person in line. "David's setting up a firing range to allow you to practice with live rounds."

Mark put his .357 Magnum back together, pulled the slide and released it. Lori was confidently reassembling the Uzi. "Let's go Lori. I'm ready to fire."

"Me too. That bear's in serious trouble after what it did to Rick." Will had made the announcement about Rick's death that morning. Many residents wanted to go after his killer immediately but Will insisted on weapons training first.

Lori gathered her ammo and they left the room.

David had commandeered one end of the machine shop and fashioned a makeshift firing range. One end was lined with batting to absorb the shots and there were make-shift partitions between the shooters. Targets were suspended from wires. All the supplies for the range had been stored at the rear of the armory. Four people could use the range simultaneously. By that afternoon it was already in use, two men outfitted with earmuffs and firing their hand guns at the targets. Lori would only be firing the Glock, not expecting to ever have any use for the Uzi and not wanting to chance hitting someone with a ricochet if she were unable to handle unexpected recoil.

David gave them each a set of earmuffs and a quick lesson in firing range etiquette.

"Keep that thing pointed toward the target." Mark cracked.

"Yeah, let's see who's the sharpshooter here," she replied and fired several shots in rapid succession each one coming further down the wall, as she compensated for the recoil, the third hitting the paper target in the center of the head. "Oops, that was cool! I didn't expect the trigger to be so sensitive!" she exclaimed.

"The Glock has a double pull trigger instead of a standard safety," David explained. "After the initial hard pull it becomes very easy to fire off successive shots. You need to watch it." Mark fired off a shot and was surprised at the recoil of the large caliber hand gun. "Whoa, it really kicks!" He said as the bullet hit several feet above the target. Firing again, this time expecting the kick, he nailed his target in the head as well.

"The problem is", David told them both, "You don't want to go for the head. Try for mid-chest, it gives you more room to shoot wide and still hit the target."

Mark and Lori broke for a late lunch and met Will for a strategy session. They wanted everyone to have practice with the weapons but, on the other hand, didn't want to wait too long to retrieve Rick's body, for obvious reasons. Quite a few of the shelter's residents were already fairly proficient with weapons so Mark felt they could go after the animal first thing in the morning since it was already late-afternoon. That is, if it was even still in the caves. Will agreed and told them he would call for a meeting that evening to brief everyone and call for volunteers.

After lunch Mark and Lori went back to get some additional target practice. They were gaining familiarity with the weapons and Lori even got off a few shots with the Uzi.

They both were doing a creditable job considering they had never fired weapons before. David was helping Mark replace his clip when the intercom summoned Mark to the Crow's Nest. "Lori, keep practicing, I'll see what they want and return ASAP." He slapped the clip home, flipped the safety on, stuck the gun in his waistband holster at the small of his back and headed up the stairs. He felt like such a cowboy!

When he entered the Crow's nest he knew immediately something was wrong. Even Micah had the look of a dead man walking.

"What's going on?" he asked.

"We have another man missing." Will told him glumly. "Bud Nagle. He and his wife took a nap this afternoon and when she awoke he wasn't there. She says it was about three-thirty. Being concerned about whatever killed Rick she paged him and he didn't respond."

"When did anyone see him last?" Mark flopped down in a chair forgetting about the gun until it stabbed him in the back. Reaching back he retrieved it and laid it on the desk feeling a lot less macho than he did a few minutes ago.

"Tyler Forbes says he went to the plant around 3:15 to check out some power fluctuations. Says he thought the tremors might be causing some problems. Just as he left the plant Bud entered. Tyler said he didn't see anything unusual."

"None of my alarms have gone off. There's no way the animal got into the power plant," said Micah.

"Shit!" exclaimed Washington from his computer console. "Take a look at this." They gathered around the screen. "This is a list of the dragon doors. There's more of them on the list than we have lights for on the monitor panel. What's with that?"

"There were some areas that had no access at all to the outside," said Will. "It wasn't necessary to have visible alarms on those doors, since we were primarily concerned with radioactive contamination. I had forgotton about them, but the only way anything could get into those tunnels would be by opening a door, which a bear couldn't do, or possibly digging through from another tunnel. A few had very thin walls from one tunnel to another."

"Or if the tremors had caused a cave-in, opening up one of the tunnels." said Mark.

"Shit!" Washington repeated.

Mark barely knew Richard Kreig. He was one of the younger guys. But Bud was one of their inner circle and Mark felt a stab of grief at the thought that something may have happened to him. "Maybe he can't hear the page. Those turbines are deafening and he might have on his earmuffs. I'm going to the plant to look for him."

"No you're not! Not until we find out what the hell is happening!" Will said angrily.

"We can't just sit here and wait for someone else to get killed!" Mark remarked jumping to his feet. He and Will locked eyes, they had never raised their voices in all the time they had known each other.

"Sorry Mark," Will said. "Let's just take this slow. Get a group of armed folks together for a search party. You can go tonight instead of waiting until tomorrow."

"Now you're talking." Mark picked up his weapon and left to carry out Will's instructions.

He entered the machine shop and saw four new shooters firing weapons at their targets. Lori was off to the side cleaning her gun. He walked over to David. "How many people have you checked out?"

"About a dozen this afternoon but we have a lot of folks that already had experience either with rifles or hand guns or both."

"Give me some names. Our timetable's been moved up. I need to put together another search party."

"Why, what's up?" Lenny came over to see what was going on.

"Bud Nagle's missing."

"Count me in!" Lenny and David said simultaneously. They went off to gather the weapons together and get Mark a list of competent marksmen.

"Oh no, Mark." Lori overheard and came to stand by his side. "I'm going with you."

"Like hell you are!" Mark said.

"I am. I can use this thing and Bud's my friend too."

He could tell by the determined look on her face he was going to be unsuccessful at dissuading her. "Yeah, yeah. Let's round up the rest of the posse."

Mark made a general announcement over the intercom for anyone interested in the hunt to rendezvous in the auditorium at

7:00 p.m. When he and Lori arrived they found over forty people ready to rock and roll.

Mark chose ten of those present to form two groups to go inside, with he and Lori making it a dozen. David and Lenny would each lead a group, the remainder of the people staying outside the power plant door in case they needed reinforcements.

"Bud may be fine, but no one's heard from him and he doesn't answer any pages. Considering what happened to Rick, we have to assume the worst and be very careful. I don't know what's holed up in those tunnels but it must be big and strong. Meet me back here in about an hour so we can issue weapons and ammo." Mark instructed.

They left the auditorium. "I want to check in at the Crow's Nest to see if there's been any news." Mark said to Lori. "I'll see you back here. You sure you want to do this?"

"Yes, I need to stand up and be counted for once."

He placed his hands on her shoulders looking down into her eyes and trying to fathom the mystery behind them.

"Lori, I don't know what happened to you, but this may not be the best way to prove yourself."

"It's a start," she said, meeting his gaze head on. "Go on and reconnoiter. I'll see you back at the auditorium."

She went to the daycare center to check on the kids. Barbara and Sandi, along with several teenage girls, were babysitting the children for movie night. She pulled them to the side and told them about Bud Nagle.

"Why on Earth would you consider going with them?" asked Barbara, flabbergasted that Lori would think of going after that thing with a gun.

"My reasons are playing over there," she pointed toward the kids. She hesitated, unsure of what to say. "Before the war, my wonderful husband used to beat us, me and Kevin, not so much Ashley. I stood by like a coward and let it happen, over and over, too scared to fight back or stick up for myself or my children, believing that somehow, it was my fault. What kind of role model was I for my little girl? I just stood there and took it! I'm through letting people I love get hurt!" She wanted desperately for these friends to know she was no longer that coward, no longer a woman that would let anyone, or anything, ever again hurt her children.

"Besides, I'll be with Mark. I'm not going to let this thing hurt him, either. Barbara, if anything happens, take care of my kids, okay?"

"Sure, but nothing's going to happen. You guys watch each other's back."

Lori had never let anyone know how she felt about Mark. She knew, though, her remarks made it clear to the others that she loved him, and she no longer cared who knew, regardless of the fact that he didn't feel the same way. She went over to where the kids were sitting on the floor before the T.V. and knelt down. "You guys be good and do everything Mrs. Thompson tells you, okay?" She kissed each of them on top their head.

"Where are you going, Mommy? When will you get back?" Ashley asked.

Lori thought, "*I hope to God I come back.*" She stood. "I have to take care of something. I'll be back soon, baby," she told Ashley and left for the auditorium.

Mark, David and Lenny loaded weapons and ammunition into the cart and delivered them to the auditorium. Then Mark returned to the Crow's Nest. "Any news on Bud?" he asked Micah.

"No word from him at all. And still no alarms have gone off. I hope you guys blow its brains out!"

"We'll get it. You can bet on it." Mark said.

"Hey, Mark. Jeez, I almost forgot. I intercepted another message but this one was from someone else! They were attempting to communicate with the government shelter we talked to earlier. It sounded like an Australian accent. Can you believe it? I've been busy with the bear thing, but as soon as you guys finish it off, I'll concentrate on making contact again. Isn't it great?"

"Good work, Micah. We'll exterminate this thing so we can all get back to work. See you later."

Mark exited the narrow staircase and ran into Will just coming out of the elevator.

"Hi Mark, I just came from Chris. She says 'good luck'."

"Thanks. Don't worry, we'll get it before it hurts anybody else."

"Mark, be careful." He came over and put his hands on Mark's shoulders. Mark could feel them shaking. Will paused, at a loss for words. "I've lost one son. I don't want to lose you too."

Mark didn't know how to answer, touched by Will's comment, he reached out and hugged the man that had been a father to him all his life. "I'll be careful." He noticed tears in the older man's eyes as he entered the elevator.

May 7, 9:00 p.m.

A large group of men and women stood outside the power plant door staring at it, trying to fathom what lay beyond. The door slid aside and the dozen heavily armed men and women jumped through quickly, guns held with both hands, sweeping left to right. Lenny instructed them to never point the weapons away from where they were looking. Moving farther into the cave they split into two prearranged groups, the first, led by Lenny would search the lower level; the tunnels, water outlet areas and first floor of the plant including the areas around and behind the turbines. The other group, led by David, would go to the second floor computer room and on through to the oil storage caves farther back in the mountain. Mark and Lori were in David's group.

"Hey, what's going on? There's water all over the place." said Lenny.

"I hope it's not contaminated." Mark answered. "Where do you think it's coming from?"

"Looks like the wall sprung a leak. Look over there!" Lenny pointed to the concrete aqueduct wall where it connected to the side of the building.

"Damn! The tremors must have caused some damage. We'll need a repair crew in here as soon as we get this thing." Mark said.

They moved forward farther into the cave and Lenny motioned to David. He, in turn, signaled to his group to start up the stairs. Mark smiled over at Lori, hoping she would stay behind them and not take any unnecessary chances. David led the way, moving slowly up the stairs, his weapon extended before him and the others following close behind.

They reached the huge open door of the plant, the vibration of the turbines setting Mark's teeth on edge. Reconnoitering at the top of the staircase, they peered into the well-lighted area beyond the door trying to see around corners. The computer room was rectangular, with a central island jammed full of 21 inch monitors that depicted the water level in the reservoir above, the acre feet of water entering the lake, turbine RPM's, kilowatts of power generated and other pertinent parameters. The equipment blocked their view of the aisle on the other side of the island.

David motioned to Mark to check out the back aisle. Mark gulped at being chosen and quickly moved around the end of the island, jumping into the open space with his weapon outstretched before him.

It was empty.

Mark let out the breath he'd been holding. He wasn't cut out for this green-beret stuff. They moved forward into the cavernous main floor of the plant, spreading into an arc, weapons pointing straight ahead. Again, there were no signs of the animal. A staircase descended through the floor to the lower level and Mark noticed the sign that cautioned "ear protection is necessary," was missing. He saw it smashed against the far wall. He pointed it out to David and the others.

This room had huge tools, 6 foot long wrenches, hanging on the wall in the event a manual shut down of the penstock valves ever became necessary. The tops of the turbines extended through the floor on the side of the room closest to the water outlets.

Beyond the stairwell a large door led to the rear of the plant, the oil storage area, an area that was darker, more ominous.

"Group two, come in." the walkie-talkie squawked. "Take caution! We've found a tunnel with evidence that something recently dug through from the reservoir. Whatever got Rick is in this cave! Any sign of Bud?"

At that exact moment Mark and David, leading the group, came upon a pool of purple, congealed blood by a bank of lockers located next to the back door.

"Oh God," Mark said. "There's blood here." They stood frozen, their weapons pointed at the darkness beyond. There were stacks of barrels filled with machine oil that extended into the mountain, in caves and tunnels few of the remnant had ever visited. Mark turned to Lori. Her face was pale but she appeared determined to follow this through with no sign of retreat on her features.

The radio reported, "We've searched the lower cave. There's nothing down here so we're coming up to join you. Hang on until we get there."

They were more than willing to wait. As they stood there, Mark suddenly felt dizzy and slightly nauseated, and being from Southern California he knew the symptoms –

Earthquake! A big one!

He grabbed the railing around the staircase as the tremor grew in strength, then diminished briefly, and – KACHUNK - intensified, as it shifted the shelter sideways, throwing them all off balance. Dust billowed into the room from the open door, loose equipment in the plant fell off shelves and glass shattered on the floor and flung shards around their feet as the violent shaking continued. Mark, trying to keep his feet, threw an arm around Lori, covering her head with his hand, his forgotten weapon pointing toward the ceiling. David slipped on the blood and fell heavily to the ground, as the other three jumped to the open doorway to take cover.

That was a gigantic mistake.

A hairy arm extended around the side of the door, raking one of the men across the throat with rapier-like claws and laying him open from ear to ear. His already lifeless body, gushing blood, dropped in place. One of the other men leaped away, whirling, firing his weapon indiscriminately into the opening. "It's in there! Oh sweet Jesus, it got Manny!"

David regained his feet, although the shaking continued, leveled his weapon, and moved quickly to the side of the door away from the creature.

"Quit firing!" David yelled. "You're gonna hit one of us!"

Mark released Lori and they both moved to David's side, weapons trained at the door. Mark could barely see a shadow through the dust, moving toward the back of the cave. It disappeared behind a stack of barrels. The shaking subsided as the other group ran up behind them.

"What's goin' on?" Lenny yelled. "Did you get it?"

One of the guys with Lenny, Patterson, spotted Manny's body, his throat grinning at them in death. "Oh man, what happened to him?" He turned away, suddenly green. The others pointed their guns at the door, hardened by the fact that whatever had done this to Manny was just beyond.

"I saw it go farther back into the cave." Mark said.

"Yeah? Well, it's going to be hard to see back there." said Lenny. "Everyone, on three, through the door in an arc, backs together. One-two-THREE!"

They jumped through the door, fanning out, weapons pointing into the back of the cavern. Patterson gave Manny's body a wide berth. They choked on the thick, swirling dust which also obscured their vision. Barrels were stacked against the back wall by the huge storage tank while other stacks extended into the large empty area in front of them.

"My group, you five," Lenny pointing to the four men and a woman, "In an arc, weapons ready, stay by the door. Whatever happens, it doesn't get past you. Got it?" They nodded in unison.

"The rest of you, come on!"

They moved away from the door and took positions against the railing. Mark looked down, back toward the entrance, and saw dark swirling water covering the cave floor thirty feet below. There was a lot more water than when they first entered the cave. The recessed floor was almost full, reminding him of Will's black-bottom pool from his former existence.

Lenny motioned them forward. "Three of you, Lori, Marcus and Sam, take positions here. You have a clear visual path and it can't sneak up on you. Just try not to shoot the rest of us." Mark was relieved Lenny had selected Lori to remain behind.

Lenny, David, Mark and Bill Jamison moved forward, still unaware of the nature of their adversary. Ten feet from the first line of barrels Lenny motioned them to stay together and go around to the left. Just as they reached them, the entire line, pushed from the back, came crashing down, on, and around them. The barrels were empties, stacked two high, prior to being moved into back caves for storage. Even empty they weighed twenty pounds apiece. Mark threw up his arm and deflected one that was falling directly at him. It hurt like hell but he managed to maintain his focus behind the barrels.

And saw the creature attacking!

"Here it comes!" he shouted to the others. He brought his .357 up and fired, but using only one hand the shot went high with the kick of the weapon. He grabbed the gun with both hands and fired off a second round. The creature screamed, more in anger than pain, but Mark thought he may have hit it. David flung a barrel aside and fired several rounds in rapid succession, also from a .357 Magnum. The Jaime creature reached Bill who had been dazed by the falling barrels, picked him up over his head and flung him toward the rail, his body landing hard on the smooth surface and sliding under the rail. Sam leaped for him but missed as Bill disappeared over the edge, his surprised yell ending abruptly as he hit rocks in the cavern below.

The creature screamed again, a thunderous, maddened scream that froze them momentarily in horror, when they finally discerned its nature, and then all three men as well as Lori, Sam, Sheri and Marcus began firing everything they had. The creature stretched up to its full height, fully seven feet, and stood there as a rain of bullets tore into it, stepping back slightly but not going down. Letting out a final primal scream it suddenly flung itself forward directly into the gunfire, lunging toward Lenny who was farther forward than the others. It slashed at him, the claws laying open a gash in Lenny's arm as the creature crashed to the floor. They stood there pumping more rounds into it until David regained his senses.

"Hold your fire!" he yelled. "I think it's dead." They all stopped firing, with the exception of Patterson, who kept spasmodically pulling his trigger, teeth gritted and his eyes wide, until he ran out of ammo, the others watching in amazement. "Nice going Patterson. Now it's deader. Hope you never need that ammo you wasted."

David approached the body tentatively, kicked at it, and jumped back. It didn't move.

"What the hell is it?" asked one of the men that had been guarding the door. "God! It looks like it's rotting!"

"Whew, and it smells like it too!" added Lori. "Where did it come from?"

"I think it must have broken in from the outside. That would explain the increase in the radioactivity we detected in the dragon caves." Mark said.

Just then the lights went out.

May 7, 9:20 p.m.

The contractions were stronger and more regular than yesterday's and Sandi was feeling pressure above her pubic bone. Moments ago, while using the toilet, she saw bloody mucus on the paper and knew it was a sign she could really be in labor. She was excited, but frightened as well, still concerned the baby may have been hurt during the attack by Clay Hargraves. She wanted to tell Pete, but he hadn't answered her page so she decided to go see Dr. Jim on her own.

She entered the elevator and pushed the button for the top floor, feeling the gentle surge as the car glided upward.

In the next instant she was thrown against the back of the car as it lurched and ground to a halt. She smacked her head, and dizzy, threw out her hand to brace herself. The car bucked, causing her to actually leave her feet. She came down hard, went to her knees and grabbed her abdomen.

"Oh no...oh no... not now. Please God! Not now!"

She tried to get to the side of the car to brace herself but it was shaking violently, scaring her into thinking it might drop. The car lurched again, this time in the other direction. She grabbed the railing and held on for what seemed like several minutes but the temblor actually lasted only 42 seconds before subsiding.

When the shaking finally stopped she regained her feet and punched the buttons on the panel. Nothing happened. The lights were all off and she realized the power to the elevator had been knocked out, maybe power to the whole shelter. She waited while she had another mild contraction then yelled to try and attract attention to her plight. This quake was much stronger than the smaller tremors they had been experiencing and she knew, if the shelter was damaged or people hurt, that there may be no one to help her.

She sat back in the corner of the car, eyes wide, big tears flowing down her cheeks.

"Pete, oh please... please help me," she whispered.

May 7, 9:40 p.m.

Barbara was making a valiant attempt to read "The Wind in the Willows" to a group of twenty three extremely frightened children. The big quake had tossed the daycare room around like a ship on a stormy sea flinging the kids to the floor. No one had been seriously injured and Barbara was trying to restore calm until parents could arrive to collect them. Tonight was movie night, many parents taking advantage of Barbara's babysitting and a chance to have a break from the little ones. She knew the parents would be here any minute to retrieve their children.

"Tigger was …," she was saying when the lights went out. Quake damage caused safety relays in the power plant to trip, even though the turbine continued to generate power. Approximately two seconds later red emergency lights came on creating an eerie atmosphere that frightened the children and sent a shiver up Barbara's spine. Kevin Arnaud started to sniffle but Ashley and Jeremy comforted him. Jeremy understood Kevin's uneasiness. Each time his mom told them everything would be alright something else happened, and the children were feeling less and less secure.

Barbara gave up on the book, gathered two of the crying children in her arms and hugged them. The others all gathered around for their hugs as Barbara gave comfort in the strange reddish glow.

Parents arrived, relief crossing their faces when they found their children unharmed. After a few minutes Barbara was left with Jeremy and Lori's two children. "Mom, when will Ashley's mother be here?" Jeremy asked.

"She's really busy right now, Jeremy. We'll keep Ash and Kevin with us for a while. Okay kids?"

"I want my mommy!" Kevin whimpered.

"I know, honey. She'll be here in a little bit."

May 7, 10:00 p.m.

"There's more radiation at the power plant." Micah said. "It's pretty weak, well below the danger level, which is a good thing since Mark's group is down there. Jeez, you know what? I'll bet it's from the water."

Micah held one of the walkie-talkies. He and Will were trying to monitor the communications between the two groups in the power plant.

"No doubt." Will said. "We need to repair the leak as soon as possible. How're you doing with the intercom?"

"I'll have it fixed pretty soon. The main system's back up, you can make general announcements, but the individual intercoms, on a separate circuit, are still down."

Will flicked the toggle, announced a meeting in the auditorium and said to Micah, "Inform me of anything you hear from Mark. I'll be back shortly."

Just then an audible alarm sounded from the computer.

"It's the door alarm." Micah said. "They must have opened a Dragon Door in the power cave looking for the bear." He hit the enter key and the alarm ceased.

Just as Will left the room the walkie-talkie came to life as the search party reported in, announcing that the creature had been slain.

"Yee-hah, good news at last!" Micah whooped. He briefed them about the radiation in the cave, assured them it wasn't dangerous and promised to gather a repair crew immediately.

***

Will hurried to the auditorium through hallways illuminated by the red back-up lights. The room was packed with frightened residents needing reassurances from their leader. Others streamed in, these late arrivals having just fetched their children, as Will raised his hands for quiet.

"Please, take your seats so we can get started." He shouted above the din. "We'll be sending a repair crew to the power plant as soon as possible and the intercom system is partially repaired." He took a deep breath. "Unfortunately, there's a problem in the power cave besides the potential damage from the quake."

"What kind of problem?" asked Vernon Richenour.

"The animal that killed Richard Krieg has apparently gotten into the power plant. Bud Nagle is missing."

The remnant sat in stunned silence.

"We have an armed search party at the plant. They're equipped with walkie-talkies and will inform the Crow's Nest as soon as they hunt it down. Then we can send in a repair crew."

"Have there been many injuries?" Freddie called out.

"I'll have to check with Dr. Jim. We'll let you know."

"What about more quakes?" someone yelled from the audience.

"Dr. Whitehorse warned us the tremors could be leading up to the large quake we've just experienced. There will undoubtedly be some aftershocks but I'm confident we can make repairs. We need to assess the shelter for any damage. It was built to withstand hydrogen bombs but the quakes put it under different stresses. We need volunteers to perform the inspection so please stay after the meeting. I know it's late but we need to get started immediately."

"What if this wasn't the big one?" asked Vernon.

"We'll cross that bridge when we come to it." Will answered. He reached up and pulled a map down just behind the podium, shining a flashlight on it. All three levels of the shelter were illustrated on the map.

"On the bottom level, here," He pointed with the light, "at the rear of the shelter is a dragon door that isn't indicated on any other maps, nor is it readily visible, being only a slit in the wall. The door has been secured until now but I unlocked it on my way to this meeting. Beyond the door the corridor goes west for 30 yards then turns south. There is a quarter mile, reinforced tunnel leading to a massive blast door that, in turn, opens into a cave. The cave is reinforced in the same manner as the reservoir and power plant caves are. The tunnels and other caves were subject to being damaged by blasts but these structures were too important to leave in their natural state."

"Why weren't we told about this before?" asked Vernon.

"I'm telling you now! You didn't need to know before."
Will was beginning to lose his patience with Richenour.

"The cave will hold all the residents of this shelter. The outside blast door will not be opened until absolutely necessary - it leads to the outside."

"Is that safe?" asked Brian Morrison.

"The radiation has fallen to levels we believe are safe and we'll only use the tunnel in the event a catastrophe renders the shelter uninhabitable. If that happens proceed through the tunnel into the exit cave."

He explained to them the reason for building their sanctuary in this lonely part of New Mexico and the hope that the radiation in the west valley would be compatible with life.

"The radioactivity in the western valley is less than elsewhere. We would be wise to remain there until it's safe to try and return to civilization. We can send out reconnaissance parties to assess the damage and they can report back about what condition the surrounding area is in. We're attempting to fully restore the intercom system. There is still significant danger so stay out of the dragon caves and especially the power plant. Try and get some sleep and we should have more news in the morning."

May 7, 10:20 p.m.

Emergency lights had come on within seconds of the power failure, powered by an emergency generator located in a third level room of the shelter. Mark ran to the railing and peered down into the darkness of the pit below. He couldn't see Bill. At the far end of the ledge where the railing connected with the wall was a ladder descending into the dark area between the lower cave wall and the concrete enclosure around the waste water outlet. Mark ran to the ladder and quickly descended. Lenny followed him and the others stood at the rail looking down. Once they were in the dark their eyes adjusted slightly and Mark found Bill's body by the wall in several inches of water, his neck obviously broken from the fall. Lenny felt for a pulse.

"He's dead Mark. Let's get him out of here." They yelled the news up to the others and heard muttered curses. Hoisting the body, they carried it to the foot of the ladder.

"Let's get some rope to haul him up." Mark told Lenny as he started up the ladder. At the top he met the others. "We need to retrieve his body for burial." Mark told them. "But let's take a look at the plant. Now that the thing, whatever it is, is dead, we'll want to get started on repairing the leak and getting the primary power back on. Did you radio the Crow's Nest?"

"Yeah, we told Micah we killed it but didn't tell them about Bill yet." David said.

"Radio for a crew to come take away both bodies and send for guys that are familiar with how this plant operates." Mark instructed. "Let's take a look at the damage." He moved over beside Lori.

They went through the plant and down the stairs to the base of the wall where rocks and concrete littered the floor of the cave creating tiny islands in the dark sea of water. Water poured through an opening in the wall approximately ten feet up.

There was a pounding at the door. The door was on the emergency power circuit but the earthquake has tweaked it and it only partially opened. Each door was equipped with a manual switch but it was on the inside. Mark and the others hurried toward the door when the sound of barrels rolling violently around on the upper level attracted their attention.

Whirling around, they stared in horrified disbelief! Standing in the ruddy light at the head of the stairs were a half dozen creatures like the one they had killed, giant rotting creatures from the bowels of Hell, one in particular catching Mark's attention. It appeared to be eight feet tall, massive shoulders, a malevolent gaze trained directly, unswervingly at Mark as though it had a personal grudge to settle with him alone.

"Damn, there's more of em! Get the door open!" yelled Lenny. He and David raised their weapons, but not wanting to provoke the creatures, they would hold their fire as long as necessary. Several more of the creatures approached from behind the others.

Mark jerked the manual lever! Nothing happened! The door jerked, ground to a stop and made a loud screeching sound that galvanized the monsters into action. They plunged down the stairs and everyone not working on the door started firing, the distance causing them to miss most of the shots.

A dim memory of the danger guns represented caused the creatures to pause momentarily. One of the men on the outside stuck a shovel through the opening and applied leverage. The door ground farther open. Mark put his arm around Lori and pulled her toward the door.

"Lori, you can get through. Come on you guys, I think it's wide enough." Mark yelled.

Lori slid through the opening with ease and most of the others followed quickly. The Arby-creature saw them escaping, his need to kill overpowering his fear of the weapons. He didn't understand it but Mark was the embodiment of all that the Arby creature had ever hated, ever murdered or raped or tortured, a representative of the "men of privilege", an ancient enemy he had seen in his dreams. David dropped the walkie-talkie and opened fire.

"Hurry, hurry... come on, go, go, go! Mark literally shoved the men through, some of them wedging in the too small opening until, pushing with his shoulder, he forced them through.

"Go Mark!" yelled Lenny. "We're right behind you!"

Mark slipped through the door, the others in the shelter pulling him through by one arm. He whirled back to the door, heard a curse as David ran out of ammo. Lenny jammed another thirty round clip into his AR 15. "David, you're out of ammo, get through the door! David tried to squeeze through but he was too big. He turned his shoulders and lunged forward. Mark grabbed him and heard him yelp as skin was scraped off his chest. He fell through into the corridor and swirled back to pull Lenny through the gap.

"Lenny, come on! Come on!" David reached through the door. His huge frame was wedged into the opening, his arm outstretched, reaching for Lenny. David saw the creatures rear up in front of Lenny. Lenny whirled for the door and David saw his face suddenly register fear, a terrified grimace... then he screamed in tremendous pain. Bright red blood poured out through his gaping mouth and soaked David's arms as he jerked them back through the opening. Mark grabbed David and desperately tried to pull him from the door.

"David, come on. It's too late!" Mark looked into the opening and froze, staring up into gleaming, red, hateful eyes. The creature reached through and grabbed a handful of Mark's shirt and jerked him toward the opening.

Something smashed Mark from the side as David tackled him, ripping him from the thing's grasp, the two of them crashing to the ground as their momentum carried them down the hall. The creature screamed in frustration adding his voice to the clamor of the monsters screeching and snarling, as they tore Lenny to shreds. Arby threw himself against the door, over and over trying to break through but it was now solidly frozen in place. The quake had twisted the track, negating any possibility of opening it further.

Mark jumped to his feet, all of them frozen in horror at the thing bashing itself against the door. They all backed slowly away from the door.

"Wow," Mark said. "We're going to need much bigger weapons!" His eyes were glued to the creature in sheer astonishment.

Lori broke the spell. "Come on! You're right. I'm going for the Uzi and we have to warn people!'

They all raced down the hallway to the staircase, burst through the door and took the stairs two at a time heading for the top floor.

May 7, 10:30 p.m.

Pete rushed into the apartment he shared with Sandi, "Sandi! Are you here? He was frantic to see if she was okay following the quake. He'd been in the machine shop with a couple of others when the quake hit and the door had stuck. When the lights went out the three of them were blind. For some reason no emergency lighting had been provided in the shop or it hadn't worked. They used a welding torch to illuminate the door so they could force it open and get out. It took a long time, too long for Pete.

"Damn." he exclaimed. "Where is she?" He checked the bedroom thinking she might be sleeping but she wasn't home.

As he left the apartment the shelter was hit by an aftershock, not nearly as strong as the big quake, but strong enough to cause his heart to skip a beat as he braced himself against the wall. He passed other residents, two almost carrying a third who was having difficulty walking, his head bleeding from a large gash.

"Oh baby, where are you?" He realized she may have gone to the doctor and turned toward the central elevator hearing excited voices ahead as he turned the corner. A crowd of people gathered around the elevator door.

"What's going on?" he asked someone at the back of the crowd. Some men were trying to pry the elevator door open.

"Oh Pete, thank God it's you!" said the resident. The quake damaged the elevator. It's stuck between floors with Sandi inside! The car's closer to the top and your dad and Dr. Jim are on the top floor talking to her. She's in labor." But he was talking to Pete's back as Pete sprinted down the hallway heading for the staircase.

He entered the dim stairwell and heard a mob of people coming from the level below. Mark, Lori and a large number of others, all fully armed and looking like they were followed by death's legions, sprinted up the stairs, catching up with him.

"Pete, where's Will. We killed the thing in the power plant,..." Mark began.

"It was horrible. . ."

"They're nine feet tall!"

"Some kind of monster!"

"Everybody shut up!" Mark yelled. "There are a dozen or so more!" He took Pete's arm urging him upstairs. "We're getting heavier firepower. Regular weapons don't stop them. The door is stuck but they may figure out how to get into the reservoir or farm caves. Everybody needs to hold up somewhere safe until we get them. They've already killed two more men!"

They exited at the top floor. "I'll tell them, but Sandi's in labor and she's stuck in the damaged elevator!"

Pete ran down the central hallway as some of the others entered the elevator to the weapons locker to get more ammo and higher caliber weapons and the others went looking for their family members to verify their safety after the quake.

Pete rounded a corner and found another large group of people. He shoved his way roughly through the crowd. "Get out of my way!"

His dad and the doctor were on their knees at the elevator door. Walter had a crowbar and the door was cracked open a few inches. "She's fine, son. She's in early labor but we need to get her out of there."

Pete leaned down to the crack. He could see the top of the elevator. "Sandi? Can you hear me?"

"Pete, please get me out!" She was crying and sounded so scared his heart ached.

"Don't worry, baby. We will."

They had enough room to get their hands into the crack. With Walter pulling on the crowbar and Pete and Jim pulling in opposite directions on the door it gave way and scraped open about two thirds of its width.

"I can get through!" said Pete. He backed into the opening with the others holding his arms and they lowered him to the top of the car which rested just below the level of the hall floor.

"Oh damn, I forgot!" he yelled up to them. "Mark killed some kind of huge creature in the power plant but he says there are a bunch more!" He kneeled down and unhooked the hatch cover. "Tell Mr. Hargraves! Everyone needs to get somewhere safe until these things are dead. They've killed two more men." He swung the cover up and dropped through the hatch where Sandi flung herself into his arms.

Walter turned and told someone to get Will Hargraves. "He's having a meeting in the auditorium. Hurry!"

Just then another aftershock struck and the elevator slipped a few inches. Sandi screamed. "Hurry up!" Pete called to them. "I need help to lift her to the hatch!"

They lowered more men into the shaft with two additional men descending into the car to help lift Sandi to the top. Pete prayed she would fit through the hatch.

"Sandi, we're going to hoist you up. Keep your body perfectly straight and don't bend over or you'll fall. Okay?"

She nodded as he and one other man each put a hand under her foot and holding on to her leg they counted to three and hoisted her straight up. The third man braced her and another reached down from above grasping her upstretched arm. Pete breathed a sigh of relief as her abdomen just cleared the sides of the hatch. He could see up through the opening as one man bent down allowing her to step on his back and up and out of the shaft.

They hoisted one of the men up and Pete made a stirrup of his hands as the second man reached up to grasp hands that extended down through the hatch. Pete was last and tried to jump to reach the hatch. As he landed the car fell another foot. He crashed to the floor.

Getting slowly to his feet he looked up and saw, to his great relief, a rope trailing through the opening. He grabbed it and wrapped it around his waist as the men above hoisted him through the hatch. As his feet cleared it, the car fell and he was left dangling in the elevator shaft. The others slowly hauled him to the level of the corridor. There was the sound of crashing metal and dust flew up the shaft as he scrambled over the edge and rolled into the hallway. Sandi fell on top of him, shaking and sobbing.

May 7, 11:15 p.m.

Hunger and the smell of blood drove Arby from the door to share in the meal. By the time his rage had subsided most of the man had been eaten. He grabbed a leg bone away from a smaller creature and sunk sharp teeth into the meat. Even a full–grown man made a small meal for the monsters. After eating, the creatures spread out, wandering around the lower level and sloshing through the deepening water, trying to find a way out. They became uncomfortable when the water reached their waists. With the water deepening, and after they'd exhausted the possibilities for escaping from the lower level they climbed the stairs to the plant's upper floor and backed out on the ledge, the noise from the turbines grating on their nerves as they crouched together alongside the door leading to the farm cave. Not knowing what else to do they squatted down, resting and waiting. They knew the creatures would return and they would eat again.

The water in the cave was now lapping at the few small steps leading into the shelter. In a matter of hours it would begin to spill over, through the stuck open door, into the interior.

May 8, 1:00 a.m.

The infirmary looked like a warzone. At least thirty residents had been injured in the earthquake, Sandi was in labor in one of the exam rooms with Pete attending her, and in the operating suite, a body bag held all they could find of Rick's remains. Mark had led a party to the dragon cave off the reservoir to fetch Rick's body and they had been in constant fear that the creatures in the power cave would hear them and come to investigate. Apparently, though, they still were unable to open the doors between caves and were unaware of the tunnel wall that had been breached.

"Is there anything I can do to help you guys out?" he asked Aaron.

"I think we should just dispose of Rick's body in the burial chasm and worry about a memorial service later. We can combine services for Rick, Bud, Bill and Lenny. Can you get some help and take care of that?"

Mark was beginning to feel like a Coroner. "Sure, Aaron, that's a good idea."

He recruited help from the healthy group that had brought in the injured and, using a gurney, they transported Rick's remains to the cave they had used for burials. The earthquake had caused the chasm to widen even further and rather than trying to jump across they rolled the body, bag and all, over the edge of the chasm and let it fall. Mark almost felt it was sacrilegious but conditions in the shelter had altered dramatically and concessions had to be made. This was the fourth resident buried in this chamber and two more bodies lay in the inaccessible power cave. They had never found Bud's remains.

The Crow's nest was alive with activity when Mark arrived to check on the situation. Micah watched the alarms, hoping to detect any further breech in the dragon doors which would give them advance warning the creatures had gained access to inhabited areas. Darryl was trying to get critical environmental systems back on-line. The computer and all other systems were limited by the diminished electrical power produced by the back-up generator.

"The generator's producing uneven power. It's not that noticeable in the lights but the computer's picking it up." Darryl told Will.

"Does it show the output of the power plant?"

"Apparently the turbine is still spinning but the relays have tripped. They don't do that unless there's a real problem with the operation of the turbine. We won't be able to evaluate the problem and go back on regular power until we can get to the plant. The generator has enough fuel for two weeks, longer if we shut down some systems."

Mark advanced into the room. "Did you inform everyone about the monsters in the power cave?"

"No, I got the word just after the meeting broke up. As long as the creatures are confined, we'll let people try and get some sleep and tell them in the morning. I have told them about the escape tunnel and they are prepared to evacuate if necessary."

"Okay, I'm going back down to the auditorium. Lori and the other members of the hunting party are there. The earthquake collapsed a portion of the second level ceiling and destroyed part of the living quarters, including mine, so I'll be in the auditorium until we can get new quarters after these things are either killed or expelled from the shelter."

He descended to the first level and entered the auditorium where the vigilante group had congregated.

An hour passed, and then another, as Mark watched Lori dozing in the auditorium seat and wished he could also get some sleep. He was too keyed up to be able to rest even though he was completely exhausted from the day's events. After they left the power plant, they'd gone to the weapons locker and secured more weapons. Lori checked on the children but Barbara had put them to bed and they didn't awaken when she kissed them goodnight. They had all returned to the auditorium to reconnoiter and plan their next move. With the damage to the living quarters many of them had decided to remain in the auditorium to be ready for any eventuality.

David was alternately despondent and angry. Lenny had been like a brother to him. They'd been best friends since they were teens, joined the marines together, served as each other's best man and lent support during both divorces.

"You don't think they can get out of the power plant do you?" Patterson asked Mark.

"I don't think they can get the doors open. If they could, we would know it by now."

"Are we going back after them? There must be a dozen of them. How are we going to get them out of there?" Patterson asked.

David snarled through gritted teeth, "Damn straight, we're going after them! Those fuckers are going down!"

"Take it easy David. We don't want any more casualties." Mark said. "We'll get some reinforcements in the morning and see if we can herd them back out the way they came. I have no idea how they got that back door open, probably just by chance. Maybe there's some way to lock out the controls for the dragon doors."

"What about the earthquakes?" Lori said groggily after awakening at David's outburst. "Do you think there will be any more big ones?"

"I hope the one last night was the 'big one' Dr. Whitehorse has been predicting. Otherwise we're in big trouble. The intensity of the few we've had since then seems to be much less, though." Mark told her.

Patterson shook his head. "I was one of the ones that wanted to get out of this place, but if those creatures are what's happening on the outside, I think we should stay in here for a while. You think they're radiated mutants, or something?"

No one answered him but that's exactly what they all thought they were.

While they considered this revelation, the lights flickered and failed for a second time. They immediately came back on but the intensity was decreased. "What's happening now?" he muttered.

He and Lori stirred and again climbed to the Crow's Nest to ascertain what had happened to the lights and to see if they could lock the Dragon doors.

"Something's causing the generator to lose power so we're cutting all unnecessary functions. I've cut the power to the lights and they're now on batteries. They should last for a few hours and will recharge when we get the generator stabilized. I've cut all power to the shops, the gym, the warehouse, and all dragon caves. We absolutely need to keep power to the Crow's Nest or we lose all communications and worse, the computer. Mark, you want to go down to the generator room and find out what's wrong?"

"Sure, I'm on my way." He and Lori went down the winding stairs since the elevator was out and continued down to the lower level. "Uh oh." They had stepped into several inches of water when he reached the bottom corridor. "This can't be good."

They ran down the corridor to the generator room and saw the water leaking under the door. Mark decided not to open the door, hoping that keeping it closed would slow down the volume of water entering the room.

Back in the tower he told them what they'd found.

"How bad is the flow of water?" Will asked him.

"Doesn't seem too bad yet, and I know the generator is elevated but I don't know how bad the leak in the aqueduct is. If it gets worse we could lose the generator. Obviously, it's being affected somewhat, even now."

"When the shelter was designed, we knew that flooding was the greatest danger we faced due to the lake above and the fact that we piped the water down into the shelter for power. The blast door at the tunnel's terminus is sensor controlled to close if we flood and the tunnel slants slightly upward to keep the flooding from the escape cave. I hope that aqueduct holds out." Will said.

"I'll keep tabs on the water level and notify you if it gets worse. We can begin evacuation if that happens." Bone weary, Mark returned to the auditorium to try and get some sleep. Lori went downstairs to be with the children. Mark was partially successful, dozing on and off for the next few hours.

May 8, 6:10 a.m.

Hours had passed and the man-creatures hadn't returned. The monsters were not only hungry, but the red lights in the cave and the hallway beyond the door had begun to pulse slightly and it was disorienting, agitating the creatures. A low pitched whine could be heard from inside the building, and curious, some of them warily slunk toward the sound.

Passing through the main room, they approached the gigantic hole in the floor where the upper portion of the turbine protruded through. The noise came from the turbine, still spinning, though a thin tendril of smoke now rose from somewhere below. The deafening sound of the water rushing through the penstocks and the whine of the failing turbine infuriated them.

They wanted it to stop!

More of the creatures left the ledge and approached the turbine. One of them picked up a piece of metal that had fallen from somewhere during the quake and heaved it at the offending piece of equipment. It bounced off and others grabbed everything they could find, throwing it at the turbine.

Arby reached up and touched the penstock over his head feeling the vibration. He remembered the man's face, looking up at him, remembered him putting his arm around the female and leading her away from Arby. He screamed, a furious, frustrated scream. He whirled around, looking for something to hit. He spotted the wrench on the wall, a wrench that required a winch overhead to normally lift it. He plucked it off the wall with little effort.

Carrying it over to the penstock he swung the heavy, formidable weapon and smashed it into the six foot diameter metal tube leaving a dent 18 inches across. He swung again leaving a bigger dent. Again and again, with total fury he smashed at the hateful tube until he finally succeeded in bending the metal enough to split a seam. Water squirted out, spraying the creatures. Arby took the wrench and heaved it at the turbine. It crashed into it, bounced off and hit one of poles of the railing and bounced back into the side of turbine.

The low pitched whine increased in frequency gaining in pitch until the creatures put hands over their ears and screamed in agony. The room swayed as another large aftershock struck the shelter. Heavier dark smoke poured up through the hole and bright flashes of light lit up the room. One creature that had descended to the floor of the cave to search out scraps of Lenny's body, and was standing in waist-deep water, screamed once and then collapsed as he was electrocuted by a massive amount of electricity traveling through his body.

The sound of metal tearing itself apart filled the air and the turbine suddenly quit spinning, the ear-splitting whine ceasing completely. Except for the thunderous sound of the water, silence ensued.

Then they heard another sound of rending metal and the penstock ripped open, tons of water crashing into the plant and washing one of the creatures into the hole containing the now dead turbine. The others scurried to the rear of the room. The water flowed forward into the abyss below the plant. Unable to reason as humans but still possessing survival instinct they ran out the front opening, remaining on the second story ledge away from the water that now filled the cavern floor. The wall covering the waste water channel crumbled and whole parts of the building above collapsed into the churning torrent below. Huge chunks of concrete and limestone crashed down from the ceiling of the cavern, splashing into the deepening pool of black water.

The creatures crouched back against the wall on the second floor trying to stay away from the destruction, trapped on the ledge with nowhere to go. There was a thirty foot drop to the cavern floor and the power plant had collapsed in front of them, blocking the staircase. Water still rushed from the broken penstocks, much of it flowing into the, now, uncovered aqueduct but also onto the floor of the cavern as well. They milled around, growling and pushing one another, agitated and angry. Arby hunched down against the wall, his thoughts dwelling on the creature that had stolen the female and escaped from him. He grew restless and began to pace, swinging his arms violently as the others struggled to get out of his way, one of them inadvertently backing into the mechanism that opened the door into the tunnels connecting this cave with the farm complex. As luck would have it, this door worked perfectly.

May 8, 6:15 a.m.

Mark was jolted awake by James, who had been sent by Will, running into the auditorium with news that the dragon door between the Power cave and the farm cave had opened. Mark's back and neck were stiff and sore from dozing in the uncomfortable auditorium seat. The others started awake, wondering what the commotion was about.

"Well Patterson, you wanted to know if they could get out of the power plant cave. It looks like the answer is yes. Let's hope it was accidental and they still can't get into the farm through the Chicken Ranch. Come on let's go." Mark climbed stiffly to his feet and headed for the door, a 12 gauge shotgun slung over his shoulder.

***

"I want my mommy!" Kevin cried out again, waking Barbara from a fitful sleep. She wondered what had happened in the power plant cave during the night. Lori had told her the creatures were trapped, and they were hoping the things would retreat into the tunnels they had entered through, and that the Dragon doors could be locked to keep them out. She prayed they wouldn't have to confront them. Lori, after checking on the kids and grabbing a couple hours of sleep, had gone back to the auditorium in case they were needed.

There had been additional aftershocks, one of them rather large and the children were frightened. "Your mommy should be here before too long, Kevin. I'm sure she's almost finished." She tried to coax him back to sleep but he tossed about, unable to fall back asleep. Barbara had fashioned a bed for the kids on the couch since they had been too scared to sleep in one of the two small bedrooms in Jerry and Barbara's apartment. Lori had been able to use one of the beds earlier. Jerry sat in a chair sound asleep, his head thrown back and his mouth wide open. Barbara was on the other sofa with Jeremy beside her, his head in her lap. Barbara knew she should go to the infirmary to see how Sandi was doing, but Pete promised to let her know when the baby was close. She thought she would hear something before this, but first pregnancies often had long labor.

The intercom startled her as it announced, "This is an emergency. Everyone report to the auditorium at once!" It was Will Hargraves voice. He repeated the message twice more.

"Now what?" Jerry mumbled as Barbara woke her husband and told him about the page. They woke Ashley and Jeremy and had the three kids hold hands as they left the apartment.

Residents, ripped from their slumbers and still sleepy, filed into the room, over half of their number missing. Most areas didn't have intercom service restored. People milled around and many remained standing.

"I don't have all the details," Will announced, "But apparently there are several more of the animals that killed Bud and Rick and we think they've managed to get out of the power plant. You all need to take refuge in the exit cave until they're hunted down and destroyed and we can repair some of the damage to the shelter." Questions were shouted from the audience but he cut them off.

"Please, there's no time for questions. Get moving now! There's been damage to the power plant and the lower level is flooding. It's imperative you get to the cave quickly before the exit is cut off! I need several of you to act as runners and notify those that don't have intercom service. You'll have to go door to door. Hurry!"

Jerry hugged Barbara, "Come on honey, let's go. I'll run over and tell everyone at the infirmary. They'll have to evacuate too. I'll help them out and I'll meet you at the cave and let you know how Sandi's doing." He kissed her and hurried out the door. She stood a moment looking at the door and then, realizing time was running out she turned to get the kids.

"Oh my God!" She stood stunned. The kids were gone.

May 8, 6:30 a.m.

Mark's party, armed with AK-47s, Uzi's, AR-15s and Mark's shotgun had hurried back to the power plant. Wading through water, they carefully slid through the narrowed door into the cave, pushing against the current of the water rushing through the aperture.

The creatures had left the cave!

Much of the cave had collapsed and the plant was obviously beyond repair. A torrent of water rushed from pipes, the erstwhile penstocks, most of it going into the waste water canal but a good portion flooding the cave and pouring into the hallway through the jammed door. They wedged back through the door and again waded through the water, weapons ready, trying to figure out where the creatures may have gone. They had somehow managed to exit the cave.

"Shit, where do you think they are?" asked Doug.

"They could be in the farm or reservoir caves. If they were anywhere else we would know about it." Mark said. "We all need to evacuate before this level floods completely. Get your families and get out quickly. Good luck everybody!"

***

"Kevin, come on!" Jeremy tugged at his arm. "We have to go back. Mom'll be so mad!" Kevin pulled free, ran into the stairwell and started down the stairs holding on to the railing.

"I'm gonna find my mommy!"

"She'll come back when she's done." Jeremy followed him holding on to Ashley's hand. "Mr. Hargraves said we're s'posed to get out of here! Come on, Kevin, please!" They went down the stairs to the second level where Kevin exited the stairwell and ran for his apartment. They passed others running through the halls in the opposite direction. There were stairwells in three of the four corners of the upper level, the central elevator, now out of commission, and the large freight elevator in which they had originally descended from the outside. On lower levels, which were much larger than the first, the stairwells came out mid-way along the perimeter hallways.

They chased after Kevin as he entered the apartment and went straight for his fire-truck, having to go through the debris caused by the earthquake. He wasn't going anywhere without it.

"Okay, you got it! Now can we go back to my mom?"

Kevin looked around the apartment. He had been convinced his mother would be here.

He started to cry, "Yeah."

"Ashley, do you want to take anything?" Jeremy asked. He was back in charge. Her face brightened and she ran to the bedroom returning with her ragged Barbie clutched tightly in her arms.

"Okay, you guys do what I say, alright?" They nodded. "Let's go. Mr. Hargraves said we need to go to the back tunnel on the bottom floor. Ok?" They nodded again. "Alright, let's go."

He led them out of the apartment but he wasn't sure in which direction the tunnel lay. It seemed darker than before and they hurried to the left, back to the stairwell they used when they descended from the top floor, one that comes out at the intersection of the long hallway that goes to the farm cave and the cross hallway that bisects the lower level. The stairwell was very dark, only dim lighting shining through the door from the hallway as they entered. They held hands and slowly descended in the dark, Kevin terrified of the dark.

"Oh no." Jeremy jumped back up to the higher step. "There's a whole bunch of water down here." They hunkered down together on the steps in pitch dark not wanting to descend into the water and not knowing what to do next.

May 8, 7:05 a.m.

Chris took a last look around the farm cave. "Let's go everybody!" Sam and Rana ran out of the office, Rana carrying an armful of books. The red lights in the office and lab had dimmed perceptibly from the original intensity a few hours ago. Chris waved her arms, ushering the others toward the door. The intercoms had gone out completely and they had only been informed of the emergency when messengers had awakened them twenty minutes ago. Several of them, all having the same idea, had felt it worthwhile to save the animals. Unfortunately, communication was breaking down and the fact that the creatures had escaped the power plant wasn't part of the message.

"Come on everybody, move!" She hit the button, the door swished open and water cascaded into the cave from the corridor.

"Oh brother! Come on you guys, we're flooding!"

The entrance to the animal compound opened and groups of animals, herded by several people, tramped across the soaked crops and the wet floor toward Chris.

"Let the chickens loose, too!" someone called out. A man and woman went back into the animal area, crossed to the chicken ranch and using the manual lever, opened the door. They ran down the rows unlatching cages and pulling birds out. The birds were decidedly unhappy about the rising water on the floor, flapping their wings and flying clumsily into the animal cave.

Someone knocked on the back door. "That's weird. I'll get it." the man said. He pulled the manual lever, opening the door and giving ingress to a band of the most horrific creatures he had ever encountered.

The woman screamed as the monsters rushed into the chicken ranch. She ran for the door, the birds fleeing before her. The man's cries cut off almost as soon as he commenced screaming. Pulling the lever back up she tried to close the door but the creatures were quickly crossing the other cave having savagely murdered her companion. She turned and fled, past the corrals, to the main door of the compound. The monsters were confused and distracted by the flapping birds, giving her an opportunity to escape to the next room. The main door closed when she yanked the lever up.

"Go, everybody out! Those things are in the cave. Oh God, they killed Steven!" The remaining people quickly finished herding the animals and a few chickens that had managed to get into this cave out the front door and closed it.

"I don't think they can get through the door unless someone opens it," the woman told Chris as they shepherded the animals through the calf deep water.

Mark's hunting party had gone their separate ways looking for their families to begin evacuation. Mark and Lori started back through the hallway to go upstairs. Wading through the water and fighting their way through the frightened animals, they ran into Chris.

"The monsters are in the animal compound," Chris told them. "Come on, we're evacuating. Looks like we're out of here for good."

"We're going to make sure everyone is out first." Mark told her. "The intercom is still down in some areas. Where's Aaron?"

"He's helping the injured to evacuate. Keep your eyes peeled. Very soon the water's going to make it difficult to get out of here. Dad says the exit tunnel slopes upward. If the water gets too high and starts flooding the exit cave the blast door will activate. That means no one else can get out. Don't wait too long."

"We'll be there. Count on it! Where's Will?"

"I think he's in the Crow's nest. Make him leave, promise?"

"We're on our way."

Others joined and assisted Chris and the others in herding the animals through the hallways to the back corner, getting the dragon door open and the animals through. As each group entered the long escape tunnel the door was closed behind them.

Chicken carcasses and feathers were everywhere. The beasts crashed through and tore apart corrals and enclosures casting the debris around the cave. One pounded the door and jerked the manual lever leaping back, surprised, when the door opened. He slithered through the opening, traveling in the same direction he'd seen the humans go, the others trailing him. They trashed this cave as well, jerking down the lines in the hydroponic gardens and throwing pieces of the planter boxes through the windows of the offices. Eventually finding their way to the shelter door, Arby pulled the lever, having watched the man-things open the door this way.

Now there was nothing stopping them as eight monsters moved forward into the shelter.

May 8, 7:20 a.m.

"What do you mean gone?" Lori asked.

"They were with me in the meeting." Barbara explained through tears. "I think they went with Jerry to tell Pete about the evacuation. I missed them right after he left. I just turned around and they were gone!"

"Oh no!" She moaned. She took Barbara by the shoulders. "Listen to me. You get to the exit. I'm going to look for them. It won't do any good for you to stay behind and maybe Jerry has them after all. Go!" She pushed Barbara toward the door of the daycare where they had encountered her yelling at the top of her lungs for Jeremy and the others.

She turned to Mark. "We can search the top floor first and then work our way down toward the exit."

"Okay," he said. "Unless the creatures have found their way out of the caves it should be safe enough to split up. You check the infirmary side and I'll take the cafeteria side and check the Crow's Nest."

"Ok, I'll meet you at the second level dining room." She ran off shouting for Ashley and Kevin.

Mark ran through the eastern portion of the top floor shouting for the children. He found no signs of them. After making his way through the other hallways he climbed to the Crow's Nest to find Micah, Will and Darryl still there.

"What are you guys doing? You need to evacuate now!"

"How bad is the flood?" Will asked.

"About knee deep, but it's rising. The creatures are in the farm cave but it's probably only a matter of time until they figure out how to enter the shelter. There's nothing more you can do here! Are the sensors still working?" Still carrying his weapon he walked around the room checking the gauges.

"Some. We're trying to contact the outside, let them know what happened or find out what their status is. It will be even more important if we're forced outside."

"Will, there's no 'if' about it. The power plant's gone, the place is flooded and there are some serious bad guys loose in the shelter." He crossed the room and took Will's arm. "Please, you need to come now!" He tugged Will toward the exit. "I have to get back. Kevin, Ashley and Jeremy are missing. Lori's searching the top floor and we need to work our way down until we find them. We have to locate them before the monsters do! Come on!"

Will looked at Micah who shook his head. "Not getting anything, Boss."

"The power's failing! Water's reached the emergency gennie!" said Darryl from his position at the computer. "Communications won't work much longer anyway. I say we vamoose!" As he spoke, the computer screen went blank and the sensor displays and monitors began to wink out one by one around the room. The lights dimmed to a ghostly illumination.

"Oh man, come on, let's get going!" Mark threw open the door and the four men ran down the stairs. They reached the alcove with Darryl in the lead. The elevator, of course, was dead.

"Wait a second. I need more ammo!" Mark veered into the vault and slung a bandolier full of shells for the shotgun over his shoulder. When he reentered the alcove Darryl and Will were entering the staircase, Micah holding the door for him. Just as he followed Will into the stairwell the shelter bucked, throwing all of them to the floor. Micah fell backwards, the door slamming in his face. Darryl fell down the stairs with Will teetering above, trying to maintain his balance. Mark instinctively reached out grasping Will's shirt but couldn't prevent him from following Darryl. The quake continued to rumble, as part of the ceiling gave way.

Rocks and metal caved in all around Mark. Through it all he managed to maintain his grip on the weapon but Will had fallen back down the stairs. The stairwell above and behind him filled with debris and he scurried lower to avoid being crushed as the choking dust filled the confined space. The shaking slowly ceased and Mark detected light behind him where Micah had managed to get the door open.

"Whoa, Boss! Looks like I'm not getting out that way!"

"Come on, Micah! We'll clear it!" Mark started desperately trying to move rocks aside.

"Don't worry! You get going. I'm taking the emergency escape route." He reached through the small opening and Mark reached up to grasp his hand. He held it for a second, then Micah pulled it back. "I'll see you in the valley Boss. I'm a great rock climber."

And he was gone.

Mark descended the stairs dangerously fast, skirting and climbing over pieces of metal and rocks and dirt, around a support beam that had fallen, coughing as he inhaled the thick dust and listening intently for evidence of Will and Darryl. He was almost to the bottom when, unable to see in the dark, he tripped over something, going down hard and knocking his breath out. He lost the shotgun. It was a body!

"Will! Oh no, Will!" He felt for him in the dark, found him and pulled him close. Will was unconscious. Mark could feel something warm, wet, and sticky. The metallic smell of blood almost sickened him.

"Mark! Down here!" Darryl called from the bottom of the stairwell. I got the door open!"

"No! Darryl, come here. Will's hurt!" He heard someone hurriedly ascending the stairs and then felt hands reaching for them. Mark felt for the weapon, slinging the strap over his shoulder.

Together they lifted Will and managed to get him down to the first level where, in the dim light, they could assess his injuries. Mark could see blood on Darryl's clothing also.

"Are you hurt?"

"I fell part way down the stairs and cut myself on some metal, but I'm okay. How badly do you think Will's hurt?"

"I can't tell. Oh God!" He pulled his hand back quickly. He was feeling Will's skull for the source of the blood when he felt the side of his head sink inward. "Oh shit! Wait here!"

He ran around the corner into the deserted infirmary, grabbed a rolled up military field stretcher and returned at full speed.

"Help me get him on the stretcher! Come on, Dr. Jim and Aaron should be in the exit cave!" They tilted him on to it, each man picked up one end and they labored down the hall to the corner stairwell, descending to the hallway by the entrance to the power plant.

"Hey! Come here!" Mark recruited two men wading through the water toward the escape tunnel. "Will's hurt bad! We need help transporting him."

"Mark." A faint whisper came from the figure on the stretcher.

"Will!" He handed his end of the stretcher to one of the men and leaped to Will's side. "Don't worry. We'll get you to the doctor. Hang on, Will, please."

With great effort he whispered to Mark, "Did you find the children?"

"No, and I haven't seen Lori. We're on the lower level, and you're almost to the exit. You're going to be fine." They were still moving through the water.

Just then, they heard a scream farther back toward the shops, then another, several people screaming in mortal fear.

"Come on guys, faster!" They reached the back door and Mark looked back down the tunnel. Unless she'd found them immediately after he left her, Lori and the children were still in the shelter. And so were the creatures!

"Mark," Will called out hoarsely, "Find them. I'll be alright. Go!"

Mark took his hand, and squeezed it gently. He reached up caressed the older man's face. "I'll see you at the cave, Will."

May 8, 7:30 a.m.

In completing her search of the top floor Lori ran into stragglers still evacuating. The Thompsons, including Jerry, had left some time ago, wheeling Sandi on a gurney, and Greg Whitehorse and Brian Morrison were helping injured earthquake victims make their way to the back stairwell. Dr. Jim and Carmen had gone with the first wave of injured. Lori saw Ron and Jean half carrying a woman with a blood soaked towel around her head.

She hailed them, "Ron, If Jerry and Barbara Thompson are in the exit cave and they don't have Jeremy and my kids with them, don't let them leave! They will want to come back and search but Mark and I will find the children. It's very important that no one come back into the shelter once they've left. The creatures may break in here at any time and we may lose track of who's safe and who isn't. Do you understand?"

"Yeah," Ron told her. "We won't let them leave, Lori. I promise."

By the time Lori finished looking through the top level there was no one else around. She completed her search of the top floor and descended a staircase to the residential level, coming out by the dining room. She didn't see Mark anywhere in her travels although he was supposed to meet her here. This level was approximately twice the size of the top floor and was going to take longer to search. Mark would just have to find her as she didn't want to delay locating the kids. She ran through almost completely dark corridors, barely illuminated by the faint reddish glow, yelling for Ashley and Kevin.

Entering her damaged apartment, she checked it thoroughly, even in the closet, thinking they might be frightened and hiding. She had to climb over portions of the fallen ceiling and looked in the shadows beneath. Rushing back into the corridor, she ran past the central elevator with the doors stuck partially open, revealing the empty shaft. Just as she glanced down the shaft she heard a scream echoing upward from the level below. Her heart leaped, but it was the voice of an adult.

The monsters must be in the shelter!

She met several people coming from the dining room. "What are you waiting for? You need to evacuate the shelter, Now!"

"We needed to get some breakfast. We may have to stay in that damn cave for a long time." It was the Richenours and their friends, Bernie and Joyce Palmer. Vernon gazed with disapproval at the Uzi.

"You're idiots!" she screamed at them. "The bottom floor is flooded and the monsters are loose in the shelter. If you don't get out of here right now, you'll BE breakfast!"

Mrs. Richenour turned ghostly white, suddenly realizing the precariousness of their situation. "Vernon, please, let's go!"

"Don't worry, dear, she's being an alarmist. Come along." They turned toward the stairwell next to the dining room.

"You'd better stay on this floor to the southwest stairwell. It's closer to the exit tunnel," she warned them. "The creatures are in the farm cave."

Ignoring her warning, Vernon took his wife's arm and pulled her into the stairwell, the one that descended to the hallway outside the farm cave. The others followed them.

Lori shook her head and continued her search of the second floor. When convinced the children weren't there she descended to the lower level using the rear staircase she tried to convince Richenour to use. She barely missed Mark, as he had gone the other direction. She hesitated momentarily at the door that opened into the escape tunnel, but instead turned east until she came to the north-south corridor. She knew in her heart her children were still in the shelter.

Holding the Uzi in front of her she waded through the current toward the machine shops, the water now reaching to her mid-thigh. She passed through an intersection with a cross-corridor when she heard something, a large body, splashing through the water in that other corridor, coming in her direction. She increased her speed trying to reach the corner ahead when the creature suddenly let out a triumphant scream. She looked back as it bore down on her, slowed only slightly by the water that came up to its calves. She swung around and opened fire!

The Uzi kicked, spraying bullets toward the bellowing creature. It stopped, looking down at its chest as multiple bullets tore into it. Even in the near darkness she could see blood and bits of flesh flying. It dropped to its knees, and as she stopped firing the creature toppled face first into the swirling water.

"Yes!" She yelled "One down!" she moved quickly forward, aware the noise would have attracted the others. She reached and rounded the far corner.

"Oh damn!" Several monsters were approaching. She could see massive reptilian shapes looming in the ruddy glow, their backs shaped like an "S" as they hunched forward, quickly moving toward her. She could flee but knew they would get her in the next hallway. Her only choice was to run toward them and try and beat them to the door of the machine shop. She didn't hesitate - whooping at the top of her lungs, and firing wildly, she sprinted straight at them hoping to confuse them for the second she needed to pull the door lever and duck into the shop.

In an instant she knew she wasn't going to make it.

She was so close! But the lead creature was now opposite the door. Just as she came to a sudden halt, completely uncertain of her next move a booming sound filled the corridor, shots from a very large caliber rifle reverberating in the hallway zinging by her ear.

"Blam!" The lead creature fell back. "That's for Lenny, you Son-of-a-bitch!"

"Blam," he fired again, and the monster dropped into the water. "Take that you fucker!" The others, momentarily disoriented moved back a few steps.

David pulled the trigger again. ...And the weapon jammed.

Lori came out of her stupor and jerked the manual lever, glancing at the monsters coming at her as the door seemed to open in slow motion.

"Come on, come on, come on!" she chanted under her breath. She glanced back at David, flashed a thumb's up signal and saw him disappear back around the corner. The second the opening was wide enough she scraped through into the shop. She whirled back to the door and jumped back as hairy hands grabbed the inside edges of the door above her head, screeching, and preventing its closure.

She looked into the eyes of death. "Get back you bastard!" she shoved the muzzle of the Uzi toward its face, pulled the trigger, and blasted it out of the crack, allowing the door to close. She turned and fell back against the door, her knees wobbling, and taking in great gulps of air. She was shaking in reaction to her mad dash directly into their faces. They were banging furiously on the door. She swung around wildly wondering if they knew how to use the lever.

She quickly crossed through the shop, sloshing through the flood, discarding her clip as she ran and slamming home the one stuck in her belt. She reached the door that opened onto the cross-corridor and pulled the lever. Nothing happened.

May 8, 7:40 a.m.

Mark waded through the knee deep water around the corner into the east hallway. The emergency lights barely illuminated the corridor. He stopped dead in his tracks, his heart rate accelerating, as memories of a nightmare from a lifetime ago washed over him, paralyzing him with dread. In that instant he was back in the nightmare, all the emotions and feelings washed over him, and he realized who the people in the dream were, the people he cared for but couldn't quite place. It was suddenly so clear. Lori and the children.

With sudden comprehension he knew what he felt all these years for Chris Hargraves wasn't love; he loved her like a sister. But Lori, he loved with a fierceness he never knew was possible. How could he have been such a fool to have believed they were just friends!

His dream was becoming reality. The horrifying creature of his nightmare, with others of its kind, was loose in the shelter and the people he loved more than his own life were with them somewhere in the darkness. He crept forward through the dimly lit corridor as the lights faded perceptibly. Straining to hear anything that might warn him of the presence of the enemy he waded slowly, trying not to create splashing sounds and wondering if he were walking into the jaws of death.

The sound of silence was shattered by the rapid staccato gunfire of an Uzi! He threw caution to the wind and quickly moved forward toward the sound echoing through the corridors. He was aware the creatures must have heard it also, but he didn't care. Almost to the stairwell, he slowed, peering intently toward the corner far ahead. The door to the farm cave, on the right side of the corridor was 50 yards ahead. The latest information from Chris indicated the creatures were in that cave.

Now he heard gunfire from a second weapon, a booming rifle!

He detected movement at the far end of the hallway, barely visible in the dim shadows and he heard low growling and snuffling sounds. The sounds of rending flesh and cracking bones.

Then he heard the sound of a human child, crying in the darkness. Just like in his nightmare. Only this time he knew the voice - it was little Kevin!

A shadow emerged from the dark corridor ahead, massive, reptilian with horrifying red eyes. It didn't see Mark, as the crying had attracted its attention. The creature reached the intersection and turned left, looking at the door to the stairwell eight feet into the corridor. It turned toward the sound and cocked its head. It was the gigantic creature Mark had seen staring at him in the power plant cavern. It approached the stairwell and reached out and pulled the lever that operated the door!

The cries became louder as the door scraped open, stuck momentarily, and then sprang open directly in front of the creature.

"Noooo....!" Mark screamed! He jumped forward, all caution abandoned as he sloshed madly through the water, his weapon held over his head with both hands. "Come here you bastard! Leave them alone!"

Mark reached a point in the corridor where he could see into the stairwell - and froze as he saw the three children on the steps just above the level of the rising water. Their eyes were wide with terror, and they were crying uncontrollably as they huddled together, staring up at the Arby-thing. He heard Ashley's small trembling voice, weak with fear, "Please, please don't hurt my little brother."

"Here! Mother-fucker! Take me!" Mark screamed.

Unbelievably quick, the monster swung to face him!

Mark stumbled back several steps.

Recognition and hatred filled the eyes of the creature as it saw the despised man-thing. Slouched over, it slowly began to straighten, uncurling its back, growing to its full height of eight feet, and baring the two inch long fangs as thick, mucoid, drool, dripped from its mouth. Mark stood transfixed, his jaw dropping, paralyzed as the creature curled and uncurled its claws. It tilted its head, lips drawing back into a horrid caricature of a smile.

May 8, 7:45 a.m.

Water swirled around her thighs as Lori struggled to break open the door. She yanked the lever again and the door opened slightly. She froze, not daring even to breathe, as a huge figure passed the door going left. Readying the Uzi by swinging it from her back to the front, she squeezed her fingers into the opening and pulled with all her strength, stumbling forward as the door unexpectedly whooshed opened completely.

She raised the Uzi in front of her, jumping through the door and swinging the weapon first right, then left. Two emergency lights, casting a dim red glow, depicted a scene that created in her such tremendous fear that her tongue thickened and she made strangling noises in the back of her throat.

Directly in front of her was a reptilian monster creeping forward towards an unsuspecting Mark. Mark stood frozen, looking up... way up, at the largest of the creatures she had yet seen. The smell in the corridor was overwhelming. The decaying, putrefying, beast glared at Mark, grinning, anticipating its most satisfying kill, and behind this monster, huddled together and sobbing in the darkness, just barely visible, were her babies and little Jeremy Thompson!

"Mark! Behind you!" She was afraid to shoot with him in the line of fire.

Her scream broke the spell, and the Arby thing lunged for Mark. He pulled the trigger on the shotgun, aiming high to avoid any possibility of hitting the children, and leaped to the side!

Arby screamed as Mark's shotgun blast took him in the chest, slowing it down and causing pain, but little damage and Lori saw Mark disappear into the side corridor. She opened fire at the nearest monster. Lori saw the gigantic creature beyond start for Mark but then it saw her, and confused and enraged by her gunfire, it paused. She was still filling the closer monster full of lead when it fell into the flood leaving Arby a clear view of her. It was ambivalent, swinging its head from side-to-side looking at her and then at Mark.

Mark scrambled to his feet, from where he'd dived into the water still grasping the shotgun and trying to hold it above water. It was drenched. *"Would it still work?"* he wondered.

"Come on, you Son-of-a-bitch!" He pulled the trigger. The bullet spray hit Arby again, irritating him further and deciding for him that it was Mark he wanted. Mark had retreated down the corridor firing again and Arby followed slowly scratching at his wounds like they were mosquito bites. Mark fumbled to reload from the bandolier as he backed away. He fired once more before Lori moved into the intersection and Mark had to stop shooting or risk hitting her!

"Lori! Get the kids! Go upstairs and get to the exit tunnel that way!" He heard a roar and saw other monsters approaching from her back.

He saw her hesitate. Their eyes met - and for a moment he thought she wasn't going to leave him. Her hand came up, reaching toward him.

"Lori, for the love of God! Go!"

With sudden determination she turned the Uzi toward the ceiling. She couldn't aim directly at the thing without risk to Mark. She began firing into the exposed rock. He raised his shotgun and joined her in blasting away at the ceiling hoping neither of them would be hit with ricochet. Rocks and dirt flew everywhere and suddenly a massive portion of the ceiling gave way, collapsing on, and burying, the huge creature. She swung on the others she could hear approaching from behind her, firing everything she had, literally. The Uzi ran out of bullets.

"Arrrgh!" she screamed at them furiously, and heaving the Uzi in their faces she turned once more toward Mark. Through the dust she saw him trying to reach her by climbing around the rubble, but his passage was effectively blocked.

"Lori, go, I'll meet you in the cave! Get out of the way!" She dove into the stairwell to allow him a clear shot of the remaining monsters. He stood firing at them through a space beside the rubble, slowing them down.

She slammed the door. "Come on kids, let's go! Climb the stairs. Quickly!" She knew Mark wouldn't leave while there was still a chance she could be followed. She picked up Kevin, who held so tightly to her neck she didn't even have to hold onto him, and grabbed Ashley's hand. Jeremy ran up the stairs in front of them. She looked fearfully behind her but Mark's gunfire was holding the creatures at bay. Mark kept firing, watching monsters fall, holding them back from entering the stairwell in pursuit of Lori.

She hit the upper floor running, just as the gunfire below quit.

"Oh, please God! Please let him make it!" she prayed as they sped down deserted corridors toward the back stairwell.

Suddenly the rocks alongside Mark exploded apart as the giant creature buried in the debris reached out and clutched Mark's rifle, jerking it roughly from his hands and pulling him forward, where he fell into the deepening, now muddy, water. He choked down a mouthful of foul liquid, coughing and sputtering, which temporarily incapacitated him. The creature was trying to shake off the debris, picking up and flinging aside the rocks that held it pinned. Mark backed away, still unable to breathe. The creature would soon be free! He whirled and half ran, half swam toward the far corner. He was gaining control and making better progress as he reached the corner. Looking back he saw the monster pulling itself free from the debris. The others bellowed and surged forward but the gigantic creature turned on them, threw out its long arms and let out an ear-piercing scream that stopped them in their tracks. The man-thing was his!

Mark rounded the corner and his heart leapt as he saw Lori, David and the children enter the escape tunnel. Then he couldn't see anything as the red glow faded, the emergency lights finally failing 50 yards too soon! He heard the susurration of the air conditioning cease, as the shelter that had been their home for eight months took its last breath and died.

He was running in darkness, darker than he had ever known, had ever thought possible, as though light was gone forever from his world. He sprinted through the endless corridor with something unspeakable in pursuit. He could hear it coming closer.

Running, trying to escape its unclean grasp as water flowed all around in a tide that climbed up his legs, his hips, swirling by him on all sides, seeming to come from everywhere. The water trapped him as he moved in slow motion, as though his legs were embedded in concrete - while the thing behind him gained ground. He heard it come around the corner into the hallway he was traversing. If only he could enter the tunnel and have the door close behind him!

He smashed his face into the wall ahead of him. The escape door was on his left. Frantically he felt for the manual lever. He could hear the thing coming through the dark!

He found it and heaved with all his might, waiting while the door took forever to open. He turned sideways and scraped through even before it drew back completely.

Mark groped forward with his hand on the wall until the tunnel turned to the left. The escape cave had its own battery-powered emergency power system and Mark saw a light at the end of the quarter-mile tunnel, impossibly small, so far away it was still pitch black at this end. He heard a noise at the door behind him and whirled to see, but it was too dark to make out anything. He realized that with no power the doors had remained open. He heard, rather than saw, clawed hands grab the edges and slowly try to force them to open wider. He turned and partially swam, partially ran as fast as he could. A quarter-mile. The length of a single, oval high school track. It looked like a mile.

The tunnel slanted slightly upward, curving, gaining approximately four feet by the time it reached the cave. He sped up slightly as the depth of the water decreased, and halfway down the tunnel he looked back... wishing that he hadn't. The creature had made it through the door into the tunnel and had just come around the corner.

It was gaining rapidly, deadly silent, intent on overtaking him.

As he came closer to the light, he saw figures in front of the opening. Then two things happened, filling him with dread! One of the figures broke free from restraining arms and entered the tunnel, running in his direction.

Lori!

And the other, was that the level of the water reached almost to the level of the cave floor!

He screamed at her, barely able to breathe with the exertion of sprinting for so long through the deep water, "Get back! There's... nothing... you... can...do!"

One hundred feet...!

The water reached the level of the cave floor and started sloshing into it. Three figures had followed Lori into the tunnel and they grabbed her, dragging her back into the cave.

The huge, metal blast door began to descend!

"Oh God, no," he whispered, knowing it was sensor controlled and they couldn't stop it. It was designed to prevent the flooding of the cave in event the reservoirs were damaged. He was sure they could see the thing in pursuit of him. Fifty feet and he could hear the creature close behind!

He was so exhausted he was certain he couldn't go on, his legs were leaden, his lungs burning with every inhalation. The door was slowly sinking, halfway down now, six feet to go. He saw Lori struggling, could hear her pleading with them to release her as they dragged her back into the cave.

The opening was filled with people encouraging him to go faster.

"Come on Mark!"

"You can do it."

"Run, man!"

"Sprint!"

A thunder of voices, all pleading, cheering him on. The water was down to his calves, the door down to four feet, faces peering under it.

Twenty feet.

Through ankle-deep water he accelerated, heard the creature's bellowing, furious scream, trying to paralyze its prey with fear. He felt it grab for his shirt as he lunged forward, the shirt ripping off his back as sharp claws tore skin and fabric together, digging deep and burning all the way down his back. He juked toward the side of the tunnel and angled back toward the door causing the beast to miss its second grab and lining him up for his only chance.

The opening under the door was now just two feet high. He ran and jumped, splashed onto the ground hard, his body as parallel to the door as possible. The air whooshed from his lungs as his breath was knocked out, and he again inhaled water as he rolled under the descending door. His mind blanked out, endorphins raging, as he expected to be crushed. The only thing he perceived was a tremendous, frustrated shriek and the sound of a heavy body smashing into the barrier as he cleared the door. Hands grabbed him and pulled him along the floor. The door thunked down in its track, cutting off the flood and damning the creature from hell to its rightful resting place.

Then he was in Lori's arms.

"Oh Mark, thank God!" She was on her knees, her arms around him, her face buried in his neck.

He reached out and held her close. "I love you, Lori! I thought I was going to lose you!"

"Never, not ever," she murmured, shocked to hear his words. "I love you too." And they clung together in the cavern, as others pounded him vigorously on the back.

May 8, 10:30 a.m.

Light..., white, blinding light. The light flooding the cave had a brilliance the survivors had not seen in months, intensified by reflections off the dust particles that twinkled like fairy dust, filling the cave and puffing toward the slowly opening doors. The color was wrong. They had become used to the 3200 K wavelength of artificial illumination. It felt like the old days, coming out of a movie theater during the brightest part of the day. As the gap in the rock wall slowly widened they threw their arms across their faces to soften the glare. There was an impression of limitless blue sky and they realized this back entrance to the shelter was above the ground level of the valley. There had been no reason to wait to open the doors. The cave didn't have any monitoring equipment and they couldn't stay in the cave for any length of time.

Mark quickly glanced at Darryl who was staring at the scintillation device in his hands having purposely turned off the audible alarm that would alert others to danger. Darryl looked up and nodded at Mark with a hopeful smile. Mark realized he was holding his breath and let it out slowly. There may be traces of radiation, but apparently it wasn't in a dangerous or lethal range.

The people in the cave were immobilized, staring through the widening aperture, as though not believing the world still existed beyond their shattered realm. The only sounds were Dr. Jim and Carmen urging Sandi to push against the pain that had reached its greatest intensity, her accompanying moans, and Pete's murmurs of encouragement. Mark tore his gaze from the door and turned to Will whose eyes were fixed on the breach in the cave wall. The look of pain had vanished from his face and he now had an expression of satisfaction and joy. His eyes flicked briefly to Mark's and he smiled. Then they closed, as his breathing became labored and his head dropped back against Chris's shoulder. Mark jumped to his side, going down on his knees, and gently took Will from Chris who sat on the dusty ground, tears streaming down her cheeks and her shoulders shaking with silent sobs. Will's breathing slowed and then ceased, and Mark held his body close for a few moments before lowering it to the ground. Aaron appeared beside him, his fingers on Will's wrist. He looked at Mark and shook his head, then turning to Chris, he helped her to her feet and started to lead her toward the door.

Through tears, Mark glanced around the large cavern. Over two hundred people, their eyes adjusting to the glare, slowly edged toward the open doors. The injured were carried or helped by others. Mark rose and took Lori's hand, looked once more at Will, and with the children, they moved forward with the others. They would come back for Will and give him a proper burial in the valley below.

At the side of the cave Sandi gave a final push and Dr. Jim held up the newborn child. As the bedraggled and battered group of survivors spilled out onto a wide shelf in front of the cave they heard his exclamation, "it's a girl!", and the baby's cry echoed off the cave walls and spilled forth into their new world.

Before them lay an incredible valley, the most beautiful place any of them could have imagined. Above, shining through gaps in the rocks, shafts of golden, morning sunlight spilled over the mountain top and cascaded out onto a huge green meadow that filled half the valley and extended to the mountains on the right. A forest covered the left side of the valley and a river ran through the meadow close to the forest's edge. The river's origin could be seen as a wide waterfall flowing out of the cliffs on their left and the entire valley, except for the very far side, was surrounded by sheer mountains, most still crowned by snow.

The cave entrance was approximately fifty feet above the level of the valley floor. On the left, a path cut into the side of the mountain led down the cliff and through boulders and debris fallen from the cliff face. It traversed a rock bridge that spanned the river, crossed a meadow and disappeared into the forest. People began to move down the path, with the animals from the shelter herded before them. Mark, Lori and the children stood holding hands and staring across the magnificent valley. They could make out animals, possibly elk or deer, grazing at the far side of the meadow.

William Hargraves had led them through the shelter to this beautiful valley, where they would have still another chance to survive the holocaust that had transformed their world. Mark didn't know what the future held for any of them but he was willing to bet that Will had planned ahead to this eventuality, and they would find the tools they needed to make new lives somewhere in the forest beyond.

Coming Soon!

Look for the exciting sequel to
"Shelter"

Humanity Abides – Book
Two

"Emergence"

Read about *Shelter* and *Emergence* at:

Carolannbird.com

About the Author

This is Carol's first novel, hopefully the first of many! Carol has had a life-long interest in all things relating to survival. Even as a child in San Diego, she carried around a small canvas bag with a bottle of water and a piece of fruit, a pocketknife, a flashlight and a deck of cards. Later she enjoyed backpacking, where she could carry around a lot more stuff and even got to stay out overnight! More recently she enjoys being a "survivalist" and pondering what life would be like in a post-apocalyptic world. Joining the Army at the age of eighteen, she was the first woman to attend the U.S. Army Chemical School, and was trained in CBR, or Chemical, Biological and Radiological laboratory techniques. Carol has participated in two 10 day backpacking/survival trips and is a certified scuba diver. She has a private pilot's license and has completed a few 50k races, several marathons and many, many races at shorter distances. She graduated from California State University Northridge with a Bachelor of Science in Biology/biotechnology and has worked as a Clinical Laboratory Scientist for most of her adult life. Carol has three daughters and a son, and lives in Colorado Springs with one of her daughters, a granddaughter and her newly adopted grandson.

Made in the USA
Lexington, KY
18 July 2014